NIGHT MAGIC

Tom Tryon

Simon & Schuster
New York ◆ London ◆ Toronto
Sydney ◆ Tokyo ◆ Singapore

SIMON & SCHUSTER
Rockefeller Center
1230 Avenue of the Americas
New York, NY 10020

SIMON & SCHUSTER and colophon are registered trademarks of
Simon & Schuster Inc.

Designed by Levavi & Levavi

Manufactured in the United States of America

10   9   8   7   6   5   4   3   2   1

Library of Congress Cataloging-in-Publication Data
        Tryon, Thomas.
                Night Magic / by Tom Tryon
                p.   cm.   I. Title.
                PS3570.R9N53   1995
                813'.54--dc20
ISBN 0-684-80393-3

Contents

And Moses and Aaron went in unto Pharaoh, and they did so as the
Lord had commanded: and Aaron cast down his rod before Pharaoh, and
before his servants, and it became a serpent.

Then Pharaoh also called the wise men and the sorcerers: now the ma-
gicians of Egypt, they also did in like manner with their enchantments.

For they cast down every man his rod, and they became serpents: but
Aaron's rod swallowed up their rods.

I maintain that this is possible. It is not possible, you reply. Obviously one of us is wrong.

The Sorcerer

Who was greater in all the world than the pharaohs of Egypt, and of these who greater than great Cheops, he who was building the Great Pyramid at Giza? Pharaoh was blessed with sons, and one of them, Prince Dedefhar, was a harmless dabbler in magic for the amusement of his family and friends, and because of his prestidigitatorial talents the prince found himself a popular fellow indeed. How had he learned these things? As all magicians do, from another wonder-worker—a case of sleight-of-hand-me-down. But from which magician? For there were many such in the two kingdoms of the Nile, some of them white magicians, and some black, capable of terrible powers and great sins.

At that time, when the pharaoh ruled from Memphis, there was an old Canaanite who worked the marketplace. He came, it was said, from the coastal city of Byblos in the Lebanon, whence arrived the cedar wood for Cheops's tomb furniture and funerary boat. But he had wandered far indeed from the coast of Canaan, past the fortified walls of Jericho, across the lands of the sand-dwellers, which fringed Pharaoh's kingdom on the northeast, and down through Akkad to the ancient cities of Sumer. He had drunk from the waters of the Euphrates, he had seen the Great Palace and the Royal Tombs of Ur, he had visited Uruk of the strong walls and heard the tale of its mighty King Gilgamesh, whose beloved friend Enkidu went down to the land of the dead and whose bitter tears and dangerous quests could not avail to bring him back.

It was further said of the old Canaanite that he had been a mendicant throughout the Kingdom of the Lower Nile; but now, amid the dust, the flies, and the camel dung, he had found gainful employment as a potter, throwing clay vessels on a wheel and producing prodigies of gracefulness and character. Or for the children he would fashion little clay hippopotamuses or crocodiles, which he would fire and paint. One of these little figures, it was reported, had been given life through incantations and black magic, and the beast grew to a fearful size, twelve feet long and more; it had seized a man in its jaws, carried him off to the river, and drowned him. (Nobody cared; the man was bad, they said, good riddance!) Such were the tales concerning the Canaanite magician, who, while he worked at his potter's wheel, would mumble disjointedly in a language no one understood; people whispered that he was a sorcerer, rehearsing his spells.

When he was not muttering over his labors, he would amuse the crowd with conjuring tricks and feats of juggling. He could behead a dove and make it spurt blood, then instantly restore it to flight. He kept a cat called Thoth, for Thoth was the god who had invented magic and made the tarot. And he could make painted balls seem to hang in the air while he tossed and caught them.

Surrounded by thin-ribbed dogs and thin-faced children, he could pull yard after yard of colored silk from his rags, or bring forth from nowhere flocks of birds aflutter. Sometimes he would leave his wheel to read fates and fortunes in the tarot of Thoth, and he stood in the dust in a circle that he claimed was charmed.

When he returned to his pots at the wheel, mudding up the clay with his fingers and using a peculiar metal stylus to inscribe spiraling rings around the outside surface, he muttered and mumbled like an old fool, as if he were talking the pots into existence. Still, it was said he was a sorcerer, a man to beware.

But how had a member of the royal family happened upon so

disreputable a figure as this magician? It was simply done: one day, proceeding in pomp through the marketplace, the young prince chanced upon the Canaanite juggling his wooden balls, and the prince was amused. That, he declared, was something to learn, to juggle wooden balls so cleverly, and he asked Pharaoh that the magician be brought to the palace to teach him. But the magician proved to be an eater of pork, an abomination, who rightfully should not even have been admitted into the marketplace but kept outside the gates altogether. Still, Prince Dedefhar persisted, and at length the magician was admitted to Pharaoh's presence, where he was ordered to instruct the prince as the prince desired; and before long the magician had the boy tossing up the balls adroitly, and next had him bringing forth pigeons as if from thin air.

Still, when he had accomplished these tricks the prince remained unsatisfied, desiring now to lay out the tarot cards of Thoth and tell fates and fortunes; but this was not so easy to teach, for it was a skill requiring much thought and patience. Nevertheless, having been enjoined by Pharaoh so to instruct the boy, the magician brought out his tarot deck and had him shuffle the cards and showed him how to lay them out on the table, and when the boy had studied the colored pictures and had learned their various meanings, the magician gave him an amulet that would help him interpret their significance. This amulet was an Eye of Horus, painted in azure on faience, and a present worthy of royalty, for it was an amulet with an interesting history, possessed of strange and wondrous properties. Horus, the great celestial falcon-god who personified and ruled the sky, had for eyes the morning sun and the evening sun (though some said the sun and the moon), and a replica of his divine Eye was a mighty charm for making offerings more acceptable and rituals more potent. Such an Eye, it was said, could see both the future and the past and was an invaluable aid in matters of necromancy and in prophecy.

The prince wore the Eye of Horus about his neck and learned the tarot well, and in his turn and for the sake of practice he laid out the cards as he had been taught and proceeded to tell the magician's own fate.

The first card he turned up was that of the Hanged Man, and the magician blanched, for he had taught his pupil well. The card of the Hanged Man meant but one thing: death upon the gallows. And both prince and magician were filled with fear.

There was at that time an even greater magician (so it was said) living at Ded-Snefru, farther down the Nile, who, having heard of the Canaanite in the marketplace who had so charmed the prince, became jealous and vowed to do away with his rival. The sorcerer's name was Dedi; it was whispered that he practiced the black arts and was capable of all manner of horrors that affrighted all who saw them. It was said that this Dedi could go to the House of the Dead in the great necropolis and call forth the spirits that had departed from the dead, and that he could perform other prodigies of necromancy, bringing the dead to life and delving into their secrets. Being forced to take note of this upstart Canaanite from Byblos, Dedi was filled with hate and malice, and resolved to rid himself of so contemptible an adversary.

The manner of revenge chosen by Dedi was wicked indeed. Many spells were cast, many incantations chanted, and before long the old Canaanite's pupil, the young prince, fell ill. On the orders of his father and mother, Dedefhar was removed from the company of the magician to that of the court physicians, who labored desperately to save the boy's life. Their efforts failing, the prince succumbed to his malady, though the cause of death was not immediately determined. Since the disease was, however, first manifested by an insidious form of scrofula, Dedi caused to be repeated the rumor that the prince's contact with the Canaanite magician had brought him low. Dedi rejoiced when Cheops, believing the story, banished his rival from all the lands of Egypt.

Meanwhile, the young prince's body lay for some weeks in the House of the Dead, forbidden by ancient custom to be touched by other than those individuals and priests certified to prepare it for burial. Once this was accomplished, it was bedecked with an array of jewels, talismans, amulets, and medals, not for the sake of ornament but to give the deceased strength and possessions while wandering in the underworld: a gold ring for the little finger, a bracelet around the wrist, and, on the chest, that same Eye of Horus whose occult properties the prince had become so fond of. After the body was smeared with more magic oil and henna paste, the wrapping was begun, with each resin-soaked strip carefully and traditionally placed, forming a warp and weft of ancient configuration, the strips inscribed with prayers and marked in ink with holy symbols. To do all this properly required a goodly time.

During this period, with the stench of asafetida rank in the gloom, the corpse was watched over night and day by priests who, sleepless and unrelieved, were held responsible for its safe-keeping until it might be entombed. On the night before the remains were completely wrapped, the guardian priests fell one by one asleep, until only the last of them remained awake. Having extinguished the burning incense, this man removed the cotton wadding from his nostrils and approached the corpse, whose linen swathes he unwrapped until he exposed the Eye of Horus lying upon the prince's chest. This he sequestered, then took up a position close to the corpse, holding its hands pressed between his own and laying his shorn head upon its breast, as if absorbing what remaining life currents might still emanate from the dead. Thus embracing the prince, he continued through the night, and thus was he found the next day. Accused of defiling the holy dead, the culprit was brought before Pharaoh, where he was recognized as the magician from the marketplace who had taught the king's son to juggle and to bring forth blue pigeons from the air.

How he had breached the sacred precincts of the House of the Dead disguised as a priest never came to light, though it was said before he was sentenced to hang that he claimed to have been born during the reign of Menes himself, an unbelievable allegation, since Menes, the first Pharaoh of all Egypt, had reigned some four hundred years earlier. Such talk enraged Dedi, who was resolved to put an end to this charlatan-beggar for once and all. But first there were the rites to be performed, that Prince Dedefhar might be properly laid to rest.

No such rites awaited the magician, only the unmarked grave of the pariah; in retaliation for the theft of the Eye of Horus he was blinded in one eye and hanged before the populace, and within a month no one even recalled the charlatan who had performed tricks amid the dust and dogs and dung of the marketplace.

And Dedi, king of conjurors, ruled supreme in the Upper Kingdom and in the Lower as well.

Where was there a wiser man in all the world than Solomon, great Solomon whose wisdom was known unto all the corners of the earth? Who could make a juster, more disinterested, more sublime judgment, when it came to solving a quarrel or mending divisions, whether of lands, chattels, or even babes in arms? Who but this great magus-ruler, whose empire stretched from river to river, sea to sea, the greatest kingdom a living man had ever seen.

But in a neighboring kingdom there lived a glorious queen, the beautiful and desirable Queen of Sheba, and it was arranged that this monarch should travel to the realm of great Solomon, and there the two rulers should meet and determine what degree of mutual admiration existed between them. And so it was that mighty preparations went forward, all with the idea of making a great celebration when the two monarchs should first set eyes upon each other.

Now, it was widely known that the king and his wizards had for many years been compiling a great book meant to contain all the secrets of magic and necromancy, spells, enchantments, and the like, and when all this arcana—including the secrets of the ancient Egyptians, who were after all the first magicians—had been gathered together and written down upon scrolls, the book was known as *The Key of Solomon,* a work of enormous value, for he who could delve into its pages and learn from its lines would have power to make jealous the very gods. And jealous was the king, Solomon, who highly prized the work that bore his name, and he was resolute that none but qualified wizards and magi would be made privy to its precious pages, its formulae and incantations. For it was this compilation of wisdom and knowledge that contained all of the secrets known to man until that time.

But when the Queen of Sheba was come to Solomon's domain, and welcomed as befitted her crown, the king carefully put away his books, for he had other matters to consider, romantic matters of the sort to which any man might wish to give his full attention. And thus it was that Solomon, forgetting the cares of the day and the meditations of the night, engaged in intimate conversation with the fabled beauty who was his guest, and who so willingly offered herself to him. Meantime, and while the guards were slow witted with the wine that had been generously dispensed to one and all, the greatest treasure of the kingdom, *The Key of Solomon,* was stolen.

A cold dawn brought the realization that the king had been robbed of that which he most cherished, and, still somewhat befuddled by drink, Solomon set about retrieving from his brain all he was able to remember of the book. But the scrolls and their contents were irreplaceable, and who could possibly remember all they contained? And in his rage and misery the king sent away again the woman he had meant to make his queen, in order to spend his remaining years on earth striving to recapitulate the contents of the great *Key.* In this endeavor, wise as he was, Solomon failed miserably.

And no one, neither the great wise king, nor his clever advisors, nor indeed anyone at the palace, had taken time to notice the mendicant who had departed through the wide-flung gates, with property not rightfully his hidden under his smelly rags, property whose possession he craved as a thirsty man gulps for water, a dying man for life itself. A fraying, knotted thong hung around his neck, and suspended from that thong, against his bony chest, he wore the Eye of Horus.

He could fly!

Couldn't he?

Through the thinnest of air, he had levitated himself before the court, before Nero himself; had defied Peter the Fisherman, laughed in his face, then risen from the marble floor and floated high and free in the air while the court and the emperor sat aghast, the wine spilling unheeded from their cups. Consternation! Disbelief! Fear! A gaggle of astonished voices, murmurs, cries, applause, puzzlement, yet before their very eyes . . .

He had done this, hadn't he?

A magician from Samaria, whom the heretic Christians

branded for having begged of the apostles, those sheeplike men, to touch him with their hands and make his magical powers greater, had offered them money in exchange for this service. Naturally they refused, called the sin by his name: simony. For he was Simon Magus, the Great Magicker.

Simon's feats were truly miraculous, greater than those of that other magician, Jesus of Nazareth, who, it was said, had turned water to wine, had made the dead rise and live, the blind see, had fed a hungry multitude from some paltry loaves of bread, a fish or two. But Simon Magus—greater by far, for while the Nazarene had rendered unto Caesar what was his, the Samaritan had made docile the mad despot of Imperial Rome—by his magic had the emperor eating out of his hand, and Simon himself wore the purple, a wizard's robe with symbols embroidered in gold thread, a marvel of a garment.

There were many stories about the magus broadcast throughout the empire. This was one: Before the throne of the great Nero the magician knelt, while a centurion clutched a sword, stood over him, and with a vicious blow struck his head from his neck, and blood ran on the marble and women fainted and men turned pale; but no sooner had they bent to remove the remains than they discovered the curly-coated body and horned head of a slaughtered ram, while the magus in his purple gown and undecipherable symbols appeared amid the throng, in perfect composure and decidedly whole.

Another story: He had a mirror, a magic mirror, and that which it reflected was not necessarily real but only what one thought was real, and he made it seem that the mirror cast reflections of those things that were coveted and lusted after. There the dead and departed might be seen again, or the beauty of a woman, or all the treasures of the earth—whatever was wanted.

In the magic mirror he conjured up the vision of Helen, wife of the Spartan King Menelaus and the ruin of Troy. Not only conjured her, they said, but brought her to living life, though this poor creature was no more than a gutter whore in whose body the real Helen resided. In arrogance, and defying all morality, he washed and dressed her, gave her perfumes and jewels, and paraded her in the streets like a queen, this Helen-whore, indifferent to the laughter that the sight of her provoked among the multitude.

It mattered little, for he had the crowd's applause, the rich rewards, money given into his hand, honors conferred, not the least of these the patronage of the emperor. Of course they said the magician had hypnotized Nero, had seduced him through the fraudulent Helen and trick stage effects. A charlatan, nothing more.

For what man could have his head lopped off and still live? Who indeed could fly that was not a bird? Who could bring the dead Helen to life in another age?

It was only illusion, they said.

It was.

Wasn't it?

But who could tell what was truth, what was illusion? The magician could, though for him illusion was the true reality.

Who was mightier than Merlin, prophet, magician, and privy councillor to Arthur the King? Who but he had provided for the establishing and prosperity of the kingdom, as well as for the very engendering of the king? And yet Merlin had become a sorrowful, lonely figure, bent under the weight of his vast knowledge and terrifying because of his occult powers and his uncertain (some said diabolical) origins. Long before the events, he foresaw the hideous ruin awaiting Arthur's realm, the treachery and faithlessness, the internecine carnage, friends striking down friends, brothers slaughtering brothers, the king and his only son barbarously murdering one another in simultaneous paroxysms of rage. It was likewise with Merlin's own personal doom; the seer could foretell but not forestall it. A power, greater still then his, would seek him out. And so, it seems, he deliberately went to meet it.

His fate was not long in arriving. Her name was Viviane.

She was one of the damsels of the mysterious Lady of the Lake, and she came to Arthur's court as part of King Pellinore's entourage. From the moment he saw her, Merlin would let her have no rest; he must be at her side, he must converse with her, he must gaze into her dark and disingenuous eyes. The girl fought down her revulsion, along with her scorn, and learned what she could from this decrepit sorcerer while prudently keeping him at a distance.

So they traveled together into the forests of Cornwall, each entreating the other, he for her supple body, she for his secret wisdom. And there Merlin lured Viviane into the hollow of a great tree, where, at last, in exchange for the promise of an embrace, he made known to her certain fatal charms and revealed the magical properties of the ancient Eye that hung on a gold chain about his neck; whereupon, stepping lightly away from the tree, she spoke the appropriate charm.

Though he knew there was no escape, he could not keep from struggling against the bark thickening around him, pressing against his chest. As he tried to lift himself from the tree, his arms were pinned above him, and he felt the blood ebbing from his feet, which grew cold and stiff, anchoring him like roots to the earth. He could not speak. His breath came hard, catching in his throat, where it chilled, congealing like ice. He had foreseen it all, but not this, to be so cold. His hair swarmed above him, twisting into the branches so that his head ached and he could not turn his face. His eyes searched the narrowing gap. He saw the bright fabric of her dress, and then the slender pale hand darted through the weaving, encircling fibers to snatch the gold chain from his neck. He raised his eyes and saw above him new green shoots where his fingers had been. The next things he saw were the last: Viviane's exultant, pitiless eyes, laughing at him from the face of a man older yet than he.

Acolytes swung heavy censers, and clouds of strange, aromatic incense filled the great hall with intoxicating perfume. Silver stars embroidered on the blue damask that covered the walls of the room sparkled in the dancing light of a hundred candles. Placed at intervals along the walls, pedestals of polished wood bore statues of Egyptian deities. In the middle of the room stood an altar, and, facing it from the far wall, a golden throne on a dais covered with fine white silk. A solemn hymn begun by the acolytes was taken up fervently by the gathered faithful.

It was a noble assembly; the liveried ushers had been called upon to pronounce some of the most resounding names in France. And only in Paris could so resplendent and fashionable a gathering take place. Nowhere else were the ladies' gowns so rich, so bright, their jewels so tasteful and expensive, the men's buckled shoes and lace shirts and formal coats so exquisite and so imposing. As they stood and sang in the closed room, adding faint hints of sweat, powder, and perfume to the all-pervasive incense, they looked forward eagerly to the revelation of secrets that would regenerate mankind and change the world. They could not know that within a few years their world would indeed change, beyond all recognition; revolution was a phenomenon occurring in Anglo-Saxon countries, and the guillotine had not yet been invented.

The hymn ended, a hidden door opened, and suddenly the Grand Copt himself was in their midst and approached the throne, his unprepossessing figure made stately by his long black robe, his stole of gold brocade, and his tall, golden double crown, modeled after the pharaohs' crown that signified the unification of Egypt's Upper and Lower Kingdoms. For this was Count Alessandro di Cagliostro, Grand Copt of the order of Egyptian Masonry originally established by the prophets Enoch and Elias. He was attended by his wife, the radiantly beautiful Serafina, and it must be admitted that more than one male member of the company had come hoping to receive personal initiation into the mysteries from the countess herself.

In sonorous but heavily accented French, the Grand Copt welcomed the company, invoking the pure spirits that hovered over it. Then, after a significant pause, he plunged headlong into an ecstatic, overwhelming, not always comprehensible discourse. He was come, he said, to heal the sick, give succor to the poor, and bring about the moral and physical regeneration of the world. He would accomplish this mission through occult powers and secret knowledge arrived at over many centuries and many incarnations, a long apprenticeship that had raised him to the summit of the Great Pyramid of Being and rendered him an adept in such arcane arts as healing, prophecy, and spirit evocation. His was the white magic capable of overcoming the powers of darkness and transfiguring humanity.

He spoke at length, as though entranced, captivating his listeners with his strange imagery, his mysterious allusions, his mesmerizing eyes, the sheer force of his will. Suddenly he stopped and gestured to Serafina. The spellbound audience watched as she opened another hidden door and led out a shy young girl, dressed in a gleaming white robe with a crimson sash. This was the *petite colombe*, the "little dove" whose purity and innocence made her the perfect liaison between the Grand Copt and the spirit world. She was led to a chair surrounded on three sides by ornate screens, and she sat inside this "tabernacle," facing the congregation from behind a table that was bare except for three candles. Hypnotically, inexorably, the High Priest induced a trance in the girl, muttering to her and breathing upon her; then, supported by the cadenced chants of the faithful, he began to adjure one of the attendant spirits to make itself manifest. Finally the child, who had been sitting stiffly and silently, groaned aloud.

"What is it that you see?" cried the Grand Copt.

The girl replied in a faint, broken voice, the voice of a scared child. "I see . . . a giant man . . . in a white cloak . . . with a red cross on it."

"Ask him his name," Cagliostro commanded, his tone a mixture of reverence and authority.

The child asked the question, her voice faint and broken as before. Then her lips moved again, but what issued from them was no young maiden's voice but a resonant bass, uncanny and penetrating: "*I am the Archangel Zobiachel!*"

The crowd gasped and shuddered, but the High Priest's voice was calm. "Do not be afraid, brothers and sisters. The spirit loves us all. Ask him to kiss you, little dove."

There was a rushing, as of great wings, audible to the whole rapt assembly, followed by the distinct, unmistakable sound of a kiss. The girl's right cheek glowed brightly, and a surge of warmth flooded the hall. A few people began to sob quietly. One lady, amid the whispering of silks and taffeta, slid softly to the floor and lay in a bright heap, unnoticed and unmoving.

Such was the power of the Grand Copt, and such was the faith of his believers. Yet there were some scoffers who said that he was neither Copt nor count, but plain Giuseppe Balsamo, a scion of

Palermo's working classes, and that he had begun his charlatan's career as a peddler of panaceas and amulets, working his way up the scale to mystical communion with the cosmos. Others told tales of a direr sort, that he was in league with the powers of darkness, that his magic was black and blasphemous, that he hosted "Suppers with the Dead," where the illustrious damned sat down at table with the living.

And yet his prophecies were often accurate. Was that guesswork? He healed the sick, made the lame walk and the blind see. Was that mass hysteria, mass hypnosis? Who could tell what was truth and what was illusion? Perhaps the distinction was not clear, even to the magician himself; or perhaps when he died ten years later in one of the Inquisition's dungeons, his tortured body foul with its own filth, perhaps even then what others called illusion was his reality, and the Count Alessandro di Cagliostro, adept, high priest, miracle worker, gratefully betook himself to his next incarnation.

The men and women arriving at the great house, just off Park Lane in one of London's poshest neighborhoods, were a mixed lot, brought together by a shared interest in occult phenomena; no class distinctions exist in the spirit world. Some of those whom Mrs. Angus Macbride (widow of Professor Macbride of Edinburgh) had invited were personally unacquainted with one another, but many bore names familiar in esoteric circles. Several foreign guests lent the gathering an international flavor, and titles of one sort or another—Lord, Lady, Sir, Reverend, Captain, Professor—figured in the appellations of most of the company, but not all. Jane Cox, for example, the milliner whose trances had first stirred Mrs. Macbride's interest in the unseen, was an honored, familiar guest. Only one person was totally unknown, by name or reputation, to his companions, but the openhearted Mrs. Macbride, paying no heed to his slightly outlandish clothes and more than slightly outlandish accent, welcomed him warmly, and his gaunt, hawklike features and the penetrating gaze of his single eye exacted deference from the rest.

Before moving on to the real business of the evening, the visitors, about eighteen in all, paused to chat and browse in the handsome library. The dark, polished shelves were laden with works of occult literature, which was flourishing vigorously as the long reign of Queen Victoria drew to its close. Enshrined on a shelf all its own stood a photograph of the golden lily, perfectly formed and seven feet tall, which had been materialized at a famous séance given by one Madame d'Esperance, author of *Spirit Land*, one of the books to be found here.

At a gentle hint from Mrs. Macbride, the guests left the library and filed into the séance room. The house had recently been wired for electric light, but the maids called it "electric dark"— the bulbs were maddeningly fragile, and the light they shed was much weaker than gaslight. In the designated room a single lamp glimmered dimly, outshone by the intermittent flames of an expiring fire. The company took their seats around a large, circular table, their hushed conversation charged with anticipation. Having closed the heavy main doors, Mrs. Macbride swept aside the thin curtains that covered the entrance to an inner room, or "cabinet," revealing there the seated figure of her guest of honor: Mr. Eglinton, the celebrated medium.

Eglinton was a stout young man with a placid face, hooded eyes, and the vague expression of one tottering on the brink of sleep, unsure whether to climb out or fall in. Renowned in occult circles throughout Europe, he had achieved successes in every type of mediumistic endeavor, from levitation to clairvoyance, from telepathy and telekinesis to the various forms of spirit evocation and ectoplasmic materialization. He traveled constantly, giving demonstrations of his powers all over the world, and had just returned to his native England from a triumphant tour that included sittings in Vienna, Paris, and Venice ("a veritable hotbed of spiritualism," as he described it to his friend Mrs. Macbride).

After nodding distractedly to the gathering, the medium sat in the chair nearest the fireplace and bowed his head. The room, except for the death throes of the fire, remained utterly silent for a few minutes, then Eglinton raised his arms and extended his hands to the persons sitting on either side of him. As if acting on a signal, the entire company joined hands around the table—the one-eyed stranger did so with an air of hard-won resignation— and sat there in the gloom, striving to unite and focus their thoughts on the immaterial world. Suddenly, behind the entranced medium, who remained seated, head bowed, eyes closed, clutching his neighbors' hands, an indistinct, gauzy form materialized, seeming to grow in height until it began to resemble a very tall man. This shape passed silently around the room, shaking hands with three or four of the guests. When it had nearly completed its circuit of the table and was approaching Mr. Eglinton, he moaned loudly and staggered to his feet, where he stood swaying, half supported by Captain Rolleston, who was seated on his left hand. The form seized Eglinton by the shoulders and dragged him into the cabinet. A few seconds later, when Mrs. Macbride drew aside the curtain with a shaking hand, Eglinton could be seen inside, sprawled as though lifeless across the armchair, but otherwise the cabinet was empty.

Those of the company who had moved from their chairs took them again at a sign from Mrs. Macbride. All eyes strained toward the cabinet's curtain, below which the medium's feet were protruding slightly into the room. A few chairs scraped, the fire hissed, then silence descended again upon the gathering.

More minutes passed, heavy with wonder and expectation. Then sounds came from the cabinet, and the curtain billowed outward, taking on a shape almost human, but this disorienting illusion lasted only a few seconds before the medium emerged from beneath the curtain, having walked straight into it without drawing it aside. He was obviously in a state of trance, and for some minutes he lurched about the room among the sitters. Leaning against the wall that faced the fireplace, he began to draw out, apparently from his side, a dingy whitish substance that fell to the floor like some misshapen rope. While the medium continued to pull it out from his side, the ectoplasm—for so it was—began to increase in mass and pulsate, moving both laterally and vertically as though driven from underneath. The mass grew slowly to a height of about three feet, and then, with a sudden burst, it attained full stature. Mr. Eglinton deftly flicked away the white material covering the head of the form, and as he did so, this covering seemed to merge with the apparition's clothing. The link connecting the figure to the medium was severed or became invisible, no one could say for sure, for at this point a loud shout in an unrecognizable language brought the demonstration to an abrupt end.

The one-eyed man thrust himself away from the table and leapt to his feet, fixing Mr. Eglinton with a look of murderous contempt; the form at Eglinton's side dematerialized at once. Stepping past the shocked guests, the stranger stopped beside Mrs. Macbride's chair and bowed stiffly, snatching and kissing her fluttering hand in one rough motion. "I beg your pardon, Madame," he murmured, then turned and left the room.

Alone on the street and walking away from the house as fast as his old legs could carry him, the man rubbed his one good eye and glowered into the dark, his face more fierce and hawkish than ever. What tawdriness, what fakery, what fools! And this medium, this Eglinton, with his pudgy fingers like white worms and his indolent, stupid eyes. Ectoplasm, indeed! If he thought Eglinton was what he was looking for, his brain must be turning to ectoplasm. But how many choices did he have? The world was poised at the edge of the precipice, ready to slide down into the snake pit of the twentieth century, and weariness was laid across his shoulders like an iron yoke. His amulet was gone; his search for an apprentice, for a successor, had grown so desperate he was sitting down among idiots to admire the posturing of charlatans; and he was alone, tired, thoroughly ready to leave. He couldn't bear this mumbo jumbo, this hocus-pocus, these tricks a child could see through, especially when he knew, and when he needed, real magic; not phantoms conjured up in the dull glow of electric lightbulbs and half-dead fires, but something from nothing, light out of darkness: night magic, real night magic.

CHAPTER ONE

Saskia in Tears

The man approaching the Metropolitan Museum of Art, on Fifth Avenue at Eighty-first Street in New York City, was seedy, tall, scarecrow gaunt, clad in indifferently fitting preacher black, despite the heat. His head bobbing, he strode amid the crowd, shadowed by a large black silk umbrella as if shunning the light, like a parasol-shaded spinster. His spare form seemed to gather mass by a trick of the eye, optically, like a desert mirage, undulant, damply vaporous in the convection currents rising from the steaming pavement, a discernible aura emanating from the dark outline of his spidery figure, wobbly, insubstantial, all of it wavering in the heat.

His caricature of a nose ended in a bulbous knob, red, as though not even the umbrella had managed to protect it from the sun, and the growth of hair curling outward from around his dark red mouth—mustache and beard, both curly—glistened with perspiration. His expression was vague, abstracted, one might say almost blank, his heavily Semitic features made more striking by the eyes, one of which, if careful notice were taken, drew fine light to itself even under the umbrella, while the other was dim and lacked sheen, skewed off in its alignment, as if seeking its separate way or viewing the world askance.

The lope-gaited, awkward figure reached the museum steps, which he took two at a time, and bounded through the wide doors, loose-jointed, long, manipulative fingers swinging jerkily like slack-strung puppet's hands, his gangling stride neither taking space nor assuming it, but seeming rather to encroach upon it as he came. One might have thought that, spiderlike, he had let himself down on an invisible filament to dangle there and, after the habit of arachnids, could retract himself with ease at any moment.

He looked around over the heads of the crowd and moved across the Great Hall to the checkroom, where he rid himself of his umbrella and a large paper shopping bag: the words "Big Brown Bag" printed on its side identified it as coming from Bloomingdale's. Then he crossed to the ticket booth, his steps resounding emphatically on the marble floor. It was his shoes and his curious way of walking in them that caused this emphasis. They were hardly what might be called ordinary footgear, but of a peculiar sort, ankle-high, in an old-fashioned gaiter style with inserted elastic panels. The worn patent leather was cracked and seamed across the instep, soiled with long wear but not so much that the blunted toes did not gleam when he moved; and he moved in a peculiar way, splayfooted, with toes turned out, each heel striking the marble first, then the sole coming down, producing a splat-splat splat-splat sound, an almost comical rhythm that rebounded acoustically in the hushed hall.

An off-duty flatfoot? A burlesque comedian? Who could tell?

At the ticket booth he paid the suggested admission fee of five dollars, pinched the small tab button he received onto his jacket lapel, and entered the Egyptian wing, where he inspected the antiquities displayed in the jewelry room off the main corridor, while the uniformed guard locked the backs of his knees against fatigue. Glass cases held, on illuminated shelves, an array of gold bracelets and necklaces, other cases contained talismans and amulets, including a number of scarabs carved from semiprecious stones—lapis lazuli, jade, obsidian, rose quartz—some raised

over little squares of mirror so that the writing on their under-
sides would be legible.

Reading, the man had a peculiar way of holding his head
canted to one side, with the left eye askew in its socket, as one
might regard a single object from two separate points of view, the
white of the one walleye gray and pallid, the iris lackluster and
obliquely angled, hardly matching the right one, which peered
with the intensity of a magnifying glass focusing the sun's rays
down to the point of combustion.

His was an unhurried survey, interested but not too interested
(the guard, though bored, was watchful). One could safely say
moderately interested: the man seemed to mutter something as
he bent to study, amid the collection of scarabs, an Eye of Horus
painted on an azure fragment of faience. His thick gray brows
contracted as he peered through the glass; he put his ear to the
protective wall, compressed his lips more tightly. He placed his
spread palm on the glass, silently shook his head. The guard
came meandering in; the man ignored him, gazing at the fragment as though considering a swap, an eye for an eye, as Scrip-
ture says, that ancient visionary Eye for his more recent but
sightless one.

The guard ambled out. The visitor might ponder these pharaonic
treasures with impunity; there was no one to disturb him, the room
was now quite empty. Today, the larger share of the museumgoing
public was upstairs on the second floor, attracted by the famous
Rembrandt portrait recently placed on exhibition in the European
Painting wing at the head of the grand staircase, now thronged
with art lovers going to view or already having admired the portrait of Saskia. The appertaining brochure printed under the museum's imprimatur for the occasion stated that the priceless work,
on loan from the Rijksmuseum in Amsterdam, had been painted in
1637, just after the artist's first marriage. It hung in solitary splen-
dor against one large red wall in the second gallery to the right, the
space before it cordoned off with velvet ropes.

There it was, the partially nude figure, full of warmth and ten-
derness, well composed, offering a serene harmony of flesh tones,
a deft handling of the brushstrokes, whose rich impasto brought a

luminous quality to the features, captured in the subtle chiaroscuro the artist controlled so well, while the contours of the figure softly receded into shadow. Though bare breasted, she seemed chaste and maidenly, her features reflecting a pensiveness, even a melancholy.

Caught in her spell, the viewers gazed in awe. They spoke in hushed tones. They peered closely to examine details or stood well back to appreciate the whole, lost in the reverie that an indisputable masterpiece can evoke. And, strangely, so substantial was the artist's talent that he was able to lend that thoughtful expression a lachrymose, grieving air, a quality falling just short of tragedy. It was as if Saskia, in the bloom of youth and health, already contemplated her impending decline into illness and death: the tear just there, in the corner of the eye, how real it seemed, how wet, a single, sparkling drop of moisture, poised at the duct to roll down the face. And—more strangely—it fell, leaving behind a shining trickle visible on the canvas. It fell, to be replaced by another tear, and yet another. Tears in both eyes, and those falling. Saskia was crying. The sitter in the portrait, Rembrandt's wife, was crying.

Astonishing.

Incredible.

Miraculous.

"Saskia in Tears" was what she would be called before evening, the famous "weeping painting." The curious spectators surged forward, their voices rising in volume. In the general confusion, guards from opposite ends of the gallery hurried to restore order among the crowd. The guards halted, also staring in disbelief. In the hubbub no one noticed the bearded man with the red nose who likewise had been viewing the work, aloof from the rest, standing to one side, one eye askew, the other fixed not precisely on the portrait itself, but obliquely, possibly upon the faces of those looking at it.

Soon after, he left. Presently he would arrive at the place where he was meant to be.

CHAPTER TWO

Michael into Frog

It was the Thursday after Labor Day, a noontime of record-breaking temperatures, when the city lay sprawled as though poleaxed under the stunning heat, when people's clothing stuck like wet wash to their backs, and under a poisoned sun New Yorkers were already exhausted and cranky. Michael Hawke was performing at the corner of the park, on the plaza, under the blindingly golden statue of General William Tecumseh Sherman.

While Saskia is weeping, while the minutes are ticking by and Hawke's own wristwatch recording them, while the man with the black umbrella is approaching and Michael is working the lunchtime crowd, it will not hurt to use this time to discover some facts concerning him. Name, Michael Hawke. Age, twenty-six. Born, Buffalo, New York. Tragic childhood, parents believed dead. Brought up in Ohio by mother's older sisters. Resident of New York for almost five years. One more aspiring actor lacking prospects. His greater aspiration: to be a magician. Not merely a magician, but the Greatest Magician in the World. He bills himself as Presto the Great and dreams of doing presentation shows for large corporations; what more fitting employment for the

Greatest Magician in the World? An appealing young man with an engaging smile, earnest in his belief that he has overcome his past and is on his way to Great Things, he is confident, possessed of all the requisites: talent, dexterity, imagination, audacity. Plus the necessary guts and fortitude, and a nervy ambition to succeed. Last but not least, he has a deep-seated curiosity, a personality trait that, as we know, killed the cat.

Today, Michael was in whiteface, doing mimes. He was a street artist worthy of the name and a not uncommon attraction in this quarter of the city. Since returning from a season of summer stock, he had staked out his turf at the southeastern tip of Central Park, across Fifth Avenue from the Sherry Netherland, across Central Park South from the Plaza Hotel and the fountain, its rim dotted with idlers defying the heat, while here, in the brick-paved area margined with low hedges, the benches were filled, and all around the side gathered a catch-as-catch-can audience of watchers.

Here was Michael: an enviable helmet of dark hair, thick, shaggy, glossy, looked-after. A trained-down body, lithe, agile, quick to respond to the mental impulse, controlled by the sharply honed precision of the athlete and nurtured by the vital enthusiasms of the young. He was dressed and accoutred for his trade in close-fitting black trousers, soft black shoes, a top hat, and an oddment of costume resembling a grenadier's jacket, with gilt frogging front and back. This coat was a necessary part of his act, for the lining was a labyrinth of sewn-in pockets and cunning flaps where he had cached his store of sleight-of-hand materials, including his trick wallet, one compartment of which held the money he had saved all summer and which must that afternoon be deposited in his account before the bank's closing time.

He had a thin, almost feral face, washed out with a coat of dead-white makeup; its sweating planes and turnings were smoothed to a matte glaze, its features accented with dark pencil, outlining, widening, exaggerating the size of his eyes, his mouth painted a dark carmine, which did not precisely follow the beveling of the lips: the classic tradition of the pantomime mask, followed in every detail.

Moving, darting, dancing even, his shadow a perfect replication in this hot city high noon, he was by turns antic, doleful, mocking, manic, outrageous; but in its brief moments of repose his face reflected the look of one in control of serious, even important, matters. His talent was not in question, only his ambition, and it required but scant perusal of his audience to determine that they were responding here not to the hack but to the artist at work.

They had encountered him, a stranger, some in hilarity, some in mild humor, some against their wills, even in apathy, and from their remoteness and boredom he had fashioned—for this was his true métier—something they would remember for a moment, an hour, a day, but something that in some infinitesimal way would alter them, reveal them to themselves. For it was not Michael's desire that they should see him but rather themselves; he wanted to ignite the flash of insight that would awaken them to their own persons. It was a combination of his natural intuition and his intellect that made him a keen perceiver of individual natures and foibles, but in another fifteen minutes now, twenty at the most, he would commit a grave error regarding the man with the umbrella.

Until then, however, there was time enough for him to have some fun, and collect a little money in the hat, too. The pretty girl on the steps of the statue, the one with the flute, was Emily Chang, Michael's girlfriend; that is to say, Emily was in love with him, though Michael, whose intuitive gift for reading emotions, inclinations, desires did not always extend to his own, was not certain that he totally reciprocated Emily's feelings. He loved her; he was sure of that. But "in love" . . . ? That was a different matter and called for commitment he wasn't sure he was ready to make. Yet he appreciated her generous heart, her loyalty, her exotic good looks, her talent. She played the flute beautifully, and Michael enjoyed having his mimes orchestrated. But like all pipers, Emily must be paid; Michael thought he'd been spending more and more time with her by way of making up for the paltry sums that fell to her share, but the truth was that he enjoyed her company more than anyone else's, even his own. So they spent many of their nights together, and two or three days a week she was there with her flute, improvising accompaniments for his act and passing the hat afterward. She was bright and willing and nice to have around. Everyone in New York should have someone around.

Michael was doing one of his slow-motion routines, Emily was making music, and down the steps of the Metropolitan Museum the tall man in black was coming, holding his umbrella above him as though the sun were anathema, turning right and beginning his journey south, down Fifth Avenue, lost in thought, moving with his odd, splattering gait, halting for the light, heading toward the plaza and the eventual, inevitable encounter.

Michael and Emily working, then, and the man approaching, still unseen. And someone else en passant: a matron come from shopping at Bergdorf's. Middle-aged, stout, carelessly dressed, perfunctorily accessorized, hot and tired—and how long since a man had kissed her, publicly kissed her? Unaware of what was about to happen, she passed through the crowd, Michael's audience. In a trice he lunged for her in wolf-prowl crouch, spun her to him, and made a mock assault on her person, becoming a lecher, Groucho Marx, flicking an imaginary cigar, wiggling an imaginary mustache, leering, then Harpo, squeezing obscene quacks from a rubber duck produced from his jacket. Then he embraced her with comic passion, while she, first alarmed, then with a flush of embarrassment, swatted at him with her plastic bag, yanked away in anger, looked around at the faces, feeling a fool. Emily, trilling her flute, bobbled three notes as she laughed. Everyone was laughing except Michael, looking innocently rueful behind his makeup. In spite of herself the woman laughed too. Michael swept her a bow and regally escorted her on her way, Emily interpolating eight or so bars from "Pomp and Circumstance."

In a flash, Michael abandoned his victim for another, darting through the crowd to sidle up beside an Uptown hipster shagging along on stiltlike platform shoes, black and sassy, a cat, and Michael in whiteface mimicking his slouch, his sassy blackness, his feline self. The man, unoffended, showed a row of pearly teeth and good-natured recognition of this unexpected mirror image, stopping for a fraternal exchange of Harlem Hi-Baby hand slaps, elbow knocks, hip swings, butt bumps, while Emily piped out some jive. She finished the riff and noodled some off-key notes as Michael attached himself to a derelict drunk, instantly making himself a pal, a fellow inebriate, jabbering soundless inconsequentials, staggering, nodding, listening in blind stupefaction to the drunk's sodden queries, agreeing and disagreeing alternately, until, taking his cue, the drunk produced a pint of Four Roses and offered it, but Michael-drunk had his own, an imaginary bottle from which he guzzled blissfully.

Abandoning the drunk, Michael-sober sped to the curb to lie supine on the fender of a limousine, arms locked behind his head, knees crossed, a man of leisure. The chauffeur, concerned about the paint job, honked his horn, and a rear window rolled down, a face appeared.

"Hey, babe, get out of the sun, the heat's getting to you." Off the fender, Michael ran around to the window. It was his friend, Dazz, and next to him, a gorgeous redhead, and in the corner, a weird character, grotesquely fat, wearing about three million dollars' worth of rocks on his fingers. Michael figured that Dazz, a painter, was probably hustling the guy for a portrait commission. Out came the rubber duck again, quack, quack. The redhead laughed, tossed her hair, clanking bracelets on her arm. What a laugh, Michael thought.

"Write when you get work," Dazz called. "*Ciao, bello.*" Then, an afterthought, he held up his hand as a signal to wait, quick consultation with the bejeweled mountain in the corner, at the end of which he spoke again: "Come over tonight, seven-thirty. Bring the band. Don't worry about dinner—we're going to a party. Eat, drink, and be merry." He rolled up the window, sealing himself in air-conditioned luxury while the limousine moved on, and the big guy limply waved his rich rocks at the rear window.

The tall, thin man in black, still carrying his umbrella open above his head, observed this exchange as he approached, and with a spark of interest he watched the young mime as he turned back to the crowd, which the man himself now joined, umbrella and all.

Michael watched the car turn in at the Plaza, where Dazz would be having lunch in the Oak Room again. You sly bastard, he thought, grinning. Then, like a shot, he was back on the sidewalk. The crowd was breaking up. Had enough? Okay, magic time. He stuffed the duck back in his tunic and signaled Emily, who ran up carrying his little magician's stand with the sign: PRESTO THE GREAT. From nowhere he produced a silver half-dollar, sent it rolling across his knuckles, made it disappear, drew it again from his elbow, changed it before their eyes into a nickel the size of a small saucer. Applause. Like it? Get this one. He produced a pack of cards, fanned them expertly, offered them to the closest member of the audience, a woman. Take a card, any card; she complied. He shut his eyes while she showed it to the rest— the three of hearts—then returned it to the pack. He closed the deck again, tapped it, thinking hard. Zip, he slipped his wallet out of his inside jacket pocket, unzipped a compartment, and produced the three of hearts from within. He showed the compartment empty, returned the wallet to his pocket, repeated the trick with another person, this time having him sign the chosen card— the nine of spades. Another cut and shuffle, and the deck was closed up. Out came the wallet again; the autographed card was inside. More applause.

Like it? Terrific. Next, the silks, colored handkerchiefs magically flying from his fingertips, he knotted them, pulled them from his fists, one by one, all unknotted, then balled them up and from them snapped out an American flag, while Emily played "The Stars and Stripes Forever."

It was at this point that Michael noticed the black umbrella above the crowd. There was something in the way the umbrella was held, in the idea of an umbrella at all on such a day, that intrigued him. He took a closer look.

The tall man's ludicrousness was apparent, something just short of grotesque. Michael's practiced glance quickly noted and recorded physical characteristics, posture, clothes, mannerisms. This one was a seedy character indeed, Jack Nicholson after a bad night. The length of his trousers was inadequate for his long shanks; four inches of ankle and shin were covered only by dingy white socks. The coat pulled badly away from its single button in radial folds, and in the black lapel a touch of red; Michael failed to note it precisely, but it was a small detail. A lack of fastidiousness, a rumpled carelessness about his whole person, as though what he wore were of little consequence to him. His face long and dour behind a beard, a W. C. Fields nose too phony looking to be real but almost too real looking to be phony. Why would he wear a false nose? And the hair, like a cartoon symphony conductor's, gray, somewhat combed, but greasy, spilled over the soggy collar. Big feet, ridiculous shoes, a funny ducklike stance about him. A queer duck.

At this moment their looks connected, and Michael noted the uncanny, walleyed stare, one eye going off at an angle, but the other riveted on him. The man's expression was startled, puzzled, as if seeing something there he had not expected to see. A perceptive look, one even of recognition. Kindred spirits? Michael didn't think so. In any case, he was going to get him.

The crowd moved back as he sidled up to the man. Michael produced the pack of cards, which he offered with a confidential leer: a peddler of French postcards. He winked slyly, rolled his eyes, nudged the man, who, surprised, tried to back away. Fanning the cards out with graceful expertise, Michael silently invited him to pick a card, any card. The man did so, looked at it, was flustered. Michael snatched the card, showed it around: nude male in black socks and striped garters doing things with nude female wearing black stockings and garters with rosettes. The man with the umbrella shied, started away. Michael went after him, riffling the cards in an accordion arc, catching them neatly. He caused them to disappear, then from the man's ear produced the silver coin again. The crowd laughed, the man looked disappointed, embarrassed, tried to extricate himself. Michael let him go, momentarily, then made a wide circle, approaching from the opposite direction as if merely out for a casual stroll and coming upon an old and agreeable acquaintance. Confounded, his prey changed direction, while Michael hugged his side, aping his gait, his abstracted manner, in a perfect imitation of the absentminded professor. Now, from inside the man's jacket, Michael magically plucked out a small paper parasol, using it to mimic the larger black one, holding it with carbon-copy primness, jiggling his head, pursing his lips like an old maid.

"No, no," the man muttered haltingly, but Michael was not yet done. The paper parasol disappeared, and out of the jacket came a whole string of objects: a fan, a watch, more colored silks, sausage links, and again the rubber duck—quack, quack!—in the man's face. He shied again, turning redder, while Michael mimicked the tilt of his head, the hunch of his shoulders, even his acute discomfort was exaggerated into farce, moving the crowd to further hilarity.

The victim shuffled confusedly, first looking about as if seeking help, then hiding under the umbrella as if shielding himself from closer scrutiny. Michael circled him once more, tapped him on the shoulder; the man turned, Michael popped around and lifted the back of the umbrella. Peekaboo! The man was not amused. He turned in greater agitation, hindered by this whitefaced fool who was making a fool of him. His bony elbow forced itself up between them as if to ward him off, but Michael slipped his own arm companionably through the offered crook, describing formulae, hypotheses, theorems. They were two nuclear physicists, devising between them the atom bomb.

Now Michael was admiring the man's neckwear, a shoddy cravat, horrendously knotted. He used the end to wave bye-bye, then pantomimed the arrival of a Great Idea. He was the magician again, making abracadabra passes. From his tunic flashed a pair of scissors, and with a knowing nod to the spectators he clipped off both ends of the tie an inch below the knot, tossed the pieces away, then did more abracadabra. The tie, supposed to be magically restored, was—oh dear—not. The painted-on mouth turned down in a parody of the Greek mask of tragedy. Michael shrugged, grimaced, shot an imaginary bullet through his brain. Miming profuse apology, he yanked out and offered a brand-new tie; furious, the man rejected the offer. Michael patted his shoulder, pillowed his head on it.

"Never touch me."

The voice was softly sepulchral, wind-breath carrying dead leaves. Momentarily flustered as the man tried to make his way past the encroaching crowd, Michael hearkened to the rasping sound. Its resonances hanging in the stillness of his inner ear gave warning, one Michael palpably felt, yet imprudently chose to ignore.

He moved quickly after the strange old man, flinging himself onto the pavement to impede his passage, then coming to a crouching position to do his frog bit: feet spread flat and wide, eyes bulging, mouth stretched into a great frog-mouth, tip of the tongue protruding slightly at the corner, jaw, neck, chest swelling as he hopped back and forth before the perturbed and halted figure, japing his indignation with ridiculous frogginess.

As if better to inspect this very quality, the man bent closer, angling the umbrella over them like a canopy, isolating them from the onlookers so that beneath that black dome there was only himself in quick consultation with the would-be frog. Michael was perplexed; behind the ridiculous fake nose, transcending the demeanor that both attracted and repulsed him, he recognized a look of contemptuous pity, not unmixed with compassion, the look one gives an incorrigible little brother in trouble again through his own foolish fault.

Michael—and this had never happened to him before—was intimidated; he felt somehow diminished. In the man's bearing there was reproach, an absence of humor, an unequivocal gravity. For in trying to force the man to recognize himself, Michael had fatally recognized something in his own person, though of what this might have been he was at present unaware. Yet he felt neither chill nor premonition, but some intuitive flash, in which he perceived his fellow, his counterpart, his other self. Surely the old man felt it too.

The man gazed down. His soft-hoarse voice spoke in a tone of deep intimacy.

"Are you then a frog?"

Leering, mouth opening and closing, cheeks puffed, Michael felt obliged to give a froggy nod.

"Very well. *Be a frog.*"

Somewhere beyond the black scallop of the umbrella the city sounds suddenly stopped. Michael acknowledged something akin to a thrill, a limpid rush through his limbs, a docility, as the man now described a half circle around him, Michael still hopping, the man raising the umbrella in the fashion of a stage curtain and making his way among the nearest spectators, the crowd parting before him, Michael hop-hop-hopping after, twisting his head grotesquely, still hopping, hands dangling between his flexed, straining thighs, the frog-leer still contorting his face, the crowd trooping after, hooting in amusement, thinking it all part of the act.

With aplomb the man proceeded across the street. Michael hopped after him, along the sidewalk toward the fountain, where more onlookers gathered, all watching as the man came, followed by this ridiculous whitefaced frog-fellow, and Emily slowly trailing the crowd, clutching her flute. Though she could not tell what it was, she knew something was drastically wrong, saw Michael hop-hop-hopping, saw the old man pointing to the rim of the fountain, bidding Michael-the-Frog to hop up there and from the ledge into the water, and there was Michael knee-high in water, with that horrid face, the crowd still laughing, applauding as the man disappeared among them, leaving Michael-the-Frog ridiculously hopping-jumping-splashing in the algaed fountain, while two policemen came running and shouting for him to get the hell out of there. But he did not, or would not, or could not, for though the fun had ended he discovered to his horror that the frog business had not.

The cops waded in after him and dragged him to the fountain's rim and pulled him over it, half strangling, onto the sidewalk. Michael felt something rising in his throat, a mess of fluids in which floated the remains of his breakfast, which came roiling up and spewing forth uncontrollably onto the pavement, while, realizing something strange and awful was happening and not knowing what, the watchers stood back. Then, with foam and spittle hanging from his lips and the water drenching him cold and a terrified uncomprehending look in his eyes, he formed himself into some fetal creature as yet unborn and toppled slowly to one side and over, where he lay hunched and hugging himself in a ghastly shivering ball of pain, while his thoughts raced on into a chaos he could in no way imagine imagining.

CHAPTER THREE

Slide Show

Michael's consciousness had separated into compartments, each of them operating independently of the others. One of them knew exactly where he was, on the slope of grass just inside Central Park, and of course Emily was with him. He could see the half-drained muddy pond, the subway construction in progress at the Sixth Avenue entrance, and beyond the treetops the towers of the apartment buildings along Central Park West. He could hear traffic noises and people's voices, birds, the clip-clopping of horses' hooves, all the sounds normal to that part of the city. He could see and hear and even move, if he wanted to, yet after opening his eyes and briefly returning Emily's anxious smile, he shut them and lay still and wet on the grass, trying to establish lines of communication between the various compartments, trying to put this confounding experience into some kind of recognizable frame. Visions from his past paraded across the backs of his eyelids like slides, and he kept clicking through them, looking for the ones he needed. At the same time, there were sensations to take into account: the grass he was lying on, the smell of it, the poisonous taste in his mouth, the jackhammer blood in his head.

That's it. It wasn't the grass that was reminding him of his aunts' little farm in Ohio, but the pain in his head. The time he was playing baseball in the back pasture, squatted down behind the batter's box with the thin, tiny glove he pretended was a catcher's mitt, and he lunged upward, forward, to snatch a wild pitch, and the unaccountably swinging hickory bat caught him a vicious clout alongside the temple. Laid him out like a plank while he saw stars and tried not to puke.

That's not it, that's not enough. There was more to this dismaying episode than a suffering head. True, he found something familiar in the way his brain felt as though it were trying to beat a path out of his skull, but his general wretchedness transcended even the most memorable, monumental headache. The blur of images whirred on, then jolted to a halt. He was kneeling in the road, tears were stinging his eyes, and Charlie was lying there in front of him, beautiful and still.

Charlie was his magic cat. One afternoon when Michael was standing on the front porch of the farmhouse, concentrating hard on his magician's table and box, determined to make one of his old stuffed animals disappear and reappear, he looked up and got his first glimpse of Charlie: sprinting up the dusty drive, heading straight for him like some urgent messenger. Charlie bounded across the front yard, flashed up the steps, and came to a sudden stop on the edge of the porch, staring solemnly at Michael with his penetrating yellow eyes; Michael dropped to his knees, sat on his heels, and stared back in admiration and wonder; it was love at first sight.

From that moment the two of them, boy and cat, took their places in one another's lives as though they had made reservations. They walked together in the woods that edged the farm, sat together beside the little creek, slept together in Michael's bed. Michael slept deep and hard, seeming to fuse with the bed, but no human could fling himself into the act of sleeping so voluptuously as Charlie did, stretching and twisting his strong, lithe body into dozens of impossible, comic positions. On cold days, Michael would walk around with Charlie draped across his shoulders like a stole, his bushy gray tail slightly twitching, his four white-tipped paws relaxed and dangling. Michael made a dark blue cape for Charlie, pinned a cardboard moon and some cardboard stars on it, and solicited Charlie's assistance in the magic performances he sometimes gave for his aunts and their friends. Charlie couldn't always be counted on to take his cue, but the wise gravity of his owlish face and the elegant way he wore his cape never failed to enhance the proceedings. Michael carried on experiments outside the house, trying to make Charlie appear before him by saying his name softly, or just by closing his eyes and concentrating, and more often than not he would open his eyes to see Charlie marching purposefully toward him.

And then one day, as suddenly as he had come, Charlie was gone, though what remained of him was present enough, lying at the side of the road like a piece of litter. The car that snapped the life out of him had left only a single mark along his lower jaw, and his hind legs were drawn up tightly as though gathered for the saving spring he didn't have time to make. When Michael saw Charlie's body, he felt the same surge of joy he always felt at the sight of him, but this soon gave way to horror at the dull yellow glaze of Charlie's eyes and the unnatural angle of his neck. Bewildered, overwhelmed by grief, Michael's entire consciousness compressed itself into a single desire: to will Charlie back to life. The contest was unequal: the ferocious, unequivocal, passionate will of a fourteen-year-old boy against the laws of nature, biological necessity, the ultimate destiny of every living thing. Charlie's long, thick fur stirred, fumbled by the breeze, but for the first time there came no responding purr to Michael's stroking, no answering pressure against his fingers. His effort had been absolute, prodigious, exhausting, futile. His skull seemed fissured, his eyes felt like sticky pulp; he had experienced as never before the intensity and helplessness of his own will. Charlie's beloved body was stiffening under his hand.

"Charlie," he said, remembering the pain of that moment.

Somewhere above him, Emily was saying his name. Part of his consciousness struggled upward past the insistent images, while the rest, unsatisfied, strained to pull him in deeper. He opened his eyes and saw the pale triangle of Emily's face gazing down at him, her dark hair falling across her cheeks, her eyes blinking with consternation and unspoken questions. Her fingers made light circles at his temples, as if she knew without being told that this was where the pain was. Somehow her knowing irritated him, as her questioning would irritate him. Why didn't he like her asking, or knowing, or having seen, having witnessed the event? It was true, he wished she hadn't been there, that no one he knew had been there. He wanted to keep it to himself.

He smiled at her as convincingly as the circumstances allowed. He was dimly aware of some people standing nearby, whispering and pointing. One of them had a camera and was snapping off shots. "I'll be all right soon," Michael said. "I just need to rest for a few more minutes."

Emily leaned closer to him, nodding wanly, and he shut his eyes again. And there it was, without warning, the primal image of his life: he was sitting on one of the molded blue plastic seats in the bus station in Toledo, the soles of his shoes hanging a good ten inches above the bright linoleum floor, and his mother was leaning over him, stuffing something into his jacket pocket. "Stay right here, Mikey," she said. "I'll be back soon."

Michael touched bottom with this memory, and the recoil jackknifed his upper body. Propped unsteadily on his elbows, he looked at Emily, whose eyes expressed about equal proportions of panic and relief. "That was quick," she said hopefully, pressing the back of her hand against his forehead. "Are you going to be okay?"

Never again, he thought. "Sure," he said, more dazed than glib. "At least, I think so."

"What happened back there?" It was a logical question, and Emily's tone was almost casual, but he could tell she was frightened. "What was going on?"

He grunted, shrugged, and lay down again. "I don't know," he admitted, feeling foolish.

"You must know. That frog bit—what did you think you were doing?"

How could he say? How to explain? Or even if he could come up with an explanation that would satisfy Emily, how could he explain it to himself? He'd been doing what he always did, having some fun, trotting out the old reliable frog routine. Frog footman from *Alice in Wonderland*. But then there was this man, this Queer Duck, and that moment, that small, single, private, unfathomable moment of darkening illumination when the umbrella lowered over the two of them, and the voice, strangely bland, without rancor or even irony, asking, "Are you then a frog?" with something archaic in the phrasing, or was it merely a European turn of speech, the thinnest trace of an accent? And then, this wild compulsion to play a frog, to hop and hop and not stop hopping, to grimace and pop his eyes, no longer by any volition of his own but because having been bidden to be a frog he was obliged to accept utter and unequivocal—

Subjugation.

Michael knew, though he didn't say it, couldn't say it, that that was what it had been. A form of subjugation. It wasn't that he'd allowed himself to be a frog, not that merely, but that he'd allowed himself to give in to the will of another. The old man had exercised some incredible form of mastery over him. In that moment, he had become enslaved!

He drew up his knees, locked his hands behind them, and bowed his head, like a long-distance runner after a particularly draining race. "We can talk about it later if you want to," Emily said softly. "Let's just get out of here. Are you up for that?" On the path by the pond were a man and a woman with a dog, all three of them looking at him. Michael thought about what he must look like still in his mime makeup, wrecked now—smeared whiteface, smeared mouth, smeared eyes. Doesn't take much to gather a crowd in New York. All you've got to do is paint yourself white, become a frog, and nearly drown in a public fountain.

"Probably," he drawled, as though calculating the odds. "I'm fine except for my head and my stomach and a few other places."

She patted his abdominal muscles lightly. "That was an amazing display of virtuoso vomiting, but it was lucky, in a way. Those cops were going to make trouble, but when they saw how sick you were, they just carried you over here."

The small talk went on, so small that Michael was able to contribute his fair share without engaging more than a fraction of his brain. The rest was free to search for clues to this incomprehensible mystery. How was it possible to do such a thing, to say *Be a frog* and cause it to happen? Not really a frog, of course, that was ridiculous, but to make him continue playing at being a frog, so that he lost control of his being, his self? Leaving him over-whelmed, controlled not by any impulse of his own but by some unknown force outside himself? He searched his memory for the crucial moment, the point of surrender to a power he could not comprehend and would never have believed were it not that he knew without a doubt that it had held him in its sway. He felt hungover, as though from a deadly intoxication, one enormous bender.

"Where's my kit?"

"Behind you."

The parasol, the fan were sodden, the silks a disaster. The rub-ber duck eyed him wetly. He picked it up, then tossed it aside. "What a mess. Jesus, we forgot to pass the hat." No passing the hat, no dough. A free performance courtesy of the Queer Duck.

The light glimmered through the summer-weary trees, long slashes of a reddish yellow, with ribbony purple shadows, larger ones cast by the apartment fronts at the far side of the park. Higher up, the elegant towers where the rich dwelled rose against the sky in a wash of gold. Out on the muddy surface of the half-drained pond, purple ducks glided by ahead of rippling silver wakes. Quack, quack, queer ducks. He heard a frog—ga-dunk, ga-dunk—a big one, he thought. Aunt Priss used to say they had a catarrh in their throats; he thought she'd said "guitar." Frogs with guitars in their throats.

But maybe now he was just imagining frogs.

Ga-dunk. Little frog in a big fountain. He didn't want to think about it now. He'd think about it tomorrow. Or maybe he wouldn't. Maybe he would just bury it, pack it away and never have to worry about it again. He shook his head. Fat chance.

"Wasn't that Dazz in the limousine?" Emily asked, putting away her flute.

"Mm." He had a vision of red hair and heard a cool laugh, re-membered the conversation like something from the distant past. "Wants us to go to a party with him tonight."

"Are we going?"

"Mm. Let me see how I feel." He wasn't sure he was ready for a party with Dazz's friends, where he would be expected to interact with intensely chic types who used words like "viable" and "persona" and "mystique."

"You've still got your face on," Emily reminded him.

"I'll take it off at home."

"Can I keep the duck?"

"It's all yours." He realized that his head had stopped hurting somewhat, though its preoccupation had not diminished in the slightest. He wondered about the man again, tried to make sense of it all, failed totally. What sense was there to be made? Had he been hypnotized? Possibly. And possibly not.

He reached for his grenadier's tunic, which lay spread out to dry, picked it up, and whirled it in a circle. Jesus, no! He remembered his wallet, money to be deposited—and the banks were closed. Then, with mounting panic, he was feeling the jacket, finding all the pockets empty. He looked around wildly, stopped, and began combing the grass. It wasn't there. It wasn't at the fountain, either. It was gone. And with it, thirteen hundred bucks, all his summer's savings.

He looked back at Emily, standing apart, regarding him with a look of concern and confusion. And affection.

He shook his head. "Well, it looks like we get to start all over," he said, indicating empty pockets.

He put his arm around Emily as they started their walk back to his apartment. It was, of course, impossible to blank from his mind all that had happened, but fortunately Emily was content to talk, to allow him to be quiet, to listen. And now there was the loss of the money to ponder as well. Gone, in exchange for what? To that question, at least, he had an answer.

In exchange for a taste of what he knew he had always been looking for, though he had no name for it. He would call it real magic. Dark magic. Night magic.

CHAPTER FOUR

Kindred Spirits

Lena sat at the open window, fanning herself and trying to catch whatever breeze might be stirring. There was none. She looked mournfully at the broken air conditioner and, below it, at the shallow pan of red-brown water where metal chips lay in various stages of oxidation, some of them quite advanced. Air-conditioner maintenance, like creature comforts in general, was not high on Max's list of priorities. He never noticed things like wilting temperatures or suffocatingly heavy air. Sometimes she imagined that he was hollow inside, like an empty nutshell, dry and shriveled, indifferent to heat or cold or life itself. Yet she needed him, just as he needed her. Their relationship, like the seasons, just seemed to endure.

She could see Max's big black umbrella at the corner newsstand. As his gaunt figure drew nearer, she tried as usual to read his mood from the way he was carrying the umbrella; having observed several dips, a couple of tilts, and one nearly complete twirl, she looked forward to a relatively pleasant evening.

She heard him as he climbed the stairs slowly, opened the door, and uttered his perfunctory, general greeting, as though addressing all the heterogeneous objects scattered about the large room. Lena looked at the heavy black coat, the beard, the nose, and shook her head. "On such a hot day, why do you wear—"

He made a placating gesture, as though to avoid argument, and left the room. When he returned, he was without the beard and the rubber nose. His long gray hair was wet where he had slicked it back, and his shirt collar was damp. He carried his black coat on one arm, held it against his lap as he sat, and left it draped there as he took up his newspaper, squinting to scan the front page. Lena remained in her chair at the window but contrived a position that allowed her to observe Max without staring at him. He bent his head, turning it slightly to the light, and eased from beside his nose something that he put on the heavy mahogany table: a dull glass eye. It lay on the embroidered linen runner, staring up at the ceiling. After quickly putting on a black patch with an elastic band that he slipped over his head and adjusted, he began rummaging in his jacket pockets, drawing out first one wallet, then another, then a third. These he opened, extracting their contents, laying the cards and photographs in his lap and fingering the money, glancing with his good eye over his shoulder to where Lena sat silent and immobile, as if for a portrait. When he had counted the money, he slipped the cards and wallets into the shopping bag beside him, fanned out the bills, and contemplated them again.

Lena could no longer assist in silence at this spectacle. "Really, Max," she sighed, "I shall never understand how a man with your abilities can stoop to such things. Why aren't you embarrassed?"

He fixed her with his good eye, but her guess as to his mood had been accurate; he wasn't angry, his look was mild, without impact.

"I, on the other hand, shall never understand your fondness for the reiterated reproach," he said airily. "And you know very well that such pranks never embarrass me. Banal moralizing—now there's something embarrassing."

"Who's moralizing? I simply want you to set your sights higher. Do you get so much pleasure from stealing? And if you must steal, why not steal something large? An air conditioner, for example."

He chuckled in that eerie, cackling way he had. "My dear Galena, what would be the use of such a thing?" he asked, narrowing his single eye. "Surely you've noticed the chill in the room. *You must be cold.*"

She rose abruptly from her seat and shut the window. Casting a wounded look in his direction, she left the room. Several minutes later she returned, wearing a shawl over her shoulders and carrying two steaming cups of tea on an elaborately worked Persian silver tray. She placed one cup at his elbow, next to the eye on the table, touched his shoulder, and took the seat across from his. Putting on her reading glasses, she began to peruse part of the newspaper as she sipped her tea.

Max had been lost in thought, staring at the shopping bag beside his chair, but now he opened the bag and withdrew the largest of the wallets, the one with the monogram "M.H." Once again he went through the various cards, slowly this time, absorbing the name, the address, the scraps of information about the young man whose property he had filched, recalling his earnestness, his innocence, his hurt, surprised eyes. He chose one of the cards, a small, plain, white one, and put it into his shirt pocket.

Lena glanced up from the paper. "Where were you today?"

"Uptown." Sounding casual, as if nothing had happened uptown.

"I see. The beard. That awful nose. You were at the museum. Interesting, about the Rembrandt."

"Somewhat," he said offhandedly, but he was not interested in the Rembrandt now, nor in Egyptian antiquities. No, something else had pricked his curiosity. What had that sign read? "Presto the Great." Absurd, amateurish, but the boy himself was not. Callow, certainly, and untutored, without a doubt, yet somehow compelling, not to be dismissed. Yes, there could be an answer here. The more he thought about the young man, the more it became clear that some further action must be taken in his regard. He would not let this one go.

During their evening meal, Lena hardly spoke. Max was unaccountably, uncharacteristically voluble, though he did not mention the museum or the painted Eye, guarding it in his thoughts as jealously as any curator. He did talk about a young man he had met, who he thought looked interesting despite his immaturity, a young street magician. He seemed likely as a prospect, Max said. Then, after they had finished eating, he made the suggestion—it was too mild to be a request—that he had been contemplating all along.

Taken by surprise, Lena dismissed the notion with a flat refusal. "Tonight? You must be mad. Let me remind you of what happened last time—and the time before that. It only brings trouble. Besides, my head is aching, and my hands hurt." She illustrated her last point by rubbing her hands. "It's a bad idea."

He shrugged his shoulders, the most easygoing of men. It was only a thought. She might try finding out something. The young man in question seemed particularly likely. The final decision would of course be up to her.

"Of course," she said wearily, rising from her chair and walking over to a small, marble-topped table, on which lay a curiously carved cedar box filled with her pungent French cigarettes. She extracted one, lit it, and turned to face Max, who had remained in his chair with an expectant look on his face. "Why don't you do it yourself?" she asked, mingling pleading and recrimination. "You're the one with the power."

"Because, Lena dearest, I do not choose to. Power is different from strength; if you don't use strength, it goes away. But power accumulates."

"Like interest?" she snorted.

"Perhaps. But I had in mind something less material. Like longing, like desire." He smiled deprecatingly and stood up. "In any case, I'm going downstairs for a while. Please consider my request," he said, in the tones of a hopeful suitor, but he knew she would do as he asked. She always did.

An hour later, Lena sat again at the heavy table in the front room, smoking one of her Gitanes. Under the light, the yellow pad and pen lay ready. She smoked and looked at them and coughed. She knew she should give up cigarettes, but they were one of her few pleasures. Expensive as well—nearly four dollars a pack, three packs a day; approximately eighty dollars a week. How much was that a year? She'd never figured it up, but the expense secretly added to her pleasure.

Since Max had left, the room was stifling again, and she knew she wouldn't sleep. Sometimes, sleepless, she liked to cook late at night. Not tonight, however; the thought of a stove or an oven made her want to scratch. Besides, there was the thing he wished her to do. She sat motionless, trying to think of nothing. A television set, incongruous amid the Victorian clutter, stood across the room, but she would not turn it on until it was time for the news. She put a record on the phonograph instead: Mendelssohn's Violin Concerto in e minor, a passionate performance by Heifetz, first recorded in the 1930s. Ardent and soaring, the sound enveloped her, and she was absorbed in it for a long time.

The record ended, the return of silence shocked her into awareness. She pushed her damp hair behind her ears and arranged her blouse awkwardly as she crossed the room to turn off the phonograph. She thought about banging on the water pipes; Max would hear it in the cellar, but she knew it would do no good; he would come up when he wanted to. The strains of the Mendelssohn seemed still to hug the high corners of the ceiling and float out the reopened window, mixing with the other sounds—radios, stereos, televisions, street noises. Below, people gathered on doorsteps, under streetlights, talking in groups, or moving up and down the walk as though on a Sunday *passeggiata* in Milano. Everything was quieter than usual, hushed by the heat.

Lena sat again at the table and eyed the wallet Max had left there, then picked it up, not without reluctance. The two gold initials told her nothing. She looked inside: empty. She sniffed the leather, felt it in her fingers. Nothing was revealed, about it or its owner. What did he want to know? What could it mean, to say that the young man "seemed likely," "looked interesting"? In the years she had known him, Max had once had an assistant, but things had ended badly and the subject had seldom been mentioned again. Besides, was stealing people's wallets and searching through them any way to recruit help? Normal people placed ads, left notices on bulletin boards; Max picked pockets and examined what he found there. And why on earth did he need an assistant, for that matter? Lena wondered. Life with Max prompted an endless series of questions, most of which she was afraid to ask.

She expelled her breath so hard that it made her lips vibrate. Holding the wallet in both hands, she laid it against her cheek, then her forehead, then resumed running her fingers over it. The ornate clock on the mantel chimed; a delicate Viennese sound: quarter to eleven. She watched the little brass pendulum swinging in the painted circle on the glass door, saw the hand move a fraction of an inch. She might as well start. She stubbed out her cigarette and immediately lit another, arranged wallet and ashtray to her liking, and leaned toward the yellow pad.

The clock ticked drily in the silence as she sat and stared at the pad in the lamplight, her fingers laced in her lap, the cigarette dangling from her lips. She put it in the ashtray and watched as a little pencil line of smoke rose toward the light. When she had composed herself, she took up the felt-tipped pen, pulled off the cap, and held the pen poised in her hand, waiting.

She waited for perhaps a minute, letting everything flow out of her, so it could flow back in. Her hand moved slowly along the paper, scribbling, then more rapidly, then still faster. She could feel the working of her hand, a detached, automatic thing, uncommanded by her brain. She recognized the writing: Mrs. Carsin's, enlarging into broad scrawls and loops, then becoming erratic, until Lena's fingers fairly flew across the paper and the page became filled with script. As fast as one page was filled, she tore it from the pad and began another, until there was a pile of pages on the table.

She stopped abruptly, waiting until her breathing slowed. She put on her glasses and read the pages aloud, then thought over what she had read. Obviously Mrs. Carsin was concerned about the Rembrandt. But Lena already knew about that from the evening paper. This was not news to anyone, certainly not to her. Should she try further? The clock continued ticking as she put aside the sheaf of pages and took up the wallet again. She held it flat in the palm of her hand, then laid her other hand over it. The leather felt warm. She ran her nail over the gold *M*, and the gold *H*. She raised her hands to her forehead, the wallet between the palms, closing her eyes. Yes, there was something.

She glanced at the curio cabinet behind the piano, where something drew her attention. Something to do with the wallet? She went to the cabinet, opened it, and stared at the objects on the shelves—the astrolabe, the statuettes of various ancient Egyptian divinities, the cluster of tan pebbles lying in a box lined with cotton batting—and then her hand went to the silver christening cup on the second shelf. She set it in her hand, its round base on her palm, the wallet on the other, and held them as if weighing them against each other. That was strange, she told herself, why the cup? She waited. Nothing happened. She put the cup back on the shelf, closed the cabinet door, passed the mantel with the clock. Seven more minutes had elapsed; the clock now read eight before eleven. She wanted to be done in time for the eleven o'clock news.

Seated again, she placed the wallet between her palms, this time pressing it against her breast. Her fingers began to twitch, little tremors of energy. She put down the wallet and took up the pen.

It was Carsin again, her large loops and scrawls, more about the Rembrandt. Then, quite suddenly, Lena felt a wrench, like a soft muffled blow inside her, and her hand was scrabbling about on the paper in a series of erratic gyrations. It came under control finally, with a different sort of writing. Neater, more legible, in a smaller, more feminine script. It wasn't much, only a paragraph; then it stopped. She sighed, and her head fell forward, striking the tabletop. She heard the sound, felt the pain. For a moment— no more—she perceived only darkness, then she opened her eyes, saw the room sidewise, with her head still on the table. She lifted her head and looked down at the page, at the single paragraph written in something resembling an old-fashioned calligraphy.

I will try to tell you. There is a beginning here somewhere. Ask of John, he knows. Numbers 21, 6 and 8; 22, 18 and 19. He will reveal all, if you know your Scriptures. Alpha and Omega, in that order. This will be Greek to you but it is not difficult, I don't think. Remember the Archangel, of celestial armies Prince. This is important. He will bring a thirst and must be given to drink. You will know him when you see him, don't be surprised at that. Must he be told? I think he must. Tell M the money must be returned. All restored as was. James. James. He will know James. John through James or James through John, I am not sure which. I will have more numbers for you if I can come back. Yes, M must be . . .

Must be what? She had trouble making out the last word. It seemed to read *marred*, or was it *warned?*

She sat with her fists digging against her chest where the pain was; then she gently pressed all along her knuckles, trying to rid herself of the pain in her hands. She became aware of the odor. Not cigarette smoke; a floral scent. Some kind of flowers, but unfresh, as if wilted in the heat. She took the single page, folded it, and slid it between the pages of a book, which she laid on the shelf. She folded the Carsin pages and took them to her chair, turning on the television set before sitting. A movie was on. She put on her glasses and peered at the clock. It was still before eleven. She took up her crewelwork and was sewing when he came in.

"You're up so late, Lena. No wonder you look tired."

"I'm waiting for the news."

"The news must be over, surely." He took out his watch. "It's ten minutes to twelve."

"Then the clock has stopped."

But when? She was surprised.

He went to the mantel, tapped the glass. "So it has, so it has. Have you taken to wearing perfume?" He was lifting his nose and sniffing.

"No."

"Then what . . . ?" He fanned the air negligently as if to rid his nostrils of the smell, then casually glanced at the yellow pad on the table. "Well, what do they say, your chatty friends?" Trying to sound jovial, easy, preserving the amenities while his curiosity drove him like an appetite.

"Nothing. Nothing, really."

"Nothing?" He took up the wallet from the table, and when he spoke again, his tone had darkened. "Ah, Lena, you lie so poorly; you have no talent for it, and I even less patience. Now answer me. Did this help?" He brandished the wallet at her like a weapon.

Helplessly, her eyes slid sideways to the cabinet. *Tell M the money must be returned*, she remembered. "I'm not sure. I don't think so," she said, frowning in genuine confusion, her eyes back on his hands.

He was using the pen to work out something on the pad, a kind of doodling habitual with him when he was thinking through a problem.

"You must give the money back!" she blurted out suddenly; then, more softly, as if shocked by her own vehemence: "You must."

"Do you really think so?" he said, his voice dangerously low. His eye glittered as he stared at her, and a cold clump of anxiety began to gather in her stomach.

"Just—give back the money. And that, that too." She nodded at the wallet. *All restored as was.* Then she lowered her eyes to her work.

He doodled some more, slipped the small white card from his pocket, looked at it. After a moment he rose and, adjusting his eye patch, started for the door.

"Where are you going? It's late."

"Out," he replied, irritation in his voice.

He went, taking his black coat with him. As an afterthought he came back and took the wallet as well. When she heard him going down the stairs she laid aside her work, removed her glasses, and pressed the heels of her palms against her eyelids; saw the pinpoints of light, wavering sightless illumination; took her hands away, calmer now, saw the blurred face of the clock. Eight minutes before eleven. She went to the table, looked at the page he had drawn on, undecipherable black symbols that only he understood. She gathered the pages and tore them in half, then in quarters, and dropped them in the basket. At the cabinet again, she opened the door and took out the silver cup. The metal seemed to have taken on the heat of the day. She turned it in her hands, thinking, felt it become cool under her touch. She returned it to its place, blew at a bit of lint that had collected, closed the door. The cabinet needed dusting. Touching her fingers to her temple where it had struck the table, she went to the window, leaned on the sill, and saw Max going up the street toward the subway. Then she dialed the number for the correct time and reset the clock on the mantel.

CHAPTER FIVE

Up on the Roof

Michael lay in a bathtub filled with hot, soapy water, feeling miserable and counting the ways. Two hours ago a bright, hot summer afternoon, enlivened by the performance of a bit of street theater, a little harmless magic cleverly conceived and professionally executed, had been transformed into a glimpse of a bottomless pit. His knees and thighs ached from excessive froggery; his stomach, though certainly empty, was still lurching about queasily; his head was vibrating slowly, like a gong struck not too long ago. Overshadowing these physical discomforts, there were of course the greater, deeper griefs: loss of money, loss of confidence, loss of balance, loss of, well, identity. And apparently no possibility of making any satisfactory sense out of this cataclysm, no matter how compulsively his brain orbited around it. He flicked his toes, rippling the water, and sank disconsolately into the suds, so deep that when Emily knocked on the door all he could manage in reply was a splutter.

"Are you playing submarine?" she asked, having opened the door and looked around it. "Shall I get you the rubber duck?"

"I've had enough fun with the duck today, thanks," was his gloomy reply.

She knelt beside the tub, touched his brow tenderly, tried to meet his eyes, but they were too furtive for her. Dipping her hand into the water, she began to make a lazy, circular movement, producing a small whirlpool centered around his groin. "Ah," she said, "the hidden treasures of the deep."

He flexed a knee, stopping her hand. "Emily . . ." he began, then hesitated.

"I know," she said, reaching for a towel, "you don't have to tell me. Not in the mood. But I think it's a bad idea to lie around driving yourself crazy. Get dressed and we'll go over to Dazz's. Aren't you hungry? Dazz said there was a party, and the parties Dazz knows about always have mounds of food." At last he looked at her, and she smiled affectionately. "Come on, Mr. Wizard. Don't be antisocial. Let's go have some fun."

Michael pressed his hands against the wet hair above his temples. Maybe she was right. What he really wanted to do was to crawl alone into a small dark space and brood until he fell asleep, but he had to admit that Emily's recommendation sounded healthier. "Why not?" he murmured, half to himself; then he grabbed the sides of the bathtub and rose from the water before her approving eyes.

Jack Dazzario's studio was located up the block from Michael's apartment, on the opposite side of Seventy-second Street between Columbus and Amsterdam. In marked contrast to Michael's tiny living quarters, Dazz's place occupied the whole fifth floor of his building and even included what could pass for a roof garden, a walled-in, tiled terrace under a wooden water tower, with a copious crop of plants in tubs and pots, and chairs sawed from olive barrels. Dazz was Michael's best friend, had been since he'd got to New York. An excellent painter of the photorealistic school, Dazz had been enjoying a gratifying degree of success for several years now; quite a few of his works graced prominent private collections around the country, and one of them hung in the Whitney Museum. He was small, wiry, and intense, with a dark mustache under a brawl-smashed nose, and bright ferret eyes that compelled attention.

"The sorcerer and his orchestra," Dazz intoned, greeting Michael and Emily with hugs. "Come in, come in. Wine is being served on the terrace." Dazz presented quite a spectacle as he led the way through his studio. Inordinately given to fanciful and romantic outfits, tonight he looked positively piratical, dressed like Errol Flynn in *Captain Blood,* complete with a colorful bandanna tied like a sweatband around his forehead. All he lacked to complete the effect was a cutlass protruding from his sash.

They sat outside in the thick air, sipping some of Dazz's cold, delicious Italian wine while he recounted the major news event of the day: the "Saskia in Tears" episode at the Metropolitan Museum. "I can't believe you haven't heard about it—it was the lead story on all the local news programs." According to Dazz, speculation was rife in the TV newsrooms, and the *Post* had even deemed it worthy of a rare "special edition."

Some were calling the crying portrait the product of mass hysteria caused by the excessive temperatures, while others said the phenomenon was due to the psychological fervor of art lovers, seduced by the pensive expression of Rembrandt's sitter into believing they saw tears, much as the devoutly religious sometimes believe they have seen statues bleeding or visions of the Virgin: the wish fulfilled. Museum officials and the scientists they'd consulted invoked an inexplicable differentiation between the normal, controlled temperature of the room and the heat generated by the bodies of the spectators, causing a condensation on the varnished surface of the canvas. There was total agreement on only one point: all of the museumgoers who had been in the room—slightly over a hundred, though by tomorrow their numbers were bound to swell—were swearing they had seen real tears.

"What a load of crap," Michael growled. "They must be out of their minds."

"Who must be?"

"The so-called witnesses."

"A hundred people saw it happen."

"A hundred retards, probably all from the same bus. How can

people be so dumb? You may as well bring a flock of sheep into the museum. They'd get as much from it."

"My, but aren't we in a lousy but superior mood tonight," Dazz said, as Michael settled back, chuckling with pleasure at the image he had just evoked, a vision of dozens of milling sheep, unimpressed by the Impressionists, bleating approval before *The Peaceable Kingdom.*

Then his eyes fell on one of Dazz's garden ornaments, a big cement frog, squatting staunchly between two potted trees. His mirth stopped short, his face changed. He looked involuntarily at Emily and felt strangely breathless, disoriented. He continued to stare at her, glad that she was there, reassured; he kept seeing her in different lights—just now she seemed particularly lovely. "Hey, Lotus Blossom," he said, grinning uncertainly.

To cover his confusion, he picked up the running garden hose and began soaking some of the plants.

Dazz, sensing that the subject needed to be changed, said blandly, "Speaking of art lovers, you two sure had a big crowd today when I went by. I hope they showed their appreciation of genius at work?"

"We didn't even pass the hat," Emily said, ignoring Michael's warning look.

Dazz's face expressed horror and pity. "Art for art's sake, my least favorite kind. You gave a free show?"

Michael said bitterly, "Not just free, a total giveaway. I lost thirteen hundred bucks."

"Christ, how?"

"Well, it was in my wallet, the wallet was in my coat, and then the wallet was gone."

"Where was your coat?"

"In the plaza fountain, if you can believe it."

"What? What happened?" Although Michael bowed his head and shook it slowly, Dazz pressed him, undeterred. "Looks serious. Let's hear it. You must want to talk about it."

Michael paused. Dazz was right: he *did* want to talk about it, yet at the same time, he didn't. He got up, stretched, stared moodily up at the dark shape of the water tower looming overhead. If he talked it out, maybe the missing piece would fall into place, that one niggling thing he couldn't remember, the one word that would make sense of all the rest. Amid the dripping plants, candles glimmered limpidly, little glamorous flames in clear glass cups set about amid the foliage. On the wall near the doorway a Mexican earthenware *olla* dripped onto the tile flooring. Leaning against the parapet, he turned, gazing out at the city view and began reciting the facts. As he described what had happened, his voice gradually assumed an intensity that made Dazz lean forward with fuller attention. "It wasn't the heat, I know it," he concluded, "it was something else, something really scary, but I can't . . ."

"Exactly what did it feel like? What were your sensations?"

Dazz was completely focused, coiled like a spring on the edge of his chair.

"I don't know for sure." Not strictly true; the words lay on his tongue, too heavy for him to speak them. *Overmastered. Subjugated. Enslaved.* He shook his head again. "It really was incredible, Dazz, honest to God, but I don't know how to say it. It was just— complete compulsion."

"As though you were under a spell?" Dazz's voice was deadly earnest.

"Yeah," Michael said slowly, "a spell." He thought a moment, holding his breath. "Imagine . . ." His voice trailed off and he was back on the street by the fountain again, reliving the experience of the frog, recalling the still, soundless moment, the constriction of mind, the cessation of bodily coordination.

"Imagine what?" Emily said in a wary voice.

"What it must be like to be able to do that—whatever it was. Imagine having that power over people. Imagine what it would be like to be so in control of yourself that you could control others. Jesus, wouldn't that be something?" He was beginning to feel elated, he could hear his voice rising in the stifling air, and the street noises below seemed very far away.

"Well, yes indeed, that certainly would be something," Emily said sarcastically, getting up and moving the hose to a plant near the parapet. "A noble ambition if there ever was one. Join the Thought-Control Pantheon. Just think, your name right up there in lights along with Hitler, Charlie Manson, the Kool-Aid preacher, and my mother. Don't be so easily seduced, Michael. This man must be stopped before it's too late."

"Jesus, Em." Michael, surprised and a little annoyed by her anger, tried to make a joke of it. "I'm not in the same league with those people."

"I wouldn't have thought so, but you seem to have some of the same interests."

"I can't deny that I'm interested in that sort of thing—hypnosis, illusion, all of that. I'm a magician, for Christ's sake."

"I just wish you'd forget this particular illusion, that's all."

"No." The negative came out stronger than Michael meant it to. He looked at Emily, then Dazz. "You don't forget about things like that so easily. I'm going to find that guy."

"So you find him, then what?" Dazz asked.

Michael lolled his head back, easing his neck muscles, staring up at the tower again. Dazz was right. Then what? "I don't know. But I'd like to talk to him. He's got something, and I want to know what it is."

"Don't." Emily had dropped the hose, was looking out over the parapet at the view. "Don't do it."

"Why not?"

Emily was silent, narrow shoulders hunched, thinking. Once again, Michael felt irritation at her; how could she oppose her will to his? "Come on, why not?"

"I don't know. There was something about that man, some-thing . . ."

"Creepy?" Dazz suggested, his voice hushed. "Sinister?"

"More than that," Emily said. "Dark, dangerous, evil. He looks like a bird of prey, like some sort of raptor. Some people just have a look or a posture or a way of—I can't explain it, but he made my flesh crawl." She turned from the parapet and faced Dazz. "You didn't see him, and Michael hasn't really told you the whole thing. It was terrifying. I hated watching it, and there was nothing I could do about it. If you didn't know Michael you'd have thought it was part of the act, but I know him, and I could see that what was happening to him was terrible." Her eyes were moist. "He was suffering, and I couldn't help him—I could barely even move myself. It was terrible and terrifying and I want to put it out of my mind"—her voice broke a little now—"and I wish you would too, Michael." She looked for a long moment at him, at Dazz, then turned back to the view.

Dazz decided to do some mediating. After all, he was supposed to be going to a party with these people. "I think Emily's right, Mike, you ought to chalk it up to the mysteries of metropolitan life. How are you going to find the guy, anyway? I don't care how strange he looks, everybody looks strange in New York, especially during a heat wave."

Michael wasn't listening, but he knew what he was supposed to say, so he grunted something like "I guess you're right," thinking still that there was one little thing he couldn't remember— red, something red against the black, on the jacket, a button in the lapel; letters on the button, who's got the button, find the button, find the man, find the money . . . And in one instant of certainty he realized that the Queer Duck had pickpocketed him. While Michael had been pulling tricks on him, those long fingers had been performing their own tricks, inside his grenadier's jacket, pulling out his wallet. More reason than ever to find him. The Bloomingdale's bag was a clue. Maybe he was a regular shopper there. He could stake out the store, prowl it, maybe come up with something, maybe find out what he wanted to know.

". . . but I never saw her again," Dazz was saying when Michael surfaced. By way of getting his bearings, he glanced through the doorway to the clock on the studio coffee table. It had no numbers, only illuminated circles that turned and colored lights that changed. Surreptitiously he checked it against his watch: eight-fifty, in perfect agreement. He was starting to feel a little hungry, and no wonder. He slid a look at Emily, discovered to his surprise that she was staring at him. Dazz said, "Almost nine o'clock. The festivities should be under way by nine, so we'll go soon. I know you're going to be impressed."

"Whose party is it, Dazz?" Emily asked.

"It's being thrown by my newly devoted friend and patron of the arts, Samir Abdel-Noor, at his notorious townhouse off Sutton Place."

"Was he the fat guy in the limousine?"

"Daddy Warbucks himself, and yes, the rocks on his fingers were for real."

"How about the redhead?"

"I'm not sure that she's for real. She'll probably be at the party, so we can try to find out then. But let me tell you about our boy Sami."

"He seemed a bit strange in that little glance I got of him," Michael said, resolved to make up for lost time in this conversation.

"He's nutty as a fruitcake or vice versa, take your pick. Whatever, he's loaded. His family gave him a ton of money to disappear from Egypt. Some bad local scandal in Cairo. So here he is, rich as the proverbial Croesus, looking for creative people to help him spend his money. He gives parties twice a week, and I mean *parties!* Great food, great drinks, the works. Everybody goes, and Sami doesn't know half his guests, but he hosts bravely on."

When it came to his taste in art, however, Dazz spoke in more admiring terms of his new sponsor, from whom he had received a handsome commission to execute a full-length portrait. "This job's going to take me forever. Sami's more than willing to sit, but he never shuts up, and while I'm working he brings in the fat lady, and she hangs around talking about the astral plane." The fat lady, he went on to explain, was an American friend of Sami's, a Southerner who gets billing as a medium. There were séances and attempts to contact spirits. "She's putting him in touch with his sister," Dazz concluded with a shrug.

Emily looked skeptical. "Where is she, Schenectady?"

"She's dead, Em, she's on the Other Side."

"Oh, God," Emily cried aloud, "I'd like to get on an astral plane and fly someplace where everybody's rational."

At that moment the phone rang. As Dazz answered it, Michael and Emily smiled shyly at one another, and he blew her a kiss. "We can't, Otto," they heard Dazz saying, "we're just leaving for a party. Some other time. Thanks." He hung up and walked back out to the terrace. "That was Trashy Otto downstairs. Otto's your kinda guy, Emily—not all that interested in the spiritual aspect of our nature. He's showing X-rated movies and wanted us to join him and his guests."

Emily laughed. "If my only two choices are parapsychology and pornography," she said, leaning again on the parapet, "I'll take pornography. But I thought we were going to a party."

"So we are, so we are," said Dazz, adjusting his costume. "Arise and walk, Michael, let us go forth into the real world."

Emily, taking one last look into the street below, shrieked suddenly, then began to laugh. "I believe I'm having a cosmic experience."

They joined her at the parapet, hung over the edge, and looked where she pointed. Lower down, on the white front of the building across the street, male and female bodies performed complicated sexual acrobatics with athletic enthusiasm. They heaved in a great, tangled mass, thrusting, licking, panting, writhing, biting, while a crowd gathered on the sidewalk beneath the building, gesturing upward toward the ludicrous alfresco scene.

"How many do you count?" Emily asked.

"Six," said Michael.

"No, seven," Dazz said. "There's a girl in the upper left corner—you can just see her head bobbing up every now and then."

Silence fell for about a minute. Then Dazz said, "Oh, Jesus," and ran to the telephone, dialed, spoke. "Hey, Otto, your outdoor porn show is terrific. Sure, I can see it from here. Everyone can see it. All of Seventy-second Street can see it. Fucking all over the front of the karate parlor." Doubled up with laughter, he listened for a short while, then hung up. "He's showing his movies on a sheet hung in his front window. It's projecting right through the sheet and across the street. Let's go, kids, unless you want to . . ."

"We're coming," Emily said. Leaning against Michael as they gazed down at the frenzied, flailing bodies materialized like ghosts in rut on the building wall, she slipped two fingers inside his shirt, running them down behind the waistband of his pants. "Do you know what you want to do after the party?" she asked, her breath hot in his ear. "If you don't, I have a plan."

CHAPTER SIX

The Retentive Host

He was called the *Lis doré*, the "Gilded Lily," an appellation resulting as much from his own personal lifestyle and peculiar magnetism as from his fondness for that particular flower. The word "fabulous," in all its connotations—incredible, marvelous, exaggerated—best described the character and career of the man known as Samir Abdel-Noor. After nearly twenty years in New York, he and his elaborate establishment off Sutton Place, overlooking the East River, had become legendary in sophisticated circles, and stories about his background and personal history varied widely, both in degree of truth and in dramatic content.

It was an established fact that his family were Egyptians of extraordinary means. His sister, Syrie, for whom Sami felt a rare fondness amounting to obsession, died in the early seventies, and shortly after this tragedy, a scandal—a murder committed in one of his apartments—cast a further shadow over his life. He found himself under familial, if not legal, indictment; was provided with a considerable, not to say princely, sum of money; and told to quietly get lost. He arrived in New York with a generous complement of servants and installed them and himself in the Sutton Place house, where, already corpulent, he soon ate and drank himself into obesity, spent prodigally, entertained lavishly but joylessly, and maintained a steady turnover in the coteries of parasites that surrounded him.

As time passed, Sami suffered increasingly from digestive complications that prevented him from fully utilizing his marbled and gilded bathroom facilities for up to a week at a time. This complaint of constipation, added to a long list of other ailments, kept doctors of several specialties in almost constant attendance. Used to entertaining, Sami had not given up the notion that his house should provide the finest food and drink in the city, to say nothing of the most captivating diversions, but now he did not descend—or condescend—to share in them; more often than not he let joy reign unconfined below, while abovestairs he kept to his bed, in rich and lustrous striped pajamas, eating cream pastries and watching game shows on television, attended by Gilbert, as he called his disreputable-looking Arab body servant.

Beyond large quantities of food and television and such personal indulgences as an encyclopedic variety of exotic drugs, he derived greatest satisfaction from the idea of communicating with his dead sister, Syrie, whose loss had left him grief-stricken and whose absence, after more than twenty years, he still felt keenly. He never gave up hope of establishing some line of communication with her, and to this end he had consulted a long list of mediums, spiritualists, clairvoyants, and other seers in the city.

He was now on terms of some intimacy with a certain Beulah Wales, an obstreperous woman of Southern extraction, whose occult powers allegedly enabled her to put her rich client in touch with his departed sister by summoning up the spirit of one Alfred Jenks (born: Denver, Colorado, 1882; deceased: Denver, Colorado, 1909; cause of death: rheumatic fever) and thus bridging the gap to the astral plane, where both the said Jenks and Syrie Abdel-Noor currently resided. In addition to this absorbing pursuit, Samir had been giving thought to the condition of his own immortal soul and investigating the vast array of available religions with the attitude of a discriminating consumer for whom the sky's the limit. Born a Muslim, he had practiced nothing akin to devotion since attaining his majority; now, however, he busied himself by probing the tenets of numerous sects and faiths, looking for something not even he himself could articulate. He was, in short, "searching."

So it was that his guests included those of many and varied persuasions, all of whom were committed to proselytizing in the hope of enlarging their memberships, and who therefore readily accepted the invitations. As did a great many other people. These extremely mixed gatherings, though informal in style, took on the aura of chic East Side soirées, and no one, least of all the host himself, ever knew who might be found in attendance. Tonight, plagued by his eighth consecutive day without a bowel movement, he didn't much care.

When Jack Dazzario arrived, accompanied by Emily and Michael, the door to the Sutton Place house was opened even before the bell could be sounded, and was shut at once behind them, as if to fend off the humid heat. Dazz presented a folded, printed card to a doorman, and they passed through the dark vestibule into a large, cool, oval hallway, where a dim chandelier dripped glittering prisms. A large round marble-topped table stood before them, and on it a giant vase filled with an enormous arrangement of tropical lilies. The servant stood beside the wide, draped entrance to their left, waited for their approach, then silently withdrew. They stepped through the portal.

The room was a large, high-ceilinged, softly-lit, cool velvety half-world where guests floated like so many wraiths, indolent, dreamlike. Groups clustered in all corners, sprawled on low, wide, comfortable furniture, here washed in bright laughter, there sunk in quiet conversation. No one, including the waiter passing with a tray of drinks and the uniformed maid emptying ashtrays, paid any attention to the newcomers in the doorway. Wine-colored brocade above mahogany wainscoting covered the walls, which were further embellished with giant tapestries and paintings in baroque gold frames, which hung by thick tasseled ropes from a picture molding high overhead. In the center of the room rested a round, tufted-velvet Belle Epoque settee. There was a profusion of flowers in vases, palms in pots, flora in general.

No matter what was the occasion or who were the guests,

everything here was calculated to appeal to the senses: the sound of water flowing in rivulets, recorded music not readily identifiable but exotic in nature, heavy incense filtering through the refrigerated air. It was as if this place, with its softness and dimness and coolness, had been specially constructed as a protest against any sort of reality, a magic world where one might pursue fancies, act out fantasies, indulge private vices, all to the furthest extreme. Temperature, lighting, sound, scent all combined to produce an instant feeling of lethargy, of luxurious and indolent ease, of sensuousness that might challenge the proclivities of a pasha.

In the manner of such parties, the guests had formed various splinter groups, according to their particular acquaintanceships or desires. Beyond a panel of open grillwork stood a fashionable lot that might have been assembled to pose for an advertisement for expensive scotch: women with burnished coiffures, flashing bracelets and rings, and silky shimmering apparel that draped gracefully as they drooped and lounged, smoking long cigarettes and conversing with several males of a similar well-dressed type, bearing the sheen of striven-for elegance, talking in hushed tones punctuated with occasional bursts of mirth, while illuminating devices of undisclosed origin changed them, full face and profile, from red to amber to blue and back again, but never cast upon them any sort of natural light. In the opposite corner clustered six or eight members of the Hare Krishnas, looking as if they had been encamped there since the seventies, limp in spite of the cool air, pathetically shorn like so many lambs.

Through a gilded archway, in a candlelit alcove, on a carved high-backed chair, sat a corpulent woman of fifty, with bright red lips and heavily made-up eyes, engaged in serious conversation with a rapt young man perched on a stool close beside her, while people crowded around on either side leaned about her in auditory attitudes. She seemed to be holding court, blinking rapidly as though surprised by her own utterances, her heavy rings idly tinkling against the stones of her pendant earrings; occasionally one hand strayed to her breast, where either through distraction or by contrivance she hooked her middle finger in the scalloped edge of her bodice. Glittering ornaments on her bare shoulders clasped her gown, which fell in long folds to her gold kid sandals, exaggerating rather than hiding her considerable girth. Several curls artfully escaped from the turbanlike wrapping on her head, giving her the look of Madame de Staël masquerading as a sibyl. Her soft, slurring voice betrayed her Southern origins.

Dazz, Emily, and Michael moved slowly through yet another open doorway into a room where a buffet had been arranged on a pair of long tables lit by ornate silver, many-branched candelabra. Rows of silver-plated dishes shaped like the hulls of galleons offered a variety of hot foods giving off a profusion of odors—curry, garlic, unrecognizable spices—and towering between the candelabra on each table was a giant three-tiered silver tower laden with fruit. Grapes hung in clusters from its lip.

"Eat, drink, and be merry, for tomorrow we die, die, die." They looked up to see the Southern lady, plump, round-faced, turbaned, helping herself liberally at the end of one table. She beamed at them, her bright, tiny, china-blue eyes dancing, and licked two fingers with a smack. "Don't be shy, folks, just dig in, there's plenty more where that came from." Holding her plate high, she picked up silverware and snapped out a napkin, which she proceeded to tuck in her bosom while occupying a gilt chair too small by far for her bulk. "Damask," she said, mopping her damp chest. "Don't find any paper napkins 'round here." Again she beamed, the flesh of her cheeks causing the blue of her eyes almost to disappear. She had ensconced herself near a pair of French doors that gave onto a large terrace, where guests mingled in the shadows amid points of candlelight, and beyond bulked the swooping, filigree arches of the Fifty-ninth Street Bridge, festooned with ropes of white lights.

Michael's eyes were wrenched away from the heaped tables by the sound of Dazz's voice. "Emily Chang, Michael Hawke, meet Miss Beulah Wales of Atlanta, Georgia. Miss Wales is a very good friend of our generous host."

"Why, Jack, what attractive friends you have," she exclaimed, watching Emily's slender, outstretched hand disappear into her own. "Are you all artists too?"

"Yes," said Dazz; "No," said Emily; "Hunger artists," said Michael, all at the same time. Emily laughed, a husky ripple of merriment that Michael loved to provoke. "Emily's a virtuoso flute player, and Michael's a master magician," Dazz explained. Emily demurred modestly, Michael looked distractedly at the tables.

The fat lady's little blue eyes sparkled. "How extremely interesting," she said, mercilessly emphasizing the stressed syllables. "I want to hear more after you get yourselves some food."

They gladly dedicated themselves to the task of loading their plates. With a conspiratorial look on her elfin features, Emily tilted her head sideways and winked at Michael across the table, as if they were raiding some rich, forbidden pantry. He grinned at her in frank admiration. Plates filled, they sat, the three of them, on a small sofa off slightly to one side of the room, eating enthusiastically while the party surged on in ever-changing waves around them.

Beulah Wales bobbed her head at them in convivial approval, then rose, tugging her chair, and plunked it down next to Michael. Her bright, earnest eyes seemed even smaller and bluer than before. Sniffing dismissively at the saffron-robed Hare Krishnas, who were now lining up at the buffet, she said, "They'd best make hay while the sun shines, they won't be about the premises too much longer." She rested a damp hand confidentially on Michael's knee. "Mr. Abdel-Noor, our absent host, was contemplating a journey to India, to visit with their Swami. The poor man's looking for his sister, I know, but go all the way to *India*? All those *filthy* cities? And his sister's here all the time, all the time, I tell him."

"I thought his sister was dead," Emily said.

"She is, honey, as a doornail. But Samir wants to talk to her. They were real close, Sami and Syrie. That's why you see me about." She leaned forward, putting a finger alongside her nose and gazing briefly at each of them in turn. "We—are—*del*ving."

Emily rolled her eyes, thinking the terrace might not be a bad idea; Dazz was busy evaluating potential nude models; but Michael was interested. "So you're trying to put Samir in touch with his sister?" he asked.

"Honey, you're a delight, that's exactly what I'm doing. It's a question of reaching the Other Side, that's to say, the astral plane.

Samir's got no need to mess with those skinheads. He just feels the lure of the East, being from there himself. I think those kids remind him of home."

"And where is our host this evening?" Michael inquired.

She gave him an incredulous look. "Why, honey, he's *up*stairs. He doesn't come down. He just likes to know there's a party going on, but he *don't* come *down*. Samir's got the dreadfuls." Her listeners' faces showed curiosity but not enlightenment. "It's a chronic condition, well, *almost* chronic. He's *con*stipated." She looked briefly from one to the other to make certain her words had had their effect. "Poor man, he suffers so." She leaned against the padded back of her chair, amused at a temporarily private thought. "It's terrible to laugh, poor Samir, but—I must tell you, it's too funny to keep, if you young folks won't mind a lady using one tiny four-letter word?" Briefly she awaited their acquiescence, then plunged on. "Poor Samir. We were sitting right there, in that very room, and you take a look around and guess how much cash's hanging on those walls or that you're walking on with those rugs, and he says to me, 'Boo'—he calls me Boo—'I am a very rich man, I am known on three continents, there is nothing I cannot have, when I go to the opera I wear a fortune in jewels, there is not a restaurant in the world at which I cannot have the best table, and I would give it all up for one good, healthy shit!' "

After a brief moment of shocked silence, her captive audience laughed ruefully. "The spirit is willing, but the flesh won't excrete," said Emily. "If Samir gets everything he wants, he'll be evacuating on the astral plane."

Beulah Wales looked at her quizzically for a second; then the china-blue eyes were nearly buried in flesh as she smiled. "Well, he does want some things that are very hard to get."

"You'd think he could find some consolation," mused Dazz, watching an extraordinarily beautiful woman, a sensuous goddess, bend over the laden tables to choose the most perfectly ripe fruit.

"Money can't buy miracles, Jack," said Miss Wales. Her hand suddenly plopped back on Michael's knee. "Which reminds me. Are you really a magician, honey? Show me some magic."

"I don't really have any of my—" Michael began.

"Don't play hard to get, Michael," said Dazz. "Show the lady."

"Go on, Michael," Emily urged, her dark eyes shining encouragement.

Faced with the prospect of total improvisation, cold, from scratch, Michael felt a bit uneasy, but he slipped into his professional mode as he would into a favorite sweater. "Well, ma'am, if you insist, but first, may I ask what these utensils"—his hands moved to her gaping cleavage and extracted from its depths first a knife, then a fork, then a spoon—"are doing here? Are you pilfering the silverware?"

"Shocking," said Dazz, who had been to parties with Michael before.

"Do you think a strip search is required?" asked Emily, mockingly stern.

Beulah Wales gasped in delighted confusion.

"No," said Michael, stooping low and grasping the cascading folds of the lady's dress, "I think a good shaking will do the trick." He shook the voluminous cloth vigorously, and five or six more pieces of silverware clattered to the floor, followed, after a couple of seconds and one final shake, by a pair of silver ice tongs. "That should do it, ma'am," he said, shaking a cautionary finger, "but you ought to be ashamed. Now I'll show you some magic."

Michael walked over to the tables and removed a burning candle from one of the candelabra. "Now, Miss Wales, cup your hand like this"—he showed her how—"and blow at the flame as hard as you can." He handed her the candle.

Captivated, she did as she was told, obedient as an eager child. The flame disappeared immediately, replaced by a long, wispy coil of smoke. The sweet smell of burning wax filled their nostrils. "That's very good," Michael said, taking back the candle, "but let me show you what you can do when you've got fire in your belly." He cupped one hand around the top of the candle as she had done and expelled his breath with a sharp, hissing sound. When he removed his hand, the flame was dancing again atop the candle. He held it toward her triumphantly, nodded in regal acknowledgment of Dazz and Emily's applause and Beulah Wales's ecstatic squeals.

She rose hugely from her chair. "Don't move, honey," she said to Michael, "don't any of you all move. Sami's got to see this." She steered her bulk with surprising grace, heading for the elevator to Samir Abdel-Noor's inner sanctum.

Taking advantage of her absence, Michael steered Emily to the dessert table. "I had nothing to do with the ice tongs," Michael said. "I half expected to see the bucket fall out as well."

After a short while, Miss Wales returned, clasping her hands in anticipation. Less than a minute later the gold filigree cage, balking and shuddering, redescended. Beulah Wales hurried to open the folding gate, but she was beaten to it by an olive-skinned man of thirty, with glossy ringlets and a fierce mustache. Through the wide portal, Michael and his friends could see emerging from the elevator car a gross form, the shape and size of a giant inflated pillow, covered neck to toe by a tentlike caftan embroidered with exotic birds and beasts. As this apparition drew closer, further details became visible: much jewelry, turquoise and silver; a round, swarthy face, the eyes hidden behind dark glasses; a fez, topped by a black silk tassel; a silken scarf or handkerchief, bright green, dangling from one of the caftan's sleeves; and, below the caftan's hem, appearing far too small for their enormous burden, feet enclosed in embroidered Turkish slippers with upcurled toes.

Miss Wales, walking backward in front of him with beckoning gestures, led their host into the buffet room. He sniffed the air briefly, then at the woman's instigation walked directly over to Michael. "Good evening. I am Samir Abdel-Noor, your host. It is a great pleasure to have you here. May I say I find it always a pleasure to meet gentlemen of your profession? My friend Miss Wales informs me that you are a talented magician. What will you do for me? Something interesting? I am easily amused, have no fear. Have you eaten? Have you a drink?" He peered about with a slightly annoyed expression, as if he expected that by some invisible agency a drink should be delivered into his guest's hand.

"I have a drink, thank you." Michael raised his glass diffidently.

"You will do some tricks for me, yes? Conjuring—that is what you call it?—has always held a special enchantment for me. When I was a boy I had a tutor who was most dexterously adept at sleight of hand. And card tricks, you never saw such clever card work, he could practically slide the spots around before your eyes. But—oh, he was a dreadful thing, a rude Englishman, he would never show me anything. If you do tricks you must show me how they are done, no? Yes. One wants to know how they are done." Sami closed his mouth, his lower lip curled in petulance, his expression presaging a child's tantrum. Then he immediately smiled again, and in the smile, the coquettish tilt of his head, the fluttery play of his pudgy, bejeweled hands, there was something that told of his desperate desire to please.

His long-lashed, damp little eyes with their entreating dog-devotion could hardly take themselves off Michael's face, and several times as he spoke he touched his hand or exchanged meaningful glances with the Southern woman. His speaking voice was mild, reluctant, fluffy little billowings of sound, spongy and lethargic, lacking substance.

Michael's first instinct was to dislike this soft, stuffed man, with his small darting eyes and his cherry lips, his costume, the cloying politesse of his tone. But in his obviously sincere hospitality, his anguish to please, his desire to be entertained, his need to be liked at once, there was something touching.

With a precious look, Samir lifted a hand, showing a bent knuckle on which was squeezed a gold ring set with an enormous green gem. Was it an emerald? Michael caught himself staring.

"Do you like it? Mu'ammar al-Gadhafi gave it to me." Samir giggled at his joke, then took Michael's arm fraternally. "Aren't they dreadful, all these rocks? So vulgar, but I like them. Yet, shall I tell you something? I have all these and more. Real. The real thing, not paste—I am not like your movie stars who keep their real diamonds in the safe. I have a coat which is sable on the outside and mink on the inside. It is reversible. I have this house which you see—a small palace, no? I could buy the Chase Manhattan tomorrow if I chose. I mention all this not in the spirit of braggadocio but to make a point. Namely, that I would gladly give up everything—" He paused, his small bright eyes encompassing the guests who stood about listening, and drew Michael closer. "Everything, for one good, healthy shit. It's true. How do you call it, a 'dump'?" He spread his fingers over his large round stomach. "I feel that half an hour on the pot and I should be thin like anything. Do you know what my dear, departed friend the

Duchess of Windsor once said? 'One can't be too rich or too thin.' It is true. And one cannot have too many shits. Now, young man, your tricks, yes?"

He patted Michael's hand, released him, and sat in a large wicker chair with a high back that rose over him like a cobra's hood, crossing his ankles below the folds of his garment: an Eastern potentate, waiting to be entertained. Michael looked around; then, with a smile and a little bow, he moved to the table, where he took some fruit from the giant epergne—a lemon, an orange, another orange—which he tossed into the air and manipulated with ease. Samir pursed his lips, leaning his round chin on his sparkling hand, watching impassively. To the revolving circle of fruit Michael now added other pieces until he had five circulating, then a half dozen. He snatched a banana and balanced it on the tip of his nose while the rest of the fruit spun in a continuous arc before him. Then, one by one, he let the pieces fall back onto the pile in the epergne, caught the banana, and laid it on the table. He glanced at Samir, who sat blinking but seemed hardly interested. Michael took three plates from a stack and tossed these into the air, catching them deftly, then adding more until six of them were whirling through the air and as quickly returning to the stack on the table.

"Oh!" Samir exclaimed with a surprised look, nodding and peering about the circle of guests who had joined them in the room. "Adroit, yes, very." He nodded again, waited for Michael to continue.

Michael approached with exaggerated deference, displayed his fingers and hands, back and front, leaned toward his host, and removed from the front of his caftan a silver half-dollar. The Egyptian blinked with pleasure, the gleam of the metal drawing a gleam from his eyes. Standing erect, Michael caused the coin to do prodigies of movement across his hand, between the fingers, behind, appearing, disappearing, reappearing, seeming to gallop across his agile fingertips, now falling out of his ear, now from his mouth, now from inside his collar. Eagerly following each movement, frowning in concentration, Samir leaned forward, enthralled.

"Good! Good!" He clapped his hands, the other watchers following suit. Michael held out the coin at arm's length, and at arm's length caused it to vanish. The applause increased. He crossed again to the buffet. Stepping behind the table, he snapped out one of the blue damask napkins and spread it on an open spot before him. Picking up a salt shaker and unscrewing its top, he poured the contents into his right hand, then raised his open, empty palms. He smiled at Samir, made a quick, grasping motion in the air with his left hand, and looked up; salt was trickling from the closed fist in a thin, steady stream, then pouring copiously, at last forming a white mound equal to the contents of three salt shakers on the blue damask square. Michael shrugged his shoulders modestly amid resounding applause.

"Beautiful," Samir pronounced admiringly. "Very beautiful. Do some more."

Michael gave him a helpless look. "I'm sorry—I don't have anything with me . . ."

"Yes, yes, it is unfair, of course, a magician needs his equipment."

Seeking to improvise, Michael cast about the room, pausing briefly to note Emily's proud, expectant smile, Dazz's smug grin, Beulah Wales's vast approval. His eye lighted on a woman in evening dress, seated by a window. Quickly crossing to her, he bowed chivalrously and asked if he might borrow the evening bag that lay in her lap. She handed it to him, and he returned with it to the table, where he emptied its contents into a napkin and placed them to one side. The bag was of a soft material, with a drawstring, like a reticule, and encrusted with beadwork. He turned the bag inside out, showing the blue silk lining, then right side out again. Setting it in front of him with the bottom squashed flat, the mouth open, he leaned to the pile of eggs by the omelette pans. When he flashed his hands up, the right one was empty, but there was an egg between each pair of fingers of the left. He cracked their shells in turn, one by one, dropping yolks and whites into the open reticule.

"My bag!" the woman exclaimed. "He's ruining my new bag!"

"Hush!" Samir commanded, holding out an imperious hand, never taking his eyes from Michael, who pulled the drawstring tight and lifted the bag from the table, letting it swing in the air. It had weight and substance, obviously, and he swung it faster so that it made a circle around his hand, faster and faster, until with an abrupt motion he brought it to a sudden stop. Holding it in front of him, he loosened the drawstring and opened the bag wide. Then, with a dramatic flourish, he turned it upside down; from its inverted mouth fell, not a mess of broken eggs, but a bunch of Concord grapes. He turned the bag inside out, revealing its unscathed lining, restored it to its normal shape, replaced its contents, and returned it to its startled owner. The bunch of grapes he brought to Samir.

"Beautiful, wonderful, extraordinary," gushed the happy host, plucking off a grape and popping it into his mouth. His little eyes gleamed hotly behind his dark glasses. "I've never seen anything like it. What do you call it, this magic trick?"

"No special name. It's just the egg-and-bag trick. You supplied the eggs, but I needed a bag. I hope," Michael added, looking to the woman by the window, "your friend didn't mind."

"She is not my friend, I have never seen her before. None of these people have I ever seen before." He waved negligently at the ring of faces. "Perhaps you can make them disappear like eggs, yes?" He giggled behind his hand, his rings flashing. "Come, do something else, not for them, but for me. You will, yes?"

"I will, yes, but you'll have to help me," Michael said softly, drawing closer to Samir as though enlisting a new accomplice.

"Yes, yes, of course." Samir could barely contain his eagerness, shifting his huge body perilously forward as Michael bent toward him. "Tell me what I must do. And what will you do?"

A feeling of strength, of absolute competence, flooded over Michael. He was truly enjoying himself, performing with an ease and energy that surprised even him. It was as though, after the shock of events earlier in the day and the subsequent purging, he had risen to a new level of competence. Or could it be a new level of power?

"I'm going to relieve you of certain belongings, right in front of your eyes," Michael said to Samir. "Take off two rings, place one on each palm, and hold out your hands."

Michael straightened up. He was now wearing Samir's dark glasses, but the Egyptian, intent on carrying out his instructions, failed to notice this, or the fact that his fez was now on Michael's head.

"Keep your eyes on your rings," Michael said. Samir stared at his upturned palms. With two swift movements, Michael closed both of the proffered hands, patting the soft, plump fists. "Hold on tight," he said, "and count to five, slowly."

As his victim obeyed, Michael stood in front of him, his hands joined at his mouth, a ring adorning each index finger. "Now open your hands," he commanded.

Samir did as he was told, gasping at the sight of a napkin ring lying on each fat palm. Raising his eyes to Michael, he recognized, with mounting astonishment, his fez, his glasses, his very rings, and began to giggle uncontrollably, his flesh undulating in ripples under the caftan.

"Ah, my friend," he said, gasping for breath and drying his eyes with the green silk handkerchief he plucked from his sleeve. "Ah, my friend."

There was applause from the guests, which Michael acknowledged with an elaborate bow, indicating with a wave of his hand that his performance was ended. All his personal items restored to their rightful places, Samir sat in silence for a while, quivering and turning on Michael a look of utter fascination. "You are a miracle worker, my friend. If my doctors knew their art as well as you know yours, my problems"—he tapped his distended stomach—"would be over."

Exhilarated and energized to the point of recklessness, Michael spoke more quickly than he thought. "I can fix that too," he said, gesturing at Samir's belly.

"You can? How? Show me, show me how? You are serious, yes? Show me how you can do this." The man was practically pleading; Michael had suddenly become the glowing center around which all his hope revolved.

Incredulous in the face of such desperate credulousness, Michael decided to play along; one last, quick trick. "It's a question of visualization," he said. "Give me your handkerchief." He took it and began tying knots in it. "Imagine that this is what your intestines look like now. Here, take an end and pull hard." They pulled together on the knotted piece of green silk. "All tied up, compacted, blocked." He crumpled the handkerchief into a ball in his hand. "But now imagine the dawn of a new intestine, grand opening, a mighty river flowing"—he opened his hand and lifted the unknotted handkerchief from his palm—"free at last!"

Samir leaped shouting to his feet, clapping Michael in an embrace that made him imagine an enormous, suffocating cushion. Then Samir released him and fell back with a squishy sound into his chair. "What else can you do?" he panted. He seemed to be having difficulty focusing his eyes.

"I'm afraid I'm all out of tricks," Michael said wearily. "Usually when I'm hired for a party I have my things with me."

"Ah!" There was a pause while the Egyptian gathered his thoughts. When he looked up again, leaning back against the fan of his chair, his eyes had regained most of their customary shrewdness. "You perform at parties?"

"Children's parties, birthdays, that sort of thing."

"But you are wasted on children. No, no, no, no, you shall not perform for children. You shall perform for me at *my* party, my next *real* party. This"—he waggled his fingers contemptuously—"is a mere get-together, haphazard, slovenly. When is my next important party, Gilbert?" he asked, turning to the glossy-haired one who had remained immobile behind his chair the entire time.

Without moving his head, the Arab said, "The night of your birthday."

"But of course," Samir said joyously. "My birthday. It falls on Halloween, and I give a special party. That is perfect. On Halloween night you will come with all your things and perform magic for my guests. You will make it truly special. You are free then?"

"Yes. Sure." Michael turned to Emily, who smiled slightly and shrugged.

"And so you will come? Definitely?"

"Sure. I'll come."

"Then it is arranged." Samir nodded with satisfaction at Beulah Wales, who was hovering near him. "You hear, dear Boo, this marvelous young man will come."

"I told you he was special, didn't I, Sami?"

"Yes. You told me so, and he is. Very quick, your young man.

And very handsome. He should go far." Heaving his bulk from the chair, Samir stood before Michael and took one hand, pressing it between both of his. "Far," he repeated, then broke into a smile, holding up his bejeweled fingers. "If I were a king you should have one of these in payment for tonight." He dropped his hand and sighed audibly. "Alas, I am not a king. I bid you good night. Come, Gilbert." Followed by the Arab, he left the room.

As Michael walked over to Emily's side, he felt the strange tension that had so completely energized him drain out of him and exhaustion fill its place. It must be well past midnight, he thought, a strange day from start to finish—summer in the city. But his watch read only eight minutes to eleven. Odd, Michael thought. This was a particularly reliable watch, and it had never stopped before.

CHAPTER SEVEN

Stakeouts

It was strange weather for "duck" hunting. The heat persisted, radio and television weathermen predicted continuing excessive temperatures, newspapers headlined NO END IN SIGHT. With Bloomingdale's Big Brown Bag as his only clue, Michael took refuge in the huge department store, grateful for the air-conditioning. For several days, he staked out the place, moving from entrance to entrance, riding the escalators, the elevators, checking the men's rooms, going methodically from floor to floor, department to department. Despite the enervating weather, people were buying like crazed creatures, and the store stayed crowded. He saw many weird sights in his days there, but there was no Queer Duck.

He would, Michael figured, be easy to spot in a crowd. Mostly he looked for the umbrella, or for anyone wearing black. He flogged his brain to imagine what merchandise such a person might buy in a department store, especially one so trendy as this. He even checked with the information counter to see if there had been any particular sales or unusual promotions on the "Day of the Frog," as he now thought of it, but all he could discover were blind leads.

He set up his act outside, on the corner of Lexington Avenue and Fifty-ninth, doing hocus-pocus, and while he performed his tricks he kept his eyes peeled in every direction. He wasn't merely observing or noting characters, as was his habit, but looking through them, past them, for one particular character, a Queer Duck dressed in black, with a walleye and an umbrella, a strange-gaited, long-haired, absent-minded professor sort of guy with funny shoes and a secret. Michael went through his routines automatically, letting his hands work by themselves while his eyes examined the interminable parade of faces and his brain kept imagining what it would be like to learn the Queer Duck's trick, whatever it might be, to acquire that skill, that knowledge, that power.

Busy though he was in body and mind, he found the insistent heat sometimes broke through all the barriers of his concentration, demanding attention, and he envied the nun sitting on a camp stool next to the store's revolving door, cooled by steady blasts from the air-conditioned interior. She sat there so patiently in her long black habit and her starched wimple, a collection can tilted negligently in one hand and the other tucked under her scapular. She always kept her head slightly angled toward him, watching shyly behind her spectacles as he flashed his silks or did his coin numbers, and he wondered what order she belonged to. He was so busy looking up the street and down the street and across the street that he never noticed the tips of her blunt, shiny, patent-leather shoes, barely peeking out from under the hem of her habit.

Michael couldn't afford to eat in any of the places around the store, so Emily brought him sandwiches and juice, and when she had time she stood watch at entrances he couldn't cover. On Thursday evening, when the store was open late, they both stayed until nine and were the last to leave. Even the nun was gone by then.

Emily was by no means an enthusiastic accomplice in this operation. She had been opposed to Michael's stakeout project from the start, but all her efforts to argue him out of it, to persuade him of the illogicality of such a hunt, to point out that he could ill spare time spent in what must surely prove a fruitless search, to express the nameless dread she felt at the prospect of success, however unlikely, collided with his obstinate determination to confront the strange old man who had undone him. As far as Emily was concerned, Michael's understandable curiosity had grown into a dangerous obsession; it was beyond reason, and no good could come of it. She told herself the Queer Duck would never reappear; he had, after all, stolen Michael's wallet and a considerable sum of money. And then she told herself that if he *did* show up, Michael would need her help. That rationale, working in tandem with love, did the rest, and so against her better judgment she stood at the entrance to the store, a loyal sentinel, conscientiously scrutinizing the passing throngs for a bizarre figure she hoped she'd never see again.

On the days when Emily couldn't help him, Michael would go home by himself, hot, frustrated, and exhausted. He resolved to abandon the search, get back on the street in whiteface, pick up some cash. The whole idea was crazy, the proverbial haystack was too large, no matter how precious the proverbial needle. But then he would remember man-into-frog, the weird, almost obscene thrill he'd experienced, the total "frogginess" of those moments.

Ga-dunk.

On the Saturday night, sluggish from more useless searching, five glasses of wine, and an hour of lovemaking with Emily, he lay in the dark beside her sleeping form. Gazing at the smoky blue halo the dim outside light spread across her black hair, he relaxed completely and let fantasies shimmer across his mind. All over again, he allowed himself to be seduced by the idea of the power he sought, surrendering to the allure of the undiscovered mystery, offering himself false hopes, false promises. Yet, despite his weariness, and perhaps because he could hear Emily's gentle breathing, he saw with total clarity that he was falling in thrall to a mania, becoming a slave to a dream.

Because Bloomingdale's was open only during the afternoon on Sunday, Michael yielded to Emily's pleas and agreed to hang around the brightly gilded Sherman statue at the foot of Central

Park. She played her flute while he, not bothering with makeup or miming, performed some simple magic—the cut-and-knot rope trick, the water-in-the-bottle number—and earned a few dollars in the process.

Michael knew, as did any street performer, that working the streets, especially in a city so diverse as New York, was a great challenge. Faced with a crowd whose moods were unpredictable, and over whose movements he had no control, the street magician had to be brave, quick witted, coolheaded, and highly skilled, or he should consider other ways of making a living. But Michael had great confidence in his artistry, and he delighted in winning over a crowd, the more heterogeneous the better. He loved doing the water number, it always got the kids, and he liked the kids best. Kids and magic were made for each other.

First he'd fill an empty Coke bottle with water from a paper cup, then upend the open glass mouth on his palm, announcing that he could "control" water; and so it seemed he could. He would slide the mouth of the bottle off his hand and command the water not to pour, and it would not. Or order it to pour, and it would. Stop. Pour. Stop. Pour. The kids would take it up, chanting and laughing, until the bottle was finally empty. Even the sandwich-board man wearing an ad for the latest Donald Trump book stopped his march up and down the sidewalks and seemed to be enjoying Michael's performance.

Or the rope trick. Cutting it in lengths and bringing it out whole again from behind his palm. But those were easy dodges; he'd done them ten years ago for the Elks Club of Genesee, Ohio. Crowd pleasers, but trifles.

Michael knew he should have put on whiteface and given them the Mechanical Man number. There was more money in that, but it was too hot for makeup and all those physical gyrations.

And still no sign of the Queer Duck. Sundays at Veterans Plaza in a heat wave evidently wasn't his style. The sandwich-board man, on the other hand, had stayed on to the very end, hugging the edge of the plaza or General Sherman's pedestal, watching from behind his dark glasses. Only when it was clear that Michael planned no more tricks did he return to his job of silent sidewalk salesman.

• • •

According to an old joke, on any Sunday night in New York, the city's entire Jewish population could be found having Chinese food. The old rabbi riding the subway with Michael and Emily, however, seemed to be an exception. And then again, maybe he was on his way, Michael thought. They *were* going downtown on the Lexington Avenue line, headed for Chinatown's Mott Street and Sunday supper with Emily's parents, the Changs.

Emily had been raised in Chinatown, where her father imported plum sauce and other delicacies from Hong Kong. They were a large, wealthy, handsome family, the boys slim and somewhat aloof, American slang sounding strange in their mouths, and the girls elegant and poised.

Michael could tell that Mr. Chang objected to him, didn't approve of his not having a proper job, nor of Emily's joining him in the mimes. Her oldest brother felt the same way. Charlie Chang (Number One Son, as Michael privately called him) was coolly polite, but Michael knew Charlie knew he was sleeping with his sister and didn't like it. This veiled but palpable hostility bothered Michael only slightly. He by nature sought the approval of others, yet when forced to make a decision, he would always choose in his own behalf, even if it meant alienating others. He loved Emily, and she loved him—he was secure with that. If her family didn't approve, well, too bad.

Michael's recent general unease had made him feel more uncomfortable than usual tonight. As soon as it was feasible, he had suggested that he had a busy day tomorrow—a pronouncement that drew smirks from Mr. Chang and Charlie—and had made his escape with Emily. They walked the few blocks north to Houston Street, where they could catch a subway that would take them uptown to the West Side.

The D train was unusually crowded for a Sunday night. Emily and Michael found adjoining seats, but they were soon knee to knee with a young man who stood before them, holding onto an overhead rod and listening to his Walkman. He loomed above them as though enraptured, his eyes half closed, his lips parted, his head thrown back. His earphones fit loosely, and the volume was so high that the sound cut through the whoosh and clatter of the subway. Michael wasn't sure what the man was listening to, but he was sure it wasn't Kenny G. The added irritation of malfunctioning air-conditioning in their car served to make what was in fact a relatively brief trip seem interminable. He sat with his eyes closed, clutching Emily's hand tightly, his only goal to reach Emily's apartment as soon as possible so they could shut themselves away from the rest of the world. He was too excited by the prospect, too absorbed by his need to escape the subway with its heat and clatter to notice the same rabbi they'd seen before, sitting with his newspaper at the rear of the car.

Emily's father's money made it possible for her to live in what Michael considered luxury, a few blocks from Lincoln Center and the Juilliard School, where she studied music. They got off at the Columbus Circle station and by an unspoken agreement hurried along the sizzling streets until they were safely inside the apartment.

They made love once, urgently and athletically, in the shower, and then again, languidly and deeply, on Emily's bed, while the ceiling fan ticked like a slow metronome above them. Afterward they cuddled in contented silence. He put his nose against her neck, smelling her skin and her hair, remembering their first night together, in New Hampshire, a little over a year ago. They were both working at the Rustic Theater in a modest little summer musical production, she as part of the small orchestra and Michael as the leading man, and staying at the same boardinghouse. One night, sleepless with desire and praying that the feeling was mutual, he'd simply gotten up, tiptoed to her room, and slipped into bed. She'd started awake, raising herself on her elbows and looking at him; then she'd murmured, "My dream come true," and rolled into his arms.

Everything between them afterward had been equally smooth and trouble-free, all year long. Michael had at first thought that this was a temporary liaison, but he wasn't so sure anymore. The relationship was still undefined, still in flux, but Michael was sure that it was based on more than physical attraction and sexual energy. He felt at peace with Emily in a way that he had never known before.

As he lay next to her, hanging on the edge of sleep, each of his dwindling senses still filled with her presence, he allowed himself to realize that he was crazy about her, and for the first time in many nights it was Emily's sunlit, smiling image, and not the frightening memory of an ominous black-clad figure, that accompanied Michael into unconsciousness.

Emily was busy the next day, with classes and related matters, all neglected that past week, so Michael staked out Bloomingdale's alone, foregoing his performance and once again wandering the store's aisles. And once again he failed to see the Queer Duck. Afterward, alone in his apartment, and despite his exhaustion, he couldn't sleep, so he went for a walk, wandering aimlessly for a while through the small, triangular plot of Needle Park near the Ansonia Hotel. Though it was after midnight, it seemed that half the population of the city was still outdoors, plastered flat by the heat, lolling like melting statues on the benches, dull eyed, listless, stolidly resentful, as if come together in maleficence, felons waiting for doomsday. He passed people with fast food, eating, dropping papers and garbage; people with radios, listening; people with ice-cream cones, licking; the homeless, limp with sleepless despair.

He walked several blocks south on Broadway, stalking nothing but the night, eventually turning back north on Columbus Avenue. As he shuffled down Seventy-second Street to his apartment, having covered a lot of distance and gotten nowhere, he never noticed the man wearing an eye patch and leaning in a doorway across the street.

Upstairs, Michael stretched out on his wrinkled sheets, staring at the ceiling. His head felt fuzzy, and his thoughts jumped erratically from subject to subject, but he found that he didn't want to dwell on any of them and descended at last into a troubled sleep.

On Tuesday it was back to Bloomie's, again without Emily, again on the in-store patrol, and again without luck. Bored and fatigued by his own doggedness, he stopped at the notions counter, imagining how easy it would be to fill his pockets with shoplifted goods. He even went so far as to test his skill on a pair of small, blunt-edged scissors, taking them in his fingers, trying them out, examining them for flaws as though trimming nose hairs was a very serious business, then sliding them up his sleeve and back down again, fast, smooth, undetected. But as he replaced the scissors an uneasy feeling passed over him like a hot breath, and when he turned, he saw someone watching him: a rabbi, much like the one he'd seen on Sunday, complete with black suit, black hat, earlocks, tieless collar, and a hairy face, the eyes hidden behind dark glasses. As the man moved up the escalator, peering down over his shoulder, an amused smile seemed to play about his dark lips.

That night Michael used his dwindling funds to treat Emily and himself to Cuban food at Victor's Cafe, followed by a movie. Paying for the dinner check and the movie tickets was only a gesture; he knew Emily would reimburse him. She did, and he took the money under protest.

Back at her apartment, they made love in the dim bedroom. Later she brought him lemonade, and they lay chatting. Inevitably the conversation came around to the Queer Duck, and once again she tried to dissuade Michael from continuing his search. "You can't win. If you don't find him, you're wasting your time, and if you do find him, you're in serious trouble. Can't you give it up?"

"You know I can't. What kind of trouble?"

"I don't know—danger, something bad. The guy's spooky." Emily sat up. "Michael, what he did to you was frightening. Terrible." She paused. "And evil, Michael. Evil. That man is evil. Oh, please give this up."

Michael tried to tease her out of her anger and fear, but she was too upset to yield easily. Finally she responded to his calming entreaties, and at last she slept.

The next morning, Emily still had some practicing to do, so Michael left and prowled the streets again, as if suddenly, from around the corner, out of nowhere, the Queer Duck would miraculously appear. This was what he hoped for, all he could hope for now, really. He knew it was pointless to return to Bloomingdale's. All he could hope now was that one day he would look up and the old man would just be there.

But the days came and went, and he wasn't. Money was becoming a more urgent matter. Michael's last reserves were about to vanish, and if he didn't get back to his street act, he didn't get to pass the hat. No hat, no dough, and his landlady was beginning to hassle him.

The clue to finding the Queer Duck, of course, was the button, the thing in the old man's lapel. But what was it? Why couldn't he dredge it up? He remembered it as a common object, something he'd seen before. The trick was in remembering where.

Michael struggled to drive all thoughts from his mind but this one, and he did so successfully. In doing so, however, he entered a kind of dreamworld of exhaustion and frustration, and his actions became more and more automatic, as if he were indeed performing as the Mechanical Man, all day long. Classes were taking up a lot of Emily's time, and at night she was busy with rehearsals for a concert, so he often returned alone to his own apartment, paying little heed to the Italian beggar who had lately been hanging around his block with an outstretched hand and a whining voice: "*Niente da mangiare, cinque bambini, niente da mangiare, cinque bambini.*" Five kids? Surely the man was too old, Michael thought. He would slip him a quarter and head for his doorway, not noticing the toes of the shiny patent-leather shoes that protruded below the pants cuffs.

Alone in his unairconditioned apartment, he would try to sleep. And he would fail.

In those unsettling hours, when this alien city roared and screeched outside his open windows, Michael allowed himself a rare moment of doubt. Would anything ever come of this? Had this small-town boy, abandoned by his mother and father, finally pushed too far? And it wasn't just the Queer Duck. He would or he would not find the strange old man. In the end, that would take care of itself, probably already had, for Michael sensed the chase was somehow over. Only he wasn't sure who had found whom.

And so he sat alone, waiting—for whatever it was that would happen next. And obsessing about being ready. To stay alert, as well as to sharpen his skills, he spent much of his time working his card drills. Half-fanning or full-fanning, split-decking or under-carding, single-cutting or double- and triple-cutting, refining spreads, shuffles, pinky breaks, side-jogs, fixes, flipping up the aces where they should appear, losing and finding them again, making black red and red black, moving his fingers like machine parts, keeping them in perfect working order, improving the flow of the cards, always, always improving. Or perfecting a variation on a triple split, making the cards do everything but walk by themselves and all the time pondering how he might do even that. Or switching to half-dollars, palming and repalming, under-knuckling them, losing them, finding them, pulling them from elbow or ear or thin air, making them disappear back into elbow or ear or thin air again. Hour after hour, devising a new subtlety for an old sleight, something that would make it just a shade different, that much better, more clever and adroit.

Presto the Great, that was him. The Greatest Magician in the World.

But cards and coins weren't enough. So once more he would be reminded of his tormentor, the Queer Duck, and once again he was dazzled by the idea of utter mastery and envied it with his entire being. He felt mounting excitement, as always when he let his mind surrender to the lure of such uncanny power. What if he could acquire it, learn to exercise it—whatever it was? It seemed somehow as if it were there for him, waiting to be discovered; hypnotism, perhaps, but of a range and intensity nobody had ever seen before.

But how was it done? he kept asking himself. How do you learn something like that? You wouldn't find it in books. Then how? Of course . . .

Find the man.

One afternoon, walking toward Fifth Avenue on East Fifty-second Street, he saw Dazz coming out of La Grenouille, a restaurant Michael knew to be far too rich for his own means. Dazz was accompanied by a plump, swarthy, expensively dressed man Michael didn't at first recognize, and by the unmistakable Beulah Wales. Only as Michael approached the three, who were absorbed in animated conversation, did he realize that the other man was Samir Abdel-Noor himself, all flashing teeth and jewelry, but changed in some indefinable way.

Dazz, ushering his companions into the waiting limousine, looked up and saw Michael coming. He smiled broadly, leaned over to speak a few words inside the car, and then stepped gingerly aside to avoid being flattened by his patron, who came bursting out of the vehicle with surprising agility. Ululating joyously, he charged Michael with open arms, engulfing him in an embrace and kissing him with disconcerting enthusiasm on both cheeks. "My friend, the worker of miracles!" he exclaimed, pummeling Michael's shoulders while Dazz and the rather more ponderously emerging Beulah Wales beamed approbation. "You have made me a new man," Samir was gushing. "I am born again!"

Michael glanced quizzically at Dazz and nodded a distracted greeting to Miss Wales, who said, "Samir thinks you fixed his plumbing."

"Unclogged his drain," Dazz said sotto voce, enjoying Michael's gape-mouthed effort to understand.

"Yes, yes!" Samir yelled, shrill with excitement. "As you told me, 'Free at last.' Now I am regular like everyone else! Every day! Like clockworks!"

Having grasped at last the nature of the prodigy being attributed to him, Michael began instinctively to demur. "I'm glad you're feeling better, but I don't think—"

"*Feeling better?*" Samir shrieked. "I am transformed! Look at me!" Giggling, entirely unselfconscious, he held his linen jacket open and strutted on the sidewalk, striking various incongruous poses.

"More than forty pounds, my dear friend! In two weeks!"

Samir bent to the window of the limousine, spoke briefly to the driver—Michael recognized the brooding Gilbert—and straightened up again, holding a manila envelope, which he handed to Michael, literally brushing aside his modest attempt at a refusal. "No, no, take this, my friend. Think of it as a token of my gratitude. And don't forget my party, where you are to perform for my guests."

"Halloween night. I won't forget."

Samir shook his hand lovingly and followed Beulah Wales into the limousine. Both of them waved at him as Dazz clapped him on the back and climbed inside, winking like a conspirator. "Your lucky day. *Ciao, bello,*" he called; then Gilbert accelerated into the traffic.

Clutching the envelope against his chest, Michael watched them drive away. A little dazed by this whirlwind meeting, which had interrupted his reveries and distracted him from his single purpose, he stared at the envelope before opening it as unobtrusively as possible. A quick glance inside revealed a sheaf of hundred-dollar bills; he guessed there were about forty of them. He shook his head, disbelieving the evidence of his eyes; maybe he was a miracle worker after all. He stepped to the curb and raised his arm to hail a taxi. Emily had to see this.

CHAPTER EIGHT

The Mechanical Man and the Disappearing Duck

Despite controversy over its side effects, money possesses formidable therapeutic powers. His mood elevated, his perceptions altered, Michael settled easily into unfamiliar surroundings—the rear seat of a cab—and proceeded to enjoy the ever-changing spectacle presented by the streets of New York. For all he knew, the frenzied, unintelligible, surly Middle Eastern wails pouring from the cab's radio might be an exhortation to eradicate his kind from the earth; he smiled, nevertheless, soothed by the thickness of the envelope in his hand. Samir's gratitude had turned him into an optimist, at least for the afternoon.

Emily had planned to go to the Metropolitan Museum and attend an afternoon concert (Bach, Debussy, Poulenc) given by her flute professor and a Juilliard colleague, so Michael figured she wouldn't be home for a while. Not without difficulty, linguistic and otherwise, he persuaded his cabdriver to wait for him outside first a florist's, then an upscale delicatessen, and finally a wine shop. Laden with flowers, fancy snacks, and a bottle of very good, very cold champagne, Michael gave the cabbie a princely tip and rang the bell to Emily's apartment.

She had been home only a few minutes and was surprised to hear his voice. She was even more surprised at the sight of his offerings. Exclaiming with delight, she immediately took the flowers into the small kitchen and set about arranging them in a vase. Her back was turned to Michael, who sat on the couch, leaning over the coffee table and telling her his story of encountering Samir, while he poured the champagne and laid out the deli treats. Emily entered the room, holding the vase at arm's length and slightly to one side. "Look how beautiful!" she said. "What do you think?"

Michael admired the bouquet and, behind it, Emily's glowing face. He saw her clearly for the first time since his excited arrival. He was beginning to say, "I think they're almost as pretty as you are," but stopped in midsentence as his eyes focused on the button pinched onto the collar of her blouse.

With a joyous whoop, he jumped up, embraced Emily, and swung her off her feet, ignoring both her frantic effort to hold the vase upright and the water that splashed down his back. His reiterated shouts drowned out her laughing protests: "It's the museum! It's the Metropolitan! It's the museum!"

They were both dizzy when he lowered her to the floor, interrupting the celebration for an instant to snatch the tin disc from her collar. She barely had time to set the vase down on the coffee table, where it was relatively free from danger. "Will you please tell me—" she began.

"Museum, darlin'! Button, button, I've got the button!" He was speaking loudly, waving the little tab in front of her nose. "He went to the Met that day."

"Who?"

"The Queer Duck, of course! My magical mystery man. He had a button on his lapel. Different colors for different days, right? He went on the red day. He was at the museum! Here, let me pour us more champagne. This is our lucky day."

He set up shop at the plaza the following morning. He'd always liked it there and still did, despite its associations with frog-horror. Maybe he'd never get rich working that spot, but at least at the end of the day there was usually an equal number of dollar bills and quarters in the hat. Besides, Samir had temporarily calmed his money worries. He'd paid his landlady, set aside a few hundred dollars he owed Dazz, even insisted on repaying what he owed Emily. She had classes again today, so he was doing a solo bit, his ladder-climbing routine, feet on the ground but moving rung by rung upward into some cloudy infinity, the ladder swaying while he surveyed the terrain like a seasick sailor in the crow's nest. Tourists were taking snapshots. A black mailman sat on a bench, wolfing down his lunch; next to him a natty-looking banker type in well-creased trousers leaned on the darkly gleaming cane that he held propped under his chin.

Michael's performance was interrupted briefly by the appearance of one of New York's too-numerous street crazies, this one an aging hippie alcoholic, a man who'd obviously tippled one too many and had probably ingested more than his share of mind-altering substances in his earlier days. Whatever was left of his mind seemed fixed on being heard and being seen, center stage.

Playing with the drunk in a way that was more fun than mocking, Michael mimicked the man's unsteady walk and wild gesturing. In the end both of them got applause; Michael even got the man to join him in a bow.

Everyone laughed, the mailman, the woman feeding pigeons, and especially the banker, with his homburg, his yellow gloves, his waxed mustache and horn-rimmed glasses. He even wore spats, over shiny, black patent-leather shoes.

The next day, Michael moved the stakeout to the Metropolitan Museum of Art. The weather had cooled somewhat, promising an end to the heat wave that had gripped the area for so long now. After the ninth straight day of ninety-degree-plus temperatures, river breezes had blown some life back into the city; people seemed more normal, relieved, almost winking at one another, as if they shared some private joke.

Michael had put on his whiteface and claimed his spot outside the museum even before the doors opened. He smiled at Emily as she crouched nearby, readying her flute, and then he strode onto center stage, the landing between the first and second tiers of stone stairs. After clapping his hands to gather the passersby, he launched into his act.

From inside the breast of his grenadier's tunic he slipped out a long-stemmed rose—cloth, faded from use—the only prop he would work with. Around him, up and down the steps, beside the fountains flanking the entrance, the crowd was gathering. He placed the rose at the edge of the top step and returned quickly to center stage, where he lay flat on the cement, closing his eyes as if he were dead. He remained still for a minute; then he began to rise, transformed into the Mechanical Man. This was Michael's art in full flower. Each of his body movements was precise, robotic, slowly gauged, slightly jerky. He accompanied each operation with ratcheting clicks of his tongue against the roof of his mouth, careful never to use his lips or move his throat muscles. Emily, meanwhile, underscored the proceedings with music of her own devising, quirky and humorous, skillfully incorporating hints of *Coppélia* and *The Tales of Hoffmann.*

Michael's performance as the inanimate toy come to life was masterful, and he was proud of it. With a combination of effortless, rhythmic, slow-motion jerks, he arrived at a sitting position; his apparently sightless eyes looked first right, then left, observing his audience without seeming to. (All the while, of course, he was glancing up and down Fifth Avenue, looking for the bobbing black umbrella.) Clicks and pings, an endless variety of noises reproducing the sounds of invisible interior workings, emphasized each of his movements, as if his body housed, not human organs, but wheels and gears and chains and levers, the internal intricacies of a delicate timepiece or some incomprehensible invention.

Elbows angled, hands flat in front of him, feet straight out, he twisted his torso first one way, then the other, while his head made countermovements. Then, bending one knee and leaning his weight on a single foot, he slowly levered himself up off the cement with the discipline of a Russian dancer.

It wasn't easy to do it slowly, keeping his balance, his body rigid, the other leg straight out in front of him. He held the position as long as he could without seeming to strain or trembling, then brought the other foot into play, bending so sharply at the waist that the ends of his hair nearly touched the ground and his rear end was sticking perpendicularly up in the air—this phase unfailingly produced a laugh from the audience. Inch by inch he lifted his head and torso from the hinge of his waist until his body formed a ninety-degree angle. He held that pose for some moments, making sounds like gears shifting laboriously, then gradually straightened himself until he was standing naturally. At once he initiated a series of expertly choreographed movements, walking straight-legged to the far side of the landing, bent arms and flattened hands perfectly synchronized with the rest of his body. Clicking, clacking mechanically, he walked, spun, tipped, bowed, straightened, swiveled, bent, straightened again, walked backward, forward, side to side, until he drew near the cloth rose lying at the edge of the top step. He was reaching the peak, the knockout, the "big flash." The crowd stood motionless, fascinated. He felt strong, loose, confident, yet somewhat disappointed: there was no black umbrella in sight, and he found that he had been expecting it.

With mechanical aspect he registered the discovery of the rose, his penciled brows lifting in circumflex interest, his eyes blinking on as if electrically operated, lips forming a metallic smile. In graduated beats, he mimed joy, savor, passion, ecstasy; while, clanking, cranking, shortening the intervals between his movements—Emily's flute was picking up the tempo—and putting himself into absolute muscular control, he began to bend toward the flower, hand outstretched, an expression of ineffable joy fixed upon his face. Slowly, movement by infinitesimal movement, the robot fingers closed around the stem until they grasped it, lifted it. It was a difficult task for the Mechanical Man. From behind his closed lips he made a confusion of noises as he tried to stand upright, then repeated one sound like a broken record as Emily cued into a flute passage consisting of a single reiterated phrase. As though suffering mechanical failure, he halted all movement, frozen in this half-bending pose. Thus he remained, while the crowd burst into laughter at his predicament. Finally he managed to administer himself a knock on the back; then some drops of oil from an imaginary can restarted the mechanism. Blissfully he began to move his hand, tiny fraction of an inch by inch, intent on bringing the rose to his nostrils. Bit by bit the rose moved nearer to his face, which was marked by robotlike but boundless ecstasy. Closer, closer came the flower, each movement telling and precise, his nose quivering for the scent, his mechanical eyelids blinking like camera shutters in anticipation of the climactic moment, the flute shimmering, quivering on the brink of satisfied desire, until . . .

Alas. Distances had been falsely gauged, tangents miscalculated, degrees over- or underestimated, angles misjudged; the arm, the hand, the rose all unfortuitously passed the face, the flower's scent forever uninhaled, forever unattainable: an heroic effort, a great near miss. The Mechanical Man's blinking, puzzled expression, a mask of Chaplinesque regret, cried out against the small, sad frustrations of life.

Michael held the last moment, a freeze-frame of amazement and bewilderment, for exactly the proper length of time; then he let his body go limp, the arm holding the rose fell to his side, his head dropped. While the crowd applauded, he looked out through his eyelashes, again searching for the black umbrella. He was surprised not to see it, and surprised at his own surprise. Why was he so sure?

Wondering whether to keep the crowd or let it go, Michael turned at Emily's call, then looked where she pointed. Out at the curb, a remote television truck was parked, and a cameraman leaning against a fender had a mobile camera pointed at him. He spun around, made a bow, flashed some quick funny stuff that got guffaws from the crowd. While the camera recorded these antics, he glanced down the avenue again; still no sign of the umbrella, or of the man. The camera crew waved him a thank-you. Michael called out, "When will it be on?" The cameraman shrugged; the crew had already begun moving equipment through the front doors of the museum.

"What's going on in there?" Michael asked in an aside to Emily.

"The big Chinese exhibit's opening today."

Michael, who never read the newspapers and seldom saw television news, vaguely remembered Emily's telling him about this exhibit. It was called "Treasures of Ancient China," and it included artworks and artifacts never before seen in the West: ritual bronze vessels, bronze horses, ceramics, jade carvings, lacquerwork, tomb figures, even a few paintings, all from pre-Imperial

China and the earliest centuries of the Chinese Empire. Every piece in the show was at least fifteen hundred years old, most were much older, and the opening, combining as it did great artistic, cultural, and (especially) political significance, was receiving heavy coverage from the media. At this moment, in the museum lobby, Important People were smiling and shaking hands, brought together by the universal language of art and the presence of the TV cameras.

To keep the crowd from dispersing, Michael resorted to his ladder-climbing routine. Meanwhile, one of the TV crew had come back down the steps with a pad and pencil. "Can you give us your name?" he asked when he caught Michael's eye. "Just in case we use some of that footage?"

Michael disliked interruptions while he was performing, but the thought of some free publicity appealed to his professional instincts. As he was about to make a graceful descent from the ladder and answer the question, he caught sight of the Queer Duck. Michael had been so busy pulling stunts for the camera that he had missed the man's approach, but there he was, skirting the periphery of the crowd and just beginning to climb the steps, beard and red nose firmly attached, head hunched between the shoulders of his Sunday-black suit, carrying the Bloomingdale's shopping bag in one hand and the furled umbrella like a walking stick in the other.

Though Michael had spent weeks intensely imagining this moment, anticipating, preparing for it, when it came he could think of nothing to say. "Hey," he called out lamely, and then "Hey!" again, louder this time.

"Wait, buddy, what's your name?" The TV man stepped after him as he moved. Michael signaled to Emily, who was passing the hat, and started toward the man, who suddenly looked up and met Michael's eyes. The man's gaze froze, his head cocked in perplexity, as if encountering some unexpected situation; then he stepped back, amazed, even (perhaps) alarmed, as though the unexpected had turned to something stranger still. He made a crablike sideways movement along the step, then turned to go back down, hastily popping up the umbrella at the same time, and, thus hiding his head—unreasonably, by calling more attention to it—he tried to lose himself in the crowd.

"Have you got a name?" the TV man insisted, as Michael, oblivious of him and heedless of his inquiries, beckoned again to Emily, nimbly threaded his way through the onlookers, and began following the man.

Their prey sailed down Fifth Avenue, melting into the crowd, the umbrella pitching and dipping as it duplicated his bounding walk. He passed the plaza, reminding Michael again of the Day of the Frog, and continued south to Fifty-third Street, where he turned right, past the Museum of Modern Art, to Sixth Avenue, then Seventh, then Broadway, where he took a left, heading south toward Times Square. His pursuers, younger by far, had to work to keep up with him. Once Michael thought they had lost him, but when they got through the light and up on the curb he saw the black umbrella again, as if the man had slowed his pace on purpose. Then he turned right again, and they hurried to close the gap.

They entered a backwater area with few pedestrians on the sidewalks to block the view. Yes, there he was, up ahead, his shoulders rising and falling, you could see the flash of his white socks as his feet moved. His head was completely obscured by the umbrella, but there was in that dark, striving figure an enticement, as if he were deliberately leading them on—but where? To do—what? Yet the feeling persisted, expanded, and Michael found himself breathlessly excited, like a traveler embarking on a voyage to an unknown destination, beginning a thrilling but nameless adventure. He was holding Emily's hand, and he could feel the sweat between their entwined fingers and slippery palms, could hear her breathing as he hurried her along, could sense her reluctance and hesitation. Every now and then she made a sound like a stifled giggle, as if this whole pursuit were silly, a charade, not to be taken seriously. Her behavior appeared incongruous and even puzzling to Michael; he hadn't enough time, nor, perhaps, enough penetration, to see that she was fighting down the dread she felt at the entire undertaking, and at the same time sneering at herself for feeling it.

Then came the strangest part. They had gone many blocks since crossing Broadway, not along any direct path but by erratic jigs and jogs, two blocks west, then two south, one west again, then another three south, and so on. Never once had the man looked back, never paused at a store window to catch their reflections, but only continued on. It seemed to have become some sort of game for him. Emily's nervous giggling had turned to outright laughter. Then, suddenly, in the middle of a crosstown block, they saw him veer abruptly, his head still screened from them, and move quickly to the side of the pavement away from the curb, up against the buildings; then he passed from view.

Michael, letting go Emily's hand, started running, going fast but ready to turn suddenly or step into a doorway should the man reappear. Only he did not. The point at which he'd made his turn from the street was just a trifle beyond a sign, a long thermometer advertising witch hazel and set in a rectangular metal frame. When Michael got there he found, not the entrance to a store, as was to be expected, but an alley. He stopped, looked around, motioned to Emily to wait on the sidewalk by the entrance, and then ventured cautiously down the alley, beyond some stacked wooden skids. There lay the mystery, for the alley went, as Michael quickly discovered, nowhere. A cul-de-sac. The sides of three buildings, two of brick, one of concrete, the brick walls blank, the concrete one pierced by two windows, but each of these protected by stout vertical bars. To prove what he already knew, he gripped them, bracing himself against the wall and yanking with all his strength; nothing could budge them. He looked down toward his feet: solid paving, no grate or manhole cover. Above: sky, roof edges, no fire escape or ladder. The three sides, brick and cement. Behind him, the opening to the street.

Slowly and cautiously, Emily had arrived next to him, as breathless as he and equally mystified. "Where'd he go?"

"Damned if I know." He put a hand out and touched the brick, as if reaffirming for himself its solidity. "He must have gone up in thin air."

And they laughed together this time, for they both knew that was impossible.

Several days later, as if by accident—but not quite—the Queer Duck drifted into view again. Michael and Emily were at the Central Park Zoo, kibitzing while Dazz sketched parrots and macaws. (Samir, convinced that his new dimensions would upset the balance in his portrait, had insisted that empty spaces in the background should be filled with tropical birds.) The old man must have come up alongside them without realizing it, for soon after Michael spotted the shiny patent-leather shoes, their owner, lost in deepest thought, had moved on past the birds. He stopped at the pool to watch the seals cavorting, and then he started off again.

Clapping on his top hat, Michael turned to speak to Emily, but her wide eyes were already on the retreating black figure. Leaving Dazz, they followed the old man at a distance, keeping well behind him, stalking his footsteps as he picked his way along the walk. Moments later he came to another halt, his back to them; then slowly his head swung around. His single eye connected with Michael's two, maintaining contact for perhaps a couple of seconds. With a visible effort, the old man disengaged his look and shuffled off toward the zoo's exit. Pleasant agitation animated his stern features, as though he were an athlete thrilled at the prospect of starting up the game again; his bearing suggested that he considered himself no one's quarry, that he himself was the pursuer.

He continued along the winding path, emerging finally into the open field that fronted on the merry-go-round. The calliope's sound was far away, then nearer. When the man stopped again, without turning toward them, Michael seized the opportunity to close the gap, grabbing Emily's hand and sidling behind some trees, closer to the carousel, which was housed under a pointed roof supported by octagonal brick walls, but open to view on the side Michael and Emily were approaching from.

The merry-go-round slowed, stopped. Children got off and came through the exit, while others, holding their tickets ready, passed through the entrance and got on. The old man stepped up quickly, put down money, took a ticket, and hurried in as the merry-go-round began to revolve. Moving closer, Michael peered through the archway. There was no way out except through the exit gate. This time, Michael thought gleefully, they had him; he was trapped.

Round and round the painted horses went, and the children with their mothers, and the old man in black. There he was, coming around again, standing straight and holding on to a stationary vertical pole, looking out (at Michael?) with his features composed, bland, impassive, almost meek. There he went, the black shoulders whirling past, receding, now hidden behind the central cylinder containing the machinery and the calliope. He appeared, disappeared, reappeared, disappeared again. Michael glanced at Emily, shrugged his shoulders as if to say, "What's this old fool doing on a merry-go-round?" They waited. Round and round and round went the carousel, like a miniature world, spinning through space. The music banged and clanged like orchestrated tin, the horses pranced tirelessly, rhythmically, up and down. The man came around yet again, clutching the brass pole, then spun out of sight once more as the carousel made another revolution.

When the brass pole swung into view again, he was no longer holding on to it.

He wasn't there!

Michael ran up to the exit gate. As the merry-go-round slowed down, he stepped inside.

"Hey!" the ticket-taker called. Ignoring him, Michael made a rapid circuit of the slowing machine, came out on the other side, at the entrance.

He stopped and stared at Emily, palms thrown up in futile amazement. Together they peered back in through the portal, Michael even looking up at the overhead rafters, as if the man might have somehow and for some reason climbed up there. Each hurrying in opposite directions, Emily and Michael made a circuit of the carousel house, meeting at the far side. Michael walked up and stared at the brick walls, then touched one of them, but it was as unyielding as the ones at the end of the alley. While Emily went back to the parrot house to get Dazz, Michael sat under a tree, toying with his top hat, trying to think. There was no way he could have gotten out, no way at all, and yet he was gone.

Just gone.

CHAPTER NINE

Dreams and Revelations

Lena had the television on, a cops-and-robbers show, as she thought of it. But she wasn't really watching, only listening to the soundtrack while she stitched and occasionally glanced at the glowing little screen. She couldn't sew and watch at the same time, for she needed two pairs of glasses to handle the diverse tasks, and it was too much trouble to switch them back and forth. Bifocals, the obvious solution, had for some reason never come under consideration. So she sat and sewed, intent on her work, while the sounds echoed in the room: police squad cars with straining engines and squealing brakes careened through city streets. There were spurts of gunfire, shouts, an occasional scream; sometimes Lena wasn't sure whether what she heard came from the television set or the city outside her windows.

She looked to the doorway. Max was probably down in the basement, and who could say how long he would remain there? It didn't matter; he could stay as long as he chose. She assumed that the work in the basement, insofar as she understood anything about it, would come along as it might. She was not terribly interested in that particular enigma just now.

Just now she was more interested in the writing. Each night she had tried again but was unable to make contact. Carsin had reasserted herself and was refusing to relinquish her control; the result was sheaves of yellow pages denouncing the "Saskia in Tears" trick. Lena chose to ignore this otherworldly nagging. She had not questioned Max again about the matter, it was his business and did not concern her. But the paragraph she had received from the new control, before Carsin and her prissy remonstrances took over again, that was another thing. The money was to be returned. *All restored as was.* And she must remember the Archangel, *of celestial armies Prince.* He was coming and must be— marred? or warned? None of this was clear to her. The clue was in John. Ask of John. The numbers were verses. And the other key words: James; John; Scriptures. Obviously the King James translation, accounting for the name James. She had pored over the Scriptures, 1 John, 2 John, 3 John. But these were concise, even terse epistles, and their chapter and verse numbers didn't tally. 1 John had only five chapters, the others but a single one each. She had searched her Bible, an offering of the Gideon Society removed from some hotel room vacated in the distant past—she also owned a copy of Conrad Hilton's rather less inspired *Be My Guest*—but her diligence had so far gone unrewarded.

It occurred to her that it might be mere capriciousness, or worse. Sometimes the controls liked to have their little joke, pull her leg a bit. Maybe making her read the Bible was their idea of amusement. Still, she didn't think so. And there was the matter of the clock's having stopped at the precise moment she had gone under control, or at least as closely as she could place it.

Ignoring the yammering television, Lena laid aside her sewing and thumbed her Bible's pages again: 1 John, 2 John, 3 John. She flipped the pages, her eyes occasionally veering upward over her eyeglass-rims to the curio cabinet and the silver cup on the shelf. John's Third Epistle was followed by Jude, this followed by the last book, The Revelation of . . . She adjusted her glasses, her heart fluttering. *All will be revealed by John.* The Revelation . . . of Saint *John* the Divine. She knew the numbers by heart: 21:6 and 8; 22:18–19. She turned quickly to these sections and read:

And he said unto me, It is done. I am Alpha and Omega, the beginning and the end. I will give unto him that is athirst of the fountain of the water of life freely.

"Alpha and Omega," she repeated aloud, "*alpha and omega . . .*" Gunfire spattered briefly. Galena shook her head and read the eighth verse:

But the fearful, and unbelieving, and the abominable, and murderers, and whoremongers, and sorcerers, and idolaters, and all liars, shall have their part in the lake which burneth with fire and brimstone: which is the second death.

Whoremongers, and *sorcerers* . . . The words jumped out at her, powerful, compelling. But they made no sense. She moistened her finger, turned the page quickly to chapter 22, found verse 18:

For I testify unto every man that heareth the words of the prophecy of this book, If any man shall add unto these things, God shall add unto him the plagues that are written in this book:

And 19:

And if any man shall take away from the words of the book of this prophecy, God shall take away his part out of the book of life, and out of the holy city, and from the things which are written in this book.

Her eyes traveled along briefly: "The grace of our Lord Jesus Christ be with you all. Amen," she read.

She closed the book and sat holding it in her lap. The television, as if exhausted from so much mayhem, had now switched over to a comedy, and the unnatural sound of canned laughter stirred Lena from her reverie. She rose from her seat, flicked off the set, and gathered a few throw pillows from the sofa. Placing these on the table, she sat down and waited. When she felt ready, she took up the pen, put it to the top line of the yellow pad, and waited some more.

But nothing came. The pen remained poised, unmoving. It was her implacable rule to write nothing that was of her own volition. It must come from Elsewhere. Resolutely, she continued to wait. She listened to the ticking clock and wondered if it would stop again. She put down the pen, wishing she had the wallet in her hand, feeling that it would help. Then a thought occurred. Sometimes she stared into a crystal egg; it induced a kind of mild hypnosis. But instead of the crystal egg, she brought to the table the silver cup from the cabinet, holding it in her hand for a time, feeling the metal sides, the bottom, the rim, running her finger around the gold-washed lining. Then she placed the cup under the light and stared at it.

Presently the familiar empty, magnetized sensation mounted inside her, and she took up the pen again and placed it on the pad. She was fearful, not only of the pain she knew would come, but of the words that would come with it. Her hand began to tremble, there was a rush through her body, and she felt the seizure in her chest. Each breath ended in a hoarse, guttural gasp. She could sense them, officious and importunate, shoving at her, vying for her attention like rude children. Carsin came and wrote briefly, then stopped; then someone else, whose handwriting was unknown to her. She started to hear voices but rejected them, demanding written, not spoken, communication. Carsin came back, gave it up, and then a name appeared on the yellow page.

Miss . . . James.

Had she been wrong, then, about the King James version? The Bible clue was in John and Revelation; the James was the control? Miss James? Even though she was in pain, it amused her that it had all come to the same thing in any case. But why must they always make a game of it, why must they have their little mystery? Such silliness. Was it possible that not even death made anybody any wiser?

Miss James—what?

Nothing more came. She was staring hard at the silver christening cup when, involuntarily, her hand began moving again. Then the writing came faster and faster, until she was writing as quickly as she could—not her handwriting, of course, but Miss

James's, and Miss James tearing off the pages and strewing them over the writing table—and she could hear the sound of her own hoarse breathing and the lamplight seemed to grow dark and her head fell with a soft thump on one of the pillows.

When she came to and lifted her head, she could smell the same floral scent in the room; lilies, she thought. "Lilies that fester smell far worse than weeds." She put away the pillows, then gathered up the pages, sorting them as best she could. Then she put on her glasses and read:

> Yes, you are getting it. The clue is still John (P.S. he is divine). You must find the rest of the numbers yourself. It's not my fault, I'm taking dictation too. Something looks like a horse, it's very pale, hard to make out. The words are all lined up together. John will know. Also Daniel, maybe others. Don't forget the Archangel, the Prince. He must make careful note. Tell him when you see him. You must decide because you will have the strength. No one ever told me; it made me angry. I would want to know all about the conditions. I don't know if he does. You will see whether to tell him or not. Max is on the way. The plague is locusts, whatever happens. One woe and two woes. I am terribly sorry about this. The problem is language. You must help decide about telling him. When he comes he is for Max, but also to see you again. I think Max is either the Beast or Lev—Lev—is this Lev? Can't remember. Try Levi, he seems to have come back. Ignore the lilies if you can. No, not that. Tell Max if he has him he must care for him. He is beloved. Could I be clearer? Not Max. Max . . . Levi . . . Levi . . .

The last word was at the very bottom of the page, in the right-hand corner. She went back to the writing table and peered through her glasses, fitting the page to the rest of the word that had run off onto the tabletop. Together they spelled *Leviticus.*

This was nearly too much, but Lena's was an indulgent nature. She folded the pages and held them in her hand. When she heard the downstairs door open, she slipped them into her sewing basket and covered them with her crewelwork. Max came in briskly, not at all tired. It was not required of her to ask where he had been; she always knew when he was lively like that. She rose with her sewing and caught his eye lingering on the silver cup.

"What is that for?" he inquired.

"Nothing. I was just looking at it." She returned the cup to the cabinet, closed the door. He was examining the blank top sheet of the yellow pad.

"So. You have been writing?"

"I tried, but nothing came." He fixed her with his eye. "Nothing," she repeated.

"What? No message at all from the garrulous ghosts, the riddling revenants? Ah, Galena, my Lena." He laughed out his scorn, wagged his head at her insolently.

"Why do you ask, since you find them so contemptible?"

"Even contemptible things have their uses," he replied, looking pointedly at the television set, then the sewing basket, then Lena herself. She decided on a diversionary tactic, even though she knew such transparent devices rarely worked.

"What is it, your obsession with that boy? What is this foolishness with the costumes? Every day, those outfits . . ."

His reaction was strangely candid. "*Niente da mangiare, cinque bambini,*" he said, in a wheedling Italian voice; though he held out his hand like a beggar, there was a look of triumphant mockery on his face. "I keep my eye on him, that boy. I play a little game with him, to see how well *he* plays. He is looking for me, I am looking for him. I have found him, but he does not know yet that that is what has happened. He provides much amusement."

"I know your amusements. When it's over, no one else is ever amused. What is to happen?"

"That is what I tell myself you shall tell me—what is to happen."

She sat on the sofa and leaned back with a sigh. "You know more than you say."

"I always do. But it's nothing that concerns you."

"You should let me judge that." He made an impatient gesture, but she plunged ahead. "If you want him, why don't you go and tell him?"

"No, not yet. I will play with him a little longer. One cannot be too careful. He has determination, that is good. It would be funny, perhaps, if he tripped over me in his doorway one morning or evening. He is looking so hard I think even then he would not find me." Max smiled broadly, baring his teeth, which were uneven and discolored.

Lena, taking advantage of his unusually forthcoming mood, pressed on. "Why is he looking for you?"

"I have something he wants."

"His money. Give him back his money. He must need it."

"Perhaps he does, but he will get more. Until then, he can wait. Doing with less now will make him willing to do more later, when I need him."

"Why do you need him?"

"He is going to—let us say he is going to help me."

Lena couldn't believe her ears. "How? What should he do here? Since when do you want anyone around? Remember what happened the last time . . ."

"We will not speak of that," Max said evenly. He stepped to her in two long strides, stood before her with outpointed toes, took her hand, and placed it against his chest. "You feel there, Lena, how it beats? Strong, heh?" She could not deny it, could feel the even throb under the material of his shirt. "It is strong, always strong, yet I am tired. There is something I want to do; the time has come at last. At long last, eh, Lena? And that boy must help me do it. Do you follow me?"

She looked at him blankly, uncomprehending.

"Of course you don't," he continued, "how could you? The return of the Boy Wonder, let us say. The boy who is an old man and wants only to be free. But before that—one last time, Lena, for Merlino the Magnificent, heh? Assisted by Presto the Great. He is very clever, you never saw such hands, how he works them. Like me in the old days. So now you understand, heh?"

"Yes," Lena said bitterly. Although her answer was not completely true, she felt that she understood his main point. "You want to ruin his life."

"Do not talk to me of ruined lives," he growled, seeming to grow larger. "Life ruins itself, that is the arrangement." He slapped his hand down hard on her yellow writing pad.

Lena was confused and troubled, frightened not only by his sudden anger but also by the thick foreboding she felt welling up in her consciousness, fed by several sources. What to make of

Max's fixation upon the young man, whom he was reeling in like some sportfisherman, playing the line and admiring the prize he meant to destroy? Or that remark about how the time has come at last. What did he mean by that? Was he referring to death? And then there was the writing from the Other Side, from the coy Miss James, now, and Lena realized that all she wanted was some peace. She should not have used the wallet, no, nor the cup. She should have stayed with Mrs. Carsin and taken down recipes. She was very afraid, but she couldn't expect any soothing from Max. Sleep was what she wanted, sleep would soothe her.

"Max," she began, fumbled the book as she stood up, caught it.

His eye moved from her hands to her face. "What have you there, a Bible? What are you doing with a Bible?"

"Nothing."

"What does it mean, 'Nothing'?"

"Reading."

"So now you read the Bible? Next it will be comic books. To think your stupid lies once annoyed me, Galena." He watched her contemptuously, then dilated his nostrils and sniffed.

"Why is it, always, this smell of dead flowers in the room?"

"I don't know. You're imagining things." She put the Bible in the sewing basket with her pages, said "Good night," and walked out of his oppressive presence, already anticipating the darkness, the cool sheets, the delicious swerving into unconsciousness.

He stared after her as she left, wondering that she could see so much yet comprehend so little. All these years she had been with him, reinvented with each new lifetime, each time a blank slate. New personalities, yet always devoted—this was especially true of Galena. She was one of his favorites.

When she had gone, he tore off the top sheet from the yellow pad and held it to the light. A faint outline of script showed through, not sufficiently legible for him to decipher it. Smirking, he crumpled the paper and dropped it into the basket. Automatic writing, he thought, was the daytime television of psychic phenomena, something to keep the ladies busy between household chores. He wondered why he bothered with it at all. The boy hung like a flower in bloom, Max could gather him in at any time. The Eye too lay waiting for him, housed in its museum case. In a

few days he would claim it; then he would let the boy, that patient
seeker, find him. A little time must pass after that, but not much.
Soon, very soon, he would be ready.

Lena stumbled slightly as she left the little tobacco shop, stuffing
into her loaded shopping bag the last but not least of the items on
her list: a carton of Gitanes. She started to walk, and the heat
struck her like a blow after only a few steps. Nevertheless, she
continued grimly on, turning at Forty-second Street and heading
for home. Breathless and perspiring, she reached the apartment
at last, kicked off her shoes, changed her blouse, and sank with a
sigh of relief into her chair, holding a glass of iced tea in one hand
and a cigarette in the other. Max was not in the apartment, and
she was certain he wasn't even in the building; off on one of his
excursions, no doubt, having his fun at the expense of that confused young man.

You will know him when you see him.

Wondering over all the other things scribbled on the yellow
pages, Lena wondered most over this. How would she know him
when she saw him? Who was he, where did he come from?
Would he truly help Max, or would there be a struggle between
them?

And a horse? A pale horse "*. . . behold a pale horse: and his name
that sat on him was Death . . .*"

She shook her head and muttered to herself. Taking up her
Bible, she opened it to Leviticus. Lena was fascinated by all
religions, all systems, all lore that postulated the existence of the
supernatural, but she made few distinctions and played no
favorites. Her knowledge of such matters was undiscriminating,
broad rather than deep, sympathetic rather than critical. Still,
as she began to read this book of taboos and atonements, she
couldn't help noticing the pagan ring of its words, its author's obsession with sin, guilt, sacrifices, laws, rituals, its portrait of a
primitive society with priests in the saddle and riding hard. She
didn't see how any of this could be applicable or enlightening, no
matter how far she stretched it. Then, in the twentieth chapter,
she read

A man also or woman that hath a familiar spirit, or that is a wizard, shall surely be put to death: they shall stone them with stones: their blood shall be upon them.

She turned thoughtfully to the back cover, inside which she had jotted the word *Leviticus*. Using a pencil, she drew a line through the last two syllables, making it Levi~~ticus~~.

Under it she wrote Levi.

Under this, anagramming it, she wrote Veil.

And under Veil, Evil.

Then she closed the book and held it tightly in her hands.

As she leaned back in her chair, she was suddenly, startlingly aware of his presence. She tilted her head farther back and saw him standing behind her, peering over her shoulder. "You scared me," was all she could manage to say, and that in a whisper.

"You scare yourself, I think," Max replied, as condescending as a cardinal. "What is this you play, a game with letters? And you move them about, like Scrabble tiles, to find their secrets. Is this what you learn from your dear departed pen friends?"

"If you think it's such foolishness, why insist that I do it?"

"Ah, Lena, I have told you, even foolish things may serve. For example"—he glanced at the TV—"may we have the television?" She looked surprised; he scarcely ever watched. "I want the news—Channel Five." She obliged him, turned on the outmoded set, then took up her crewelwork again. She blinked behind her glasses, feeling eyestrain. The picture had flickered on, and they heard the newscaster's voice. She didn't watch, but kept to her stitchery.

"Look," he suggested impassively. She took off her glasses and squinted toward the screen, saw important-looking men of various races emerging from limousines and climbing the steps of what turned out to be the Metropolitan Museum of Art. The voice-over was describing the opening of the Chinese exhibit. She put on her glasses again and dropped her eyes to her work.

"Look."

She did as he said, drew her glasses down onto the end of her nose and peered over the rims. Saw people milling about on the museum steps, saw a boy in makeup performing pantomimes. She thought him clever, doing that machinelike creature. When he was finished, aware of the camera on him, he bowed. She didn't like him then. Too flashy. Cocky. Self-satisfied. She'd never cared for actors. Life with Max was enough show business for her.

Then it came to her. "Is that him?"

"Yes."

She put on her other glasses, bending closer, almost touching the screen. The face was just a face, hidden under the white makeup. She couldn't tell anything from it. "He's younger than I thought," she remarked.

"He will be useful. Don't you see it?"

Max was posing one of his riddles, but she was too tired for more games. And what did it matter? His mind was made up. She could tell. She changed her glasses, resumed her work. When he turned off the set, it sputtered, blinked, the light contracted to a single dot, was extinguished. Max left the room without a word, and after some inner debate she moved to the table, where she took up the tarot cards and laid them out and studied them. The boy, that was the Knight of Pentacles: a black-haired, black-eyed young man, materialistic, methodical. As she knew, the card indicated the coming or going of a matter. And, certainly, what she was preparing to grapple with was a coming matter.

But the other card, the Hanged Man, came up crossing her, against her. She could not understand what decisions lay in the balance, what new directions her life was poised to take, and her curiosity led her to ponder not merely the how of the matter but also the when. She never thought about the why. Clearly, if it was in the cards, that was enough.

Lena was a staunch believer in fate. She put the cards into their case, busied herself briefly in the kitchen, and settled gratefully into the sofa with a freshly brewed cup of tea. It was fine tea, her own mixture of herbs and spices. It comforted her, but perhaps it also caused her to dream; it sometimes did, she felt sure.

It was a strange dream, with strangers in it, and in the dream she was *sitting on a bench at the edge of a small park in a big city and wearing a gay dress yellow as goldenrod and closing her eyes and raising her face to the bright summer sun, and a small voice said, "Wait a*

*minute," and she opened her eyes to see a beautiful young black-haired
boy walking toward her with her straw hat in his hand. He held the hat
out to her and said in the same voice, "It blew off the bench," and she
said, "Why, thank you, my handsome young man," and their eyes met
and they smiled at each other. A grim-faced couple approached, and the
man gave her a curt nod, while the woman grabbed the boy's arm like a
leash and hauled him away. She wanted to call out after him but did not
know his name, and then she did know his name but couldn't call it. The
boy looked back at her, over his shoulder, his short legs hurrying away,
and their eyes met again just before he disappeared into a bus station.
She followed inside and when she saw him again her eyes weren't smiling and there were two men in different uniforms standing on either side
of him, pulling him out of his seat and saying, "You have to come with
us." He wanted to ask the lady with the kind face and the yellow dress
and the straw hat to help him, but the men dragged him toward the
doors, and all he could do was clutch the envelope his mother had stuffed
in his jacket pocket and try not to cry so much and keep repeating again
and again, "She told me to stay here! She told me to wait! They're coming back for me! They're coming back!"*

Michael started awake and sat up, trying to imagine who the
woman in the yellow dress could possibly have been. Had he
dreamed a dream of a memory, or was he now recalling the memory of a dream? Thunder rolled in the night, or was he dreaming
that too? He listened harder and realized the thunder was not
from the sky but low-planed along the streets, where steel axles
humped the faulted paving, bounding off stone buildings, cueing
windowpanes into quick vibration, echoing in closed alleyways,
dying somewhere out there in the heat, distantly, leaving him
with the tag ends of thoughts, the selvage of raveled dreams.

After her nap, Lena cleaned the room, emptying the ashtray and
picking up glasses. She dusted the tabletops, straightened the
sofa pillows, briefly swept. From outside, where the trucks ran on
the West Side Highway, she heard rumbling noises: thunder, yet
not thunder; it only sounded like it. When she had finished she
set aside the broom and cloth and sat quietly with her hands
folded in her lap. She sniffed the air, noting a smell of camphor,

like mothballs. And she thought she heard someone crying. After a while she rose and put away her cleaning things, absentmind-edly munched an apple, then switched off the lights and went to bed but did not sleep. It was too early, and she was too tired. She still heard thunder where there was no thunder, and smelled mothballs where there weren't any, and heard someone crying when no one was there.

CHAPTER TEN

The Eye of Horus

The gallery guard was hardly conscious of his fixed habit of whistling his boredom away as he rambled in the general vicinity of his prescribed station: Egyptian wing, second gallery, against the wall of the archway. People had come through in droves today, many more than usual, all day long. Since the "Saskia in Tears" affair, the number of museumgoers had trebled, and with the added interest provided by the new Chinese exhibit, visitors were flocking to every section of the museum, including Egyptian antiquities, in greater and greater numbers.

The guard paid them little attention, except for the occasional celebrity he could pick out. Last week Martin Scorsese was there, and yesterday Connie Chung, whom he recognized from television. The rest were merely faces in a crowd, and he wondered if any of them ever came more than once, except for the funny old geezer who was a regular customer.

He was in there now, in the jewelry room, where he frequently hung about, making notes and whispering to himself. The guard felt pride of ownership in the priceless items he guarded, and he liked people who enjoyed them, showed interest in them. Still, he knew he had to keep an eye out; there was no telling what people might take it into their heads to do. Especially these days.

An unescorted group of children came through, jabbering, giggling, and shoving. He busied himself in quieting them, and when they had been reduced to a semblance of orderliness, he allowed them to pass into the jewelry room and followed behind them with a watchful eye. The old man, wearing his usual black outfit—some kind of preacher, maybe?—was bending over one of the glass cases, holding a magnifying glass, closely examining, not the multitudinous scarabs, the major interest of most museumgoers, but a particular Eye of Horus, painted on faience, a large staring eye outlined in black, against a background of azure blue. (An information card affixed to the case explained, in words taken from *The Book of the Dead*, the occult powers attributed to the Eye: it was a mighty amulet, used in casting spells that enabled a deceased person to speak and to know magic formulas, allowed him to retain his memory and his heart, and provided warmth for his head.) The children had scattered at once to all parts of the room, while the guard remained in the center, letting his gaze rove about. Having noted his presence, the man beside the display case glanced up, pocketed his magnifying glass, and left abruptly.

A short while later, upstairs in the European Painting wing, a woman, one Mrs. Arthur M. Mason, who had driven in from Scarsdale to view the famous "Saskia in Tears," blinked in disbelief. Mrs. Mason was not alone in such an action at this particular instant, but it was she who first voiced the shocked concern that many in the crowd of spectators were beginning to feel.

"Look!" she said, rather loudly, and upon hearing her own voice she became instantly embarrassed. Still, unbelievable though it might seem, she certainly saw what she was seeing. Everyone, of course, had been looking at paintings, but now they all looked at this particular painting in a different manner altogether. Another woman cried out, and immediately the visitors gathered themselves into a tight knot, then began pushing and shoving.

"What's happening?" someone toward the rear wanted to know. "What is it?" No one quite knew the answer to these questions, but clearly something very strange was taking place.

"*Fire!*"

Smoke was issuing forth in wispy swirls from the painting, around or behind it. Sinister tendrils were curling upward to the light. No one moved or did anything, they all stood staring. "*FIRE!*" The dread word was shouted again. A guard hurried in, shoved his way through the wall of backs, and stopped before the picture, staring with unbelieving eyes. He began to propel people away from the area, then called out to another guard, who came charging into the group and rammed his way through it imperiously.

A third guard arrived, there was a hasty conference, and even as they looked at the portrait, the canvas seemed to leap into flame. In panic, people started shoving their way toward the exit. The guards spoke in loud, authoritative voices, warning the crowd to move quickly out of the gallery, cautioning order and safety. The odor of burning varnish permeated the room—everyone could smell it. Those intent on escape converged with those who hoped to get a better look, forming an eddying mass; elbows were brought into play, followed by hands, voices were raised to a tumult; one woman screamed, then a second, horrified at the sight of the yellow flames licking at the canvas like hungry tongues. Within half a minute the painted features of the figure dimmed, grew dark, were obliterated entirely, and as the fire engulfed the canvas its carefully judged, harmonious forms blistered, melted, and dissolved before the eyes of the stupefied people in the room.

Then the alarm sounded, loud and long, triggering general pandemonium.

Downstairs, in the Egyptian wing, the guard heard the bell and abandoned his post, hurrying into the Great Hall. He saw people thronging their way down the marble staircase, while others stood about in clusters, looking up. Keeping well to the side, the guard started up the stairs. Halfway along, he was vaguely aware of a familiar figure, tall and somberly dressed, among those rushing downstairs, but it was only in retrospect that he recognized the strange old man, his regular customer.

At the foot of the stairs, the man moved toward the Egyptian wing. It was emptying rapidly; everyone's attention was on the firemen who burst through the entrance, dragging hoses and equipment. Several museum guards brandishing fire extinguishers preceded them. No one took the slightest notice of the old man as he slipped into the deserted jewelry room and approached the glass case where the Eye of Horus was displayed.

Since the zoo incident a few days previously, Emily had been able to persuade her indefatigable hunter to relax his pursuit a little. The Queer Duck's game was a blind alley, a brick wall, a merry-go-round, spinning tirelessly but going nowhere. Perhaps the way to win, she had suggested, was to refuse to play. Besides, if they went to the Chinese exhibit at the Metropolitan Museum, Michael could always fit in a bit of stakeout after admiring the wonders produced in the ancient land of Emily's ancestors. He agreed, not so much out of interest in Oriental art as in the belief that a change in tactics might be called for.

So it was that the two of them were strolling up Fifth Avenue, hand in hand, at about the time of Mrs. Arthur Mason's astonished shout; they paused for a traffic light, seizing the opportunity for a quick kiss, at the very moment when the crowd of appalled visitors watched the canvas burst into flames; and they arrived at the museum simultaneously with the fire engines. Police were already there, holding back the spectators outside, while a TV camera truck disgorged its remote unit, the cameraman shouldering his portable equipment as a crew member guided him through the clamoring, craning throng. Firefighters clutching large hoses attached them to fire hydrants and ran up the steps. No one seemed to know what was happening, other than that there was a fire inside the building. Michael, wild-eyed, leaned away from the building as though struggling to neutralize an overpowering force and turned to Emily. "He's in there," he said, "I know he's in there."

"Who? The Queer Duck?"

"Yes, I can feel it. You hang around here and watch for him. I'm going inside."

"But wait." She hesitated, thinking, He might be right, and

thinking, He's lost his mind. "What happens if we lose one another?"

"Meet you at Dazz's," he yelled back to her, already pushing his way up the steps through the crowd. Finally he reached one of the doorways and was so intent on getting through it that he failed to see the old man exiting through another one.

The man started down the steps; then, seeing the television camera trained directly on him, he averted his face and made an involuntary motion with his hand, as if grabbing for something: his umbrella. A look of dawning realization spread across his face, and he turned back to the door he had just come out of.

"Can't go in there," a guard said, holding out his hands.

"I forgot—"

"Get it later."

The man backed off slowly, a dazed expression on his face, and then, as the television camera whirred, he ducked abruptly and jostled his way through the press of people around the door.

Emily had skirted the main part of the crowd and stood on the top step, some distance from the entrance, scanning the tumult in the hope of spotting Michael. She saw someone she recognized, though she wished she didn't; it was the old man, Michael's Queer Duck, who burst clear of the obstinate bodies impeding his passage and hurried toward her, without noting her, across the crowded landing. He wasn't like a duck at all, Emily thought, nor was he, despite the earlier impression he had made on her, as powerful and streamlined as a raptor. He was too disjointed, too bumbling, more in the manner of some dark, gruesome, carrion-eating bird, like a crow or a vulture, jerking across the stone steps while his loose black clothes billowed up around him and his one good eye rolled upward: a creature suited to the air, yet curiously bound to the pavement.

She took one step, then another, as he bore down on her, heedless of her but moving directly toward her. When he looked down to assure his footing, they were standing face to face.

This is it, Emily thought, as she registered the contemptuous, impatient grimace that twisted his thin lips and the dismissive gesture of his hand.

.

This time she would let him know what she thought of his hide-and-seek game with Michael. But as harsh words rose to her consciousness and she parted her lips to speak, all she could see was his one eye and all she could do was see it. She was frozen in place, helpless, unable to move a muscle. The eye was chilling, like an icy blade; it probed her, recognized her, dismissed her, as though she had been cut open and tossed aside. As the blood thawed around her heart and she came to herself, she felt absurdly ashamed, as if she had waked to find herself standing naked in a public place. The old man was gone. She looked around anxiously and saw him just below her, plunging through the crowd, down the steps, then darting between two fire trucks parked at the curb.

Propelled by an impulse that dismayed her, thinking all the while, Why am I doing this? she pushed her way down the steps after him. People came hurrying from all directions, and she had to struggle to ward them off. He crossed the street, heading east on Eightieth toward Madison. Without waiting for the light, Emily followed him.

In the meanwhile, Michael stood in the Great Hall, looking upward with the rest. The fire, apparently, was somewhere upstairs. A passing guard shouted at him, among others, to get out of the building, then hurried busily on. Michael stepped to one side and looked around. Somewhere in the sea of faces he felt certain he would see the Queer Duck.

A lone fireman was standing against the gallery railing above, waving his arms. A whistle blew, and then the ringing alarm bell suddenly stopped. "It's all right," the fireman shouted down.

"What's goin' on?" another called up.

"False alarm, I guess." He shrugged his perplexity and left the railing. In a moment firemen began descending with their equipment. A pair of uniformed guards came down together and spoke briefly; then the first guard walked toward the Egyptian wing, while the second one headed for the information desk. Michael stepped quickly after him.

"I'm with the *News*," he said, fast-talking the guard. "What's happening up there?"

The guard was dialing a telephone. "Damnedest thing I ever

saw—*if* I *saw* it—" He broke off and spoke into the mouthpiece, reporting that the fire was out. A moment later the first guard appeared in the entrance to the Egyptian wing and rushed shouting toward the information desk, intercepting a man in a seersucker jacket as he came. The guard spoke intensely and rapidly, the other listening, and together they came up to the desk. The guard on the telephone was just completing his call. The man in the seersucker jacket took the phone, dialed, and spoke.

"There's been a robbery in the Egyptian wing."

The first guard looked at Michael. "What do you want in here?"

"Press. Can you give me some details?"

"You got credentials?"

"Sure." Michael made a great show of feeling in all his pockets. Avoiding the guard's eye, he looked past his shoulder in the direction of the checkroom. Through the aperture in the partition, he noted something sitting on the nearly empty rack. Stepping toward it, he said, "Guess I must have lost them in the—" He made a vague gesture, then began moving more rapidly to the checkroom.

"Hey, wait a minute!" the guard called after him. Michael put on a smile and called back, "Forgot my umbrella. And my package." He pointed to the two items on the rack and strode purposefully toward them. The guard had turned briefly to speak to the man in seersucker. Michael lifted the gate, grabbed the umbrella off the hook, snatched up the Bloomingdale's bag, and headed for the entrance.

"Hey, wait a minute!" the guard shouted again. "You got a check number for those things?"

"Yeah," Michael called back, "it's with my credentials."

"Say, you, hold on there!" The first guard was after him, the other one following. The one in the lead tripped over the hoses being lugged out by some firemen, the other tripped over him, and Michael made a dash for the door. At the last moment he turned to look at the guards extricating themselves from the hoses; then he leaped through the doorway and was lost in the crowd.

•   •   •

Some hours later, Michael was sitting with Dazz in his studio, waiting for Emily. Between nervous glances at the clock—it was nearly six—Michael stared at the objects spread out on the coffee table. The ordinary-looking umbrella, well used though it was, offered no clue as to its ownership. The contents of the Bloomingdale's shopping bag had proved to be a shoe box, which contained a pair of new shoes: black, patent leather, narrow, with leather soles, rubber heels, elastic side panels, and eyelets for laces. Manufactured by the Bilt-Well Company. Little enough to go on.

Dazz had risen to go to the kitchen when the doorbell rang, and he and Michael were standing at the door as the elevator arrived and Emily stepped out, looking somewhat uncertain. She smiled weakly, but all she could say was "Hello" before Michael took her in his arms and squeezed her breathless. "Christ, I'm glad to see you," he said, leading her inside. "What happened?"

"I saw him—yes, *him*," she said, trying not to let Michael's immediate reaction, transfixed eagerness, annoy her. "He came out of the museum right after you left to go in. He got through the crowd, and all of a sudden we were facing one another. I looked him in the eyes—eye, I should say. It made my blood run cold." As she was speaking, she shook her head and walked to one of the tall windows, stood for a moment, staring out across the street at the karate parlor, then turned back to them with a strange expression on her face. "But I followed him anyway, I can't tell you why, I sure didn't want to. And, naturally, I lost him again."

"Where?" Michael asked.

"On a bus." She flopped down on the sofa and began blotting perspiration from her face and throat with a handkerchief. "He went down Madison and got on a bus. I had almost caught up with him and I got on a little after him; maybe four people got on between us. The bus took off, I pushed all the way to the back before it stopped again, and he wasn't there."

"He couldn't have gotten off right after he got on?" Dazz asked.

"Not possible," she said, rotating her head wearily on her neck. "The bus was packed, he would have had to get all the way to the back in two seconds. Not possible." She continued moving her head around slowly, then gave it a few definitive shakes. "There was no place to go, and he wasn't there."

Dazz whistled softly. Michael hugged Emily and looked at the clock. "Vanished into thin air, his favorite habitat. Let's go turn on the news."

They went into the room off the kitchen that Dazz used as a study. Holding the shoes, Michael sat on the warped sofa and scowled moodily at the television screen as the six o'clock news began. The story of the museum fire was in the lead, and the newscaster made liberal use of such words as "incredible," "hoax," and "mystifying," throwing in several "apparently's" as qualifiers. The video showed the camera being jostled by the crowds on the outside steps, firemen fighting their way through the entrances. Faces appearing, disappearing, the microphones picking up traces of conversation.

"Look! There he is!" Emily pointed at the screen, where the old man had suddenly appeared amid the crowd gathered at the entrance. He glanced at the camera, shied away, made an odd gesture, then turned back as if to go through the doorway again.

"He realizes he's forgotten his stuff," Michael muttered.

Dazz started to ask a question but was sternly shushed by the other two as the individual reports began. The main lines of the story, pieced together out of various ill-assorted facts and eyewitnesses' statements, were the following. One: the painting had not burned at all. (Eyewitness accounts, however, were at variance on this point, for many people, including several museum guards, had seen flames consuming the canvas.) Two: at the same time the painting was believed to be burning, or shortly thereafter, a priceless object was discovered missing from its case in the jewelry room of the Egyptian wing. The object was described as an ancient Eye of Horus, painted in azure on a fragment of ivory-colored faience. Three: the exhibition case was unharmed and showed no signs of tampering; the lock on the sliding panel had not been touched, nor had the glass been cut or broken. The guard on duty attested to the fact that he had seen the Eye in its proper place only five minutes before the "fire" broke out upstairs. The report continued with the pertinent information that an unidentified male individual had been seen near the display case, and police were investigating this lead. No one was certain whether any connection existed between the theft—or loss—of the Eye of Horus and the alleged fire. Finally, the head curator of the museum appeared briefly to emphasize that "Saskia in Tears" had not been damaged in any way. He hastened to assure the Dutch government that the painting on loan would be returned in the same condition in which it had arrived.

Some forced chat from the news anchors, a man and a woman who looked very much alike, heralded the arrival of commercials. Heaving a sigh, Emily rose to her feet and moved in the direction of the bathroom. Michael sank deeper into the sofa, closed his eyes, and groaned. "This sure is some strange stuff, babe," Dazz observed, "but look at it this way. You've got yourself a fine new pair of shoes."

"Great," Michael said, barely moving his lips. "And what am I supposed to do with his shoes?"

Emily stopped, leaned in the doorway, pulling her hair off her neck with both hands. "You're supposed to return them to him."

"How am I going to do that?"

"You'll find a way," she said sorrowfully. "He knows you will. And so do I."

CHAPTER ELEVEN

Lost and Found

Michael sat down with the Yellow Pages of the Manhattan telephone directory and turned to Shoes, Retail, but careful perusal of this section, followed by Shoes, Whol. & Mfrs., offered no information concerning the provenance of the Bilt-Well patent-leather gaiters. Neither Bloomingdale's nor any store in its immediate neighborhood carried Bilt-Wells. According to the National Association of Shoe Manufacturers, reached after a long telephonic pursuit, the Bilt-Well Shoe Company of Cleveland, a victim of bad economic times, had folded some time ago and sold its entire stock to a chain of liquidation stores.

From this point, things became more difficult. Abandoning the telephone, Michael took to the streets with resolution in his heart and the shoes in their white cardboard box. He began systematically visiting shoe stores, making inquiries.

Many places sold Bilt-Wells, but not that model, many more didn't sell them, period, and all had free advice: try down on Delancey Street, try some of the remainder outlets south of Canal, try Macy's at Herald Square. How about tuxedo rental houses? Or one of those cheap places on Fourteenth Street where the

Puerto Ricans shop? Try uptown/downtown/crosstown. Try
somewhere else.

It was worse than the Bloomingdale's stakeout, far worse than
the long hours spent in the plaza or in front of the Metropolitan
Museum. He was close, he knew he was nearly there, but
stymied, stuck in place.

He examined the shoes minutely, letting his imagination play
over them. Something about them made him think of show business. People didn't wear shoes like these without a reason; they did
something while wearing them, they had a purpose when they put
them on. Maybe he should try a theatrical costumer. The thought
led him to the theater district, where he wandered about for a
while looking for an appropriate shop. He found one between a
deeply soiled delicatessen featuring PASTRAMI SANWITCHES and a
sparkling porno theater showing *Psychic Bimbos*. Yes, the shop-
keeper said, they carried Bilt-Wells in this style and others, had recently purchased them from a liquidation company, but an
inventory check revealed that none of the ones like Michael's had
been sold. The man suggested a costumer who turned out to be located on the same floor as Lou Tannen's Magic Shop in the Loew's
State Building. Michael was elated; this was the best lead yet.

He brought the shoes in, laid them on the counter. Yes, the
clerk said, eyeing him suspiciously, they specialized in "character" shoes for dancers and carried a number of cancelled Bilt-
Wells. So why did he want to know? Was there something wrong
with the shoes? Were they stolen?

No, Michael explained glibly, he'd found them on a park bench,
thought they were perhaps expensive and the owner might be
someone working in the neighborhood. The clerk was still dis-
trustful. People didn't go around trying to return a pair of shoes
to an unidentified owner. Was he a cop or something? Look,
Michael said, go next door, ask Lou, he knows me. I'm a magician, see, just trying to do a favor for a guy.

The man took up the shoes and inspected them for the third
time. Well, if he was a friend of Lou Tannen's . . .

"You know Wurlitzer?"

"Wurlitzer? The Great Wurlitzer?"

The man shook his head doubtfully. "Well, let's say the once-great Wurlitzer. Nutty old geezer. Got that rundown museum, whatchamacallit, Egyptian hall around the corner. You never heard of it?"

He hadn't; had heard of the Great Wurlitzer, though. He mentioned the pictures in his collection, the man of many disguises, Merlino the Magnificent.

"Yeah, that's him, same guy. He uses a couple different names, but his real one is Wurlitzer, Max Wurlitzer. He bought these shoes offa us. He's been buyin' here for years. Used to be two pairs a year, now it's one every three or four. I always wait on him myself. It's funny, this has been going on since I was a kid, yet he never seems to get any older, know what I mean?" The man gave a sort of snorting laugh and began flipping through the cards in a small file box on the counter. "Nah, old Max's been lookin' about a hundred years old since I first seen him. Acts kinda crazy, too. Some people're afraida him, but he don't seem so scary to me. One thing's for sure, he don't make no money at that place. Aw *right*, I finely found his address. I'll write it down for ya. You take him his shoes, he'll be glad."

Not half as glad as I'll be, Michael thought.

He came upon the place from the opposite side of the street. He passed a newsstand on the corner, then continued down the block until he saw the red doors. He stopped in front of a coffee shop and looked across. It was a sorry tenement district west of Times Square, beyond the "bad luck" theaters like the Martin Beck, where no one wanted to run Broadway shows anymore. A miserable-looking building. A portal in fake Egyptian style and a sign: THE LITTLE CAIRO MUSEUM OF WONDERS. Old, dilapidated, seedy. Above, three floors of what looked to be apartment rooms. He caught a sign of movement behind a second-story window; a woman peered out; then she dropped the curtain but remained standing behind it. He sensed something furtive in her movement, something worrisome, something familiar, something . . . nothing. He crossed the street and approached, eyes sweeping the vista. Next to the two red doors, in an exterior alcove, a box-office window, boarded up. Below: THE GREAT WURLITZER. APPEARING SAT. & SUN. 3:00 & 7:00 P.M. Above the doors a faded mural in circus-poster style: paintings of a flea circus with fleas the size of cockroaches, pulling chariots and climbing ladders. A strongman bending a bar. A snake charmer. A fortune-teller with a silver globe. Recessed from the street next to the theater doors was another door, also red, but dingier, with a brass knob that looked as if it had been polished. The name on the insert plate, also brass, also shiny, read LENA WURLITZER. He rang. Waited. Rang again. Still no one. He stepped back to the curb, looked up. He could see the woman behind the curtain. She moved away. He rang again, waited. Still no one came. He recrossed the street to the coffee shop and stood with the box under his arm and looked. There was no sign of anyone. He went inside, sat at the counter, and ordered coffee.

"And where is he now, Lena?"

"Still in the coffee shop." She looked worried, uneasy. "He's carrying a shoe box. Do you think he's got your shoes?"

"Yes, I do believe he does. He'll be returning them soon." Max relaxed in his chair, smoking a pipe and leafing through a magazine. "It shouldn't be long."

When his pipe went out, Max laid it aside, along with the magazine, rose from his chair, and left the room. He returned carrying a small package wrapped in brown paper and butcher's string, handed it to Lena. "The bell will ring again," he said. "You may answer it this time."

"What should I say?"

"Nothing is necessary beyond the usual amenities. He will offer you the shoes. Take them."

She looked fearful, and he made a placating gesture. "Why are you afraid, Lena? He is only returning them."

"You left them at the museum. If the police know it—"

"The police know nothing, as befits them," he said dismissively, adding, wearily, "What can you think of me, Lena?" He drew himself up, taking on height and breadth, and said in a strong, terse voice that set off little echoes in her ears, "There is no reason to be afraid. Do what I say. I have waited long, and now the time has come. Take the shoes, give him this"—he handed her the package—"and send him away. Do not let him in, do not speak more than is necessary. Do you understand?"

Lena, who had been feeling the package, replied distractedly, "Is this his wallet at last?"

"Yes, it is, and"—she opened her mouth, he held up his hand to forestall her—"yes, everything is returned as it was."

She turned again to the window, and Max reoccupied his chair. Soon the bell rang. They exchanged meaningful glances, and Lena left the room, walked downstairs, inhaled deeply, opened the door to the street, looked into Michael's handsome, anxious face.

"Good evening," he said, and smiled appropriately (he hoped). The woman had a kind face, not unfriendly or haughty or anything he had feared. In fact, she reminded him of someone, he wasn't sure who, but someone he liked. "Is Mr. Wurlitzer in?"

Lena hesitated before answering, not because she lacked the required words, but because the young man seemed so unexpectedly familiar to her. It was a familiarity without context, its origin difficult to pin down, gliding around in the upper reaches of her consciousness like a bird surrendered to the wind. Her memory told her she had seen that face before, but whether in reality or in a dream, whether in imagination or in desire, she could not say. "He's not available at the moment," she replied. "May I help you?"

The young man, perplexed but unwavering, nodded toward the box in his hands. "I wanted to give him these shoes. I believe they belong to him."

Lena said, "Why, thank you," and as she took the box from him, their eyes met and they smiled at each other. She tucked the box under her left arm and extended her right hand, the one holding Max's package. "Mr. Wurlitzer asked me to give you this. He says it belongs to you."

Michael took the package, not bothering to conceal his bewilderment. "Can I . . . may I speak to Mr. Wurlitzer?"

Lena, still smiling, stepped back inside the door and began to shut it. "No," she replied, "he isn't available. Thank you for your time." Both of them lingered for a moment on the point of speech, their eyes meeting again, and then she closed the door.

Michael walked back to the coffee shop with the small parcel. Seated again at the counter, he tore off the string and stripped away the paper. His wallet was inside. He unzipped the back compartment; it was filled with money. In the front were his license, his cards. Hunching his shoulders, he counted the money, slowly and carefully: it was all there, every dollar. And something else. Pinned to the bottom bill was a card. It read, simply, *The Great Wurlitzer. Now Appearing at the Little Cairo Museum of Wonders. Saturday and Sunday. 3:00 and 7:00* P.M. The 7:00 was scratched out, and underneath, in pen, was written *Saturday. Expected.*

CHAPTER TWELVE

Face to Face

The poster, vividly reproduced, showed two male figures standing face to face, their right hands holding glasses of dark red wine, their right arms raised and linked in an intimate toast. One of the figures wore a sort of costume, with a flowing cape and a strange pointed cap like a jester's. Both cap and cape were of the same deep crimson color as the wine, and his swarthy features, further darkened by the shadow he stood in, were hard to discern clearly: a long, straight nose, a pointed beard, teeth bared in a smile and faintly glimmering. The other figure, dressed in evening clothes and resting his free hand on his hip in an attitude of relaxed confidence, was gazing serenely at his diabolical companion as though acknowledging a trusted accomplice. In the background, against an orange sky, oddly shaped birds, some of them resembling pitchforks, whirled and glided. Across the bottom third of the poster, huge white letters, outlined in burnt orange against an indigo background, spelled a single name: WURLITZER.

"The Great Wurlitzer," Michael said, "known to a select few as the Queer Duck." His bed was covered with overflowing scrapbooks, various magazines, and several large, heavily illustrated books. He passed one of these to Emily, who was sitting on the other side of the bed. "What do you think?" he asked, tapping the open page.

"Well," she said, pondering the imposing image, "it looks exactly like him, but it can't be. This picture's at least fifty years old, right?"

"At least," he agreed.

"Then how can it be the same person?" she asked. She made a conscious effort to keep her increasing annoyance out of her voice. "This man looks as old as the Queer Duck does now."

"I can't figure it out either. Maybe when he was young he disguised himself to look like an old guy and now he's an old guy who really looks like the character he disguised himself as when he was young."

Emily laughed at this tail-chasing logic, but Michael went solemnly on. "Or maybe it's got something to do with his willpower. Maybe his will's so strong he doesn't age the way normal people do."

"Oh, please, Michael," she said, gesturing at the radiant, toasting figure. "Be reasonable. Maybe the Queer Duck is this guy's son."

"No, he can't be." He swept a hand over the books, the yellowed newspaper clippings, the back issues of *The Sphinx, Abracadabra,* and *The Magic World,* among others, that lay scattered across the bed. "Look at all this. I've been collecting stuff about magicians since I was a kid. If the Great Wurlitzer had a magician son with the same name, there'd have to be something about him in my collection."

Emily's skeptical look intensified. "How can you say that? You didn't even know this famous magician was still alive, if that's who he is."

Michael took back the book and held it open on his lap. "That's who he is, all right. I can't believe my luck." He flipped quickly through the book, stopping at another poster reproduction. This one showed Merlino the Magnificent, resplendent in long white druid's robes and a high, cone-shaped cap covered with astrological symbols. His snow-white, waist-length beard was lifted as by a strong wind, and portions of his robes streamed out behind him.

One of his eyes, dark and penetrating, seemed to fix the viewer with its hot glare; the other was covered by a black patch decorated with a stylized eye, such as one sees in ancient Egyptian art. His right hand was extended before him as though in warning, and a dazzling white light radiated from the center of his upraised left palm. Behind him desert sands stretched away to a point where a pyramid stood outlined against the distant horizon.

Silence fell as the two of them contemplated this image. Then Michael spoke, in reverential tones that made Emily's jaws clench: "This man is one of the greatest magicians in the world. He's been everywhere, he knows all kinds of magic—card tricks, sleight of hand, mind reading, illusions, you name it. Think of what I can learn from him." He trailed off dreamily, his eyes on the ceiling.

Emily was gazing at a photograph in *The Illustrated History of Sorcery.* "I see he even levitates Chinese princesses," she said drily.

"Right," Michael said, coming back to earth. "Chinese princesses used to be all the rage in the magic world. Because of their mysterious charms, no doubt." He reached to stroke her neck.

"That reminds me," she said, closing the book. "We still haven't seen the Chinese exhibit at the museum."

"Emily," Michael replied, still absorbed in his collection, "compared to real magic, how interesting can all those relics be? What do they have in that show? Prehistoric woks, jade chopsticks, stuff like that?"

Her spine stiffened, and her eyes narrowed. "They have art objects," she said, "beautiful works of art. Made by people who lived in a civilized society while *your* ancestors were running around the woods in animal skins, foreign ghost."

Michael knew that this expression literally translated a Chinese expression of xenophobic contempt, but it never failed to make him laugh. " 'The heathen Chinee is peculiar,' " he recited, " 'Which the same I am free to maintain.' "

Emily jabbed a heavy book (*Wizardry and Illusion*) hard into his ribs, and they wrestled briefly but intensely on the cluttered bed. "Wait," Michael mumbled, forcing the word past her shoulder, and then "Wait!" again, louder this time. She paused, adjusting her position to gain better leverage. "No, stop," he said. "You're going to cause major damage." He rolled away from her and began to pick up the materials on the bed, handling each item as though it belonged in a tabernacle. "Besides," he added as an afterthought, "it's too hot to fight fully dressed." Except for the large volume opened to the poster that depicted Lucifer and Wurlitzer about to drink each other's health, the bed was now completely cleared. Michael removed his shirt, expelled his breath loudly between half-closed teeth, and stretched out again next to the book.

Emily was sitting on the chair by the bed. She looked at Michael and shook her head. Why bother to fight him? She had lost already. Once his mind was made up, nothing could change it. "So what's next with him?" she asked, jerking her hand in the direction of the book.

"What's next?" he repeated, his eyes once again on the ceiling as though it weren't there. "I meet him on Saturday. I persuade him to take me as his apprentice. He agrees to help me become the Greatest Magician in the World. I learn about all his props and equipment. I learn everything he knows." He paused; then, in a soft voice heavy with intention, "And especially I learn night magic." He paused again for effect, then added matter-of-factly, "And I learn the Frog Trick."

"For Christ's sake, Michael," Emily groaned. "You hated it! You want to do *that* to someone else?"

He didn't flinch but said, without hesitation, "Yes," and this simple reply seemed so threatening to her that she held up her hands as though she might ward it off.

"I don't understand you," she said, almost whispering. "I don't understand what you want."

"What's to understand?" He turned his eyes to her, smiling. "You've had teachers. You know what it is to learn. Remember what you told me about your first music teacher? How she inspired you? Well, this man has knowledge, and I want him to pass it on to me. I want to learn what he knows and be able to do what he can do. That's all."

"Even if what he does is bad, or wrong, or hurts people?"

"I don't want to hurt people," Michael protested. "I don't think of it like that. All I want is to be a powerful magician. Right or wrong has nothing to do with it."

Emily scowled. "Right or wrong has everything to do with it," she said flatly.

Michael sat up on the bed and closed the book beside him. "You want people to say you're good, don't you? You want the attention, the applause, don't you? So what's the difference?"

"The difference is," Emily said carefully, "that I could be the greatest musician in the world and it's not going to hurt anyone. It's not going to humiliate anyone, Michael. No one is going to be reduced to vomiting helplessly in a public fountain." She paused while the memory of Michael's cruel enchantment rose between them. "At least, I hope not," she added.

Michael sat staring at her, sullenly.

"It's not applause you want," she said. "It's power. Isn't it?"

"Of course it is," Michael agreed. "A magician has power. That's what makes him different from the rest of the crowd."

Emily got up and went to the window. She could hear the whine of a siren, then the sound of raised voices, a man and a woman shouting at one another, but though she scanned the pavement she couldn't see them. "Power over what?" she asked. "Over everything? Over me?"

"If you're in the audience."

She smiled wanly. He was being careful, she thought, avoiding an argument; he disliked confrontations. She felt she was getting nowhere; then it occurred to her that she didn't know where she wanted to get. Michael had opened his book again and was examining the picture of Wurlitzer with an expression of bemusement that irritated her. He's like a child, she thought. "Why do you think he's interested in you?" she asked.

"I don't know that he is, particularly."

"Sure you do."

"Maybe he thinks I'm promising."

"Right," Emily agreed. "And maybe he wants a son as much as you want a father."

"What are you getting at?" Michael said sharply.

"You lost your parents when you were a child," Emily said. "It wouldn't be surprising if you were unconsciously looking for a replacement."

"I didn't think you were interested in amateur psychology."

"I'm not," Emily admitted. "It just shows how desperate I am." She stood leaning against the window frame, her arms folded. A thin smile raised the corners of her mouth.

Michael frowned. The tale of his dead parents, killed, he had told Emily, in an automobile accident, was one he'd given out so regularly over the years that he almost believed it himself. It explained why he lacked what everyone else had. It was neat, innocent, a catastrophe that could have happened to anyone, and though it elicited the required expressions of sympathy, the follow-up—I don't remember them—set everyone's mind at rest, including his own.

He had never told anyone the truth. His aunts had known, of course, but they were kind, moral women. Once he'd moved into their house, neither they nor he had ever mentioned how he came to be there. They were too horrified, he thought, and he was too superstitious. The truth was bad luck. When he'd started giving inquisitive people the story of the tragic accident, his aunts had assented to it without comment.

Emily didn't speak. Her intuitions were good, Michael thought, she knew she'd hit a nerve. Instead of pushing on, inadvertently forcing him to swallow one more time the lie at the center of his life, she simply waited, watching him quietly with a smile that he might once have characterized as inscrutable but knew now to be made up in equal parts of patience and affection. He realized that barriers might make sense with other people, but not with her. Tear them all down, he thought, then we can see each other.

"My parents didn't die, Emily," he said. "As far as I know they're still alive."

"There wasn't an accident?" she asked.

"No. That was just a wish I had."

She came away from the window and sat down on the bed next to him. Outside, another siren screamed by. Michael waited until it had passed. "They left me in the bus station in Toledo," he said. "My mother gave me an envelope with a bus ticket to Genesee, twenty dollars, and a piece of paper with my aunts' address and phone number on it. No note. They said they'd be back, then they left."

Emily had taken his hand in hers. "God," she said softly.

"I was eight years old," Michael continued. "I wasn't some baby left on the orphanage steps. They knew me. And they threw me away."

Unable to speak for several seconds, she squeezed his hand, staring dumbly at her whitening knuckles. She envisioned Michael, eight years old, all innocence and trust, betrayed, rejected, abandoned among strangers, and then she imagined the smiling faces of her own parents, who she knew would have stopped at nothing, literally nothing, to keep and protect their children. The stark juxtaposition of these images wrenched her heart, and she reached out and embraced Michael, sensing as she did it that a chasm had just opened between them.

Michael passed a bill through the slot to the fat girl sitting behind the window in the small box office. She punched up a ticket, sliding it to him with the bill. "No charge," she muttered, keeping her eyes on her book; then, almost as an afterthought, she added, "You're expected." She looked quickly down again as Michael started to reply, thought better of it, backed away, and shoved through a turnstile that revolved only with urging.

He walked through the left side of the pair of badly chipped red-painted doors and entered the museum. The dim interior proved to be a warren of passages whose smokehouse-black ceilings were glazed over with a sticky gum to which adhered scuds of fuzz like dust bunnies under a bed. A wainscoting of stamped tin, kicked and dented, painted a murky coffee color, ran along the lower walls, while the plaster above was a swabbed sickly green, with an entire manic geography of cracks delineated over its moldered surfaces.

There was a paucity of light; red bulbs, mean in their wattage, glowed above several safety exits. The odor could have been indigenous only to such premises, a mixture of burned fuel, lacquer, sanitary precautions in a lavatory, and something Michael thought smelled like boiled cabbage. Yet, in its shoddy attempt at theatricality, its desire to remain what it once was, with no attempt at modernization, he detected a nostalgic stubbornness. Something in the ersatz Egyptian motif—painted columns decorated with faded gilt and fake hieroglyphs, sphinxlike plaster figures, paper palms with tin fronds, faded murals of romanticized Nile scenes, a plethora of jackal-headed beings—reached and touched Michael, made him think of the dilapidated movie house in Genesee, and half consciously he felt he had somehow been here before, had known of the museum's existence.

A young man his own age, but larger, fatter, with round, unblinking eyes and a cretinous stare, tore his ticket in half, and when Michael asked where the magician was performing, his attention was directed to a placard reading AUDITORIUM, with a pointing arrow beneath. Presently he found himself in a narrow corridor so feebly illuminated that its termination melded into some hazy infinity. The linoleum along the floor was buckled and warped, and in some places entirely worn away so the boards showed through. Dark corners made happy haunts for spiders whose abandoned webs spanned the angle between the cornices, festooning dust-covered lightbulbs.

Following arrows with AUDITORIUM stenciled beneath, Michael continued to the end of a passage, where two blank doors presented themselves. Beyond, he could hear the murmur of voices, at first a startling concept, for it seemed unimaginable that people would find this place unbidden and without a guide. Yet once inside the auditorium he found rows of folding chairs, partially filled. The patrons included young mothers with children in chattering groups, several elderly paired spouses, and other random individuals. The air felt close and carried aromas similar to those he had smelled outside. At the far end was a small stage, its fire curtain lowered. Carrying out the Egyptian theme, the stage proscenium was flanked by pairs of tall plaster columns, while at the center of the arch the face of a goddess peered down in faded glory from between twin feathered fans. The plaster arch itself was draped in worn burgundy velvet and hung with fringe that had seen better days. The fire curtain on which was painted a badly faded representation of a Nile river scene, complete with pyramids and a sphinx, rose to reveal the tired burgundy velvet stage curtain, while Michael stood at the back of the hall, deciding where he should sit.

A quartet of youths looking like extras from a Spike Lee movie filed incongruously in, occupied seats in the center of the mid-most row, and engaged in some good-natured jostling. As Michael came down the aisle to take a seat in front of them, one of the youths made a harp of his thumb and finger, put it between his teeth, and gave an ear-piercing whistle. Michael flashed a look at him, then sat.

Presently the lights dimmed, and music began; he recognized the "Triumphal March" from *Aida*. When the hall became dark, a sudden, grating scratch truncated the music, the curtain rose with a whoosh, and without prelude the magician entered from stage right, making swooping, birdlike movements, coming directly to center stage, where he bowed to a smattering of applause. Michael's chair creaked as he leaned forward in rapt anticipation. It didn't seem possible that he was actually going to witness a performance by Merlino the Magnificent. Yet there he was, exactly as he'd appeared in the posters and the newspaper and magazine photographs in Michael's collection. The long, flowing beard, the conical hat, the voluminous gown of antiquated velvet—Michael was quick to notice how its hue and age seemed to match those of the stage draperies—hanging to the floor in ample folds and spangled with suns, moons, stars, and occult symbols that caught the light.

Enfolding himself from the waist down in a three-panel screen, the magician stared out at the audience without moving; then, raising the screen and stepping quickly aside, he revealed on the boards, the floor of the stage, an enormous glass bowl filled with water in which half a dozen goldfish swam into the light.

He continued with several small tricks, with five playing cards appearing and disappearing at his fingertips, and Michael saw that though there was dexterity there was also a trembling of the fingers, and the execution of the sleight lacked deftness and precision. From the cards he proceeded to cigarettes, one of which materialized from nowhere and which the magician puffed at, scattering a shower of sparks on the stage; then the cigarette disappeared—but not without difficulty: there was some clumsy fumbling, awarded derisive hoots by the four boys—and reappeared, he swallowed it, then produced it again between his lips. The smoke troubled him; he began coughing and for a moment was forced to turn his back and rid himself of phlegm while the hoots began again. Michael turned in his chair and tried to stare the noisemakers down; but got the finger for his pains.

Now Merlino was doing silks, pulling them from an empty cylinder the size of a beer can, yard after yard of them, the stuff falling around him in billows. As he moved, the fabric got caught in the folds of his gown, causing him more difficulty and impeding his movements. He managed several other minor feats that amused the young fry in the audience but left Michael flat and feeling disappointed. Was this really Merlino the Magnificent? The audience was restless. The youths were passing remarks back and forth, and laughing outright.

The magician, clearly, was not at his ease. His card fans were sloppy, his use of props unclean, nor was there economy of gesture or any flash. It was as if he were plodding, just trying to get through the performance. He finished the hat trick and moved from behind the fringe-draped table at the side of the stage, advancing to the center, where he held his arms out and bowed. There was hardly any applause. Michael began clapping loudly, until the magician turned his head and stared at him. Michael broke off, returning the stare. What was it? Something he was reminded of . . . that look . . . Before he could pinpoint it, the magician made a quick move, still holding his arms spread wide, and the velvet gown vanished. Another quick turn and the beard and hat were gone as well, with them the white eyebrows, and, now in tails, he bowed, a short, quick bow, then stepped offstage. A moment later a familiar figure appeared in his place; Michael stared in wonder.

It was his old friend, the Italian beggar. "*O sole mio,*" he sang, crossing the stage in his baggy checkered pants and corduroy vest, his battered fedora, over to the opposite side and off into the wings, but not without a meaningful glance at Michael.

No sooner had he gone than from the same wing appeared another fellow of Michael's acquaintance: the dapper banker with the spats. It was all there, the spats, the well-creased trousers, the yellow gloves, the cane. Even the flower in the buttonhole. Traversing the stage rapidly, he doffed his hat to the audience, and executed a polite bow to Michael. The banker was replaced in quick succession by the nun with her collection can and the sandwich-board man. As they came on and exited, each in turn giving Michael a look, his mind reeled, trying to make sense of it. Something was growing in him, a narrowing-down of thought to some conclusion. Then the rabbi entered, unmistakably the same rabbi with the earlocks that he had seen in the subway and the department store. "*Oy vey*," called one of the youths, and the others laughed. Off went the rabbi (at the end of a trick), and on came . . .

. . . *the Queer Duck.*

There he was, red nose; black suit; black beard; black umbrella, identical to the one Michael had taken from the museum checkroom; the duck-footed walk—and the Bilt-Well shoes. Not the old ones, but the new, shiny patent-leather gaiters with blunt toes. He walked to center stage, collapsed the umbrella, and from it drew forth a string of objects: an hourglass, a music box playing "Waltzing Matilda," glassware, silver service, half a dozen teacups, a fur piece, a box of cigars, and—a rubber duck. This he held out toward Michael and squeezed it. "Quack, quack," said the rubber duck, and the Queer Duck turned and strode offstage to applause.

This was it, then, Michael thought; his search was really ended, though "search" was not the accurate word. The magician's performance revealed to Michael that he had been, all along, more the prey than the hunter. The old man had never, as he had imagined, been in flight from him. It was Michael who had been running, straight and true, along a path laid out for him—directly into what was, at best, a harsh joke, or, at worst, a devilish trap. He tried to put it all together, failed miserably, and even as he attempted to sort it out the magician was back, and before him stood the real, the true, the one and only, the Great Wurlitzer!

He wore a base of theatrical makeup, carefully powdered, which gave the skin a matte tone, though this covered only the long oval of his face; the neck and ears were pallid and in odd contrast to the deeper tones. The nose—the real one, this time—

was of a prominent Hebrew mold, with an excess of nostril, but pinched above in little clefts, flaring with a kind of equine arrogance; the brows, not bushy but lending a saturnine aspect, as though he wore about him an invisible aura of darkness. The lips were dark, too, with a good deal of blood in them, and thin, which with the beak of nose—sharp, incisive, as though used to pecking and devouring—made Michael think of a large, fierce bird.

But it was the eye, of course, that compelled him. Not the dull one, off at an angle, but the bright one, drilling out from its socket, darkly shining, while the face maintained that same blandly questioning air he remembered from under the umbrella.

Are you then a frog? Very well, be a frog.

Are you then a magician? Very well, be a magician.

Michael felt a little shiver of anticipation as with a quick gesture Wurlitzer produced a top hat at his fingertips, clapping it on his head, and slipping a monocle into the socket of his bad eye, giving himself the look of a seedy man-about-town, a shabby rake. He smoothed the shiny lapels of his tailcoat, an outdated and badly-fitting model, hopelessly wrinkled at the bend of the elbows and pulled tight at the waist. The shirt collar was an old-fashioned wing type, with a narrow bow tie held in place by an elastic band, and in his buttonhole he sported the same flower the banker had worn.

Under the jacket he wore a vest, or rather a waistcoat of equally dated cut, and across his concave front was looped a gold chain of some weight and substance. Quickly, and with a faintly quizzical air, he turned back his cuffs, one, two three, in the time-honored magician's gesture, assuring his audience he had nothing up his sleeves. Drawing from inside his coat a narrow black wand with ivory tips, he tapped it three times in his palm, then removed his hat. Quickly replacing it on his head, he rolled his eye waggishly as the hat began to grow, taller and taller. When it stopped he reached up and tore it from his head and scaled it into the wings. Another hat appeared at his fingertips, and he put it on to replace the first one.

It was his expression that Michael found most fascinating. It seemed to betray the man's unease at performing, as if such work came most unnaturally to him. The thin lips were drawn back, not in a smile, but in an uncomfortable grimace. Yet there was something sadly wistful about the manner in which he tried to disguise his discomfort, the attempts at flash, the sloppy fingerwork. He must be a tippler, Michael thought patronizingly, watching him fumble another one.

With one elongated hand the magician gestured toward the wings, and now there appeared from stage right a Chinese princess, bowing to the audience as she came onstage with frittering steps. She wore an elaborate headdress and a black wig, but under the makeup Michael detected features he recognized: the woman who had returned his wallet, the face he knew from somewhere else. Standing next to the magician, she stiffened her body and he lowered her onto a bench, where she lay supine. The magician covered her figure with a light cloth so that only the form showed, and then, without the usual hocus-pocus gestures commonly employed in the levitation trick, she began to rise until she was suspended three feet above the bench. Using a large hoop, the magician made passes with it from one end to the middle, and then from the other end. Now holding the hoop and standing back, he caused the form to rise farther, to some ten feet in the air. The audience was still; not a sound could be heard. Then, with a quick gesture, the magician reached up, caught the corner of the cloth, and yanked it away. The princess was gone. He flourished the cloth, then insolently tossed it aside, strode offstage, shortly to reappear pushing a wheeled sedan chair in whose interior sat the selfsame Chinese princess. He brought her out and bowed with her; then, while she bowed alone, he again exited and returned, rolling onstage a large cabinet, elaborately painted with colorful Chinese scenes and gilt scrollwork.

He returned the princess to the sedan chair and lowered a small curtain, hiding her from the audience. There was a puff of smoke, and when he drew the curtain up again the princess was gone from the sedan chair. The doors of the cabinet were flung open, and out she stepped, to more applause. She bowed again: then in broad pantomime she whispered in Wurlitzer's ear and indicated the audience. He cocked his eyebrow at the suggestion, pondered for a moment, then approached the audience, inquiring if there might be one among them who desired to join him on stage and assist him in a trick or two? He looked—pointedly, Michael felt—to the rear of the hall, but that didn't stop Michael from volunteering, with arm outstretched, rising at the same time. With a little flick of annoyance the magician suffered him to come up the steps at the side of the stage and join him in the spotlight.

"An eager volunteer, ladies and gentlemen," the magician said with a hint of sarcasm. Then, in an oilier voice: "Welcome, my young friend."

Quickly he produced a fresh pack of cards, fanned up the four aces and asked Michael to insert them at random points in the deck, indicating that the four cards that would then appear at his fingertips would be these same four aces. Michael did as he was requested to do, but when the cards appeared there was not one ace among them. The magician threw his assistant a quick look, then turned back to Michael, his confusion only brief, covering the error with patter and a joke, which the audience heartily enjoyed. Next, Michael was asked to select another card, show it to the audience, and then slip it back into the deck, which the magician reshuffled. Giving Michael the pack, he instructed him to deal the cards face down onto the table, announcing that whenever he chose to stop, the card in his hand would be the one he had shown to the audience.

Only it was not.

Michael dealt, stopped, the magician lifted the card, while the audience tittered nervously; it was the wrong card. Hoots and catcalls came from the four boys, and loud foot stompings. The magician shot Michael an admonitory glance, then produced another fresh pack of cards, from which Michael was asked to select two and show them to the audience. The cards were returned to the pack, which was then wrapped in a piece of colored tissue. Michael was offered a knife and told to insert it through the wrapping and into the pack, which when opened would reveal the blade between the two selected cards. But it did not.

While the audience now roared outright at his expense, the magician turned to Michael with a look that gave him pause, though he returned it unflinchingly. This exchange lasted no more than a moment; then, turning again, the magician went to the cabinet, whose doors he opened and with a flourish of his hand invited Michael inside, between comments addressed to the audience. He told Michael merely to stand there with his hands at his sides and to remain relaxed, that he had nothing to fear; all would be well. With these comforting words, he enclosed him in darkness. From inside the cabinet, Michael could hear the whispers in the audience and the magician's stage patter as he explained that as a matter of scientific experimentation it would be of interest if his young friend could be urged to reappear in the nearby sedan chair, reversing the progress of the Chinese princess.

Michael, who knew a thing or two concerning these cleverly structured stage props, quickly moved his feet, placing them on the stringers at the bottom, one in each corner, and holding on to the ones at the top with each hand, he made his body rigid, bracing his shoulders against the sides, head ducked down, resistant to whatever trick lay in store for him.

Outside, the magician addressed the audience. "He is clever, our young friend, is he not? I suspect he is a magician himself. At least he knows one or two tricks." He paused, stalked rapidly away from the cabinet, whirled to face the audience, waited. There were restless noises, bodies shifting, feet scraping the floor. The magician glanced at the house over his shoulder, making no sign to interrupt the disturbance. His brows were slightly contracted; a faint frown evidenced some heavy thought on his part. He waited again; then, laying his finger alongside his nose, he drily took the spectators into his confidence.

"I think perhaps we are making too much noise. It may be disturbing to our young friend, heh? One may wonder what he is doing inside there," he said, nodding toward the cabinet, "or if indeed he is there at all." His words were offered in the spirit of fun, the lightest hint of suggestion merely, but even as the magician turned upstage again the doors of the cabinet broke open and were flung wide. Michael, with a dazed and stricken expression, his hair in disarray, his shirt yanked out of his pants and all awry, was catapulted onstage in a violent bound. He paused for only a moment, staring frantically at the magician, and then, wheeling, he looked back at the cabinet. He backed away, a strangled cry escaping his lips. With one hand clamped over his mouth he turned again, dashed in terror, blindly, for the stage steps, and with all eyes upon him raced up the aisle and hurled himself through the rear doors.

"Yes," said the magician as questioning eyes turned back to him, "he is a very clever young man. He should go far. Very far. Now, if one may ask it, shall we resume?"

CHAPTER THIRTEEN

Help Wanted

Michael sat in the coffee shop across from the Little Cairo Museum of Wonders, watching the entrance and sipping from a shaking cup. It rattled as he set it on his saucer, and to keep his hands busy he smoothed his hair and readjusted his shirt.

What had happened while he stood in the cabinet, braced, he thought, for any eventuality? He tried to recall the exact progression of feelings and events—the magician's unctuous, mocking invitation, his own confident acceptance, the darkness inside, the waiting. Then the sudden, desperate combat: something, like a pair of human hands, seizing him, pummeling him about the shoulders and neck, not a pair of hands exactly, but some invisible force fastening upon him, an uncontrollable flexion of muscles, a set of purely physical sensations without any accompanying mental processes. How had it been done? How had there been time? Suddenly he'd found himself in the cabinet, wrestling for his life against something dark and powerful, something that buffeted him ruthlessly, flinging him like a sack against the sides of the narrow space, until one vicious, final blow, one last humiliation, like a disdainful kick in the rear from a giant foot, lifted him up bodily from behind and propelled him staggering back onto the stage.

He felt his neck, his arms, shoulders. All the muscles were sore, as if they had been brutally wrenched and pounded. His eye hurt where it had been struck; he thought it might be swelling. And he was convinced that the area from his lower back to his upper thighs was covered by a single deepening bruise. The Queer Duck had got to him again, and again had done it in some unfathomable way. Sitting up as straight as his throbbing body allowed, Michael realized with a thrill of fear that it was going to take more than a thumping in the dark to sway him from his purpose. Now more than ever he was determined to do whatever might be necessary to acquire the skill, the art, the power—it made no difference what you called it—possessed by this uncanny, bumbling, arrogant, absurd, dangerous old man.

The woman, most recently seen as the Chinese princess, was standing calmly outside the coffee shop. Michael saw her through the window, looking once again as she looked when she returned his wallet. He paid for his coffee and went out quickly to her. She smiled a kind smile at him and made a regretful gesture. "I don't want to disturb you," she explained. Then she added, in a knowing voice, "I'm sure you could use a few restful minutes."

Michael made a humphing sound, half laugh, half snort. "I'm all right so far," he said, and paused, letting his features express an unspoken question.

"He wants to see you," she said. She was a small woman, and as she looked up at Michael she blinked at the bright sun behind him.

"Lead the way, please," he said. She turned and crossed the street, he following six feet behind, concentrating on each step and wondering where it was leading him.

The audience was gone. The magician stood on the stage, solitary and spectral under the harsh glare of the worklight overhead. He gave no sign to Michael, but only stood smoking, an elbow cupped in his hand, and leaning back on one leg like a fashion model. The glass eye had been replaced by a black patch, the elastic caught at the back so one tuft of hair reared up like a cowlick. Two gold chairs sat on the bare stage, and with a negligent wave of the hand he indicated that Michael should join him. Michael looked at the woman, who backed away, shutting the auditorium door after her. He turned and walked down the aisle, marched up the steps and onto the stage, keeping a wary distance. The old man, exhaling fumes like dragon's smoke through dilated nostrils, observed him closely. At last Michael heard not the gaily sardonic stage voice but that bleak, moribund tone that reminded him of dead leaves in the wind.

"I thought I should enjoy a *private* meeting as well, with so *clever* a young man," the magician said, leaning on adjectives as though they were threats. "You are a *clever* young man, are you not?"

"I don't think so."

"I must trust your judgment. Sit."

The curt abruptness of this order caused Michael to regard the indicated chair; then, to his own surprise, he crossed to it and sat. The old man folded himself into the other one, smoking wordlessly and staring through his single, narrowed eye. Michael found this long scrutiny disconcerting; the magician seemed to be examining him, like a careful buyer appraising a possible purchase. Michael was determined to break the uncomfortable silence, though he had not yet decided how to do so when the old man finally spoke.

"Yes, I suppose we must begin," he said, almost reluctantly. "First of all, satisfy my curiosity: what made you try to spoil my act?"

Michael dropped his head, contemplated the undone lace of his sneaker. "I suppose I wanted to impress you."

"You try to impress me by ruining my performance? When the audience laughs at me, you think I am impressed?" There was woefulness in the voice, and self-pity, but the magician's bearing belied them. Even his sham attempt to conceal his irony was ironic, a complicated charade carried out for some undisclosed effect.

"The laugh was on me, I think," Michael said. Though he felt foolish and guilty for having tried to show up the old man, he couldn't bring himself to regard the other as the injured party, not when his eye was swelling painfully and his battered body ached. "How did you do that?" he asked, his voice earnest, almost pleading. "In the cabinet, I mean. What did you use on me?"

Wurlitzer snorted in an unpleasantly liquid way. "You have a vivid imagination, my young friend. I 'used' nothing. Whether through clumsiness or claustrophobia, you lost your footing and bumped your eye. Then you burst out and ruined another trick. You seem quite incorrigible."

Michael almost smiled at this bland, carelessly insincere rationalization. Trying to justify himself, he said, softly, "*You* spoiled *my* act, remember?"

"I? You mean your little street pantomime?" The voice was mildly reproving, that of an innocent man unjustly accused, but the eye was hard and cold. "You do not know how to cut your material. Your frog impersonation went on much too long. It is a matter of timing, merely." Wurlitzer rose abruptly to his feet and leaned toward Michael, who for a single terrible moment felt again the swooning helplessness, the blank surrender he had experienced once before when this strange figure loomed over him. But no compulsive hopping ensued; the moment passed, the magician merely ground out his cigarette under his heel and continued speaking. "Of course, timing is a skill that is learned. It comes with experience. You have had some stage experience?"

"A little." Michael admired the way the old man had finessed his questions about cabinet-thrashing and frog-horror, as though he knew nothing of such matters.

"Acting?" Wurlitzer asked in a prodding tone as he resumed his seat.

"Yes."

"And a conjuror as well. A man of parts." He brought a deck of cards from a pocket. "Show me."

Michael, though tempted, shook his head in refusal.

"Very well." Wurlitzer's look was cunning, as if Michael's weak defiance provided him some trifling amusement. "It is not necessary. I know what you can do"—he paused significantly—"and what you cannot." A noise made them both glance toward the wings, where the woman was padding about industriously, gathering costumes from where they had been flung during the magician's quick changes and putting them on hangers on a wheeled rack.

The old man returned his attention to Michael, looking him up and down as though taking his measure. "So where do you come from?" he asked. "Surely not New York."

"I grew up in Genesee, Ohio."

Wurlitzer repeated the unfamiliar names with questioning annoyance. Then he said—it was more a statement than a question—"But you enjoy living in New York."

"Yes," Michael said, sensing that short answers were being called for. "I like it."

The magician cocked his head oddly to one side before he spoke. "A young man is very brave to live in New York these days, I think. Criminals are everywhere."

"I'm not brave, I just smile a lot."

"Yes-s-s, you do." Wurlitzer released the words in an aspirated sibilance, squinting his eye sardonically, as if assessing a potential enemy or ally. "Your smile is most charming, but you use it too much. Smiles should be only for the fond, or for the wonders of the world. You are perhaps one of those wonders, heh?" His lips sketched the wisp of a smile as he laid his long finger against his long nose, a gesture Michael found precious, something an actor might use to convey roguishness. He decided that there was much of the actor about the Great Wurlitzer.

He resumed the conversation, again in his mocking tone. "You gave little shows in your hometown, correct? For the Rotary Club, perhaps?"

"Elks."

"The Elks, to be sure, the Elks. And you know some card tricks. What else?"

"You've seen my tricks." Michael pointed to the rack of costumes, the nun's habit, the banker's natty jacket, the Italian beggar's baggy pants.

Wurlitzer waved his hand in an impatient, dismissive motion. "Yes, of course, my little deceptions, so I could observe you at my leisure. But I'm not talking about tricks or deceptions," he went on, repeating his contemptuous wave with increased forcefulness. "I'm talking about genuine magic."

Michael kept his eyes on the worn boards of the stage. "You mean night magic?" he asked quietly.

The magician registered vague surprise, raising his visible eyebrow a few millimeters. "An interesting expression. Yes, that is what I mean, night magic. What can you show me?"

"Nothing," Michael admitted ruefully, ashamed of his ignorance. Then he looked up, and all the intensity of his desire was in his eyes. "But you can teach me," he said.

The old man's reply was a long time in coming, but at last he said, bemusedly, "Perhaps I can." He sat still for a few moments, slumped in his chair. Then, abruptly, he straightened his back, and the cold edge returned to his voice. "And you are now a professional conjuror?"

"In a minor way. I've done shows for small groups. I work at parties sometimes."

Wurlitzer considered this briefly. "And you have your street routines, your little pantomimes. Very savage, your mimicries," he said, his eye seeming to narrow at the memory. "Very savage indeed. And quite accurate. I could hardly tell you from myself." He paused to light another cigarette, but Michael's lighter was flaming in front of his face before he managed to extract a match from the box he had fished out of his pocket. "Very kind," he said, spewing out a long stream of smoke. "Now, then, to continue. What else do you do, how do you spend your time? Tell me more about yourself. For example, you haven't even told me your name."

"You know my name. It was in my wallet."

The old man did a broad pantomime of perplexity, as though playing to the cheap seats, followed by an impression of dawning light. Finally he said, "Ah, of course, I had forgotten. Michael, is it? Michael—" He whirled his long fingers, trying to draw the name out of the air.

"Hawke."

The old man repeated the name softly to himself, his head engulfed in smoke, which he batted away with a hand. "A sturdy Anglo-Saxon name," he said without enthusiasm. "Ah, well, at least it's not German. Tell me about your parents."

Michael winced. "I lost them when I was a little boy."

The pressure of Wurlitzer's gaze intensified, as if he were seeking the kernel of truth in Michael's declaration. "I see," he said, in a tone so penetrating that Michael thought the words must be literally true. "That explains your—how shall I say it?—not just your independence, that timeworn American virtue, but your so inadequately disguised melancholy."

Michael's eyes opened wide in astonishment, but the old man made his dismissive gesture again. "Yes, yes, your black bile, your dark nights of the soul. But let us touch on less obvious matters. For instance, I should be interested to learn something about your Asian assistant."

Michael stiffened. "Emily?" he said, suspiciously.

"How should I know?" came the bland reply. "The Asian girl, the flute player. She was with you the day you lost your wallet."

Michael was loath to say anything that might spoil his chances with this presumptuous, humbugging old boor, but he was weary of being interrogated, patronized, mocked. "I didn't lose it," he said tersely. "You stole it from me."

" 'Stole' it?" Wurlitzer's look was infuriatingly droll, as if now things were getting really interesting. "Are you accusing me of being a pickpocket?"

"Picking pockets is easy if you know sleight of hand. Magicians make good thieves sometimes."

"Perhaps you have had experience there, too, heh?" the old man asked, heavily insinuating.

Michael flushed; he recalled the rabbi at Bloomingdale's, laughing at him as he practiced at the notions counter. Something fell into place in his mind, too solidly and clearly to be denied expression. "I've shoplifted a thing or two, mostly to see if I could," he admitted, the contrite young sinner confessing to the virtuous elder. Two can play this game, he thought. "That was a long time ago, though, and I was never serious. Not the way you are."

"About what?" Wurlitzer asked at once, in his bleak, sneering voice.

"About theft," Michael said flatly, paused for two deliberately measured beats, then pressed on. "I'm a real amateur. For example, I've never stolen anything from a museum."

The sentence hung in the air between them. Michael cringed, fearing he had gone too far, but then the magician suddenly began to laugh, a horrible cackling sound like the background noises at a witches' sabbat. "You are very foolish, my young friend," he said with a discomfiting leer, "but you are also very brave. I noticed this at our first meeting. We shall discuss the museum another time." He fell silent, lost in thought, then chuckled again. "Yes," he said, as though answering a question only he could hear. "Yes, yes." He looked directly at Michael as he murmured these words, an eager, avid look the younger man found both flattering and disquieting. "Yes," Wurlitzer was saying again, "you are very brave. And very talented, with your frog and your other pantomimes. And your clever costume, your top hat and your military jacket. Your little robot routine is very well realized." He seemed decided now, and determined to please.

"Thanks," Michael said, puffing up slightly. "I call it the Mechanical Man."

"Good, good." Head tilted back, Wurlitzer had lifted his black patch and removed a wad of cotton from the eyeless socket. Quickly covering it with a cupped hand, he began to massage the periocular region, gently, as though it pained him. "You mentioned acting," he said, still rubbing. "What roles have you played?"

"I just played El Gallo in *Fantastiks.*"

"Whatever that may be," Wurlitzer murmured, clearly unimpressed. He brightened. "Yet it seems you have laid the foundations for a well-rounded career, doesn't it? All you need is a bit more skill, a bit more discipline. Well, well." A fugitive smile played upon his lips as he replaced the cotton, drew down the patch, leveling his single eye at Michael. Embarrassed, the younger man gazed around the stage, fixing at last upon the lacquered Chinese cabinet, which stood off to one side, near the wings. He felt certain that Wurlitzer was on the verge of some proposal, one whose nature was not immediately apparent, for there was a shadowy movement in the wings, and the old man peered offstage in annoyance. The woman stood back behind the curtain ropes, beckoning.

With a peremptory "You will excuse me," delivered in his curtest tone, the magician unfolded himself from his chair and shuffled across the stage, his walk ducklike, his patent-leather shoes gleaming in the light. He drew the woman behind the leg of a velour stage return, and for a moment there was silence.

Michael quickly rose, using the opportunity to examine the cabinet from which he had so recently been ejected. The doors stood askew on their hinges where he had broken through them, and the box looked like nothing so much as a well-used stage prop. He thrust his head inside, gingerly, flicked his cigarette lighter on, feeling around the sides with his free hand. Wood panels, painted black, with stretchers and corners reinforced by metal angle irons. He bent and looked at the flooring: nothing but an empty cabinet.

But—there was something about it. He got a distinct feeling, eerie, spooky, that he had no way of identifying. Something, he thought, like the idea of encountering a ghost in a haunted house; or perhaps like the encounter itself. A noise behind him startled him badly. He turned to see Wurlitzer standing on the bottom step of the stage stairs. Michael had no idea how long he'd been under observation, and he was sheepish as he acknowledged the old man's presence.

"Forgive the interruption," Wurlitzer said airily. "I trust you have not been bored in my absence?" His tone was bland, yet with that hint of mockery in it. "You were admiring my little cabinet, I see." Michael grunted, bending to retie his sneaker lace, as the old man pattered volubly on. "Come, come, no need for modesty here, we are all friends, or soon shall be, heh?" Michael found the "hch," emphasized by a jerk of the chin, peculiarly annoying. He was being baited, for sure. But for what reason? At least the old man seemed to want something from him; Michael supposed this was a good sign, whatever the something was.

"Come along, then," Wurlitzer was saying, gesturing to the wings and leading the way. "Enough of the stage, we shall go upstairs and enjoy the small refreshment that Lena is preparing. Perhaps she can also give you a cold cloth for that nasty bump over your eye. You must learn to be more careful."

"Upstairs" was gained by means of a large iron staircase, curving from the stage-right wing to a point high above the stage itself. Wurlitzer's soles clacked on the perforated metal steps as he climbed. He didn't look back until he had rolled aside the small iron door set into the brick wall at second-story level and entered an upper room, where he waited for Michael to pass him.

"Lena, Lena, we are here," the old man called, urging Michael ahead and indicating that he should go to the end of the passageway. Here another door, which had been left open, admitted them to a second passage on the right side of the stage wall. From this passageway, Michael could see down the staircase to the ground level and up to other floors overhead.

"Just to the end, if you please," Wurlitzer said. He passed Michael again, held open the door at the far end of the hall, and showed him in. "Here is Lena's parlor," he said, gesturing his guest toward a chair, "and music room, I should add, for that is what she calls it." Michael looked around the room, which was crowded and cluttered with old furniture, shelves with books and papers, a large table under an overhead lamp, a piano, a music stand, and, everywhere, antimacassars.

"Galena!" Wurlitzer shouted through the doorway, then went and stood by the clock on the mantel. "Sit down, my boy, sit down," he said. "She is surely coming. In the meantime, where were we?" He seemed to become all vague and bumbling, absently patting his pockets, fingering his stiff collar, stretching his neck, shrugging his jacket up and down. For a moment, Michael thought of a harmless, absentminded professor: Einstein wondering where he'd left his notes. The painful tightness around Michael's eye when he smiled at this image caused him to revise it. Absentminded, perhaps; but definitely not harmless.

At last he settled in a well-worn armchair, placed at an angle to the sofa where Michael sat, and slowly turned his head to face him. "Ah, yes, I recall," the old man said, sitting up ramrod straight and riveting Michael's gaze with his searching single eye. A cold, unnerving force seemed to flow out of him; every element of caricature, of absurdity, fell from him like a shed disguise. "Let us pass directly to the heart of the matter," he said, his bleak voice like an ominous wind in Michael's ears. "I have a serious proposition for you to consider."

Michael sat bolt upright, perched on the edge of the sofa like a bird poised for flight, his position mirroring the old man's, all his faculties concentrated on this moment, these words. Outside, the city's fevered pulse raged on, its cacophony shifted from crescendo to crescendo; inside, in Lena's parlor, time moved with glacial slowness, and silently.

"I have lived for a long time," Wurlitzer began. "I am weary of this theatrical life, of this world of trickery and illusion. I wish to make a final, permanent exit from the stage." He paused again, as though contemplating his own words with a hint of regret. Then he continued. "But before I take my last bow, I require a helper, let us say a kind of apprentice. Such a person must be talented, clever, and ambitious. On the first two counts, I am fairly satisfied with you, but I know nothing of your ambitions. What are they?"

This was an easy question. "I have only one," Michael said earnestly. "To be the greatest magician in the world."

The old man's fierce gaze relaxed, became almost indulgent. "And what are you willing to go through to realize this noble, if somewhat solemn, ambition?"

Michael found this one easy too, though the answer frightened him. "Whatever it takes," he said.

"It is as I thought," Wurlitzer replied in his dry, rasping voice, like a prosecutor handed a clinching piece of evidence.

Silence fell between them again. Michael sat stiffly, staring at Wurlitzer in astonishment. Surely it couldn't be this simple. All his hopes, his dreams, all those imagined conversations with the Queer Duck, thus neatly tucked into a package, as though his wildest fantasies were being delivered to him, made to order. "I would be your assistant?" he asked hesitantly, fearing to break the spell.

"Yes-yes-yes, assistant, helper, whatever you choose to call yourself." The old man spoke impatiently, desiring to have the matter settled.

"How would I assist you?" Michael wanted to know.

"As you must have observed, there is much to do here, chores for which I need your brawn more than your brains. There are things to be built, items to be repaired. To say nothing of rehearsals, working out new routines, and the like. If all goes well, then we shall prepare for the Grand Finale."

"The Grand Finale?" Michael asked, as he was clearly meant to do.

"My farewell to the stage, upon which I have strutted and fretted long enough." The old man, absorbed in his own imaginings, shifted his gaze to some indefinable point above Michael's head and spoke eagerly, pridefully. "I am planning a spectacular show, the likes of which no magician has ever performed. That show will be the ultimate goal of our—what shall I call it?—partnership."

"I'm extremely interested," Michael said, "but I still don't understand the terms of the proposition. What would the pay be?"

"Pay?" Wurlitzer looked amazed and spoke sharply. "Who talks of pay? Of late you have discovered that money comes when you need it. Your pay will be in what you can learn."

Michael could scarcely contain his joy. "So you'll teach me what you know?"

The magician gave a wary answer, though whether the wariness was feigned or genuine Michael couldn't tell. "There will of course be some transfer of knowledge and techniques, as always happens when members of our profession come together. Personal style, to be sure, cannot and should not be tampered with. You have your own tricks, as I have mine. Yours do not interest me particularly. Mine, however"—he broke off, his eye piercing Michael like a laser beam—"I have many stage routines that will be of interest to you."

Michael felt himself too near the goal to be deflected by coy double-talk. "This all sounds good, but I have to be sure of what I'm getting," he persisted. "I'll do whatever you want. But in exchange, I want you to teach me."

The magician made a snorting sound, short and contemptuous, mirthful yet humorless. "As I've said, I imagine I can teach you one or two little tricks, yes. You are quick, you should learn fast."

"I don't mean sleights. Or illusions." Michael rose to his feet, leaned closer to the old man, and spoke in a charged, intense voice. "I mean another kind of magic."

"What other kind?"

Michael bent still closer, enduring that terrible eye at short range, mindful of nothing but his own will. "The kind you do. Like the frog. Night magic."

This time the magician laughed outright, a harsh cackle that literally took Michael aback. "Do not speak to me of such things," Wurlitzer said. "They are not—transmittable."

"You must have learned it somewhere," Michael said.

"Oh, eh, somewhere. One learns everything . . . somewhere. There are many kinds of magic. Still, it's all illusion, really. And how can one teach illusions?"

"Isn't it a question of what's behind the illusion?"

"Yes, of course, and also what's in front." Pausing, Wurlitzer seemed to be considering some urgent matter. Michael watched him carefully. He's drawing me in, the old fraud, Michael thought. Just where I want to be. Then, abruptly, the magician spoke again. "Let us put an end to these negotiations. I will teach you stage magic. You will help me as I need you, and we will rehearse. You will learn the workings of many astonishing illusions unique in the history of magic. In the process, perhaps I can convey to you one or two . . . ideas. I will further your ambition as I can. Are we agreed?"

He remained seated, proffering no handshake, searching Michael's face. "Agreed," the young man said.

"Then it is settled." Wurlitzer rose and went to the doorway. "Lena, come in now," he called, muttered, "Where can she be?" and left the room.

Michael stood at the window, feeling a great sense of triumph, a flush of well-being, a tingle of excitement. He had bagged his Queer Duck, he was sure of it. The bargain had been struck. Not only would he learn what stage illusions were to be discovered, but he was sure that his apprenticeship would lead to other things, through that door he had thought of so often, that baffling, shadowy door that would now swing open for him. The old man had the key; if he kept it hidden, Michael would find it, steal it if necessary, but the door *would* be opened. And behind it lay his entire future. Beyond hocus-pocus, beyond abracadabra. Presto the Great. The Greatest Magician in the World.

He looked out at the street. It seemed alien, different. Inside this room, this building, the theater downstairs, this was the world he wanted to enter. What took place outside the window was for the ordinary, the commonplace, the everyday. For Dazz and Emily and his landlady and his aunts. Here, in this place, dim and smoky and smelling of cabbage, this was the near side of the door. He lifted the lace curtain, held it back from the glass. Directly across the street, at a second-story window, a fat woman was watering some plants. She leaned on the sill, her fleshy arms cushioned by a pillow as she searched for something interesting to observe. Look here, woman, he thought; see me. Presto the Great. See the magic. A dog came and pushed its muzzle under the woman's bosom, and she made room on the cushion. Ordinary dog. Neither noticed him, dog nor woman, they were looking to the corner, where a truck dropped off wired bundles of papers at the newsstand. Ordinary news. But here, behind the glass, in this ordinary room, things would take place, matters would proceed. Here, among the books and papers, the dusk, the shadows, a little night magic.

Steps at the doorway. He turned in profile. The old man came in, followed by the woman, who carried a tray on which were glasses, plates, things to eat, a bottle of wine.

"Now, we must celebrate," the old man was saying. He stepped back to clear the way to the table. Michael turned farther from the window toward the woman called Lena, and their eyes met. Elation shone in his, but hers were sorrowful, pitying, damp with remorse. She held the tray awkwardly, as if she didn't know what to do with it. "Well, Lena," Wurlitzer said briskly, "put it down, can't you?"

She murmured inaudibly and set the laden tray on the table. Then she stood erect, her eyes full on Michael, as Wurlitzer said, "Mr. Michael Hawke has agreed to join our small company, Lena. Welcome him."

She held out her hand, darting her eyes to it as to something she didn't recognize. "Welcome, Mr. Hawke," she said in a weak voice.

"Michael," he said, gently taking her trembling hand.

"Michael," she repeated. "I wish you good luck, Michael." She freed her hand and turned to leave.

"Won't you stay with us?" he asked, surprised.

She faced him once more. "No, you have business matters to discuss, and I have some chores to do. We'll see one another again," she said, and her kind, sad face reminded Michael of the woman in the bus station, the one who had tried in vain to help

him as the men dragged him away. She gave him one last, regretful look and stepped through the doorway.

"Lena will not be always shy," the old man said as he poured
two glasses of crimson wine. "You will get to know her after you
move in," he went on, handing Michael a glass and raising his
own in a toast. "To magic."

Michael stood with his glass raised, too stunned to drink.
"Move in?" he asked in disbelief.

"Of course," Wurlitzer said, as if nothing could be more self-
evident. "Your room is already prepared. I am certain you will
find it quite comfortable."

"But I didn't think—"

"My dear boy, I may require your services at any hour. Do you
wish to renege on our agreement?" The sneer of cold command
had returned to his voice.

"No," Michael stammered, "it's just that I have things to take
care of, my landlady, friends—"

"Your apartment will be no great loss, I think," the old man
said. Then, as if struck by a sudden insight, he continued, "But
you are worried about your little flute player. Is that it?"

Michael looked at the floor, formulating a reply, but the magician anticipated him. "Let me remind you of your purpose, as
you have stated it to me. You say you have ambition. You wish to
rise to the pinnacle of your profession. You wish to learn all I have
to teach, even to my deepest secrets. You are willing, you say, to
do whatever is necessary to accomplish your desires. Do I over-
state the case?"

Michael looked up but could not meet the old man's flaring
eye. "No," he mumbled.

"Therefore," the sepulchral voice went on, "I give you your first
lesson. The path you have chosen requires isolation, discipline,
singleness of purpose. You must withdraw from everything, even
your ordinary self. You must love nothing more than what you
wish to achieve. Before I go—"

"Go where?" Michael interrupted, his thoughts in disorder.

"That is, before I leave the stage," Wurlitzer said irascibly, "before I retire, I will try to convey to you certain things. I will try to
teach you how to raise your mind until it transcends itself, how to

fix it, more intensely than you can now imagine, upon the images you seek to evoke. If your mind is divided, you shall fail. I ask you again: do you wish to cancel our agreement?"

"No," Michael said softly, and then, more firmly: "No."

"Then drink up, my boy," the old man said jovially. "And don't fret. Things of minor importance can always be suitably arranged."

Twenty minutes later, Michael stood on the street, confused and disquieted. He had accomplished his purpose; so why did he feel so uncertain? He *was* willing to do whatever it might take, that much was true enough; so why was he so unwilling to break this news to Emily? He sighed, slouched, straightened his shoulders and began to walk, resolutely, step after step. Steps on the way to becoming the Greatest Magician in the World.

CHAPTER FOURTEEN

Night School

Supine on his new bed, closer than ever to his heart's desire, Michael was nevertheless staring joylessly at a picture on the wall, a framed reproduction of a fresco: *St. Francis Preaching to the Birds*. None of the last forty-eight hours had been very pleasant. His landlady, reconciled without difficulty to the idea of losing him as a tenant, had proved more intransigent during the ensuing negotiations concerning the return of his damage deposit. Dazz had replied to the announcement of Michael's plans with questions about stipends and box-office percentages; Michael's answers left him shaking his head in uncomprehending disapproval, convinced that his friend was making a bad career move. Telling Emily had been, of course, the worst of all. He tried a display of enthusiasm; he had, after all, gone out and gotten exactly what he wanted—but Emily saw through it, right into the uncertainty he knew he must not entertain, and she was quick to pull from him the information he least wanted to give her, that Max had made it clear Michael would not see anyone else for an undetermined period of time.

Her sad, hurt look filled him with guilt, nearly swaying him from his purpose. But she remained silent, as though disdaining to press so cheap an advantage. While he was vowing to keep in touch, indeed to call her as soon as he was settled, her features hardened from dismay into resentment. "Don't make any promises you can't keep," she said bitterly. As he stood by the door, preparing to leave, she kissed him on the mouth, then embraced him tightly, her cheek resting on his shoulder. "You can still walk away from this," she whispered before she let him go.

After that, transferring his few belongings had seemed a relatively painless, though certainly time-consuming, ordeal, and the spacious, attractive room that was his new home had been an agreeable surprise; he was braced for something altogether more monastic, or more menial. Wurlitzer, reading his face, assured him that mortification of the flesh was not a requirement of the magician's discipline. "You were expecting some dreary cell?" he asked sarcastically. "Perhaps your own personal sackcloth? No, no, my boy, it is distracting to be uncomfortable, and I require your concentration. Life brings enough discomfort as it is. Especially," he went on in a musing tone, "to the old—and the ambitious."

Truthful words, Michael thought, as he lay on the tufted chenille bedspread, fatigued by the labors of packing and moving, weary from two nights of restless dreams, convinced he had earned the right to fall asleep at once, yet held back from oblivion for a long, impatient while by the echo of Wurlitzer's voice, the memory of Emily's face.

On another count, the master, as Michael now thought of him, had spoken the unvarnished truth: there was plenty of work to do. Props and equipment were scattered everywhere—in the wings, behind and under the stage, in various storerooms and workshops in the basement—and nearly all of them needed refurbishing or repair: boxes, cabinets, trick tables for various sawing, vanishing, and levitation illusions, safes, cages, chains, ropes, locks, multifarious arrangements of lights, containers and compartments of every description, Chinese linking rings, weapons, cauldrons for magic brews, even a couple of gallows. Wurlitzer had been famous for gruesomely impressive performances in the course of which he appeared to be executed, died on stage, but rose again before the end of the act. There was likewise an incredible array of all sorts of costumes and enough conjuror's gadgets to keep Michael enthralled, and busy, for months.

It was, however, not only the magician's equipment that languished in need of renovation; his act itself, as he freely admitted, was stale, tired, outmoded. Michael was to help him revamp it, to provide fresh ideas and techniques and variations for it, to join in the creative process, to transfuse the magic shows at the Little Cairo Museum of Wonders with his youth, his energy, his enthusiasm and skill. The stage act must improve, beginning almost at once and progressing steadily until, in a few months' time, they reached the immediate goal: a brand-new, scrupulously professional, revived and reinvigorated magical experience—"born-again sorcery," Wurlitzer called it, cackling horribly—for the loyal patrons of the Little Cairo. But this achievement would be as nothing, he averred, mere conjurors' artifices compared to the grandiose spectacle he envisioned for his farewell to the stage. Should their collaboration prosper, should they do well as a team (it was clear to Michael that when the old magician said "we" in this context he meant "you"), then they would begin the even more intense preparations necessary to produce the Grand Finale.

Besides all this manual work, besides the innovating sessions, the solo practices, the rehearsals, besides learning as much as he could about Wurlitzer's equipment and stage repertoire, there was the matter of Michael's training, his magician's education. This took a variety of forms, not one of which failed to surprise him.

Meditation, for example. He was required to sit for at least an hour every day in a strange, pyramidlike structure located in an otherwise empty basement room and there to concentrate the whole power of his mind on . . . nothing. According to the master, nothingness—the pregnant void, nonthinking, nondesiring, nonbeing, consciousness turned inward and so purged, so purified that it no longer distinguished itself—was a mental state devoutly to be wished. Only after he had gained control over his conscious mind could the magician empty it of all images and replace them with the one he required. There was a vast potential in nothingness.

The power of concentration, of self-generated intensity, was one that Michael possessed in a superior degree. Though these exercises left him drained, mentally and physically, he made some interesting and peculiar discoveries while sitting in the pyramid: the attraction of the abyss, for example; and the mind's continuous effort of subversion against itself; and the sounds of his blood, pumping around inside him. He learned there some things he decided would be better kept from Emily, and so a week passed before he called her from the coffee shop across the street.

"Michael," she said, when she heard his hesitant hello. "At last. Are you okay?"

"Sure," he replied. "Just getting settled. There's a lot to do here, and I don't have a phone, so it's hard to call."

"Don't the Wurlitzers have a phone?"

"Yes, but my room is really separate from their apartment, so I don't feel comfortable inviting myself in just to use the phone."

"I see," Emily said. Michael detected a note of resignation in her voice. She'd got the message—I can't call you, you can't call me. "And how is your room?"

"It's fine. It's great, in fact, very comfortable."

"I miss you," she said flatly. "Can't you get away, even for a few minutes? I could come down there."

"I miss you too," Michael replied at once, and as he said it he realized how true it was, how lonely he was already and what a relief it would be to return to being a normal young man again, if for even just a while, to sit down somewhere with Emily, just to talk to her, to see her laugh, to laugh himself. The master was fascinating but seldom amusing. Magic was entertaining for the audience, they gasped and laughed helplessly, laughter with a little nervousness mixed in, but for the magician it wasn't funny. It was work, serious work. He knew that now; it was what he hadn't known before. "But it's impossible," he concluded. He heard Emily's sigh of exasperation explode against his ear. "I just can't yet. Not yet," he added weakly.

"I don't understand, Michael," she said.

"I know you don't," he replied. "You can't. I don't myself. But just be patient, Em, okay? Just bear with me awhile until I figure out what I'm doing here."

"Okay," she said quietly. "Okay. I can do that."

"I've got to go now," he said. "I'll call you again soon."

"All right," she said. "I'll be here. Goodbye, Michael." She hung up.

Michael stood holding the buzzing receiver for several moments, looking out through the coffee-shop window at the building across the street where the master was waiting for him, moving slowly, ponderously among the bits of scenery and machinery backstage, waiting for his student, his unusual, talented, promising student, to whom he would reveal, in time, even his darkest secrets. At this thought, Michael hung up the receiver hurriedly and rushed out into the street.

One day about a week later, Michael was invited for the first time to lunch at the Wurlitzers'. Gratefully abandoning his plan to grab a sandwich and a milkshake across the street, Michael followed the master into the living room. There the old man left him and plodded down the hall to the kitchen; murmurs of conversation barely reached Michael's ears. He glanced around, taking in various items in the cluttered scheme of the room, dwelling briefly on two framed decorations on a wall. One was a monochrome of the Gérard painting, *Napoleon Confronting the Sphinx*. The second, hung below it, was a carefully stitched coat of arms, comprising symbols he thought unlikely for such an emblem, and, below, a motto: ALTERIUS NON SIT QUI SUUS ESSE POTEST.

He sat in a chair and took up a book lying nearby, a selection of essays by Montaigne. The air was stuffy. The room itself was silent, except for the ticking of the clock on the mantelpiece. He thumbed the pages of the book, mostly looking at the titles of the different pieces—"Concerning Solitude"; "Concerning Cannibals"; "That to Philosophize Is to Learn How to Die"—and then he shut his eyes, his hands and arms relaxed. He was trying to envision that "nothingness" that Wurlitzer had described, that vivid, pregnant state of unbeing. He saw pictures printed on the retina of his eye, images, shapes. The face of the Sphinx presented itself. Then the coat of arms with its curious symbols. And the motto. His Latin could hardly be said to exist; something about the "power of oneself," perhaps? Then among the identifiable shapes he was aware of one that swam insistently before him, seeking precedence. He made an effort to evoke it more clearly. Roundish, bright, not precisely a light, but more like the reflection of light, an image he was retaining from normal vision. He tried to concentrate more, to trap its fuller shape or design. It came nearer, then floated away. He attempted to associate the object with others, with his own senses. He had the distinct feeling of thirst, that his mouth was dry and he wanted to drink.

He opened his eyes, looked around, laid the book aside, and got up. He had the feeling he was playing the childhood game of Hotter-Colder, where someone tries to discover an object chosen by the group but unknown to him. He moved from the chair to the table, then to the piano, eventually to the curio cabinet beyond it. He stared at this imposingly handsome piece of furniture; then, scarcely aware of his actions, he turned the key and opened the glass door, his eye roving from object to object on the shelves. Then he saw it: he took it out and held it in his hand. It was suntouched, somehow, and warm, a small silver christening cup with a monogram, much like the one his aunts (one of whom was his godmother) had kept on the mantelpiece over the big living-room fireplace. That cup always reminded him of his parents, perhaps because it was one of the very few visible proofs—outside of his living, growing self—that he had ever been connected to a mother and a father. He was musing now as he held this similar cup, turning it toward the window, letting the spears of light dance around the room. He wondered about the provenance of such a thing. It became his immediate fiction that the cup had once belonged to a child of Wurlitzer and Lena's, one who had died and of whom they never spoke, but who was the source of Lena's secret sorrow. Aware of sudden movement, he turned to see her standing in the doorway, wiping her hands on a dish towel and studying him with her sad blue eyes. When she recognized the object he was holding, her face took on a resigned, knowing smile.

Michael mistook her placidity for forbearance and hastened to explain what had led him to invade her cabinet and finger her bric-a-brac. Lifting the cup toward her as though proffering it, deserted by his usual glib resourcefulness, he managed to stammer out a couple of broken sentences. "I hope you don't mind . . . This looks like . . . something I remember . . . We used to have one like this . . ." His voice trailed off into a mute plea for forgiveness.

Lena bobbed her head slightly. "I'm not surprised," she said benignly, moving closer to him. They stood opposite one another for a moment, their eyes on the little silver cup. Then, by unspoken agreement, the moment ended, and Michael turned to replace the cup in its cabinet. "Will you tell me more about it?" Lena asked quietly. "What does it remind you of, Michael? Why are you drawn to it?"

Her tone, her presence, soothed him, subduing his habitual tendency to obfuscate the details of his past. "After I lost my parents, I lived with my aunts, and they kept the cup from my christening on the mantel over the fireplace. It looked almost exactly like this one. I used to stare at it a lot"—he faltered briefly—"because, because it reminded me of my parents. I guess I thought if I looked at it hard enough I could bring them back."

Lena reached out and took his arm, gently. "Where is it now?" she asked.

"What?" Michael said, confused by the memories that were competing for his attention. "Oh, the cup. I suppose it's still in my aunts' house in Ohio."

"You didn't take it with you when you left?"

"No. It belongs there," he said simply.

"In Ohio," Lena mused. A pause followed, during which she scrutinized Michael's face. Then, in a tone of convinced expectation, she asked, "Did you live in Toledo?"

The very name evoked the most painful memories he possessed, the ones he kept bound and sealed and stowed in a corner of his mind as a criminal might stow in an attic or basement the evidence of his crime. Yet as he looked at Lena's glowing face, a blurred, bright vision pierced those shadowy recesses and floated above them, a vision of a yellow dress and a straw hat and kind, compassionate eyes. "No," he said at last. "I was there once. In the bus station, mostly. But my aunts' house is in the country."

"Once I was in Toledo too," Lena said. "I remember a little boy there. Maybe it was you."

"Maybe," Michael said, and they stood silent for a time, their minds straining to recover the irrecoverable past.

Then, with a start, Lena returned to the present. "We must go," she said. "Lunch is ready, and Max is waiting."

Lunch, simple and delicious, followed what Michael would later come to recognize as a virtually unchanging pattern: Lena sweet, silent, and a little distracted, as though her real business were brooding, and Wurlitzer voluble and mercurial, wielding his conversation according to his mood. On this first occasion, Michael, feeling very hungry and somewhat awkward, did little but chew and listen. After lunch, Wurlitzer stood before one of the bookcases in the living room, selected a small volume, and proposed to Michael that they go down to the theater. As they descended, Michael recognized the book: the *I ching*, the *Book of Changes*. More than once he had seen Emily consult her copy. She used it facetiously, as a kind of party game, declaring it several notches above, say, the horoscopes in *Cosmopolitan*.

A slide show was set up in the theater. Before turning off the lights, the master showed Michael some of the hexagrams in the book. Then he switched on the projector; a form, a specific design, appeared on the screen. Michael recalled it from the series of hexagrams Wurlitzer had just indicated to him. Then the cartridge clicked, the image disappeared and was replaced by a photograph of a box, wooden, with a hinged lid, and bound with an intricately knotted rope. He thought immediately of the Gordian knot. He got the idea at once; the problem was to know the contents of the box by application of the hexagram pattern, which in another moment reappeared on the screen, replacing the box. This was repeated several times, the hexagram, the box, hexagram, box, then both were superimposed together, long enough for the combined image to register; then they again alternated: hexagram, box.

Following the master's specific instruction, Michael waited until the screen went blank, and on the still-lighted rectangle he tried to visualize the recalled image of the hexagram, and when he could trace its outlines clearly in his mind he now imagined the box, mentally outlining its proportions, and clearly envisioning both the rope that bound it and the intricate knot securing it. The wood, the metal hinges, the coarse-fibered rope all appealed to his tactile sense, and these items he easily comprehended in their more elemental substances. But, he realized, the idea was not simply to know the box as a *box*, but to reveal to himself its hidden contents. An imagined box, whose imagined contents he must mentally grasp. Either he must imagine physically opening the box and exposing its contents, or he must imagine his consciousness inside the box and conduct a mental search. It was an exercise requiring the deepest concentration, but the revelations of the box's contents could not be attained without the use of the hexagram image that was the key to the knowing of the box.

Michael had to exhaust himself in many slide sessions, staggering away with his brain as hot as an overloaded circuit, before the day when, Eureka! it happened. It was, upon later reflection, really a simple matter, like forever trying to unlock a door with a set of keys that failed to fit, trying one after the other in frustration, and knowing all the time that none of these keys would do the job, and then being handed the proper key, and how easily it fitted into the lock, how effortlessly it turned, and with what satisfaction he heard the click that signaled its opening . . .

Yet it was not precisely like an opening. It was a going in, an act of entering, the sensation of being present in the box but at the same time standing aloof and removed, seeing himself—or was it only his mind—inside the box. The knot he could never hope to understand, it would require Alexander's sword to solve it, but the hexagram he seemed now to know, to comprehend in all its esoteric meaning. He understood it as he understood a key, and this he could employ in the formidable use it was meant to be put to.

Thus the unknowable became, for how long he could not tell, the knowable. He *knew* the box, he comprehended its "boxness," and he *knew* what it contained. The knot was undone, the ropes slipped aside, the lid lifted, and inside he found, as he now knew he must, another box, exactly like the first, only smaller, this one bound by similar rope gathered into the same hopelessly tangled knot. But the application of the hexagram had worked, and he felt satisfied in the knowledge that the hidden meaning of the box stood revealed to him.

Now he found that he could successfully plan the same experiment in other circumstances, regarding other objects. Choosing various hexagrams, he rigorously applied his newfound ability to imposing them on other imagined forms: a subway entrance, for example, himself standing above, not seeing down into it, but then little by little finding himself able to move from one imagined point to another, to the steps, down them, to the change booth, purchasing tokens, clanking through the turnstile, noting the people waiting, glimpsing newspaper headlines: SECRETARY OF STATE RETURNS TO MIDEAST FOR TALKS, catching fragments of conversation: "An' I says to her, look, I says, you gotta get aholt a yaself," hearing the cry of the train as it slid into the station, the doors opening, and himself getting on, being carried away into darkness.

Downstairs, in the main workshop, there was a black door which, as far as Michael could tell, was the only locked door inside the building. After nearly three weeks of slide sessions, Michael decided to make this door the subject of an experiment.

He made a careful selection of the hexagram he would employ in his endeavor. Having no certain way of determining which one might be the correct one, he indulged himself in a bit of a psychic crapshoot, leaving the choice to fate, or to whatever he imagined might be fate.

Having made his selection, he copied it and taped the copy to the mirror over his bureau, then sat hunched on his bed, back to the wall, eyes fixed on the hexagram. When he could feel its elements like hot lines etched across his eyeballs, he closed his eyes and stamped the image on his brain, opening them again to check for accuracy, then shutting them and reproducing the lines inside his head once more. After he felt certain that he knew the symbol, he undertook the long journey from his third-floor room ("in the attic," as the Wurlitzers said), down the private stairway that both he and his hosts considered an outstanding feature of their arrangement, along the basement passageway into the workroom and from there to the black door. He pulled up a chair and sat staring at this door, forcing his eyes to remain open until they watered, then shutting them and repicturing the door. Open; close. Door; door. He repeated this process several times, then went to the door and felt it with his hands, the metal sheathing, the hasp, the lock. He stuck out his tongue and pressed its tip to the metal, actually tasting it. He leaned against the door, shook it, rattled it, listening to its impermeableness rebuff his desire to penetrate. He slid it the mere half inch it would give on its rollers, listening to the sound. He even sniffed the door: an oily, metallic scent, equally unyielding. At last he returned to his room.

Ignoring the hexagram on the mirror, he sat on the bed and closed his eyes, gently rubbing his temples as the master had demonstrated, bringing into focus the symbol, then his vision of the door, symbol, door, until the two images were clear, the symbol superimposed on the painted metal. He knew enough now to relax and not try to force entry, but to let it happen, a little at a time, not pushing but easing himself into it, and when he felt this ease, accompanied by the knowledge that what he was doing could actually be done, he discovered that though he had no sense of having unfastened the lock it was sprung, the hasp was free, and the door was grating on its track and sliding aside as he moved toward it, and then he stepped through. He took up a pad and pencil and began to write.

This is me, here on the bed. I'm in my room on the bed. I'm here. At the same time I'm in the workshop. The black door isn't locked, it has opened. I'm passing, not through the door but through the opening of the door. I'm in the room. It's not at all as I imagined it. I see that it's a room that isn't a room. There is light, but without light. M's things are here, his papers and books. There's a desk, some chairs, a stool, filing cabinets. A coat stand in one corner. His green coat sweater hangs on a hook. I can smell his pipe tobacco. I will sit here in this chair and experience the room. Why did I imagine it differently? The alchemist's laboratory? It's just a room. I'll sit here and wait.

In the room he sat and waited, while back in his own room he sat on the bed, writing, his consciousness in two places at once. Two trains on parallel tracks. This was now. Was it really now? Or something in the past, or in the future? Had he been here before, or would he come here again at some later time? Being here now

seemed anchorless, lacking reality; he must search for some identifiable marker. A digital clock was on the desk, the aquamarine
glow of its digits incongruous on this venerable and weighty an-
tique, with its rolltop, its rusty drawer handles, its jumble of pi-
geonholes. The last two digits on the clock changed suddenly,
making him jump: 3:30. He checked his wristwatch: 3:30. A.M. or
P.M.? Some papers and drawings lay scattered about the writing
surface of the desk, but the center had been cleared to make way
for a dark velvet cushion, on which an object dully glittered. Two
pious pictures hung above the desk. In one Jesus walked on the
water, in the other he commanded the storm.

Michael moved closer to the desk, closer to the object on the
velvet cushion. As he did so he seemed to pass into a part of the
room where the air was first thinner and colder, then very thin
and very cold. He was aware of his widening eyes, his accelerat-
ing heartbeat, the suddenly intaken breath probing his throat and
lungs with a hundred little icy burrs. The object was drawing
him, and part of its fascination was a steadily increasing component of terror. He stood over the desk, looking down, trying to
bring into focus the frigid glimmering thing on the cushion. It
was smooth and thin and flat, a piece of fired clay, its surface
glazed with bright opaque colors. He stared down at it and saw a
single, stylized eye, heavily outlined in black against an azure
background. He recognized, without surprise, the stolen Eye of
Horus; he was, however, totally unprepared for its effect. It returned but did not meet his helpless gaze, looking through him,
past him, neither beckoning nor encroaching, not even waiting,
simply *there,* the Eye of the inevitable abyss, cosmically indifferent
and cosmically cold. It stared out of nothingness into nothingness; its element was utter negation.

A devastating sense of his own absurd futility occupied Michael's
entire consciousness like a giant wound. He felt himself yielding,
sliding into the abyss, merging with the heatless dark, but a great
cry burst from deep inside him, and the recoil sent him reeling
away from the desk and from the Eye that lay upon it.

The room became darker. He was alone, more alone than ever
before. That is, he *sensed* that he was alone—but he perceived that
he was not. Someone was there with him. Affrighted, he looked

around but saw no one. Nonetheless, someone, something was there. He could see it if he chose; he did not choose, willed himself not to choose. Yet he knew. If he wished, he could turn and see it. By his will, by his magic will, he had the power to choose what he saw; he would not see this. He whirled around suddenly and saw it, over there, hulking in the corner, yet beyond the corner. In the room and out of it. All right, then, he acknowledged its presence but would not look at it.

The whole room had grown cold. He would not look, would leave the room, the exercise was over. All at once his head jerked around and he was staring into the corner, through the corner, into a pair of huge, wild eyes, shot with streaks of bright red blood that vibrated against the bluish pallor of the surrounding skin. He had an impression of immensity, of horns, of infinite alienation. He began to shiver; the pencil snapped sharply in his hand. He rose and tried to leave the room but slipped and fell heavily against the wall, striking his elbow and his head. At once he started flailing and thrashing, desperate to pound his way through the wall and out of the room; in his terror he forgot to breathe, and his blood roared in his brain, demanding oxygen.

He rolled onto his stomach, then rose abruptly to his knees, smashing his head against the underside of the desk. This fresh impact sent him sprawling facedown on the floor, accompanied by a variety of unidentifiable objects that crashed and tinkled around him. He crawled for his life, felt his ankles grasped by a pair of enormous hands, kicked himself free and scrabbled in a frenzy of fear across the floor, rebounding off another solid object, ignoring the gouges in his arms and chest, at last over the grooved threshold to safety. He flipped onto his back and sat up, one hand clutching his knees and the other rubbing his skull, his breath coming in great searing sobs. He was outside the room, his room, and through the doorway he could see St. Francis, calmly exhorting the birds.

Later, when Wurlitzer took to wearing the Eye of Horus on a golden chain around his neck, Michael would shrink from the sight of it as from an icy hand on his spine. Yet the amulet fascinated him, drawing him in as it had drawn him when it lay glimmering on the desk in the room behind the locked black door.

• • •

Meanwhile the master proved a source of both amazement and frustration. First, there was the matter of his health, which as he himself had indicated was not of the best, a fact made obvious by his wan, drawn features, his rattling chest, the occasional, violent cough that sounded like a ghastly intensification of his cackling laugh and often concluded it, his trembling hands, his slightly plodding gait. With his glass eye and the unpredictable clumps of wild gray hair that clung to his bony cranium like grass to a rock, he often seemed ludicrously old and patched together, a run-down mechanism in need of winding to make him go. One of the many mysteries surrounding him was the existence of enormous reserves of energy stored somewhere in that failing frame, and the indefinable plastic resiliency that allowed him to swoop domineeringly into rooms from which he had last been seen exiting, drained and decrepit, as though tottering off to the nearest coffin. Exhausted by long rehearsals, the maestro would retire early, only to reappear the following morning crackling with animation, brisk and imperious, ready to attack the day.

Though seldom in what could be called a conversational mood, he often spoke with stifling fluency on a variety of topics, all of them somehow related to the world of magic and the magician's endeavor. Many of his monologues ended in personal anecdotes or object lessons or sententious generalizations, but Michael soon accepted a certain bumptiousness as part of the old wizard's style, certainly preferable to his flashes of temper or his mordant sarcasm, and listened closely to his words, hoping to find in them the instruction he sought.

Wurlitzer seemed fascinated by the subject of onstage deaths and often spoke of the beautiful Hungarian girl whose accidental demise he had witnessed in a theater in Budapest and of his acquaintance Chung Ling Soo, né William Ellsworth Robinson, who performed his famous Defying the Bullets act for nearly twenty years to great applause, until the evening in London when the shots rang out as usual and the stunned magician, still holding the china plate he used for a "bullet-catcher," collapsed glassy-eyed to the stage, dying in his bloodstained silken robes.

Yet Wurlitzer was in his turn a good listener, producing that circumflex arch of the brow, digesting information, his eye flicking over Michael's attentive features, then away, up, down, or inward to his own nose as if contemplating the long end of it. Any fact he discovered about Michael must be probed, details must be given. How did he sleep, did he dream? Who was Dazz, was he talented? What was Samir like? What had Michael done at his party? What were Michael's plans for Samir's Halloween/birthday party? Could Michael play a musical instrument? Did he enjoy music, attend the opera, ballet, plays? He questioned Michael's use of words or why he had liked such and such a film. In time, the master seemed to be scrutinizing him at every moment, marking everything about him, the sound of his voice, the way he walked, his gestures, even the pattern of his thoughts.

Michael felt plumbed, prodded, analyzed, like a specimen of some sort. The interrogation might come at any moment, and if it seemed that he had said it all, that there was no more of himself to expose, Wurlitzer would find something else, his eye boring into the very depths of the young man's brain. That single, delving orb, Michael thought, had an independent existence of its own: bright, shiny, gem-hard, containing both light and dark, and the extremes of fire and ice (for it could flash intermittently warm or cold), at times opaque, at times fulminating. Like a predator's, it missed little, and it was rarely at rest.

Then there was the peculiar event with the bird. One morning Michael came up to Wurlitzer as he bent over to raise a window sash in the living room, and there was a little bird perched on the sill. Instead of flying away—the natural thing for it to have done—the bird remained stationary, then began to work its head from side to side. The old man stared at it, bringing his face steadily closer, while the bird ceased even the movement of its head and stared back. It remained in the same position, without moving, for some moments after the master had taken his chair and begun talking; then, as if struck by an afterthought, he glanced once at the bird and it winged away.

There was moreover the equally odd business of the group in the movie theater. One afternoon Wurlitzer amazed Michael by suggesting they take a break and go see a film over on Broadway.

There were only a few people in the audience that day—the movie was nearing the end of a long run—but the old man insisted they sit upstairs, in the first row of the balcony. The only other people there, seated behind them, were two couples, fun seekers who from their conversation had driven in from New Jersey and were warming up for a night on the town. From the beginning they were annoying, obscuring the dialogue with rude remarks and inane jokes, as though they were home watching television. Michael twice asked them to be quiet, but they ignored him. He shifted forward in his seat, his ears intent on the soundtrack, and was only half aware that Wurlitzer had leaned back and was muttering a few words to those behind. After a brief period he turned again to the screen, and when Michael peeked over his shoulder the two couples were sitting there in frozen silence. Not another sound was heard from them during the movie. Later, when the lights came up and Wurlitzer rose and shuffled up the aisle, Michael took a good look. Immobile, eyes bugged, mouths agape, the four sat clutching half-eaten candy bars, half-empty popcorn boxes, watery drinks. He watched them from behind for a few moments; they still hadn't moved when he turned away and hastened to catch up with the Great Wurlitzer, who was exiting past the concessions counter and the drink machines.

The greatest mystery, of course, was the old man himself. Undeniably, as a magician he possessed great powers, but his public performances exhibited an erratic unevenness that Michael sometimes found painful to watch. Onstage, Wurlitzer projected an indefinable sense of impending action, of an alarming surprise in store yet continually withheld, some unaccountable obscure immanent force waiting to manifest itself. Whatever it was, it failed to materialize, remaining like the signs of a storm in the distance, hints in the air, breezes stirring, a grumble of thunder, ticks of lightning, but no storm arriving: a false alarm, in other words, a fizzle. In his feats of prestidigitation he was adroit enough, even with his case of the shakes and impaired eyesight, but severely lacking in the style or panache of other older magicians Michael had seen, and compared to Michael himself he was a ham-handed fumbler. The first performances Michael witnessed were most ordinary, merely a conjuror doing tricks, and old ones at that. There were no cleverly conceived stage illusions, none of the breathtaking marvels Michael associated with magicians. He craved a stage peopled with fascinating and theatrically sinister types dressed in outrageous costumes of substance and authenticity; he wanted glitter and glamour and flourish; he conceived of a stage that was another world, bathed in the soft pink glow of footlights. He wanted painted scenery, no matter how old and cracked, something to create mood and evoke atmosphere—the sensuous gardens of the Alhambra, the disciplined fountains of Versailles, a Chinese torture chamber. He wanted mandarins in silver brocades and pretty girls in tights, with parasols; he wanted scarlet drama and black mystery, gilded romance and brilliance, if only on a small scale. And, naturally, he wanted something more . . .

What he got instead was a shoddy stage, stingily furnished and indifferently dressed, carelessly maintained props, neglected lighting, and haphazard costuming. Nothing was defined, nothing was dramatic, nothing was theatrical. When, before long, Michael asked if he might offer a few criticisms, the old man squinted happily. "But of course, my boy," he exclaimed. "I welcome your suggestions. As I have told you, this . . . this insubstantial pageant has grown stale for me. To be sure, I confess I liked it once. There used to be the thrill of capturing and holding an audience, but one becomes bored with it all, one stops caring. I am sick of stage cleverness, of seducing minds so willingly seduced. And my physical equipment, as you see, is running down. There are not many performances left in me, but with your help things will improve. Then, perhaps, I will be able to leave the stage in a blaze of glory. And after that," he added, with a kind of creepy cheer in his voice, "you will be on your own."

One of the many astonishing features of his new life, Michael discovered, was the increased vividness and intensity of his dreams. His dream life had always been fertile, but now it was teeming with lurid images and abrupt scene changes that often overwhelmed him. One night he awoke from a frightening dream to find himself curled around a peacefully sleeping Emily, a position that seemed so natural and so comforting that he lay awake beside her for a long time, trying to recall exactly the content of the troubling dream. Then, without warning, he woke up altogether, Emily was gone, and he was left disoriented, uncertain about everything, even about whether or not he might still be adrift in a dream.

It was 6 A.M., a gray morning, judging from the dim light sifting through his curtained window. Coffee might help resolve the matter. He got up and pulled on his clothes, fumbling with buttons and zippers, still dazed by his dreams. His room seemed unfamiliar; he wanted to get away from it, and on the trip down the stairs the clatter of his shoes against the wood was too loud, nearly deafening, yet he could not make himself slow down or tread more softly. The bright ordinariness of the coffee shop as he approached was a relief to his senses. He was awake after all, in an ordinary world on an ordinary day. There was Jerry behind the counter, already hard at work flipping eggs on the grill, and there was his usual seat at the counter, and there the Formica tables and there the phone on which, if he wanted, he could call anyone. He could call Emily and tell her about his dream.

How long had it been since he had spoken to her? Would she be awake? He glanced away from these questions as he dug a quarter from his pocket and jammed it into the phone. A moment of prestidigitation on the number pad, the sound of bells, and then, presto, like magic, there was her clear, confident hello.

"Emily," he said. "It's Michael."

"Oh, Michael," she said brightly. She wasn't asleep, then. "I think I knew you'd call. I dreamed about you last night."

"What do you know? I dreamed about you too," he said.

"What are you doing?" she asked eagerly. "And why haven't you called? I'd almost convinced myself to forget about you, and then there you were in my dream. And now you call. When will I see you? Can you get away now? Can you come up? We could have breakfast like we used to? I don't have to be at school until nine."

From where he was standing, Michael could see the door to the Little Cairo. And he could hear Emily's soft, expectant breathing through the wires. For a moment he felt his head was being torn apart, yet through his brief panic the serenity of the dream—

Emily sleeping peacefully beside him—steadied him. He turned his back to the theater and said, "Yes. I could. I'll be there in twenty minutes."

"Good," she said. "How do you want your eggs?"

At first everything went well. Emily greeted him enthusiastically, with a hug, a brief, almost sisterly kiss, a quick inspection. "You look different," she said. "Have you lost weight?"

"I don't think so," Michael said. "I eat as much as ever." He followed her into the sunny familiar kitchen; there were flowers as always on the little table, the rich smell of coffee filled the air, and as he pulled out a chair and sat down, he felt he was easing himself into a warm, welcome bath after a long bout of physical exertion. Emily looked terrific. She was bustling at the counter, pouring the coffee into cups, one of which she brought to him, then chopping up peppers and onions. She was talking about school. She'd gotten an unexpected scholarship; it was a real coup. How she had wanted to call Michael to tell him this good news.

"That's great," Michael said, sipping his coffee. "But I'm not surprised. You're a terrific musician."

Then, as she worked, she told him about Dazz and Sami. The portrait was turning into Dazz's life's work. Sami wanted side panels now, full of animals, all the animals of the world, if possible, all admiring Sami. Dazz spent every free minute at the zoo.

As Michael listened he felt how completely cut off he was from the world in which he had once, he admitted, been comfortable and happy. And what had *he* been doing lately, he thought. Well, sometimes he sat in a pyramid and sometimes he scared himself into unconsciousness trying to imagine what was behind a closed door. And sometimes he listened to a mad old man who told him anything was possible.

Without thinking, he reached into his jacket pocket and pulled out the pack of cards that was always there. He split them, fanned them, made them stand up on end. Emily had stopped chopping. She stood watching him, a smile of such delight on her lips that Michael, meeting her eyes over the cards, couldn't help smiling back.

"Do that one I like," she said softly.

Michael laughed. The cards marched together on his palm, then seemed to take a dive off the side of his hand. "The old waterfall," he said. Down went the cards until it seemed they must pour across the floor, then at the last possible second they were, miraculously, all back together in his palm.

"Oh," Emily said. "It's so good to see you. Would you do it again?"

"Sure," he said. "But I've got lots better tricks than that."

"I'll bet you do," she said, as the cards leaped out of Michael's fingers again. "I'll just bet you do."

Later, as they sat together eating the breakfast that Emily had prepared with such ease and care, Michael sensed an unstated question lying on the table between them: would they, at the conclusion of this convivial meal, go off to Emily's bedroom together? Michael toyed with his food, eating slowly as if to postpone that moment when the dishes might be cleared away and they had nothing to do but what they had always done before. Emily chattered about her family, her teachers. It wasn't long before she asked him about his life at the Little Cairo.

"It's great," he said. "But the theater's a mess. Mostly I work in there."

And did Max Wurlitzer really know something about magic that Michael didn't know already?

Michael shifted uneasily in his chair at the mention of his teacher's name. He didn't like to hear it spoken in such a cheerful domestic setting, and it struck him that the master was, at least in his own imagination, associated with shadows, with the dust and confusion of the theater, the overfurnished heavy gloom of Lena's sitting room. He could not say the words that immediately sprang to mind in answer to Emily's question—he knows things that scare me—because he did not, just yet, maybe never, want to let anyone, even Emily, in on the secret of his fear. In part, he thought, because he expected that fear to go away. Knowledge would cast out fear, it always did. It was clear that the master was not afraid of what he knew, though sometimes he seemed weary of it, of knowing it, whatever it was. Michael swallowed a mouthful of coffee, avoiding Emily's candid steady gaze, and said weakly, "Oh, yes. He knows a lot."

"What sorts of things does he know?"

"He knows about the discipline of magic. And how a magician sees the world."

"And how is that?"

"Differently."

"Differently from what?"

Michael chewed a forkful of potatoes. He could see where Emily was leading him, what she was getting at, but he found he didn't really care. "Differently from ordinary people," he said.

"I see," Emily said. "Would you say Max is a happy person?"

Michael frowned. "He's old, he's tired."

"Does he have any friends? Does he see anyone else?"

Michael was annoyed. "No, Emily, I don't think he does. Just his wife, Lena, and me. But I can't say for sure, because I don't watch him every minute of the day and night. Sometimes he goes out at night, but I don't know where he goes, because I don't think it's any of my business, frankly."

"Or mine," Emily said quietly.

"Right," Michael agreed. A moody silence fell between them. It occurred to Michael that in all the time they had known each other, they had never had a real argument.

Emily watched her own fork, which she pushed around in her plate disconsolately, without taking anything. "What do you think he wants with you, Michael?" she asked after a lengthy silence.

"He wants me to help him put on a terrific show, his final show."

"But that's not all."

"Why couldn't that be all?"

"Because if that was all he wanted he wouldn't have gone to so much trouble to get you. He wouldn't have frightened you the way he did with that frog thing, and he wouldn't have followed you around and created all this mystery about who he was and where he was. He would have just come out and asked you."

"He's a magician, a great magician. He doesn't do anything in a straightforward way."

"Well, that's just my point, isn't it? And also, if he didn't want something else, something besides this big show, why would he take you completely away from your friends, why would he forbid you to see anyone?"

"I made that choice, Emily. He told me it would be best, as part of my training, to be completely isolated, so I can concentrate all my energy . . ."

"Does he know you're here now?" she interrupted.

"No."

"Are you going to tell him?"

Michael fell silent. He was angry, he knew, too angry to speak. But he was also silent because he didn't know the answer to the question. He tried to imagine telling the master, in some offhand way, "Well, I had breakfast with Emily this morning," but he couldn't really picture it, it would be too awkward.

Emily set her coffee cup so roughly into the saucer that it made a sharp rapping sound that startled Michael and caused him to shudder. Emily was staring at him grimly. "You look a whole lot like a married man to me," she said. "And I'm starting to feel like the other woman."

"Don't be ridiculous," he replied sharply.

"You have to sneak off to see me, can't say where you've been when you go home." She got up from the table, pushing her chair back, taking up her dishes as she went. "What's the difference?" she concluded.

"You just have to be a little patient," Michael protested. "It won't be forever. I think what I'm doing is important."

"And when will it end, Michael?" she said, her back to him as she lowered the dishes into the sink. Then she turned again and faced him. "And how will it end, how will you know?"

"I'll be a great magician," he said. "That's how I'll know. And you'll know too, when you see me."

She shook her head. "You'll be as devious and deceitful as that old man. That's what I'll see. That's what you want."

Michael dropped his head into his hands. "I'm ambitious," he said. "I have a gift, I want to use it. I've found a magnificent teacher who can show me how to use it. How can I not take advantage of that? I'd be crazy not to try. Why can't you understand that, Emily?"

Emily leaned against the sink, looking down at him; an expression that combined sympathy and irritation furrowed her brow. "If I had a teacher who told me I couldn't see you, Michael," she said evenly, "I'd give up music."

Michael sighed. "It's not the same, Em," he said. "It's just not the same."

"I think you'd better go," she said. Michael roused himself. He felt extraordinarily tired, confused and depressed. "I will," he said. "You're right. But promise me one thing, would you?"

"What is it?" she said.

"Promise me you'll come see me at Sami's party on Halloween. Come and see me and then tell me if you think I'm wasting my time." He got to his feet slowly—like an old man already, he thought—and followed Emily to the door.

"I promise," she said. "I'll be there. But you promise me you'll think about what I've said."

"I will," Michael agreed.

"Get some rest," she said, easing him out the door. She kissed his cheek briefly. She wants to get rid of me, Michael thought. "You look terrible," she said, and with that she closed the door, and Michael turned his steps toward his new life, the one he knew, more and more, he'd had no choice but to enter.

On his trip back downtown from Emily's, Michael wrestled with his feelings and finally subdued them into a manageable sense of annoyance accompanied by a mild headache and the re-iterated conclusion that Emily simply didn't, couldn't under-stand. Her remark about his resemblance to a married man had stung him, and his thoughts returned to it, as one's tongue will seek out repeatedly an aching tooth, accepting increased irrita-tion in exchange for the satisfaction of probing. Finally, as he came up out of the subway to the busy, crowded sidewalk, he dis-missed the matter entirely. If by married she meant committed, she was right, and why shouldn't he be? No one got to be the best at anything without putting ordinary life on hold now and then. If Emily were offered a year-long tour of performances, she'd be off like a shot, and he would encourage her to go, though it would mean a long separation. She was being selfish, and narrow, but in time she would see he was right. As he turned the last corner near the coffee shop, exhilarated by his vision of vindication, he nearly collided with the master, returning at 8:30 A.M. from who knew where.

"It's a pleasant morning to be out and about," the master said. "But I think you should begin your working day with a cup of Lena's coffee. Come with me." Michael nodded; work was exactly what he wanted. Eagerly he followed the master, across the street and up the narrow stairs.

Michael sat in the living room, waiting for his coffee and idly trying to balance a cup on a saucer in the most preposterous way. Wurlitzer entered the room, stepped briskly to the coffee table, and snatched away Michael's expensive toys, one with each hand. "Really, young man," he said in a pathetic voice, sounding to Michael for all the world like one of his vexed aunts. This was certainly a new way of perceiving the master, and he listened with a smile on his lips while Wurlitzer invoked Lena's love for her china. Again, Michael was struck—he had seldom heard (or seen) his mentor consider Lena's feelings. An unusually—how should he say it?—*approachable* mood, he concluded.

"I'm sorry," Michael apologized. "I was daydreaming. Are you having coffee too?"

"I am," Wurlitzer said. "Lena will bring it soon." He took something off the mantelpiece before settling into the wing armchair he favored. "Do you know what this is?" he asked, holding up a pear-shaped earthenware pot, strangely marked, and open at both ends.

"No," Michael answered, turning the thing around in his hand. "What is it?"

"It's an aludel, an alchemist's vessel used in sublimating metals."

"Right," Michael said, smirking. "Lead into gold—what dreamers."

"We do wrong to judge earlier, benighted centuries by our own advanced standards," Wurlitzer pronounced, making a clucking sound.

Michael shifted to a more receptive position, upright but relaxed. The master was getting ready to deliver a lesson, or at least a lecture.

"The alchemist," Wurlitzer went on, "is generally derided, either for his ludicrous greed or his ludicrous science—"

"Or both," Michael interjected.

"Or both," the old man assented. "But what the best of them were trying to do was not to change base metals into valuable ones but to transmute their own personality, to discover the limits of the possible and then transcend them. They were trying real magic."

"What is real magic?" Michael asked at once.

Something almost like a smile of indulgence for Michael's impetuous youth crossed the old man's face. "First of all," he said, "it's a matter of learning to see things differently, as you are doing in the pyramid and our little slide shows. Once you learn that, at certain times it's possible to enter a world—a fantasy world, if you like—where you can do things ordinary people consider mysterious. To the magician, however, they are only clear and natural, because he brings his imagination to bear on the ordinary and makes his fantasy real. Ah, thank you, Lena," he said, looking up as she brought in the coffeepot.

"Thanks, Mrs. Wurlitzer," Michael echoed. Lena smiled at them both and withdrew. The whole family seemed to be in an expansive frame of mind.

In between sips, the old man continued talking. "It is ironic," he mused, "but the magician can go so far along this path that he, like his audience, has difficulty distinguishing reality from illusion." He leaned closer to Michael, and his tones took on more gravity. "How do we know that we are sitting here talking in the real world, and not some dream world, some fantasy? Pinch yourself. Go ahead, pinch."

Michael pinched the back of his hand and looked at the magician.

"Yes, you smile, it is such a natural thing, you feel the irritation of the nerve ends, and by this means you convince yourself that you are alive, that you are here. But what if the next moment you awake as from a dream and discover that all of this was merely illusion? I will tell you a story. A man lives in London, city born and bred, yet all his life he has received intimations of a place he has never visited, a country place, with a river. It is purely imaginary, but he sees it clearly. The river has a particular bend with trees growing at the edge, weeping willows with drooping branches. The trees too seem familiar. At a later period he travels to India, and while walking through the countryside he arrives at a river. He walks some way along it; then he comes to that particular bend with the weeping willows, the scene he has imagined for so long. He seems to fall into a trance beside the river. A light touch awakens him, and he discovers himself to be, not an Englishman at all, but an Indian, and the person who has awakened him is his wife, telling him that an hour ago he had come to the river for water and fallen asleep beside it. Interesting, is it not?" He searched Michael's reaction.

At first he was speechless; the story was so like his dream of Emily that he had the shattering feeling that Wurlitzer could read not just his thoughts but even his dreams. He forced his voice to sound normal. "Very interesting," he said—an understatement.

Wurlitzer nodded archly. "You see the possibilities. Perhaps we are all merely dreaming and may awake at any moment to discover that we are not ourselves as we know ourselves to be, but other selves, leading other lives." He laughed abruptly, harshly. "I offer these facile speculations by way of suggesting to you the power of the imagination, for that is where real magic resides. By allowing the imagination to work, one can work magic. You have surely experienced this already—the imagination of the magician working on the imagination of his audience?" he said, fixing Michael with his single eye.

A vision of himself, squatted down on his haunches like a frog, hopped across Michael's mind. "I think so," he said.

The eye seemed to see the frog too, and its gaze relaxed as though in empathy. "Quite so," the old man said. "And therefore you have felt the power of the magic will. Paracelsus defined magic as the working of spiritual power on the externals of nature. I quarrel only with the word spiritual, because, as you must know, magical power is often physical, a matter of energy and force fields and the like. Perhaps this is merely a semantic quibble; but that power, however it may manifest itself, is rooted in imagination, and it gives the true magician his mastery. His audience believes him, they have no choice; he forces them to believe, he bends them to his will." He pointed to the needlepointed motto under the engraving of Napoleon and the Sphinx. "There is Paracelsus's motto: *Alterius non sit qui suus esse potest:* 'Let him not belong to another who has the power to be his own.' As you develop that power, you will find yourself capable of greater and greater feats."

"Like the frog?" Michael whispered.

The master sighed. "You must study patience, my boy, along with all your other disciplines. It is most important. For now, focus on this: real magic—what ordinary people call miracles—is born out of the imagination, out of the mind; but the mind must be trained. Pulling rabbits out of a hat is nothing. But the rabbits of the mind—those are a different matter entirely. Nevertheless, I have hopes of your success. You are young, healthy, intelligent, energetic, independent. You have no immediate family"—he paused significantly—"and no serious love interest." He paused again, staring at Michael blankly, with no question in his voice or his eye.

Though the effort left him incapable of speech, Michael held the old magician's gaze. Now, certainly, he could not tell him of his early visit to Emily. Why did he feel so guilty?

"Moreover, you are ambitious," the funereal voice was droning on, "and you have demonstrated a certain courage. This is necessary, for if you pursue your chosen path, you may glimpse things that will terrify you. If you haven't already," he added, arching one mocking, quizzical brow, the one over his glass eye. As Michael remained silent, thinking about the room with the black door, Wurlitzer returned to his discourse.

"We—we magicians, I mean—are explorers of terra incognita, like Columbus, obliged to a quest for what most frightens us. Should you draw back from it, from the possibility of whatever exists beyond the possible, you shall remain . . . ordinary, safe, untouched, like the people who pass you on the street, who will never be touched because they have no imagination. You will explore no unknown lands, but you will have peace of mind."

"I don't want peace of mind," Michael heard himself saying.

"I know, my poor boy," the master replied, his voice nearly free from irony. "That is why we are together. You have joined me in a conjuring act, a little hoaxing of the public's desire to be amused. But you still wish, do you not, to join me in a greater undertaking?"

"You know I do," Michael stated flatly.

"Good," the old man said. He pressed his fingertips together and made of them a prop for his chin. "It will be like a trip, a voyage of exploration. And on the way, who knows? We may catch a frog or two."

Sometimes Wurlitzer reminisced colorfully about other conjurors he had known from what he called the Golden Age of Magic: Horace Goldin, the Great Nicola, Cefalu from Italy, Levante from Australia, Sorcar of India, the ersatz Oriental Fu Manchu, and the Americans, Dante, Thurston, Blackstone. He had known them all, the great stage illusionists, sleight-of-handers, coin manipulators, mentalists, quick-changers, the crystal gazers, the mediums, the Chatauqua magicians.

"Did you know Houdini?" Michael asked one day.

"Certainly. A true daredevil. He started small, with cards, as so many do. But he had a great deal of imagination, along with incredible stamina. He even escaped from the stomach of a dead whale, believe it or not."

Michael whistled, trying to imagine the logistics of *that* magical performance. "Escape artists interest me. Did you ever have anything like that in your act?"

"I've made a few escapes in my time," the magician answered wryly.

"But you don't want to do them anymore?" Michael pressed him.

"Not in this life," came the reply, followed by an outburst of raspy cackles.

Michael ignored the master's apparent conviction that he had made a fine joke. "How about the rope trick? Did you ever see that when you were in India?"

"No one has," Wurlitzer snorted scornfully. "It is nonsense, a fairy tale like 'Jack and the Beanstalk' The only thing to remember about the Indian Rope Trick is that at no time since the formation of the Himalayas has there ever been a single report from one reliable witness verifying its execution. Unreliable reports, of course, abound. So who is tricking whom? The one who does the trick, or the one who reports it? It is an absurd world, with many absurd people in it. But some find it difficult to tell the difference between a fakir and a faker, if you catch my meaning. You have heard the stories of Indians walking on coals, have you not? A bed of burning coals, a pair of naked feet, and you have a stunt. The tourists enjoy it vastly, tell their relatives in Keokuk how they saw this fellow walk on fire as if on ice. And how is it done?"

"A trick."

"Not at all. They *do* walk on coals, but they don't feel them. There is no trickery involved. It is done by faith. Not in one's self, you see: in whatever the coal walker calls 'God,' though you and I would not. The faith that moves mountains and brings about other assorted miracles. A good fakir will tell you, 'This will not hurt, believe me,' and drop a hot coal into the palm of your hand, and it will not hurt or leave a blister. But as we know, fire burns, it must; that is its inherent property. Shall I illustrate this for you? Light the candle there."

Michael took the matches, lighted one, and touched it to the candle.

"Draw it to you. Just so. Now, do exactly as I tell you. Do you trust me?"

"Yes."

"You shouldn't." His grating laugh ended in odd sucking sounds, somewhere between wheezes and giggles. "Remember," he said after a few moments, "exactly as I tell you." Michael waited, soberly regarding that single eye. Yes, he would feel some power, some triumph of the will, some transcendence of heat and energy and light. He was ready. "Turn your head, look directly at the flame. Look at it, see it for what it is, nothing more than carbon dioxide in combustion. Now—exactly as I tell you, remember—pass your hand through the flame, slowly, at a distance of perhaps an inch above it."

Bending to gauge the measurement, Michael flatted his hand and moved it above the candle, thus suppressing the convection currents and causing the flame to elongate and draw upwards, where it came into contact with his skin. He cried out, snatched his hand back, and shook it with a resentful grimace.

"It burned!"

"Of course it did. Did anyone say it wouldn't burn?"

"You said—"

"No, the fakir said it wouldn't, not I."

"But you said to trust you."

"Did I? It is amazing how two eyewitness accounts of the same event can differ. In any case, you have learned something. Never trust anybody." He gave Michael a look of complete self-satisfaction.

The young man sucked the burn, feeling the blood rush to his face but trying to stifle his anger. The—he couldn't think of a word—the *caddishness* of the whole thing enraged him. "You owe me one," he boldly said. "When are you going to show me?"

"What should I show you?" Michael did a quick frog pantomime. "Ah, of course, the frog, your bête noire. I must admire your persistence. The matter is not very difficult, really."

"Is it hypnotism?"

"I know little of hypnotism. Mesmer had certain facts to hand regarding magnetic energy, but they have proved mostly fallacious. Perhaps it had nothing to do with me, that little episode. Perhaps it had everything to do with you. You may have had a mystical experience."

"Mysterious, maybe, but mystical, no." Michael reminisced briefly about his hopping spasms and the cannonade of retching by the fountain. "No mystical experience."

"Then what could it have been?" said the master, getting up and bending over him.

Their eyes met. Michael hooked his ankles around the legs of his chair and grasped the edge of the table with both hands. Wurlitzer stooped across him and picked up the matchbox. "I'm sorry, frog-boy," he said sardonically. "No jolly springing about today. Remember: amphibians must be approached from the rear, not from the front."

As the days and weeks passed, Michael's absorption in his new life deepened. His mental and physical exertions, ever more intense, often left him muddled, fatigued, edgy. He was burning, he had no doubt, with a brighter flame, but there were times when he thought it might consume him. His powers, his skills were growing constantly; still, he felt fearful. This fear revolved around that terrifying glimpse Wurlitzer had cautioned him about—the monsters that might bestride his path. Michael had been dared to dare, and in this regard he was no coward; he could dare as well as the next, or better. He had been warned of the abyss; to look down was, the master had suggested, the end of the beginning, but it could be the beginning of the end as well. He had seen demonstrations of real magic, performed before his very eyes; and seeing was believing. As to his own capabilities he was far from sure. Sometimes power surged through him, his eyes burned, his capillaries tingled; sometimes all he felt was a great void. Sometimes he was able to make at least partial sense of what he was feeling and seeing, and sometimes none at all. Looking ahead was frustrating; there seemed nothing beyond but a thick wall whose solid mass he could never hope to penetrate. Lift the veil, the master had said; but Michael wondered how many veils he would have to lift before his progress gave him the capacity to affect anything or anyone other than himself. Meditation, complex mental exercises, boxes within boxes, horror lurking inside locked rooms: what could all that produce besides, at the very best, a headache?

Michael had no doubt that he was being led somewhere, like a horse to water, and being led he was willing enough to drink. Belief, Wurlitzer had said, was not necessary, only the constant performing of the exercises, which through mere repetition would create a force of habit; and from force of habit would come other things. But what things? He was wandering in the dark, through a maze—the labyrinth, Wurlitzer had said—following the slenderest thread, and somewhere in that dark labyrinth lay confrontation. Of what? Theseus had tracked the Minotaur, slain it, followed Ariadne's thread back into the daylight. But what if his, Michael's, thread should break? What if he were left to wander alone down there in the dark, following the turnings of passages that led he knew not where, to discover around every corner some terror . . .

Wurlitzer wanted him to accept terror as a necessary hazard, something to be got through, as a sailor accepts the possibility of violent storms. They were merely conducting an investigation, the master had said, taking a little trip together. The Quest. Its setting was, after all, only the basement of the Little Cairo. Yet that underground expanse held its own mystery, and among those dim corners, those lightless rooms, those unexplored spaces, it was not difficult for the imagination—that was what the master had said: *use the imagination*—to offer itself up to fear; and beyond fear, terror, beyond terror—who knew? The abyss, the old magician had said. But the successful pupil must dare, dare to look, and dare to *do.* There was little Michael would not dare, little he would not do, if, daring and doing, he could find his way upward and outward, through the darkness and into the light. Light meant power, and power meant, among other things, that he could make a man act like a frog. Wurlitzer denied it, but surely the secret lay in some form of hypnotism?

Thus Michael, if he did not proceed headlong, at least proceeded, hesitating and recoiling, by fits and starts, a step forward, two back, day after day. *Piano, piano,* the master had said. It would come. It would. Let it come.

It was after three in the morning. Michael saw the luminous hands of his clock as his eyes came open. He had been asleep, in a deep, dreamless sleep that was his infrequent reward for hours of meditation in the pyramid and interminable rehearsals of magic routines. Awakening, he felt certain that someone was in the room. Somewhere in sleep he had heard sounds, someone moving along the corridor, stealthily, coming toward him, the door swinging inward, someone, something entering. He kept his head on the pillow, not moving; waiting. There was stillness again, yet he knew the door had opened. No sound came; he knew something was there, breathing—although breathing sounds weren't part of it—using the air in the room. He moaned as if still asleep and dreaming, and threw himself across his pillow, angling his arm over his face so he could see around it. Saw darkness, then faint light leaking through the doorway, shadows in the room but nothing in the shadows, nothing casting them. And even as he looked out from under his lashes, seeing nothing, hearing nothing, he felt sleep dragging him back. His eyes closed; he returned to where he had come from, slept. Or thought he did. For, sleeping, he thought he knew still that someone had come into the room. He turned his head, arm still flung across his forehead, and opened his eyes. *Jesus!* It was like looking into a mirror: the eye staring back at him. Close, so close he could touch it without reaching. He must have cried out then, he heard the sound he made, scrambling back to the corner and sitting up in one quick movement, clutching the pillow like a shield, knocking things off the night table, finally turning on the light.

CHAPTER FIFTEEN

All Hallows Eve

Emily hardly recognized him. She'd kept her eyes on the entrance ever since arriving at the party, and she'd watched a steady stream of guests, some of them quite startling, emerge through the brocaded drapery; but none of these apparitions, however strange, had prepared her for the sight of Michael. She watched as he took a few steps and paused, cocking his head slightly as if to concentrate on the swirling Egyptian music that was pouring into the huge room from stereo speakers placed high on the walls. Through the crowd of party guests, she stared at him as if she were staring into a tunnel, heedless of everything but him, scrutinizing him for familiar features, straining to identify the reasons why he seemed so different, so changed. It wasn't just that he had lost weight, nor was it the unhealthy pallor of his face. It was his eyes, febrile, glittering, oddly remote, as though fixed on something only they could see. The eyes of a consumptive, she thought, or maybe a maniac.

Still, as she began to make her way toward him, she had to admit that he looked striking, even beautiful, with his ethereal paleness and his hectic gaze, and something tightened in her chest. Michael's costume, apparently modeled on the impeccable wardrobe of Mandrake the Magician, included a lustrous black dinner jacket, a silk top hat, and a short black velvet cape with a crimson satin lining. Emily groaned inwardly as she recognized behind Michael the tall, unmistakable figure of the Great Wurlitzer, whose formal evening attire, complete with tailcoat, was complemented to particularly sinister effect by a black eyepatch, a large, floppy-brimmed slouch hat, and the black cloak, operatically long, that hung from his shoulders almost to the gleaming uppers of his patent-leather shoes.

The two magicians, young and old, began to move slowly into the thronged room. Clutching her flute with both hands, Emily stepped toward Michael, blocked his path, and waited. Her heart was beating hard, and then at last those feverish eyes, the eyes of a stranger, came to rest on her. She spoke firmly, though perhaps somewhat louder than necessary, "Hello, Michael."

His immediate smile of delighted recognition disarmed her. "Emily," he said, measuring the syllables as though he relished the sound of her name. He moved rapidly to her, and she raised her head to accept his kiss, sagging against him a little as he embraced her. "It's great to see you," he murmured.

"It is?" she asked, genuinely bewildered. "Then why has it been so long?"

Michael's smile turned rueful, but instead of answering he stepped back, opening the space between Emily and Wurlitzer. "Let me introduce you," Michael said. "This is my teacher, Max Wurlitzer." He turned to the master. "I don't believe you've met Emily Chang."

The slouch hat inclined briefly in her direction, and from under its brim came the sepulchral sounds of the old man's voice. "Our paths have crossed," he said.

Emily heard the mockery in his words, perceived the sardonic flickering of his shaded single eye, and a scornful smile spread over her face. "They certainly have," she said. "But this is the first time I've seen you when you weren't in a hurry."

"Indeed?" came the hollow voice. "As a matter of fact, I'm in more of a hurry than ever before." He nodded again, curtly, dismissively, and appeared to shift his attention to a spot beyond her shoulder.

"So who are you?" Michael asked her, looking at her tights, her cape, her huntsman's hat, the flute in her hands. "The Pied Piper of Hamelin?"

"I gave that some thought, but actually I'm Tamino, the prince in *The Magic Flute*." Swiftly raising her instrument to her lips, Emily struck up the opening measures of the melody with which Prince Tamino charms the birds. When she stopped and raised her head, she saw a look of pleased surprise on Michael's face, as though he were delighted to discover that she played the flute. His eyes, however, remained restless, always on the point of turning aside; he seemed to be making a conscious effort to hold them in check, to keep them away from what they really wished to contemplate, so that the effort itself became an object of contemplation. He might as well be wearing dark glasses and a Walkman, she thought. She reached for one of his hands, held it, squeezed it. "I really miss you," she said before she knew it; then, as the words stubbornly remained in the air between them, she added, "And I wonder if you miss me too."

"Of course I do," he said in a weary voice. Despite his pallor, he looked extremely hot, though none of the warmth radiating from his forehead and his eyes reached her. "I told you when we had breakfast. I've got to . . . I can't take my attention away from what I'm doing."

"You mean you don't call me because you're afraid I might, heaven forbid, *distract* you?"

He turned to her with the air of one just back from a long trip. "Isn't that what you want to do?" he asked. There was a time when such a question would have been a defiant joke, a provocation calculated to cause outrage or laughter or, preferably, both, but that time had evidently passed into oblivion. No joking now, no outrageousness, at least none of the deliberate kind. Emily imagined a sign displaying the word IRONY inside a red circle and crossed by a red line. The image brought a smile to her lips, but before she could formulate a response appropriate to Michael's new, humorless state, stentorian Southern tones announced the irruption of Miss Beulah Wales into their midst.

Miss Wales was costumed as a well-fed witch. A broom on an unusually stout stick, obviously designed for heavy loads, was slung like a rifle across her back. "Well, well," she gushed, paddling their hands, "the magic man and his lovely lady. If you two ain't the handsomest couple I've ever seen! Does Sami know you're here?"

"No, we just arrived," Michael said.

Miss Wales seemed perplexed. "That's strange," she said to Emily. "I thought you came in with Dazz, honey."

"I did," Emily said, and felt chagrined by this trivial confusion.

"I meant the two of *us*," Michael explained, pointing first to his own chest and then to Wurlitzer's long, narrow back. The master stood facing away from them, scanning the crowd like a roosting hawk.

Miss Wales, knowing but benevolent, shook her head as she glanced from Emily to Michael. "You two tryin' to make each other jealous?" she asked. Emily found the comment tiresome, though not so tiresome as the hooting giggle that followed it.

"No," Michael answered, having considered the question. "This is my teacher. I'll introduce you." He murmured something Emily couldn't hear and touched Wurlitzer's shoulder.

His black cloak flaring behind him, the master spun around in a single, swooping motion and fixed his sudden eye on Beulah Wales. The leftover mirth vanished from her face as her tiny china-blue eyes widened in fear. Gulping audibly, she took a step backward.

"This is my teacher, Max Wurlitzer," Michael said with a hint of pride. "And this is our host's friend, Miss Beulah Wales," he went on, apparently not noticing her deepening distress. She was now nearly six feet away from Wurlitzer, standing in a kind of huddled crouch with her eyes locked on his face and her mouth resting open atop her pile of chins. Emily watched in amazement the triumph of a proper Southern upbringing over stark terror. Miss Wales quavered, "Pleased to meet you," and held out one plump and dainty hand. For a few seconds it trembled there, exposed and alone, as all four of them stared at it; then Miss Wales snatched it back to the safety of her bosom, said in a stuttering whisper, "I'll go fetch Samir," and fled away toward the elevator.

The look of sovereign contempt on Wurlitzer's face galled Emily. "Don't you think it's warm in here?" Michael said. She couldn't tell which of them he was addressing—perhaps neither, because he answered himself. "I do. Let's go find something cool to drink," he said to them, then turned and led the way through one of the gilded archways.

Emily followed him immediately, not waiting to see if Wurlitzer was joining them, though the erect hairs on the nape of her neck signaled that the old man was right behind her. As they were passing through the milling guests in the next room, she was aware of a sort of release, a slackening of tension, as though the distance between herself and her nemesis had increased, and she turned to see him standing near the elevator and looking at a colorful reproduction of an ancient Egyptian tomb painting, stylized figures in procession through serried ranks of hieroglyphs. Relieved, she stood next to Michael in front of a table in yet another room and asked the uniformed bartender for a large, stiff drink.

"Where's the master?" Michael asked.

"The 'master'?" Emily echoed incredulously. She took a long pull at her drink, not wholly certain that she wasn't about to start screaming. "The *master*, as you call him, is admiring some of the art in the other room." She wagged her hand toward the door they had passed through.

"I'd better go get him," Michael said.

She caught hold of his sleeve. "Are you afraid he'll misbehave?"

"No, it's just that he doesn't know anyone."

"Oh, as for that," Emily said airily, "there's no problem. I'm sure such a charming man makes friends wherever he goes. Michael, when will I see you again? When you left my apartment that morning, I had no idea it would really be this long. And you haven't even called."

She paused and looked at him. He said nothing, but stood looking around nervously.

"At first I was angry," she continued. "I told myself I didn't care, but I couldn't stop thinking of you. I'm worried, Michael. In some ways I'm even scared. When will I see you again?"

His eyes met hers for a second, then seemed to lose focus. "I'm

not sure," he admitted haltingly, like a man confronting a per-
plexing problem.

She released his sleeve, felt equal proportions of sorrow and
anger enter her bloodstream and rise to her face. "How can you
answer me like that?" she asked him. "What's happened to you?"

"Nothing. I mean, of course, a lot has happened, a lot, I told
you"—he drifted away, frowned, came back—"but none of it has
anything to do with you."

"Good. Come spend the night with me and tell me all about it."

He seemed to be doing his best not to writhe. "God, Emily," he
said. "It's not that I don't want to. I just can't . . ."

"Can't what?"

"I can't divide my thoughts," he explained. "I asked you to
wait, to please try to understand. I don't think you realize how serious I am."

"I'm starting to," Emily said. "You're very serious." A distant
commotion served to remind Michael of obligations. He muttered
something unintelligible in Emily's direction and strode hastily to
the open archway that connected the rooms. Lagging several feet
behind him, she observed his solicitous approach to Wurlitzer,
who was still examining Samir's display of Egyptian art.

But it was Samir himself who engaged everyone else's attention. Resplendent in angelic garb, gleaming like a snowcapped
mountain, he had just emerged from the elevator and was accepting birthday felicitations from his guests. His robe was of the
whitest, purest silk, decorated at sleeve and hem with golden
bands; two fluffy pink wings protruded from his shoulder blades;
a halo had somehow been fitted to his fez; and a small golden lyre
hung from his left shoulder on a blue satin cord. Gilbert, sullen as
always, hovered nearby, dressed like a pirate of emphatically
murderous temperament, perhaps one of those Barbary Coast
buccaneers whose intransigent hostility drew the United States
Marines to the shores of Tripoli.

Emily watched as Samir, giggling and waving, parted the
crowd around him, moved to where Michael and Wurlitzer were
standing, and engulfed Michael's slender body in a cushiony embrace. "My dear friend," Samir said excitedly, "I am so glad to see

you. When Boo told me of your arrival, I said to her, 'Now my party can begin.' Have you inspected your equipment?"

"Not closely," Michael replied. "I just saw it from a distance. I'm sure it's all right."

"Your instructions were exactly followed." Samir rubbed his hands together, grinning ecstatically, like a child about to receive a double helping of his favorite dessert. "We will begin the show in half an hour. Meanwhile, consider yourself at home—eat, drink, and feel merry. If you don't see what you want"—he gestured around the premises—"you have but to ask."

"Thank you," Michael said solemnly. Holding his arm out toward the baleful figure at his side, he continued, "Let me introduce you. This is my teacher, Max Wurlitzer. And this is our gracious host, Samir Abdel-Noor."

The old man stepped forward and bowed, touching his fingertips to his forehead, then raised his head and spoke briskly to Samir in an impenetrable language Emily thought sounded like Arabic. Samir started visibly—even Gilbert's ordinarily impassive face registered surprise—but before long, after a squeal of delight, Sami responded with a stream of equally incomprehensible sounds, and soon magician and sybarite, an oddly matched pair, were deep in conversation.

A hand squeezed her shoulder. "The Pearl of the Orient," said Dazz's voice. "What do you think about Magic Breath over there? Looks kinda overwrought to me."

"He looks like his eyeballs are melting," Emily said, "but he hasn't noticed it yet. I'm worried, Dazz. I'm afraid he's really sick."

"Have you talked to him?" They were both watching Michael, who was standing off to one side, raptly contemplating a small empty space about two feet above the master's head.

"Yes. Or at least I tried. I think his body has been taken over by an alien from another galaxy."

Dazz smiled sympathetically. Most of his wardrobe consisted of parts of costumes, but the way he mixed them together always made it difficult to divine the artist's intention, assuming there was one. Tonight's ensemble included a belt made of what looked like feathers, lederhosen, and a World War II aviator's cap with chin strap and earmuffs. "Aliens are my specialty," he said, and quite loudly called Michael's name.

"Dazz," Michael said after a smooth reentry. "How are you?"

"I'm real good, babe," Dazz said as he hugged him. "How about yourself? You get a pass before you left the ward?"

Michael, nonplussed, adjusted his tie. "I feel fine, Dazz. Let me introduce you to my teacher."

Emily sipped a fresh drink and watched Michael and then Dazz speak to Wurlitzer. "Thank you," she heard the old man say, almost civilly, although Emily thought he withdrew his hand a shade too quickly from Dazz's grasp. She was farther away now, screened by several people who had joined the group around Samir, Wurlitzer, and Michael. Emily particularly noticed a honey-blond young woman who carried her large breasts as though aiming them. Her gauzy harem pants and skimpy top offered little obstruction to those who wished to admire her deep tan, and the golden asp on her crown seemed to hiss as Emily stared at it.

Emily was thinking, *How does he reject me? Let me count the ways,* as Michael stepped lightly away from her and glided toward the far wall, where his table and other equipment were set up on a low platform. His show was about to begin. The fact that he had declined her offer to provide musical accompaniment for his performance might have been tolerable in itself—she liked to think she would have borne the rebuff with stoic calm had it been softened by a hint of gratitude or a regretful word—but what rankled was the *way* he had turned her down: "I don't do that kind of magic anymore." Her hands squeezed and twisted her now redundant flute, one more element of his past that Michael was apparently determined to leave behind. Not for the first time this evening, she resisted an impulse to scream.

She sank into a low couch and sought distraction among her fellow guests, where there was plenty of it. People had begun to occupy the chairs that a platoon of white-gloved servants was arranging in rows across the room. A stranger-looking audience could hardly be imagined; many wore costumes more or less traditional to Halloween: witches, warlocks, skeletons, corpses in various stages of decomposition, ghosts, goblins, black cats of both sexes, a pair of jack-o'-lanterns. Others, such as the vampire couple who were kissing passionately despite their formidable fangs, the ingeniously elaborate Headless Horseman, and a surprising muster of swamp monsters, had elected less trite ways to fall in with the general spookiness of the occasion. Still others, including Emily herself, viewed the proceedings as an invitation to let fancy run free, unfettered by conventions. The resulting variety diverted her, held her attention, kept her from unhappy musings. There were, she noticed, a great number of animal costumes—not just the black cats, but also a kangaroo, a gorilla, two bears, several snakes, a cowardly lion, and a wolf in sheep's clothing. But no frogs, she thought. At least not yet.

A tall, cloaked and hooded figure nearby turned slowly in her direction until she could see clearly his disturbing, hollow-eyed, skeleton face, so lifelike, or deathlike, she thought, that it gave her a start. In one hand he held an equally realistic scythe, which, with a nod, as if asking her permission, he leaned against the couch where she sat. Then with both hands he grasped the white seam at his chin and began slowly peeling the rubber mask away. The face that emerged from beneath the skeleton's grim visage was comical, myopic, equine, pale-eyed, and curious. He pushed back the black hood as well, revealing an abundance of thick blond hair. His surprised eyes met Emily's, and he smiled shyly. "This thing is smothering me," he said, flapping the mask in her direction. "I can't breathe."

"It'll be the death of you," Emily said.

He grimaced at her joke. "Do you mind if I sit with you for a moment?" he said. "I'm hiding from Sami."

"Does he want to see you?" she said, moving to make a place beside her.

"He always wants to see me, but he never wants to see me. I'm his doctor." From the folds of his cloak he extended a hand, which Emily took briefly in her own. "John Mortimer," he said.

"I'm Emily Chang," she said.

"Alias Tamino."

"You guessed it," Emily replied gratefully. "Everyone else thinks I'm the Pied Piper."

"I don't think it was a flute the Pied Piper played," Dr. Mortimer said, blinking his fretful eyes at the instrument on her lap. "And certainly not one of that quality."

"Do you play?" Emily asked.

"A little. Not much. Not well." His eyes darted about the room as he spoke. Suddenly he pulled his hood forward and shielded his eyes with one hand, crouching over his knees. "There's Sami," he said. "I just don't want him to see me."

"Is he angry with you?"

"No. But he'll go on at me about this magician, and I don't want to hear it."

"You mean Michael?"

"Is that his name?" Dr. Mortimer straightened up, looking out from under his hand cautiously. "There he goes. He's going up to start the wretched show."

"You're not a fan of magic," Emily observed.

"I'm a fan of science," he said. "I'm the enemy of magic."

"Then you don't believe in Sami's magical cure."

Dr. Mortimer gave a snort of contempt, rolling his eyes back and blowing out his lips in a way that amused Emily, he was so like a big, impatient horse. "An outrage," he complained. "Both the illness and the cure were pure hysteria. And before hysteria science stands with its hands tied."

"Surely what Michael did was harmless enough," Emily protested.

"Oh, do you think so?" Dr. Mortimer replied. "He created a believer, didn't he? A convert. That's never harmless. And here's the result, this ridiculous performance. Watch what happens next, then tell me how harmless it is."

Emily, thinking of Michael's new pallor, his hectic eyes, nodded in agreement. "You're right," she said softly.

Gazing out into the crowd, Dr. Mortimer continued his tirade. "It's like religion, only worse. If it didn't do so much damage, it would be funny. By the way, there's a young man in the front who seems to be trying to get your attention."

Emily followed her companion's gaze to the row of chairs near the stage. She saw Dazz standing on one and waving his arms at her, stiffly, like a semaphoring signalman.

"Excuse me," Emily said. "That's my friend."

"Not at all." Dr. Mortimer smiled at her amiably as she got up from the couch. "I hope we meet again."

Before sitting down in the chair Dazz had secured for her, Emily slowly scanned the odd, expectant assembly once more. No sign of Wurlitzer; was that good or bad?

Michael, looking serene and confident, was sitting apart, in a chair turned toward the audience. His smoldering eyes were narrowly focused now, examining, probing, evaluating the spectators; his whole manner expressed the hauteur of a superior man prepared to astonish the multitude.

"I have to say," Dazz said, "the boy is certainly projecting a more professional image these days. I sure don't miss those shabby pants and that *pathetic* coat."

"I do," Emily murmured, then bit her tongue, for she saw Dazz's pained expression. Objective appraisal of sound marketing techniques meets subjective truckling to myopic sentimentality. She started to explain—maybe even to apologize, though she couldn't think why—but Samir, who was enthroned almost directly in front of them, rose, simpered at the audience, and began to speak.

"My dear friends," he said, and again, "My dear friends," projecting much more forcefully the second time and rising a little on the balls of his feet. Light glinted from his halo. "Thank you for helping me to celebrate my birthday. I always get many memorable birthday gifts, so this time I give all of you something you won't forget. Ladies and gentlemen: here is a superb magician, my friend Presto the Great."

Michael stepped swiftly onto the platform and acknowledged the polite, curious applause by doffing his top hat and sketching a bow. His eyes glistened still more feverishly than before, but his intense, authoritative presence instantly dispelled any impression of weakness.

Five-branched candelabra stood at opposite ends of his magician's table. Reaching inside his hat, he extracted a long candlelighter with a burning taper and quickly lit all ten candles. After he had done so, he looked up and addressed the audience, meanwhile inserting the candlelighter, which had somehow become a long-stemmed rose, into a tall vase on the table.

"Good evening. I thought we would begin with the imagination. Here is a pack of cards." He held up an empty hand, displaying the imaginary deck to the audience, then began to shuffle, all the while continuing a kind of laconic patter and producing, it wasn't clear how, the rustling, whiffling, slapping sounds of real cards. Still shuffling, he moved around to the front of the table. Emily had always found the mere sight of him thrilling; now she found it heart-wrenching, and she gasped a little, as though from a stitch in her side. A soft chorus of similar sounds came from various points in the room. Some women among the standing guests began to mill and fidget.

"Now I am going to ask someone to pick a card," Michael said, but before he got to the end of the sentence Samir was on his feet in front of the platform. "Any card," Michael said to him. "Don't show it to me." Samir plucked an insubstantial card from the fanned-out air above Michael's hands and stood holding it with a look of joyous enchantment on his face. "Now whisper what that card is to someone. Very softly."

Samir, still clutching the imaginary card, stepped a few paces to Miss Wales's chair and whispered briefly in her ear. "Good," said Michael. He pulled a real deck of cards from his hat, broke the seal, and spread the pack out under Samir's nose. "Now put your card back. Thank you. Now, this deck," he continued as he shuffled it, "contains two identical cards: the one you just put into it, and the one that was already there. Look at the cards"—he spread them again so Samir could see them—"and tell me if you see any duplicates."

Samir studied the cards for a few seconds, then gave a shrill shout. "The queen of hearts! The queen of hearts! Look, Boo, there are two of them!" "And what card did he pick, Miss Wales?" asked Michael.

"The queen of hearts, of course."

"Of course," Michael said, and bowed.

He performed several variations on this theme, with a number of different guests, before its cumulative effect began to set in. The imaginary card drawn by the volunteer always appeared in a different way—on the top of the deck, on the bottom of the deck, in the volunteer's purse or pocket. One young woman was sitting prettily on her card; a portly gentleman in a devil's costume watched his flutter down from the ceiling. When one last volunteer found the chosen card in his own wallet, Michael bowed to ringing applause. Emily was impressed, and Dazz, she could tell, was bowled over.

Now Michael was standing in front of the table again, idly shuffling the pack of real cards. "I've been trying to learn how to do this next trick with imaginary cards, but so far I still need real ones." He took two steps forward from the table, turned his back to the audience, and began flicking cards at the candles in the two candelabra, snapping their wicks, extinguishing them in rapid succession. He missed once, in a way that made you think he'd done it on purpose. The last card was still in flight when he whirled and bowed deeply to the audience.

The applause was enthusiastic, if a little stunned. Michael stood behind the table, leaned to the vase, and removed the long-stemmed rose, which was now a candlelighter with a burning taper. As he lit the candles once more, he said, "Lights, please," and the room lights were dimmed by an unseen hand. He replaced the candlelighter, once again a long-stemmed rose, in the vase and doffed his hat to the audience. Back on his head, the hat grew up suddenly to three times its height. He snatched it off and flung it down onto the table, where it shrank to its former size. Another hat appeared at his fingertips; he put it on in place of the first one, but it was too wide and came down over his ears. He snatched this one off in its turn and scaled it into the audience, where the swamp monster who caught it found himself holding a black dunce's cap. Michael thrust out his arms, and a top hat appeared at the fingertips of each hand. The look on his face, Emily thought, was slightly contemptuous, but it changed at once, because someone behind her had risen noisily from his seat and begun shouting.

"This is too much! This is too much! This I cannot tolerate!" The lights became suddenly bright again. It was Wurlitzer, she saw, all the way on the end of a row, about ten back; somehow she had missed him when she looked over the room.

"It's all right, ladies and gentlemen," Michael said sharply, "Mr.

Wurlitzer likes to perform before an audience." He looked at the master and hissed, "Please sit down," through clenched teeth.

"No, I will not sit down! You invade my home, take over my life! And now you steal my act! This show *must* stop!"

"Sit down, old man," Michael said, with a cold hatefulness in his voice that Emily had never heard before. "Your day is over. Senility and magic don't mix."

Wurlitzer sent his chair crashing against the wall, out of his way, and started marching toward the makeshift stage. One hand flashed inside his cloak and reappeared holding a gun. *"This must stop!"* he shouted again.

During this confrontation—Emily and Dazz later estimated that the whole thing took about ninety seconds, from beginning to end—the audience sat as though spellbound. Hardly anyone moved, though a few women screamed. Emily kept thinking dazedly, This doesn't make sense, this doesn't make sense . . .

All at once Samir lurched to his feet and stood in front of the platform, screaming at Wurlitzer in Arabic, wailing the words like a muezzin's prayer. The old man barked an answer, clipped and hoarse, and Samir reeled backward, raising one hand to Michael's table for support. At the same time, Gilbert burst from the group of standing onlookers across the room and began running toward Wurlitzer, howling like a banshee and brandishing a club like a policeman's billy which, though no magician, he had produced from the folds of his clothing.

Michael screamed—Emily wasn't sure to whom—"Don't be a fool!" as the old magician pointed his pistol at Gilbert and fired, sending him spinning and sprawling. Michael yelled, "You lunatic!" and vaulted in one smooth, feline motion over the table. He jerked the long-stemmed rose—it was now a heavy baton with two white tips—out of the vase and threw it at the old man, who swept it clattering against the wall with his free arm and fired three more shots, very close together. The first one struck splinters from the table near Samir's white-knuckled hand; terrified, he did a belly flop onto the platform and crawled behind the hanging tablecloth. The second shot propelled one candelabrum resoundingly to the floor; some guests near the front later claimed they saw the tablecloth catch fire. The third shot shattered the empty vase. The old man was running toward Michael now, only to be met by a barrage of heterogeneous objects—sticks, balls, knives, saucers—that Michael pulled, seemingly out of thin air, and hurled at him with both hands. Wurlitzer stopped and fired again. The impact lifted Michael off his feet, snapping his head like a whiplash and launching him onto the tabletop. He fell on his shoulder blades, flipped himself heels over head, and knelt on the table, smiling broadly, unnaturally. He held this pose for a long time, a maniac's grin frozen on his face and a small, dark lump of something clamped between his teeth. Then he plucked out the object and held it up to the audience. "The bullet, ladies and gentlemen," he said, sprang lazily off the table, and bowed, gesturing toward the master. He too bowed, standing to the left just in front of the platform. Smoke still curled up from the pistol in his hand.

As before, the audience was too stunned to recover quickly into applause. Dazz was the first to begin, followed at once by Miss Wales, and eventually the room was a tumult of clapping, which grew louder as the blur of events became clearer in the memories of those who had witnessed them. Emily, made uneasy in a way she couldn't as yet describe, ventured a little generic applause, though by now Dazz and many others were shouting, stamping, pounding their hands together. Pandemonium broke loose when Samir, like Leporello after the devils have dragged Don Giovanni away from his supper and down to hell, crawled out from behind the tablecloth and looked about him with bewildered eyes.

Emily watched Michael as he stood unruffled, unsurprised, smiling a little, accepting the approval of his audience as though it were an unsatisfactory gift, a shirt the wrong size or a book already on his shelves. Then he held up his hands for quiet and stepped behind the remaining candelabrum. "Lights, please," he said, and all the lights in the room were dimmed. Emily looked around for Wurlitzer, but he was nowhere to be seen; his chair lay where he had flung it. With the candlelight flickering on his face, Michael began to speak in a vibrant, compelling voice, another voice Emily had not heard before.

He talked concisely, eloquently, about the Celtic Halloween and the Christian All Hallows' Eve, and about parallel celebrations on this date in other cultures, such as the Mexican *día de los muertos*, when the dead return briefly to dwell among the living. On this night, he explained, the spirits of the departed seem to hover close by those they loved in life, and it was only fitting for the partygoers to think for a few moments about their own dead. Not, he said, as we normally think of those who have died, with sadness and regret; think of them as though they were alive, present, enjoying life as we are, still loving, still beloved.

As he spoke, the audience subsided and grew quiet. The air in the room was languid with their absolute surrender. His listeners were enraptured by his words, enraptured yet more by the images he called upon them to evoke from their memories and their imaginations. Emily, dazzled and afraid, felt that she too was falling under Michael's spell, she who used to abet the spellbinder. Michael had undergone, she saw, some real transformation; power radiated from him, from his weaving, expressive hands, from the bright pallor of his forehead, from his exalted, effulgent eyes. Emily thought of her grandmother, dead now for a dozen years, who used to braid her hair for her when she was a girl and tell her Chinese fairy tales. She could hear that dear voice now, feel the gentle tugging at her scalp . . .

Christ, he's doing it to *me*, Emily thought, feeling like Mary Magdalene—or Eva Braun. Michael had asked for silence, and the room was utterly still; everyone seemed lost in contemplation. "They are here," Michael said. "They have come to greet you."

A swishing, rushing sound, like the beating of many wings, filled the room, and for a moment Emily saw her grandmother's face beaming at her while with one hand she stroked her hair. Vaguely, she noticed that many of the people around her were on their feet, some gasping, some sobbing; loud smacks, like hearty kisses, could be heard on all sides. Emily clearly recognized Samir's ecstatic voice, shouting, "Syrie! Syrie!" and then the rushing sound came again, louder than before, rising in a crescendo and ceasing abruptly, harshly.

"Lights, please," Michael said in his normal voice, then waited for them to come on, smiled coolly at his stricken audience, and bowed. The applause, when it finally came, was deafening.

Michael held up his hands for silence. Emily stole a glance at

Dazz, who was absently daubing a tearstained cheek with his aviator's cap. Michael began to speak, and she shifted her gaze back to him.

"Ladies and gentlemen, for my final demonstration, I need the assistance of someone in the audience. No, no, thank you," he dissuaded a pair of young women sitting near the front. "I need someone very strong and very brave." His eyes passed swiftly over the onlookers, came to rest on Gilbert, who was standing near the wall, apparently recovered from the effects of the earlier gunfire, but tense, wary, hostile. "Gilbert," Michael said. "Come here."

Gilbert gave him an incredulous look and folded his arms. A long moment of silence was broken by Samir, who struck his hands together and spoke in rapid Arabic. Snake-eyed and reluctant, Gilbert shuffled over and stood in front of the table.

Michael stooped quickly. When he straightened up again, he was holding what appeared to be a large iron weight, shaped like a giant flatiron and fitted with a metal handle. He swung it easily onto the table, where it landed with a shuddering thud. He moved around the table, carelessly picking up the weight as though it were an empty purse, and set it on the floor at Gilbert's feet. "Gilbert," he said, "you are a strong man, a proud man. Show us your strength." With his foot, Michael nudged the weight several inches closer. "Pick it up."

Glaring fiercely all the while, the tall Arab bent down and grasped the handle. A tentative pull, followed by a jerk, failed to budge the weight. Michael sarcastically urged him on; Gilbert straddled the thing, planted his feet, and pulled upwards with both hands. His eyeballs bulged, the veins in his neck swelled, his forearms flexed until they seemed about to burst: the weight did not move. Straining and sweating, locked in combat with an immovable object, Gilbert sank slowly to his knees, still clutching the weight, wrenching it with both hands.

Michael stood over his victim with an exultant, contemptuous smile on his face. A low moan, more like a whine, escaped from Gilbert's lips; he continued to haul on the handle convulsively, but whether he still hoped to raise the weight or simply wished to free his hands no one could tell. His eyes, filled with hatred and fear, were fixed helplessly on his tormentor. Michael laughed out loud, nastily, shockingly. He's *enjoying* this, Emily thought, and could no longer bear to look at his face. At last he said, "That will do. You're not as strong as I hoped," and gave Gilbert a slight push that detached him from the weight and left him sprawled in a sitting position on the floor. "The next time I'll choose a better man." Michael lifted the weight with two fingers, dropped it crashing onto the table, and gave Gilbert one last, disdainful sneer. "That's all for this evening, ladies and gentlemen. Thank you for your attention," Michael said, and stood bowing to the swelling applause.

Dazz was ecstatic, overwhelmed. "I can't believe how good he is," he shouted several times into Emily's ear, a little breathless from his frenzied clapping. "He's gonna make *millions!*"

Her thoughts were blurting at her, all she could do was blurt in turn. "But he's hateful!" she yelled.

"How do you mean, 'hateful'?" Dazz asked.

The applause had finally subsided, replaced by a babel of voices. People were standing in groups, talking excitedly. Michael basked at the center of a large and growing circle of admirers. Emily felt shaky, sad, and her distress increased at the thought that her reaction might be taken for jealousy. She determined to make Dazz understand.

"I mean *hateful*—rude, arrogant, unfeeling. You know he's not really like that."

"That's just part of the act. People like to watch ego displays. He's really good and he knows it. So what?"

"Oh, sure, he's a great magician," Emily admitted, "but it's wrong to use talent like that. He just wants to control people. He reminds me of some tyrant. That old man has ruined him."

"If you ask me, that old man has made him a star. I thought it was a bad move, going to live there, but God was I wrong. We are looking at major earning potential here."

"Terrific. He'll be a *rich* sadistic egomaniac."

"Emily, don't you think you're being a little—"

"No, I don't," she interrupted him. "I know Michael. He hasn't had an easy life, but he's come through it gentle and kindhearted, so far. Maybe a little sad. But he's not this sneering zombie we saw tonight, I know that. I've got to help him."

Dazz rolled his eyes enormously, as though at the hopeless unreason of all womankind. " 'Help,' as in 'bitch at'?"

"As in whatever it takes. I want him back the way he was. I'll beg him to let me play for his shows again. I've got to be with him." She stood up suddenly. "I want him back," she repeated. Ignoring whatever reply Dazz was making, she started pushing her way through the crowd around Michael.

It's that old man, she thought. The Queer Duck. His "master." As she drew closer, a young woman was earnestly confiding to Michael, "I *love* magic. I think I was a shamaness in another life." On his other side, the blond Cleopatra Emily had noticed before, she of the honey-colored hair and heat-seeking breasts, said in a voice heavy with hope, "Do you do hypnosis?"

Emily backed away, unwilling to join this particular chorus. Why not go straight to the root of the problem? Let poor Michael continue his absorbing chat with the former shamaness, or hypnotize Cleopatra until she surrendered her asp; she, Emily, would confront the real cause of her misery, the real villain of the piece. She shoved her way free of the crowd and began searching everywhere for Wurlitzer.

She spotted him, enveloped in his black cloak, his face hidden by his slouch hat, hovering near the Egyptian tomb painting. Taking a deep breath, not at all certain what she meant to say, Emily began to cross the floor to where he stood. Her way was blocked by a smiling, uniformed servant who thrust a silver salver toward her. She took one of the elegantly printed, cream-colored cards that rested on it. The card read:

THE GREAT WURLITZER
(a.k.a. Merlino the Magnificent)

now appearing with

PRESTO THE GREAT

Little Cairo Museum of Wonders
Wednesdays, Saturdays, Sundays
7:30 P.M.

Emily gritted her teeth and approached the forbidding figure. As she did so, Wurlitzer turned and faced her. "Excuse me," she said.

He stood tall, arms extended downward, hands gathering his cloak, condescending to her presence. "Ah, the flautist. You can no longer contain yourself. You must speak."

"You've guessed my secret. Now tell me yours. What have you done to Michael?"

" 'Done'? I'm helping him realize his fine potential, as he desires me to do. Do you not find him improved? The show was not to your taste?"

"That wasn't entertainment, that was abuse. Taking advantage of people."

The old man shook his head, pitying her. "You have too little faith in the young man, my dear."

"Maybe I do, if you mean those tricks work only on the credulous."

"That is indeed what I mean," he said sardonically. From the shadows beneath his hat brim, his bright eye caught and held her. Everything in her body seemed to stop—blood, breath, thought— everything but consciousness, revolving around that eye. Then she was free again, and he was cackling softly. "Only on the credulous, as you say. Yet you must admire his skill. He is a man of great talent, a superior man."

"The superior man seeks knowledge, not power."

"I've always considered the Wisdom of the East overrated."

"All barbarians do."

Wurlitzer nodded gravely, his lips pressed together, as if savoring her riposte. "What is it you want from me, my dear?" he said.

"I want to be able to spend a little time with Michael. I want you to let me work at your theater. You won't have to pay me. I'm pretty good with scenery, I can work on costumes, I can provide musical accompaniment. I just want to be around him. You have nothing to lose, unless you're afraid I'd distract him."

Wurlitzer looked at her the way a chess master looks at the opponent he's about to play blindfolded. "Nothing can distract him now."

"Then he's safe from me. Let me work for you."

"He may have some views on the matter."

"He'll agree if you do."

The old magician pondered for a moment, then bared his teeth in a tight smile. "Why not?" he said. "We can always use a Chinese princess."

CHAPTER SIXTEEN

The Sorcerer's Apprentice

The icy winter winds, becalmed at last, had burnished the air of the city into a transparent, vivifying brightness that seemed to irradiate every object under the sun, and Washington Square was teeming with living things welcoming the arrival of spring. Squirrels chased one another in dizzy spirals up and down the trunks of the quickening trees; pigeons lurched like windup toys along the ground or rose aloft in great flapping flocks; the statue of General Garibaldi commanded a squadron of sparrows; dogs romped and scented, overjoyed by the luxury of unpaved surfaces; a few bold cats, defying the dogs, cadged food or eyed the pigeons. Human beings of every age, size, race, and description loitered on the grass, sat on the benches, strolled about, gathered in groups to laugh or flirt or argue. Panhandlers drifted here and there, demanding, cajoling, or pleading, according to their nature or degree of desperation. A few drug dealers muttered their lists of available wares to anyone who came close enough. Guitars, harmonicas, a lone kazoo added a musical layer to the ambient sounds. Some of the men in the park had removed their shirts, exposing skin unwarmed by the sun for many months; there were even a few young women with bare breasts and defiant eyes. A couple of Frisbees floated lazily in the lucent air.

In the center of the park stood the great circular fountain. For years dormant and unused except as another place to sit and lounge, the fountain had been refurbished and brought back to life at the end of the preceding fall. Today the pump was turned off, but the brimming pool, its water as clear and fresh-looking as if it had just been piped in directly from crystalline springs high in the mountains, lay placid and dazzling in the noonday sun. Many people were sitting on the rim of the pool; occasionally someone reached, dipped, withdrew a hand, then watched the droplets, sparkling like tiny jewels, fall back into the fountain one by one. The great arch, not far away, dominated the scene, imposing, welcoming, somehow whiter than usual.

Michael and Emily strolled toward that gleaming arch on this bright day. Emily was, as usual, a step or two behind Michael, the better to watch him. And that was what she did now, she thought; that was what everybody did who knew him: they watched Michael. There certainly wasn't any way to get close to him, to talk to him, to get his complete attention, though he seemed willing enough and friendly enough. She spent what spare time she had, which was admittedly not much, at his side, in the theater mostly, but sometimes on errands, or even upstairs in Lena's sitting room, drinking coffee, while the old man, whom Emily thought of as a kind of shadow that had fallen over her life, fixed her with his glittering eye, his sardonic smile, and called her "dear Emily" or "our princess." She hated him and he knew it, a fact that seemed to delight him. He knew also that she had to carry the burden of her hatred around in silence, because Michael would not hear a word against his master.

Now and then, when Wurlitzer's imperiousness stretched the limits of endurance, she and Lena exchanged looks of consternation, but that was it. She had given up confiding her fears, her outrage, to Dazz, because he persisted in only one line: Michael had made a great career move. The old man was strange, he agreed, but Michael was a big boy and when he was ready, Wurlitzer would disappear like magic. "Think of him as away at school," Dazz suggested. "Maybe you shouldn't go down there until he graduates."

Another thing she had to keep silent about was the nonexistence of their once active and always exciting sex life. She thought Wurlitzer knew, how could he not? Emily usually came downtown in the afternoons and returned to her apartment alone in the evenings. Michael walked her to the subway, kissed her, thanked her, sent her away. She had not even seen his room, where, presumably, he spent his nights alone. At first she tried to persuade him to come uptown with her, but he refused, gently, always holding out the promise, "not yet." Then she got tired of asking and settled down to waiting and watching. He seemed happy to have her with him most of the time, and she functioned both as an assistant and a liaison to Sami, who was financing the refurbishing of the Little Cairo. But though beside her, Michael was seldom entirely with her; he was always at attention, one ear cocked, waiting for a word from his master, like a dog, she thought, smiling to herself. When he was working he was different, she had to admit, he was amazing. His anxiety seemed to vanish, and he was in total, perfect control of his audience. He looked different, Emily thought, older somehow, and wiser, exuding confidence and an aura of mystery. She found herself watching him, her mouth open, bursting into delighted applause along with the strangers around her.

So she stayed on, fascinated, in spite of her distaste for Wurlitzer, her fear of Michael's obsession, her frustration at the loss of what had been for her an exciting love affair. And full of dread, a step or two behind Michael, she watched him and waited for something, she didn't know what, something to change.

They had come to Fifth Avenue when Michael stopped, turned, and waited to cross the street. Emily said, "Why are we going into the square? I thought we were shopping."

"Well," Michael said, "I don't need to do any shopping." He looked ahead avidly, like a hunter who has spotted a deer, at the crowd milling about in the square. "I thought I'd do some street magic. It's been a long time."

Emily hurried to keep up with him as he dove into the traffic. "What are you going to do? You don't have any of your stuff."

"I don't need 'stuff.' I'll improvise, it's more of a challenge. It'll be like the old days, except . . ."

"Except what?"

He gave her a crafty look. "Except better. There's something I've been wanting to try." They were through the arch now, heading for the fountain; he gave her shoulder a quick pat and strode on ahead.

He quickly reached the fountain, turned around, and faced the arch with his heels touching the concrete basin. He swept the crowd with his gaze, on the alert for that momentary hesitation, that spark of interest or curiosity, that eye contact he used to build an audience. Meanwhile a silver dollar danced on the fingertips of each hand. "It's magic time, ladies and gentlemen," he cried, and began a prodigious demonstration of dexterity, making the coins walk across his knuckles, disappear from one hand and reappear in the other, twirl and spin and flip as though attached to his fingers by invisible wires. People took notice, a crowd started gathering. Public displays in Washington Square Park were commonplace, but free shows that featured such a talented performer were not. Emily watched Michael work the crowd, intriguing the onlookers, astonishing them, pulling silver dollars from their ears or pockets, making a smooth transition to card tricks, some old routines she had seen before, but more refined now, polished, brought to perfection.

Before long, most of the spectators were charmed and delighted. A few raucous young men sitting on the rim of the fountain not far from Michael indulged themselves in some puerile heckling, but the magician ignored them, and his audience was giving him all its attention. Michael was working at a feverish pace, intense, confident, focused, never ceasing to test the crowd, push it, overwhelm it, measuring its susceptibilities, gauging its inclinations, waiting for his moment.

It was provided, as he had hoped it might be, by one of the idle hecklers. After a stage-whispered conference with his friends, this young man rose to his feet and swaggered alongside the curve of the fountain in Michael's direction. Michael was bowing deeply to the applause that followed a breathtaking series of card sleights. As the clapping and whistling died down, the heckler stepped in front of him. "Spare change," he said, holding out a grubby palm.

He was a tall, broad, dull-eyed young man, towering over Michael, crowned by very dark, greasy hair that probably would have been a different color if washed and a Mets cap set backward on his head. The sleeves of his black T-shirt had been ripped off to reveal a pair of meaty shoulders. On the front of the shirt, a half-torn breast pocket flapped above big white letters: I'M STONED. WHAT'S YOUR EXCUSE? His blue jeans were an arrangement of various-sized holes held together by a few frayed pieces of denim.

Michael smiled up at him as though overjoyed at the sight. "Excuse me?" he said solicitously, in the voice of a man who knows he's missed something important.

"I said, 'Spare change,' " the other repeated, thrusting his hand out more emphatically, just under Michael's nose.

"I haven't got any on me," Michael said, and felt his pockets with a regretful air. "But wait"—he reached up and plucked a silver dollar from the young man's scaly ear—"you probably forgot you had this."

The young man tried to snatch the coin, but Michael was quicker, evading the grab and tucking the silver dollar into what was left of his antagonist's shirt pocket. "There you go," Michael said, patting the other's large chest. "Now you won't misplace it again." He turned back to the crowd, ostentatiously shuffling the deck of cards that had reappeared in his palm, leaving the tall young man standing beside him with his hand pressed against his breast pocket as though he were pledging allegiance to the flag. He remained that way for a few seconds, plainly unsure of his next move, then began digging inside his pocket for the silver coin; but the pocket yielded nothing to his fumbling except a few more stitches.

"Hey!" he yelled at Michael, who, apparently oblivious of him, was addressing the audience on the subject of his next trick.

Michael stopped and slowly turned his eyes to the other's face. "Yes?" he said mildly.

"Gimme back my dollar."

"It's in your pocket."

"No it ain't, you took it. Give it back. Now."

Alarmed by the man's mounting belligerence, Emily started making her way through the crowd to Michael. Several members of the audience were annoyed at the interruption and let their feelings be known in ways New Yorkers were especially fond of.

"Screw you!" the man screamed in their direction and took a few threatening steps toward the nearest members of the crowd. His friends were suddenly a lot closer, some glaring, some whooping and egging him on.

"Go for it, Jason!" one of them hollered. "It's Friday the thirteenth!"

"Please, ladies and gentlemen," Michael said in a penetrating voice, raising his hands and gesturing to the audience. "Relax. Everything's all right." He turned again to Jason, who was still hulking obstinately at his side. "I'll tell you what—" Michael began.

"Don't tell me nothin'. Gimme my dollar."

"You can have your dollar if you give us a show."

Jason looked astonished, then suspicious, but his scowl returned at once when one of his friends laughed. "I ain't givin' no show. You give me my money."

Michael's mocking smile clashed with his wheedling tone. "Come on, it won't take long. You seem like a good sport. Why not join the fun? Tell us what your favorite animal is."

"I hate animals," Jason said, eliciting guffaws and high fives from his more exuberant friends.

Michael persisted, negligently raising one hand to the onlookers for patience, the mockery in his smile now coloring his voice. "But suppose you were an animal," he said as though looking at one, "what would you be?"

Emily gasped, then held her breath, suddenly aware of what Michael planned to do.

The crowd was growing restive, as was Jason, who glanced at his grinning, expectant friends. "A big, mean dog," he said.

"Show us," said Michael, folding his arms and appearing to grow taller, bulkier.

Jason threw his head back, opened his mouth, and howled, very lustily, very convincingly: "*Ow-ooooo!*" Some nearby dogs paused in mid-romp and pricked up their ears. The howl lasted a long time; Jason's face was brick red when he stopped. He shook his head savagely and took a step backward. "Hey!" he yelled at Michael. "What was that?"

"You want to be a dog, right?"

Jason shook his head again. "Yes! I mean no!" He stepped closer to Michael, who still stood with his arms folded, unmoving.

"Which is it?" Michael asked imperiously, staring into the young man's eyes.

"I'll be a dog, you'll be a bone," Jason growled.

"You first," Michael said with a sneer. "*Be a dog.*"

At once Jason flung himself to the ground and began to scurry about on his hands and knees, barking and snarling, his tongue hanging out, his eyes fearsome and wild. He nipped at the heels of a few people in the audience, narrowly dodged a kick, backed off with a strangled growl, and loped to the fountain, where he lifted one leg clear of the ground and stood in a three-point stance, looking off into the distance, panting hard. His friends followed him, but he barked fiercely at anyone who approached.

Michael's face was radiant with elation. "Any other volunteers?" he asked the audience. He glanced invitingly at the people nearest him.

A large-breasted, broad-hipped girl with braided hair and big brown eyes said timidly, "I've always thought of myself as feline."

Michael watched the movement of her gum-chewing jaws for a second. "Are you sure you don't mean 'bovine'?" he asked, looking intently into her eyes. "Don't you really want to *be a cow?*"

"Moooo," she replied, her eyes glazed over, and she plodded away, chewing contentedly, to a shady spot where she could scratch her behind against a tree.

People in the by-now large crowd applauded; some laughed nervously, not sure if what they were witnessing was a put-on, something funny or something monstrous.

"Anyone else?" Michael said urgently. "Who's next? Step right up."

"Stop, Michael! Please." Emily approached him. "This is ugly. This is terrible! Please stop."

"Oh, Emily, come on. These people are having fun," he said. "What's the harm?"

A few more people approached him, one by one. A girl wearing a ponytail went clip-clopping off, the bit between her teeth and the reins hanging free. A big gorilla turned away, beating his chest and making threatening displays. A shy-looking turtle crept under a bench, pulled his shirt over his head, and froze.

Then two little boys came up to Michael, brothers, each of them pulling one of their father's hands. "Come on, Dad," the older boy pleaded. "Can we? Can we?" And the father, reluctant, hesitating, uneasy, but not wishing to deny his children the possibility of validating themselves through a life-enriching experience, gave in. "I suppose so," he said with a groan.

"Monkeys!" the brothers shouted together, jumping up and down. "We wanna be monkeys!"

"If you want to be monkeys," Michael said, bending down over the two of them, "then you should just *be monkeys.*"

Off they shot, piping gibberish to one another, heading for a tree with low branches.

Next, three young people, members of three distinct races, stood in a row before him: obviously NYU students, despite the fact that one of them was carrying a book. They couldn't quite make up their minds—they hated to give preferential treatment to any one species over another—so he left them huddled together, bleating sheepishly, and stepped back to admire his work.

He had succeeded. He had penetrated the will of another—of several others—comprehended it, conspired with it to control its owner. Rejoicing in his power as never before, transported by success, Michael raised his arms to the skies like an athlete celebrating a victory. But as he savored his triumph, shaking his clenched fists above his head, happily surveying the misbehaving animals, he noticed something he hadn't foreseen, something strange and wonderful, as if it were a confirmation of the irrestible force of his will: the phenomenon was repeating itself. Transformations were starting to occur unbidden, spreading from one person to another like a contagion.

Over by the fountain, Jason and his friends tumbled together in a desperate, roiling pack, biting and snapping at one another, growling like demons. An amphibious couple, half in and half out of the water, performed a frenzied alligator dance across the rim of the pool. A large black man, sleek and powerful, bellowed a pantherish roar at some young white girls, who fled before him like frightened gazelles. Panhandlers sat on their haunches and begged, with dangling forepaws and lolling tongues. A kangaroo family leaped about wildly; the terrified baby bounced and jolted in the pouch slung across its father's chest.

Michael stood at the center of all this whirling action, his exultation gradually changing to alarm. The park was literally turning into a zoo—but where was the keeper? He saw what was apparently a bull, thick-necked, heavy-shouldered, red-eyed, snorting furiously and pawing the ground. Michael moved toward him, speaking all the while: "Stop! That's enough! *Be a man!* Stop! It's over!" But the bull lowered his head and charged, forcing Michael to jump aside in order to avoid being gored. His eye caught Emily's; she was kneeling on the ground, sitting on her heels with her hands on her thighs, rapt in utter amazement. From the welter of emotions inside her, one was beginning to emerge and dominate: fear. Michael gestured helplessly and had time to shout "I can't" before the thunder of hooves announced the bull's return charge and he once again had to dive out of harm's way.

A pretty woman lay on her side on the ground, suckling a baby at her breast; both of them were purring loudly. Michael tried to speak to the mother, but she hissed at him and scratched his outstretched hand. He straightened up and turned away, only to confront penguins on the march, a group of eight all dressed in black and white and waddling in a column toward the fountain. Michael stood in front of one teenaged girl, grabbed her shoulders and yelled for her to stop, but her terror-stricken eyes looked through him and he released her to waddle on. He clapped his hands to his temples, felt his sweat-drenched hair, and covered his eyes.

When he removed his hands, three representatives of the New York Police Department were bearing down on him. "What the hell's goin' on?" one of them demanded roughly.

Michael managed a weak smile. "It's a jungle out here," he said.

"You tellin' me," the cop replied, bared his teeth, and charged yipping at a couple of black cats, one male and one female, who were mating frantically beside a bench, yowling and screeching in concert. The other two officers began to chase one another around the fountain, barking furiously.

The whole park was an uproar, uncontrolled bedlam, paradise inverted; these were the beasts of the apocalypse, chaos was come again. Violence and pain were everywhere, people were bleeding from bites and scratches. Every now and then an animal emerged from the tumult and presented itself to Michael, as though seeking help or instructions, sometimes pleading inarticulately, half-human, half-feral faces twisted by agony and terror. But soon they would gallop, trot, bound, crawl, slink, slouch, creep, leap, or bolt away, back on their driven, unfathomable rounds. Most of the animals were quite ready to be humans again, but something prevented them, something unimaginable. This wasn't a trick. This wasn't a game. Something was wrong—enough of their faculties were intact to tell them that. Panic was spreading among them.

Panic gripped Michael's heart too, as the full realization of his powerlessness to undo what he had done came over him. He gasped as a frog hopped past him, eyes bulging, thighs pumping; "Rrib-it, Rrib-it," said the frog, and plunged into the fountain.

Michael sprinted after him. The pool was a foaming, seething turmoil of splashing water and thrashing animals. Many were vomiting, several were struggling for air as though drowning. Horrified, gagging, Michael started pulling animals bodily out of the pool.

Emily was still on her knees, too dismayed and frightened to move; she was conscious only of mortal danger and of her will to survive it. She put her hands on the ground, trembling to the marrow of her bones, the hairs on the nape of her neck standing up like fur. She had become pure instinct, a small machine that processed sensory information and acted upon it without reflection. Her nostrils dilated as she sniffed the air, and then the fear finally propelled her to her feet and she was running fast, fast as a vixen; she felt the wind sting her eyes as she darted to the arch, through the arch, across the street—her instinct identified the honking, squealing cars as a lesser danger than what was going on in the park—until she came to a sudden, joint-rending stop and found herself, her conscious, human self, looking up into Wurlitzer's disdainful single eye.

"Tally-ho, my dear," he said merrily as he shuffled past her. She leaned breathless against a building, watched him cross the street and pass under the arch.

Michael was in the fountain, standing in the now filthy water and hauling two drowning ducks by their collars to the side of the pool. With mighty heaves he draped first one and then the other over the rim. He was crying now, shattered, desperate; one of the ducks, quacking insanely, slid back into the water, and Michael began to slap and buffet him. Pausing for breath, he looked toward the arch and saw the lean somber figure of his master standing under it, arms akimbo, calmly pondering the shambles before him. Then, still looking around thoughtfully, he threaded his way between two rampant lions, past a suffocating python, a herd, and a couple of packs, toward the fountain. Halfway along he finally looked directly at Michael, who stood dripping and cringing in the pool, each hand propping up a draped, heaving, weakly quacking duck.

The master was near enough to speak. Fierce laughter glinted in his eye as he said, "Saint Francis preaching to the birds, I presume?" Then he lifted his chin, raised his arms, and shifting slowly from his hips turned from left to right as if taking his unheeding audience into his strong embrace.

The uproar subsided, ceased. All through the park, the cries of raging animals gave way to human groans, human coughing, human lamentation.

The master somewhat gingerly helped Michael out of the pool, then pulled out a handkerchief and, with a grimace of distaste, wiped his hands. "A little learning is a dangerous thing," he quoted. He stopped, glowered, seemed to expect a reply.

None came. Michael hung his head and plucked debris from his drenched clothing.

"A truly abominable display," the master went on, "the inevitable result when imperfect knowledge joins forces with presumption."

Unable to meet the master's eye, Michael remained silent, save for his rattling chest and compulsive sniffling. The tears came again, and when his eyes were blinded by them he felt capable of looking up. "I'm sorry," he quavered.

"As well you might be," the master said, but his voice was softer, and Michael's blurred vision registered what might have been an avuncular smile. "On the other hand," he concluded, gesturing vaguely toward their surroundings, "I must observe that you're making good progress. Your technical abilities are quite, how shall I say it"—he contemplated the erstwhile kangaroo family, who lay together in a tight clutch on the pavement nearby— "impressive."

The master paused, and both of them considered for a time the pitiful spectacle of the park. The dozens of people still in the fountain clung wearily to its rim, wheezing and choking, too dazed, too exhausted to recapitulate evolutionary history by dragging themselves out of the primeval slime and onto dry land. Elsewhere, the ground was littered like a battlefield with bodies—some writhing, some twitching, some flat on their backs, gazing confusedly at the bright sky, the emerging leaves of the trees. Only Michael and the master, of all the bipedal primate mammals in Washington Square Park, stood erect.

Sirens wailed, jarring discordantly with the keening of the former animals. The master bestirred himself, made the negligent hand movement Michael had come to recognize as his manner of bidding farewell, and took a few steps toward the arch. He turned once and said in his most sepulchral, most sardonic tones, "A little more discipline, and who knows what you may be capable of." Then he made his departure, moving with that odd, shuffling gait, leaving Michael alone among the wreckage he had made, shaken, devastated, covered with shame.

And exhilarated.

CHAPTER SEVENTEEN

Come into My Parlor

"So if I step inside, will I disappear?" Emily asked, eyeing the open Chinese cabinet.

"Not unless you want to," Lena answered with a smile.

They were backstage, readying props and equipment for the imminent and much-heralded reopening of the Little Cairo Museum of Wonders. This event, eagerly awaited by a public whose numbers had steadily increased during the six months of Michael's association with Wurlitzer, promised to do justice, and more than justice, to the spectacular metamorphosis that the theater itself was undergoing. Nearly a month of renovations had transformed the old place, and at least on its newly glistening surfaces (whatever might have been the case in its more hidden recesses), nothing dingy or shabby remained. Fresh smells pervaded the auditorium and offstage areas—paint, varnish, polish, virgin upholstery, disinfectant soap, filtered circulating air.

The most satisfying result of Emily's partially successful attempt to attach herself to the tiny troupe at the Little Cairo had been her growing intimacy with Lena. Despite large disparities in their ages and outlooks, the two women were sympathetic, compatible, mutually appreciative, each having tacitly recognized the other as a fellow passenger on the same strange boat. Now Lena was padding about in her curled Turkish slippers, folding costumes, checking mechanisms, oiling hinges and grooves, adjusting screens. Emily, fascinated as always by the cabinet, was not being much help.

"Let's see," Lena said, furrowing her brow. "They want different wands. Where are we putting the wands?"

"Magic wands," Emily declaimed, as though reciting a lesson. "Small Storeroom Number One. Hanging on the back wall in some kind of quiver."

"Thank you, dear," Lena said as she shuffled across the gleaming floor to S.S. #1. "I wish I had a memory like yours."

She returned at the same pace, wands in hand. Emily was still examining the Chinese cabinet, pulling the sliding screen inside back and forth on its track. "I love this thing," she said. "Michael told me I'll get to disappear in it at the big performance."

"I know it works," Lena said. "But I don't really know how."

"Where did it come from?" Emily asked. She was half inside the cabinet, feeling along the shifting slats in the floor. "Is it really Chinese?"

Lena stood watching her; an apprehensive smile flickered at the corners of her mouth. "I don't know that either," she said. "It could be. Max has had it for as long as I've known him."

Emily came out of the cabinet, snapping the double doors closed behind her. "And how long is that exactly, if you don't mind my asking?"

"Oh, a long time, I'm afraid. Over forty years now."

"So you were both very young when you met."

"I was young," Lena said, looking wistful. "And very naive. But Max was . . . well, Max has always been as he is now."

"He was always old?"

Lena nodded pensively. "Yes, in a way, I think he was."

"So how old is he now?"

"I don't know," Lena replied. "I've never asked. It never seemed important. Max is a special man, with special gifts. I recognized that at once. I never cared about his age."

"I guess his sweet temper keeps him going," Emily said. She

smiled at Lena's mildly reproachful look. "Did you meet in New York?"

"Yes. I was just a girl, but I used to go from town to town giving psychic demonstrations. When I came to New York, I met Max Wurlitzer."

"What's a psychic demonstration?" Emily asked.

"Oh, you know, spirit writing, contacts with the astral plane, that sort of thing. I traveled by bus. I started in Seattle and made my way east on Greyhound buses. Max called it 'Spiritualism on Wheels.' "

"And he came to one of your demonstrations?"

"Yes," Lena said, gazing off into the wings of the stage as if she saw herself, young, impressionable, but talented and very willing to take advantage of her own peculiar, unexpected abilities. "Yes, that was how we met. When I saw him enter the room, I felt a shock"—she touched her breastbone, then her forehead—"here and here, a bolt, like electricity, and I saw a queer blue light around him. I knew then we would not part."

Emily looked skeptical. The idea of Wurlitzer inspiring anything but a visceral distaste strained her credulity. "Was he trying to contact a departed loved one?" she asked.

"No." Lena's dreamy gaze went hard and she looked away from her imaginary scene, turning to Emily. "No. He was looking for an apprentice. Or so he said. He may only have been looking for me."

Emily raised her eyebrows. "You mean he's been looking for an apprentice for forty years?"

"There was another one," Lena said. "A long time ago." She looked about the room nervously, then continued. "But that didn't work out."

Not surprising, Emily thought, given the questionable charms of Max Wurlitzer, that he should find only one other dupe as susceptible as poor Michael in a lifetime of searching. Only the other one had the sense to get out. To banish these thoughts, which she knew she couldn't share with Lena, she took up a set of Chinese linking rings and began twisting them this way and that. "I'm going to figure these things out if it kills me," she muttered. Lena busied herself arranging the quick-change costumes, while Emily continued to struggle with the rings. But they remained as they were, cold, glinting, inseparable. At last she gave up, and the two women passed through the wings. After Lena had switched on the houselights, they stood on the stage.

Everything was clean and bright, polished and painted, rejuvenated and revamped. The seats, burnished wood, elegantly appointed with maroon velvet upholstery, arranged in perfectly symmetrical rows, waited with an air of stately expectancy, as though serene in the knowledge that soon they would bear witness to momentous events. Emily and Lena turned to face the painted fire curtain, a minor masterpiece of restoration carried out by Dazz in accordance with Wurlitzer's explicitly detailed instructions: a Nile scene, as before, but richer in detail, more robust in execution, its vivid colors vibrant and shimmering in the refracted light. Above the pyramid, exactly at the focal point of the composition, an Eye of Horus projected into the empty house its blank, inhuman stare.

Emily bridled at the sight of it. "That wasn't there before, was it?" she asked, pointing at the Eye.

"No. Max asked your friend to add it. He did a wonderful job," Lena replied, then lapsed into silence as she admired the play of shape and color.

Emily stepped closer and scrutinized the disembodied orb. "It looks just like that piece of slate Max wears around his neck," she announced.

"It's not slate, it's earthenware," Lena murmured, adding suddenly, in an unnaturally bright voice, "Would you like to come upstairs for a cup of coffee?"

Emily was not distracted from her confrontation with the Eye. "Why does he wear it all the time?" she asked harshly.

Lena began to shift her weight from one foot to the other, launching herself into the swaying motion that meant she was uncomfortable. "It's a kind of magician's amulet," she answered with reluctance. "He says it increases his power."

Emily sighed. "I suppose we're lucky it's not a voodoo doll." She turned away from the curtain and faced Lena, who was by now listing perilously to either side. "It's almost obscene, the way he keeps stroking it," Emily burst out. "I think he even talks to it.

And it's so valuable. If someone who knows where he got it ever sees it, he could get locked up."

At these words Lena's head jerked back and she stood stock-still, regarding Emily with horrified, beseeching eyes.

Emily laughed softly and gave Lena's arm a gentle shake. "Don't worry," she reassured her. "I'm not going to turn him in, even though I should." She chuckled again as Lena's eyes grew even wider. "Come on, Lena," she said. "You think I don't know Max stole that thing from the museum? I figured that out the day it happened. So did Michael. But what I want to know is, what's he doing with it? Why is it so important?"

Lena considered her answer carefully. "Well, I think it has something to do with Max's farewell show . . ."

"The famous Grand Finale. What's an amulet got to do with that?"

"Can't we go backstage?" Lena said weakly. "I want to sit down."

They passed through the wings in silence and settled backstage, side by side, in two thronelike chairs that Max and Michael used in some of their more relaxed—or more magisterial—routines. Emily waited for Lena to raise her head, then pressed relentlessly on. "Now tell me about the Eye."

"I really don't know much. Max wants to pass it on to Michael as some sort of symbol, like passing a torch."

"He doesn't treat it like something he intends to give away."

"He plans to give everything away, I think," Lena said. "That's what worries me. He talks about it all the time—quitting the scene, leaving everything behind, saying his last goodbye. But he doesn't talk about what he's going to do afterward." Lena's voice trailed off into a whisper. "Sometimes he sounds as though he's making plans to die . . ."

Emily remained quiet, brooding on her throne, going over Lena's remarks, the story of how she met Max, his fascination with the Eye of Horus, his preoccupation with death, his Grand Finale, at which he planned to make both a glorious comeback and a permanent departure from the stage. Why was he doing it, why bother? He wasn't famous anymore; only magic fanatics like

Michael had even heard of the Great Wurlitzer. People would be coming to the show to see Michael, not the mad old has-been who purported to be his master. "The master," Emily said, imitating Michael's breathless, almost girlish tone when he spoke of Wurlitzer. She glanced at Lena, who was sunk deep into her throne, looking, Emily thought, miserable and cold. "Are you tired?" she asked. "Do you want to go upstairs now?"

"I am," Lena replied. "But it's more than that. I have something I feel I should tell you, though Max would be angry at me if he knew."

"I won't tell him," Emily said. "What is it?"

"It's about the other apprentice. It was a long time ago. He was a very talented young man, very intelligent and earnest."

"Yes," Emily said. "Like Michael. But he didn't get on with Max?"

"No. It wasn't that." Lena paused, looking hesitantly at Emily, who detected something in her voice that wasn't weariness but fear; and, as Emily recognized it, that fear suddenly gripped her like a cord pulled tight across her chest.

"What happened to him?" she asked softly.

"He was killed," Lena said. She leaned on the arm of her chair and rubbed her eyes with one hand. "It was an accident. It was onstage, during a performance."

"Jesus Christ," Emily said, through clenched teeth. "How did it happen?"

"Oh, I don't know. I don't know," Lena protested. "There was an inquest, of course. Max was exonerated entirely."

Emily got to her feet shakily, then fell to her knees before the older woman, reaching up to take her hands in her own. "But it was his fault, wasn't it?"

"Oh, no," Lena said. "No. That couldn't be true."

"But it was," Emily insisted.

"Max was devastated," Lena replied. "He blamed himself, but it wasn't his fault."

Emily frowned, bowing her head. She had to tell Michael.

"He didn't perform again for years," Lena continued. "He couldn't bear it. He said, more than once, 'It should have been me.' "

• • •

Emily, wild with impatience, jumped up when Michael entered the coffee shop across from the Little Cairo. These days, it seemed, she had to make appointments with him in order to see him at all, and she couldn't wait to speak to him, hardly pausing to respond to his maddeningly friendly greeting and affectionate kiss.

"Michael," she began at once, "Lena told me something horrible this evening."

"Oh?" he said, absently stroking her arm. It was a way he had adopted with her in recent months, a means of placating her, appeasing her, calming her down; he could do it and seem attentive without actually giving his full attention to whatever she was saying. "What did Lena tell you?"

"She told me the old man's last assistant was killed in an accident—onstage."

The slow stroking continued at exactly the same rate. "Yes, I know all about that," he said in a voice without affect. "A freak accident." He paused and thought for a minute, his eyes on the small laminated menu that was wedged between the sugar jar and the paper-napkin dispenser. "I believe I'll have some iced tea for a change. How's school?"

"Michael," Emily said, "the last person who did what you're doing with that weird old man died doing it. Don't you see you're in danger?"

He was patting her hand now. "That was a long time ago, Emily. And the guy who died wasn't nearly as good as I am. Don't worry about me."

"I worry about you all the time," she said bitterly, moving her hands out of his reach. "I've worried about you since the first moment you set eyes on him. And I'm not alone; Lena's concerned about you too."

"Why? Things couldn't be better. People can't wait for the theater to open again. And the master's farewell show is going to be—I can't describe it—it's going to be the most amazing magic show anyone's ever seen. Well, you'll see when we start working on it."

"Michael, I'm afraid to start working on it. Lena says Max is acting strangely, not eating, talking about death all the time. And his fixation on that Egyptian thing he stole is just sick."

"Well, it's true he seems preoccupied with death." Michael paused, contemplating this minor disloyalty, then went on. "He's kind of morbid these days. To tell you the truth, I'm a little worried about *him*. He's the one you ought to be concerned about, not me." He stopped abruptly, failed to respond or even react to Emily's snort. She followed the direction of his gaze, and the two of them watched the lean, somber, sidling figure of Wurlitzer as his peculiar gait took him past the window of the coffee shop.

Michael, his eyes fixed as though magnetized on the master's retreating figure, his expression a study in perplexed foreboding, rose suddenly to his feet. "What's he doing out at this time of night? He told me he was dead tired." Without looking at Emily, he said to her, "Sorry. I've got to go," and rushed out into the street.

Ahead of him, chin to chest, shoulders hunched, and lofting the big black umbrella over his head—a thick, persistent drizzle had started to fall—the master shuffled along the wet sidewalk. He wore rubbers over his patent-leather shoes, an old coat, and a velour slouch hat. Michael saw him cross to the southeast corner of the street and slow down; his umbrella angled to the side, and his head swung around, the glass eye flashing in the light from the streetlamp. Then he continued on, heading toward Fifth Avenue.

Emily came out of the coffee shop behind Michael just as he began to run, sprinting out into the traffic, ignoring her call, the angry horns, darting across the street, intent on closing the gap. When he was satisfied that he had the tall, lean figure within following distance, he slowed down, keeping to the doorways so he could duck should the old man turn around again.

Wurlitzer was moving now with a more rapid, more purposeful stride; as he gradually came upright, all trace of shuffling, all suggestion of infirmity, disappeared. A cab passed, its tires slickly pinwheeling the wet from the pavement, then another; he made no move to hail them, merely quickening his steps. The shiny black tar reflected in a melting blue the garish reds, yellows, greens of flickering neon signs. The umbrella bobbed overhead, deflecting the steady rain, as he moved diagonally across the city in a series of long straight stretches and abrupt turns. Past Union Square, close to the river, he turned right on a dark street where drunks lurched in doorways, helpless against the increasingly heavy rain. At the next corner, without slackening his pace, he turned again.

Michael, squinting past the dripping hood of his jacket as he turned the corner, was sure the master would have disappeared, but no, the umbrella was there, up ahead. Halfway down the block it slowed, paused. Two figures emerged from the shadows, and their umbrellas came together with the master's in a brief and (Michael thought) sinister conversation. A dim light glimmered above a doorway where the three—one of them was a woman—gathered, and a hand went out to ring a doorbell. The door opened immediately, they went in, the door closed behind them.

Michael hurried from the corner, lengthening his stride until he came abreast of the entrance. A small brass plate discreetly identified the place: the Urban Clement Funeral Parlor. Michael frowned, backed to the curb, and looked over the façade. The door, a single curtained window, nothing else. He caught sight of movement at the corner and looked to see another figure approaching. Michael quickly crossed the street and trotted down a low flight of steps into a deserted archway, where he could watch without being observed.

The figure directly approached the door, rang, collapsed his umbrella, and shook it. He was admitted at once, and the door closed again. Its chipped green enamel glinted slickly, wet beads runneling the panels, and, as Michael continued to watch, during the ensuing quarter of an hour it opened three more times. When Michael saw a woman in a raincoat approach along the sidewalk on his side of the street and stop for a moment at the corner while a car whirled by, he abandoned his cover and followed her closely to the funeral parlor door, where they both gained entrance without challenge or question.

Once inside, he followed her at a few yards' distance, imitating her progress through the dim interior. They moved in silence down a passageway, sliding their hands along the wall, feeling for hooks where wet coats and umbrellas were hung. Another door at the end of the passageway led to a large room, clinical, antiseptic, surgical looking, where a single light burned, casting bright gleams against chrome and nickel and squares of white tile. In the tracks of his mute companion, Michael crossed to the opposite side of this room, slipped through a door, closed it, and found himself in another passage, whose termination revealed yet another door, through which he passed, again closing it behind him.

The room he and the unknown woman had just entered was apparently the desired goal, the center of the labyrinth. Michael spotted a little grove of potted palms, where he quickly secreted himself so that he might take in the room without being observed. It was a high-ceilinged space, and it had about it a certain shabby yet overstated glamour, resembling the lobby of a medium-sized hotel at the turn of the century in a fashionable spa, say Saratoga Springs. Or it might have put one in mind of the salon in a moderately stylish bordello, a room of substance, furnished with straight-backed chairs whose seats were identically upholstered in tufted velvet, worn to exhaustion by continual use. At present, most of these were occupied by men or women who sat talking in subdued tones. Other than the desultory talk on topics of small moment, however, they were simply waiting. Their clothes were as much at variance as their faces; some looked well-to-do, some were of an obviously middle-class background, some even caught in straitened circumstances. Some seemed intelligent, others bland, others dull. A wide-ranging mixture reposed in decorous tableau. Waiting. Everyone was waiting. And then Michael saw him: standing among them, rubbing his hands together, the abstracted gesture of a man who holds himself in anticipation of some looked-for event, the master waited too.

Michael stared at him through the palm fronds, but not too intently; he wasn't sure that he wanted the master to feel his eyes and become cognizant of his presence. But then he smirked inwardly at this inane precaution. Surely the master knew he was there, surely he had led him deliberately to this very place? By ways apparently but not actually devious, by means of a cavalierly transparent subterfuge—which was no doubt part of the lesson—the master had brought him here, where he wanted him to be. But why? He would find out in time; meanwhile, he resolved to do what was obviously expected of him: to wait and to watch.

The hour had grown late. Somewhere beyond the heavy oak sliding doors a clock sounded with dull resonance, a kind of knell. A woman clenching a cigarette leaned toward a man and wordlessly asked for a light, receiving it and blowing a stream of blue smoke into the gloom. Someone looked at her with disdain and coughed; another, as if unable to resist the impulse, echoed it. The master, looking fatigued from his long walk, sat in a chair placed beside a pillar. The black patch now covered his sightless eye. As Michael watched him, he crossed his legs with professorial calm and laced his long fingers around his knee, looking down at the nails of his thumbs.

He did not look up when the oaken doors slid open and the quiet was broken by the sound of wheels rolling across the floor, onto the rug. Michael thought he must be aware of others rearranging themselves about the room, his half vision glimpsing waists and feet moving over the arabesques of the patterned rug. The master straightened his back slightly in the chair, drawing in a soundless breath, expelling it slowly through parted lips. Around him there were light, sliding movements, the rustle of women's garments, the brush of shoe leather across the carpeting. Someone went out, closing the oak doors behind. Among those waiting there went a chain of whispers like a persistent breeze, to die in silence, rise briefly, die again. In the quiet and the whispers they waited.

At last the master lifted his sunken chin, like a minister after the invocation, contemplating his assembled congregation. One-eyed, he looked at those nearest him, but did not acknowledge them. They were still waiting, but now Michael understood that they were waiting for him, for the master. Here and there a face was turned expectantly toward him, most turned away in some unspoken etiquette established among them to accommodate such occasions.

The master got up from his chair and stood and looked as though unseeing around the circle of heads and moved through it. No one touched him as he passed among them and proceeded to the center of the room, where the rubber-wheeled table had been placed. He paused, looking down, then with his thumbs and forefingers lifted and folded back the sheet, perhaps a foot, one neat fold, the economical gesture of a hospital attendant. Again a whisper riffled through the gathering around him. Heads craned.

Michael heard someone say the face was a good face tonight. Under the taut, opaque skin the flesh was like gray marble, with opaque shadows the color of oysters surrounding the eyes, sooty smudges lending a bruised, tired expression. The ends of white fibers showed faintly at the nostrils where they had been plugged with cotton. The mouth was relaxed into a neutral expression, the lower lip drawn back slightly under the upper, both bloodless, with a purplish cast. Then there was the odor, not unpleasant, something like the scent of a freshly diapered infant.

The nares of Wurlitzer's nose seemed to widen as, bending, his face suspended above the face beneath him, with a graceful movement, lost in dreamlike languor, he drew the sheet further down, draping it loosely at the foot of the zinc table. The cloth slid, and someone made a quick movement, caught it before it touched the floor. Murmurs rose as the naked and marmoreal form was disclosed. The hands lay along the sides, palms cupped upwards, fingers curled. The chest rose in bony prominence above the flattened abdomen, the midsection modestly covered by the width of a towel. Below the towel the legs lay aligned in parallel, the knees, calves, and anklebones just touching in classic symmetry. It was a good body, someone said, a fine body. The veins showed bluely under the skin, along the forearms and the fronts of the lower extremities.

The master straightened, raised his right hand in a reflective and passive gesture of commitment, then let it slip down so the fingers rested on the dead thigh. He slid the padded tips along in tactile concentration. Behind him little glimmers of light had burst, matches tipped the wicks of candles, and the electric sconces were switched off with audible clicks. The room shone with a soft amber radiance. Someone had brought a chair, which now rested several inches behind the master's legs. He bent his knees and lowered himself into the seat, his meager weight making the tufted cushion give only slightly. He sat in the candlelight, leaning toward the horizontal form, the pale shoulder just at his own shoulder but not touching. He angled his head so he looked upon the face sideways.

There was a stirring among the watchers as he languidly moved his hand along the exposed inside of the bare arm, letting his fingertips come at last to the opened palm, where he thoughtfully studied the creases in the flesh. He traced them with the rim of his nail, pressed slightly along the mounds, delicately touched each finger in turn, then gently enclosed the hand in his own. His eye closed, he sat like a doctor beside a patient, brooding, aloof, coldly pondering a difficult diagnosis. The fingers of one hand now rested firmly about the curve of the ribs; the other hand closed tightly around the Eye of Horus, which hung around his neck; then he laid the side of his face against the breast, just at the level of the frozen heart, and in this position he remained, motionless and scarcely breathing.

Beyond the paired doors the clock struck again. Several people were smoking now, and tobacco smoke drifted down from the ceiling. No sound came from outside the walls of the red-papered room. In frieze, those attending watched, grouped about the room. Two or three, including Michael, as if fearful of venturing into the light, however dim, lingered behind the arching branches of the palms.

Waiting, watching, those assembled sounded among them small, muffled signals, denoting a community of desire, softly uttered murmurs that became low moans, hanging in the room like laments that increased gradually in volume, and as if these sounds of themselves had induced movement the watchers began moving, rubbing their hands with a miser's covetousness as slowly they entered now into themselves or outward from themselves, succumbing to whatever profane ecstasy they had assembled to experience.

Though beyond the doors the clock had tolled, in the room itself there was no time. They waited, who could tell how long, with almost courtly diffidence, waited until the old man, whom they seemed to look upon with unspecific reverence, lifted his cheek and sat staring down at the marble face. Then he rose, and the chair was solicitously withdrawn from behind him. He turned away, the moist coating on his eye catching the candlelight, dancing, then disappearing into darkness as though a light had been extinguished, and all that might be seen was the black patch, which seemed visionary of its own accord.

Then, as Wurlitzer moved farther away, not looking back, the watchers closed about. They grouped themselves around the rubber-wheeled table, whose metallic surfaces rayed light against the ceiling plaster. A woman sank down on the rug as if unable to support herself, another lowered her body beside the first, and they clasped hands, their free hands reaching up to touch and feel, their eyes shut in inarticulate passion, moaning, whispering secret thoughts, lost in a dreamless dream.

After these two, the rest joined in, a choir of hands reaching with spread fingers, trembling, groping, to touch the holy object of their awful adoration. A frenzied energy had begun to communicate itself through the room, from person to person, a tangential awareness, but each was locked in a solitude of lonely joyfulness, private and unfathomable. One, more eager than the rest, came close against the far side of the table, and leaning over the prostrate form, bent to it, and as the first living mouth was pressed against the dead one a single cry of muted but uncontrollable passion was heard.

Through the palm fronds, Michael saw the master wait for a time, watching, inhaling the tallowed smoke that drifted about the candle tips; then, abruptly, he left the room. Michael's principal instinct was to follow, yet something compelled him to move forward, to see at least what it was the master had done, what it was that held these people transfixed. And then he saw—the dead man's chest rose and fell, exhaling the breath of sleep. He was alive!

Michael turned and hastened through the same door by which he had entered what seemed an eternity ago. Outside, the rain had lessened, but there was a cool breeze, and he quickly realized he was chilled to the bone. The street was empty. When he reached the corner, he looked back, peering down the block, registering the little light still glowing above the wet green door.

Pulling his hood down to his eyebrows, he headed in the direction of Union Square.

He was angry and frustrated without knowing why; and both fascinated and frightened, for reasons he knew perfectly well. And exhilarated. Suddenly he was running, not on the sidewalk but along the gutter, jumping with both feet in the puddles and splashing them and cursing aloud. It didn't matter; there was no one to see or hear him. His pants were soaked to the knees as he waited for a bus to take him across town.

He transferred at Eighth Avenue and took the uptown bus. When he got off it had begun raining again, and he made short work of the half block to the theater. He let himself in next door, wiping his feet on the mat and slipping out of his wet jacket as soon as he entered. Turning, he saw the black umbrella, neatly rolled and cinched with its cloth fastener, exactly where it had been earlier. He touched it: it felt dry. The large black rubbers sat under the hall tree; they too were dry. Upstairs, the light from the sitting room slanted into the hall, and he could hear the drone of the television set.

He came into the room and pulled up short, his mouth agape with surprise. Lena was in her chair, stitching while she watched a late movie. And, impossibly, the master sat in the chair in the study alcove, a book on his lap, his face half obscured by his green celluloid eyeshade as he examined something with a magnifying glass. He wore his vest, and his feet were slid into his old leather slippers; at his elbow a smoking pipe lay in the ashtray. Lena looked up as Michael came in, smiled a greeting, then returned her eyes to the television screen. Max's head lifted, he pushed back the eyeshade and waved Michael in. Michael stood staring at him. The old man's face betrayed nothing, but there was a hint of something in the voice. "Well, home again, eh? Did you enjoy yourself?"

"Yes."

The master's eyes flicked downward. "Your feet are wet. Is it raining?"

"A little."

"Well, it's that time of year."

Michael stared. "Yes, it is . . ." he mumbled, watching the master, but getting nothing from him. This might well have been an exchange between parent and son, only Wurlitzer was not Michael's father. No, he was a man—*was* that what he was?—who Michael had just witnessed give life to someone who was dead. That *was* what he'd seen, wasn't it?

He glanced at Lena, and when he looked back, Wurlitzer had lowered his shade. He saw the eye swivel upward for an instant, briefly green. "You will perhaps not be surprised to learn that Emily called."

"Okay. Thanks. I'll call her tomorrow."

Michael started for the doorway, yanking his handkerchief from his pocket to sneeze.

"*Gesundheit!*" the master said.

Lena looked up. "You must be careful you don't catch cold with those wet feet." Were there traces of humor in her tone? Before he could reply, she had looked back at the flickering screen.

How was it possible? Surely he'd seen the master in the funeral parlor, had followed him there, yet here he was, back home, warm as toast, and as dry, without a sign of having left the room. Michael decided he had to know the truth, had to confront him. He waited in the doorway for the master to look up again, and when at last he did, Michael said, "May I speak to you for a moment?"

"Certainly, my boy. I was just thinking about retiring."

When they were halfway down the hall, Michael stopped abruptly and said, "Why did you ask me if it was raining?"

"One likes to know something of the weather."

"But you know it was raining. You were out in it."

"I? Hardly. As I told you, earlier in the evening I felt extremely weary. Later I revived somewhat, Lena and I enjoyed some amount of conversation, she watched the television, I worked a bit. The time passed quickly and quite uneventfully. Nocturnal excursions in the rain are for the young and vigorous, not the moribund."

He smiled crazily, turned his eye on Michael and made him feel its full force, but Michael stubbornly refused to accept the denial. "I saw you. At the funeral parlor. With the dead man."

The master shook his head in mild amusement, his smile became passive. "I never stirred. You must be imagining things."
They returned each other's gaze evenly. "Still," he hastened to
add, "that's the whole point, isn't it?"

"What is?"

"To use your imagination. Even if it wished to put a man in two
places at the same time. In any case"—he was shuffling away by
now, and the words came over his shoulder—"one would have to
be extremely clever to manage such a thing, wouldn't he?" He
continued on, rubbing his hollow eye socket. Then he stopped
and turned, looking directly at Michael. "Very clever indeed. And
what one saw, or imagined he saw, might never have happened at
all, or might not have happened as he saw it, if indeed he saw it at
all. You young people are always looking for miracles, looking for
new ways to cure the ill, even to raise the dead. Well, my son, you
have a vivid imagination, and that is good. But perhaps it is too
vivid. I never left this apartment tonight, so you could not have
seen me. And whatever else you imagined you saw was only
what you imagined you saw. And now you must excuse me. I am
old and I am tired. Good night."

Michael stood watching him as his halting steps carried him
down the hall and through the door to his room. Then Michael
walked back past the living room, said good night to Lena, who
didn't hear him, and left the Wurlitzers' apartment.

At the foot of the stairs that led up to his quarters, he stood still
for several minutes, lost in thought. He should, he knew, take
things in order, starting with what he had seen, with the evidence
of his senses. And what had he seen? A funeral parlor, where a
heterogeneous group of people, apparently led by the master, had
engaged in some kind of communion with a corpse. The gathering had been joyless, the people curiously aloof from one another;
the master, their leader but not their friend, had like each of them
seemed isolated, separated from the living and drawn to the
dead. And so he is, Michael thought; lately he showed contempt
for everything alive, his conversation was filled with death . . . But
then what had happened tonight? The ritual, for that's what it
was, had gone on for what seemed an eternity. There had been no
high point, no epiphany—or if there had been, then Michael had

not been aware of it. Yet when it ended, if that's what had happened, a dead man was a corpse no more, but lay there in . . . what? A state of sleep? Whatever it was, his part in the ghoulish ritual over, the master had left, and now claimed absolute ignorance of all that Michael had witnessed. Why? Could the whole thing have been an illusion? Michael thought of the gray, naked corpse, the ghastly moaning of its adorers, the waxy, powdery smells in the room—all unmistakably, unforgettably real, as real as the master, with his ostentatiously dry shoes and umbrella, his questions about the weather, his coy allusions to bilocation.

Michael gripped his hair in two handfuls and pulled from sheer frustration. What could it mean? That the power he sought was somehow linked with death, that night magic entailed the clasping of cadavers as well as the performance of miracles? Well, if it came to that, Michael admitted with a shiver of horrified recognition, he would probably be willing to embrace any number of dead strangers.

CHAPTER EIGHTEEN

The Incident in the Garden

The day after the strange, almost surreal visit to the funeral parlor, Michael was restless, moody, unable to concentrate on his work, even peevish with Lena and sullen when the master inquired, with his usual edge of irony, if anything was bothering him. That afternoon he called Emily to apologize for running off so abruptly the day before. He got her answering machine, however, so he limited his remarks to a brief apology. He had really wanted to talk to her—he needed to discuss the events of the previous evening with somebody.

In the evening he went to his room and sat alone, awake in the gathering dark, listening to the dim voices from Lena's television, the sound of the master moving through his dreary apartment, closing and opening doors. I'm above it all, he thought, and this made him smile, although he wasn't sure why. He stayed there, his back against the wall, listening and waiting until the whole building was quiet and still. Later he woke up; he was listing sideways, about to hit the floor. He was stiff from sitting. Unable to stand, he crawled to his bed and pulled the blanket over his face, as he had done as a child, gratefully.

In the morning, he found Wurlitzer in the theater, crouched over the wind machine for the Tempest Illusion, his head tilted at an angle so that he could scrutinize the control panel with his one good eye. As Michael approached, he unfolded himself creakily, dusting off his inevitable black jacket with impatient flicks of his arthritic fingers. "You don't look well," he said, with such sincerity that Michael felt a moment of alarm for himself. "You haven't slept."

"I slept," Michael said coldly. Then, because the master continued to survey him with an expression of concern, he looked away, toward the empty theater, this narrow, overwrought world which seemed to him at the moment perfectly devoid of magic, and added, "I'm just restless."

"As well you might be," the master agreed. "You've been working too hard. I've been working too hard. Let's take the day off and go find something really interesting."

"I don't know," Michael said. His thoughts turned to the grim scene at the funeral parlor. What would it be today, the city morgue? Perhaps a dissection at the medical school?

"Nothing morbid," the master said, reading his thoughts, as usual. "I want to go to the Cloisters and see the unicorn tapestries one more time. Have you ever been there?"

"No," Michael admitted.

"A fascinating place, a park, a castle, full of artistic wonders. The sun is shining today, the trip will do us good."

Michael agreed, though somewhat warily, and after breakfast at the coffee shop they boarded the IND at the Forty-second Street station. The master sat hunched over in the crowded subway car, his long hands dangling between his spread knees, his head lolling loosely on its long neck, his lips moving silently as though reciting some prayer or incantation. Today he had foregone the black patch in favor of the glass eye, and his pate was covered with an incongruous plaid cap.

Hanging on to the strap, Michael tried to imagine the master's body unclothed; without his rumpled black suit, his tieless white shirt, he would appear somehow obscene. These items were as essential to him as the vestments of a priest, the uniform of a policeman, an English barrister's robes and wig: emblems of office.

They got off at 190th Street, and followed along behind a group descending the long incline toward the Cloisters, the part Italian, part Spanish monastery that Rockefeller money had brought from Europe and reassembled stone by stone in that part of Manhattan. The structure seemed nevertheless entirely indigenous to the promontory on which it sat, overlooking the Hudson River. A tree-lined esplanade led past dozens of benches, where city dwellers, hungry for sunlight, fresh air, and the sight of grass and trees, sat squeezed together shoulder to shoulder, four or five to a bench; Michael and the master walked past them, eventually reaching the steps that led into the museum.

Inside, the exhibits were set out in lofty, uncluttered spaces. As he and Michael moved from one to the other, there was little that did not attract the master's roving eye. They had purchased a catalogue, and he read aloud snatches of descriptions, pointing items out to Michael, and adding bits of his own polymath knowledge. Then he led the way into a room on whose walls hung enormous tapestries, marvels of splendid design and workmanship, featuring fantastic unicorns, fanciful snow-white beasts with delicate equine features and noble carriage, proudly displaying their long, spiral horns. The old man gazed at them for a long time; Michael was impressed by his frank, unfeigned admiration.

At last the master turned to him with a look of unwonted serenity. Nor was that the only distinction; when he spoke, his voice seemed to have taken on a kind of noble gravity, without any trace of his habitual irony or cynicism. "Unicorns are truly magical animals," he said. "They show the imagination working at its purest and most delightful. No one ever saw one, yet everyone believed they existed; faith in them produced nothing but pleasure, and they inspired such charming works as these. Our own magic is rough and crude in comparison," he concluded, shaking his head regretfully.

When they had seen all the rooms, and the master showed signs of fatigue, they went down to the lower level and out into the Trias courtyard. As they opened the small wooden door and stepped outside, Michael thought they had suddenly moved backward in time. A quadrilateral arcade with carved pillars supporting graceful arches surrounded a well-proportioned fountain, where colorful spring plantings had been set out between gravel walkways. There was bright light, and dark shadows, and a sudden air of tranquility. The fountain splashed softly into its basin, music could be heard from concealed speakers, a quartet of clear, harmonizing voices raised in Gregorian chant, and it was not difficult to imagine monks at their prayers, or a brother walking the arcade with a breviary in his hands, murmuring glories to God.

They moved from the courtyard into the adjoining garden, which faced southwest to the river. Two elderly ladies with sequined glasses and blue hair marveled over a statue in the center of the quadrangle, while beyond the surrounding wall, amid books and papers, a group of students was gathered on a grassy slope within the enclosure formed by a small orchard of dwarf apple trees with bright new leaves. One of the students pointed a camera at the George Washington Bridge, which could be seen through the branches. Out on the Hudson, with the Jersey Palisades for a backdrop, a solitary sloop beat its way upriver, the wind filling its sails and setting it spanking.

Michael turned to discover that the master, in order to get out of the freshening wind, had gone to sit on a stone bench in a protected corner of the garden. With evident enjoyment he sat quietly absorbing the chanting voices, his fingers laced over a crossed knee, his lips forming the O shape that was habitual with him when he was thinking. The pair of women drifted over to the wall, nodding and pointing, but the master's eye remained on the statue they had been viewing.

The figure was life size, rough hewn from gray stone, and encrusted with spots of dark, moist-looking mold. The bearded face was mantled in a heavy cowl, the form draped in loose-fitting robes whose voluminous folds lent grace to the bulkiness of the work. One hand clasped a tome to the chest, the other held the ends of a cord serving as a belt from which depended a simple crucifix. Under the beetling forehead, with its heavy, patriarchal brows, the eyes stared blankly, the head turned to one side as if the statue were looking out to the river.

Michael took a seat on the bench beside the master, and they sat wordlessly for a time. Then, abruptly, the old man began to speak, recalling a monastery in Greece where, while traveling with his friend and colleague, the roguish Christatos, he had seen a similar statue in an equally inviting garden. "The monks invited us to dine and spend the night. After a midday meal that seemed anything but ascetic, we went into the garden, a place not unlike this one: colonnades, fountains, and several carved statues, one, in fact, something of a brother to the one you're looking at now." He nodded toward the statue and paused to light his pipe. "The pride of the monastery, however, was a small gold ikon of the Virgin, specially revered because of its miraculous powers. Christatos expressed a pious interest in this ikon, and we were edified by an account of the various occasions on which it had wept real tears. Interesting, is it not? You see how little new there is under the sun. An ikon—a Rembrandt—it is all the same, is it not?"

He paused again—for effect, Michael was sure—puffing his pipe and giving a scratch or two, looking up to where some birds shot across the roof into the plane of sunlight that was already moving into shadow. Michael waited to learn the connection between the miraculous ikon and the equally miraculous "Saskia in Tears."

"Well," the master continued at last, "as a token of gratitude for the monks' hospitality, Christatos arranged that we would put on a little magic show in the garden and devoutly requested that the holy ikon be carried there to bless our undertaking. Somehow he persuaded the abbot to accede to his request. Our alfresco performance was an impromptu affair, since we had no props, but we did well enough with silks and coins and such sketchy materials—as you know, real magicians can work under any circumstances.

"The good brothers admired our efforts quite thoroughly, and finally, as the sun was beginning to set, Christatos announced a special treat for them: we would demonstrate the true efficacy of their gold ikon. He directed their attention to the statue at the far end of the garden, enclosed in a circle of yew, light enough to see, but melting all around into shadows. With elaborate apologies he borrowed the ikon from the abbot, who had stood there clutching it to his bony chest the whole time, and held it up before him. He adjusted the angle so that the fading rays of the sun reflected off the ikon and cast a golden beam onto the drab face of the statue.

All eyes were on it as it turned its shoulder ever so slightly and inclined its head in a most quizzical manner, as if saying, 'Why are you so surprised, you little Greek monks? I am stiff in my neck joints and must give them a creak or two.'

"This remarkable demonstration set the brothers abuzz, and they leaped to their feet to view the miracle more closely, but by the time they could inspect it the statue had resumed its original form and nothing could make it budge. Then there arose a debate among the monks as to the nature of the miracle: had Christatos's wizardry induced those particles of stone to shift themselves, or was it truly the miraculous power of the weeping ikon? But the outcome of that debate is another story, and so is the fate of the ikon, which, as you must have guessed, Christatos had managed to spirit away during the confusion."

The master sagged and sighed, moving his shoulders around in his coat and recrossing his knees. Michael looked around the garden and saw that everyone else had gone; they were alone, and the master had stopped talking, but it was clear that the lesson was not over. "When did this happen?" Michael asked.

The master emitted his melodrama-villain's chuckle. "Long ago, my boy, long ago. Let us say some time before you were born." This pronouncement seemed to amuse him, and he chuckled still more fearfully.

"Okay. And you actually saw the statue move?"

"I did."

"The same way the people at the Metropolitan saw the Saskia cry?"

"Something like that, perhaps. There is always the possibility of hypnotism, or mass hysteria, though I confess I myself find it doubtful."

"Did it have something to do with the beam of light? The sun reflecting on the ikon?"

"As we know, the sparkle of gold had misled many a man; perhaps the monks were even as simple as they professed to be. Perhaps it was their faith that believed the ikon wept and the statue articulated its joints. A miracle, or magic—who can say? The miraculous is always magical, and the truly magical is ultimately miraculous, but which came first? And what do such deliberations reveal except the extent to which our thoughts are circumscribed by language? I'll ask an easier question: are you expecting that statue to move?"

The customary sardonic edge, returning to the master's tone, cut through Michael's reverie and made him aware that he had been staring at the carved stone figure for some time. And that somewhere in the back of his mind a struggle was taking place between his boundless aspirations and his certainty that they were impossible dreams.

"The need for belief is part of the essential nature of man," the master continued. "He must, with all his heart, believe in something. If you wish that a statue should move, even that one, if you believe it is possible, I say to you that such a thing can be done, for as I told you I have seen it myself. What I saw was, perhaps, not a holy miracle, but a question of Christatos's ability to attune his audience to his magic will. The ordinary man wills that he shall not believe, the magician wills that he shall. Which is stronger? It is a question of belief, the magician's against the ordinary man's. Like every other human being, you have much to learn, but there is little else that I can teach you. You have been a most satisfactory student; if I could be sorry, I would be sorry to leave you, but let this be our last formal lesson. I am tired now. I'd like to rest for a little while before the darkness finally falls."

He fell silent at last, slipped his pipe into his pocket, and leaned back against the wall behind the bench. Michael recapitulated the story while it was still fresh in his mind, but he soon gave up any attempt to determine how much of it might be objectively true. The master's little anecdotes and parables contained their own nuggets of truth—it was a question of digging them out.

He glanced back at the old man. His lids were closed, he had turned up his collar against the late afternoon chill and appeared for all the world to be dozing. Yet Michael doubted it; he was waiting for something that was yet to happen, some little event that would put its seal on the day. The sun had dropped behind the rooftree, spreading a heavy shadow across three quarters of the garden. The air smelled new and green, the hopeful fragrance of spring, though experience showed that such hopes were often nipped in the bud.

Something propelled him to his feet, then induced him to movement. He went and leaned over the wall, gazing out across the water. It was gray, going to black, and looking cold. There were lights: a large boat was moving downriver, buildings on the Palisades showed yellow windows, headlight beams moved slowly across the span of the bridge. The wind was rising, tugging at the young untested leaves of the apple trees. The outlines of low-lying objects—certain hedges, the newly manicured gravel path—were beginning to blur, and the gray stone of the statue had gone blue in the twilight.

The garden lay deserted, the courtyard empty. Everyone had gone, and the place had taken on a melancholy air. In the dark of the arcade it seemed there throbbed mystery, even frightfulness. Michael felt a deepening pang, wishing he were laughing with Dazz, wistfully imagining he was doing street mimes and looking for an Equity job, not doing a magic act and living in the house of a strange and perhaps mad old man. The thought of Emily crossed his mind like a promise of salvation. What did the master want from him? What was the purpose he was being trained and molded for?

He felt isolated and frustrated and stymied, like a man nearing the top of a high mountain only to discover that his joints ache, he can't breathe, the view isn't all he'd hoped, and the way of descent is obscured. Whatever strange capabilities the master possessed, whatever Michael had managed to glean from him, suddenly seemed to have no merit. What was this power he sought so desperately, and what would he do with it should he attain it? Heal the sick? Raise the dead? Make statues move? Such notions were the leftover pathetic dreams of a lonely boy, fantasizing about controlling a world in which no single element responded to his will. Fine for a boy, but for a grown man? He had exercised that coveted power in some degree, had felt it surge through and out of him, and yet he had no idea of its limits, no sense that he could ever wield it with total mastery; unlike himself, it was inexhaustible. A vision of the fiasco in Washington Square came to him, the howling and the flailing, his despair at having freed some savage thing he could never recapture or tame again. Could he ever control his power, if indeed it was his, or would it always control him? If a magician makes his audience believe a statue can move, who moves the statue, the magician, or his believing audience? The master was just preparing him to be subject to many masters, never to be his own. And what profit had the old man had of his own power? He was cut off from everything alive, he embraced corpses among strangers, his mind was fixed on death. Rightly considered, the magic will seemed to include the will not to an enhanced, fuller life, but to death, to the chaos and disorganization of death. In an agony of doubt, Michael imagined the master offering him a large cup brimming with some bitter-smelling liquid and instinctively turned away his head.

A gust of wind swept past him, and he shoved his hands in his pockets, abandoning the wall. It was then he realized that the master was no longer on the bench. He looked around. There was nobody there. The place had a ghostly air about it, and he could hear the echo of his own shoe leather on the pavement as he moved. He stopped again. In the corner of the arcade where darkness gathered, he caught a glimmer of white. Framed in an archway stood the master, his shoulders hunched up around his long neck as though drawn in against the cold. He was waiting. Waiting . . . for what? Michael started forward, then halted again as the master's arm moved. His hand came up, pale bony fingers splayed against the shadowed colonnade, a theatrical, ambiguous gesture. The dark, brooding shape of the statue, heavy, mordant, enigmatic, stood between the two of them. The statue's cowl caught the last rays of the dying sun, which washed it in a warm glow, bleeding onto the side plane of the face; brow, cheekbone, nose, beard, all took the light. Michael glanced at the master, then back to the stone face. And in that instant, before it happened, he knew it was going to happen. As his eyes remained fixed on it, the statue became animated. The head swung slowly toward him. The features were brought into full relief in the light, the cowl shifted slightly as real fabric might do. The blank, carved eyes stared out of the wash of sunlight, and then, quite naturally, as if the light had sensitized them, they blinked. Neither hand had moved, but as Michael's eyes remained riveted, the right shoulder raised perceptibly and the head withdrew slowly into the cowl, as if it too felt the cold. Then the face turned away again, and the figure once more became stone.

Moving quickly toward it, Michael heard his feet crunching the gravel, but by the time he was within reach of the statue the sun had fled, leaving the face in shadow. The stone felt cold to Michael's touch, and dew had already dampened the carved folds. He withdrew his hand and rubbed it against his jeans. Still looking up, he circled the base, then continued along the path to the colonnade. Ahead, he saw the wooden door just closing on the master's heels. He looked again at the statue, whose hand came up in a slow, forlorn wave of farewell. Even as he looked, dumbstruck and afraid, Michael told himself he was being tricked—hypnotized; and, as he watched, he told himself nothing could be further from the truth. Then, as though the show were over, the hand came down and resumed its original position.

Overhead, the bells in the campanile tolled, and the bronze notes floated out over the rooftops. Michael did not look back again until he had opened the door to pass through. Then he turned once more. The statue was only a dark hooded shape seen through the row of pillared arches, and a pair of birds shot from out of the darkness and dropped lightly to perch on its shoulders. Before the door swung shut behind him, he heard it: the low laughter that came with the birds' chittering, rising upward to meet the sound of the bells.

CHAPTER NINETEEN

Hail and Farewell

AVE ATQUE VALE: the large letters were set in a curving line that formed an arch at the very top of the poster. Within this arch, more uppercase letters of a slightly smaller size and in a different typeface announced a GALA FAREWELL PERFORMANCE! The illustration—Dazz had modeled it on the colorful, evocative posters favored by magicians of international repute early in the century—featured a lean, sinister figure in a black cape and slouch hat draping a golden chain, from which depended a large Eye of Horus, around the bowed neck of a younger, dark-haired man in evening dress: the master passing on the amulet, symbol of his power, to his successor. At their feet, several lines of copy exhorted the reader to come and see these wonders in person:

THE GREAT WURLITZER
yields the stage to
PRESTO THE GREAT

—Experience the Tempest Illusion—
Earth Water Fire and Air
as you've never seen them before!

Little Cairo Museum of Wonders
Saturday, June 14
7:30 P.M.

Copies of this poster, placed at strategic locations in Manhattan, had combined with extensive word-of-mouth publicity to produce a packed house at the Little Cairo on this pleasant night in late spring. Indeed, many people had been turned away, to their great disappointment; however unorthodox and even disturbing the magic shows at the theater might have been from time to time, they had played to larger and larger audiences since its reopening, and even though the renovations sponsored by that canny investor and patron of the arts Samir Abdel-Noor had involved a significant increase in the Little Cairo's seating capacity, it wasn't nearly enough to satisfy the demand of a public eager to witness the most famous, not to say notorious, magic act New York City had boasted for many a year.

Samir himself, of course, was there, along with his retinue of friends and attendants: Jack Dazzario, the fashionable young painter; Miss Beulah Wales, medium and confidante; Gilbert Ramadan, bodyguard and factotum; and, reluctantly, Dr. John Mortimer, physician and enemy of magic, required by his patient's delicate constitution and excitable nature to be near him precisely at such a spectacle as this, whatever he might think of Sami's childish enthusiasms. There were, moreover, several colleagues and friends of Emily's, a few young actors who knew Michael from his musical comedy days, a large number of amateur and professional magicians, and even some longtime patrons of the Little Cairo, to whom the recent transformations both in the theater itself and in the shows presented there seemed magical indeed. All these and others, many others, were in their seats; and the vast majority of them, particularly those who had seen the two magicians' work in the past, awaited the beginning of the show with an avidity bordering on impatience.

Backstage, too, a certain amount of tension was charging the air. Emily, holding herself unnaturally rigid while Lena added some final touches to her sumptuous Chinese princess costume, seemed apprehensive and nervous; ever since the revelations concerning the fate of Michael's predecessor, the sight of Wurlitzer and Michael onstage at the same time filled her with dread. The thought that this show was to be their last appearance together did nothing to allay her uneasiness, and she frowned at herself in the mirror as she watched Lena pin a single orange-pink hibiscus into the thick hair above her right ear.

Lena too was nervous, though for a different reason: it was already 7:25, and she hadn't seen Max since shortly after lunch, if that was what she should call the cup of coffee and the single dry biscuit that were all he had consented to swallow. When she reproached him for being so careless of his health, he had smiled and said, almost tenderly, almost as though he really pitied her, "Poor Lena, so determined to keep me alive. What difference can food make to me now?" The memory of these words echoed like a knell in her brain, summoning up images she couldn't bear to contemplate.

"You look splendid, dear," she said bravely. It was, after all, true: Emily was a vision of grace and beauty, her richly embroidered satin robe perfectly complementing her shiny black hair, her pale face, the natural dignity of her carriage. Lena raised an affectionate, slightly trembling hand to Emily's long braid. "Our magicians are lucky to have so beautiful an assistant." She looked distractedly at the big wall clock and said in a worried voice, "I do wish Max would come."

Michael, too, though sitting patiently in his dressing room, wished that the master would come, that this most anticipated of nights would finally begin. His outward calm masked a small but tenacious component of misgiving that had nothing whatever to do with stage fright. Never before had he felt so confident in his abilities, so extraordinary in his powers, so fully in control, as he did this evening. In their fanatical preparations and endless rehearsals, he and the master had left nothing to chance: every movement in the show was choreographed, every syllable weighed, every gesture measured, every effect planned. Profoundly conceived, thoroughly orchestrated, the show could not fail. Nor could he. No, the tiny needle of uncertainty that was attempting to prick his concentration had its origins elsewhere. In Washington Square, perhaps, or in those hallucinatory minutes in the funeral parlor, or in the locked room in the basement, or in that incident at the Cloisters, or in the thought of Emily's unshakable love—for each of these elements conspired against his ambition. His decision was taken, there was to be no turning back, he would walk the path he had chosen, for better or worse. Tonight would be a great triumph, with more and greater triumphs to follow, even to his heart's content. But not unalloyed, apparently, not without some risk, some tinge of regret . . .

The master's patent-leather gaiter-shoes rang on the iron steps that led down to the backstage area. Michael rose to his feet, quickly checked the mirror; everything was in order—the perfectly fitting black silk tuxedo, the snow-white, tastefully ruffled shirt, the slightly oversized black bow tie. He stepped through the door and joined Emily and Lena. The wall clock read 7:29.

Striding purposefully, straight and tall, the master swept toward them. Over his formal attire he wore a midlength black cape, lined in scarlet satin, flaring out behind him like a blaze. The Eye of Horus, at the end of a long golden chain, bounced gently against his chest. He looks healthier, thought Lena, touching her breast. I can feel his power, thought Michael, filling his lungs. Why isn't he wearing his eye patch? thought Emily, wincing.

The master came to a halt and briefly surveyed his little troupe with his single eye, shifting it rapidly from face to face. Its lively glitter contrasted queasily with the murky dullness of its glass counterpart. At length he spoke, in his hollowest tones: "Good evening. I see that everyone is ready and eager to begin, as am I. This will be a memorable night." He turned to Michael. "Shall we take our places?" And, not waiting for a reply, he addressed Emily: "Tell the sound booth we go on in sixty seconds." Then, to everyone's surprise, he stepped toward Lena and embraced her. "Wish me luck," he said, spun on his heel, and walked into the wings.

From the very first moment, the master's farewell performance proved to be a spectacular presentation, the grandest of finales. The master and Michael, entering from different sides of the stage, bowed simultaneously to the audience as the processional fanfare that opens Handel's *Music for the Royal Fireworks* filled the air; then, with the music mounting and bursting around them, pouring into the auditorium from the brand-new, state-of-the-art computerized sound system, they began to juggle a set of brightly colored balls, plucking them from nowhere and throwing them higher and higher while gradually approaching center stage. Soon the two of them were facing each other from a distance of just a few feet, and what seemed like a dozen glowing balls, each a different color, were spinning through the air between and above them, passing from one to the other of their four flashing hands, soaring impossibly high, until at length, in perfect coordination with the swelling music, the balls began to explode in the air above their heads, each vanishing in a flash and cloud of smoke that matched its color, replaced at once by another and another as new balls appeared at the magicians' fingertips, flying and flashing, some of them sailing out over the audience and exploding there, the air dense with multicolored smoke and heavy with sweet fragrances, until finally the last two spheres, apparently bigger than the others, rose together as one and detonated simultaneously with the loudest, brightest burst of all, and then the master and Michael stood shoulder to shoulder, bowing to the applause through the pall of vivid smoke.

There followed a series of dazzling routines with knives, crockery, and Chinese linking rings, the last handled so skillfully and intricately that the crowd began to shout as each level of complexity was overtopped by the next. Impossible though it seemed, the two magicians, the aged and the youthful, were equals in dexterity, coordination, and quickness of reflex. Michael had long since come to realize, not without some chagrin, that the master's initial clumsiness, which he had found so embarrassing and patronized so gently, had itself been an act, part of the snare laid to catch his own tender feet. Those two gnarled hands were as sure as his young, smooth ones, that single eye saw more than both of his.

Their exertions left the audience, though not themselves, nearly exhausted, so the magicians passed from these strenuous demonstrations to a bit of comic relief. They roamed about the stage to the sugary strains of Respighi's *The Fountains of Rome*, touching spots at random with their magic wands; from every spot a thin column of colored water spouted forth. Occasionally one of them stooped and, picking up a waterspout that spewed on undisturbed, moved it to another location on the stage. The fountain routine ended with the two of them standing near the footlights as a rainbow of water droplets glistened over their heads.

After the applause had died down, the two magicians clapped their hands together, and the music changed to a long, ethereal sequence of Chinese flute melodies, arranged, performed, and recorded on tape some weeks earlier by Emily. The master and Michael stepped apart and gestured downstage, where two objects not previously visible now stood: on one side, an enormous copper cauldron, suspended from a tripod by a stout metal chain and hanging over a pyre of firewood neatly stacked and ready for ignition; and on the other side, a long table, draped in a delicately embroidered silk cloth and bearing the recumbent and apparently slumbering Princess Chang Li, known outside the magic world as Emily Chang. Michael moved to her side, catching along the way a large, seamless metal hoop that came flying from the wings. With a nonchalant flick of his wrist, he snatched off the tablecloth and tossed it aside; the table vanished as well, but the princess, supine, rigid, as motionless as a corpse, remained. Michael made several passes with the metal hoop over her body, using the levitationist's time-honored method of demonstrating that suspension has no part in his mystery, and soon, at his commands, the lovely princess was floating above the stage, higher, lower, left and right, her body unflinching, her expression of marmoreal calm unchanged.

As she drifted there, the master busied himself with the cauldron, igniting the firewood below it with a gesture of his wand. The leaping flames soon brought the cauldron's contents to a bubbling boil, and the old man, his features intent and menacing in the glow from the fire, began to extract from the smoking pot a seemingly endless series of the most heterogeneous objects: silk scarves, flags of all nations, vases filled with flowers, a mountainous coil of rope; a large cooked turkey, steaming on a platter, and a large live turkey that ran gobbling into the wings.

Meanwhile, the princess was sailing above their heads, higher and higher, until finally she rose to the flies and vanished from sight. At that precise moment, Michael and the master approached the boiling cauldron, reached deep inside it, and extracted—the princess herself! They set her down—alive, awake, unscathed, smiling—near the footlights, and the three of them bowed to a storm of applause.

When the performers turned once more to their work, the audience could see that the boards had been cleared of all their former encumbrances—cauldron, tripod, fire, scarves, ropes, flowers, flags, fowl. In the center of the stage now stood the Chinese cabinet, its lacquered surfaces glistening darkly, its four carved legs like griffin's talons, its ornate double doors closed. The music changed again—to a brooding, elegiac quartet by Shostakovich, the outcry of a soul in torment—the stage lights dimmed, and the mood of the show and of the audience grew somber and somehow ominous. Many of those present, when they later tried to describe their experiences, said this was the particular moment when they began to feel that something terrible, something tragic, was going to happen.

The princess stood demurely aside as the master and Michael each grasped one of the cabinet doors and opened them wide, displaying the empty black interior to the audience. Then they turned to the princess, gesturing, indicating that she should climb inside; she refused; their gestures became more insistent; she refused again and started to walk offstage, but a simultaneous sign from her two tormentors froze her in her tracks. They seized her stiff body as though it were a board, thrust her into the cabinet, and shut the doors. The cabinet began to shake almost at once; they opened the doors, but found it empty. Michael stepped inside. The master closed the doors, opened them, and Michael stepped back out, perplexed; the princess had vanished. Then, standing on either side of the cabinet, the two magicians began to open and shut the doors rapidly, revealing, in quick succession, a gesticulating Chinese demon, a skeleton clutching an orange-pink hibiscus between its teeth and dancing in time to the dirge-like music, a vase filled with orange-pink hibiscus, a water tank in which floated a large fish, the skeleton again, two gesticulating demons, and a vase filled with wilted flowers. They opened the doors a last time, and a flood of water came gushing out, but inside the cabinet stood the princess, deadpan and dry. She bowed and exited at once, moving with swift little mincing steps, leaving the master and Michael to acknowledge the applause.

After it died down, the diabolical shrieks and squeaks that signal the beginning of the "Witches' Sabbath" from Berlioz's *Symphonie Fantastique* could be heard. The magicians stared at their audience for a few seconds; then Michael stepped aside, gestured, bowed, and the master, his red-lined cape flaring behind him, climbed into the cabinet. At once the stage was flooded with light from what appeared to be a ring of fire suspended several feet above the cabinet. Quickly, Michael yanked the doors open, but there was nothing there, and in one balletic movement he faced the onlookers and flung his arms upward toward the fiery ring, through the center of which the master, sitting cross-legged and dressed now in flowing white robes embroidered with ancient Egyptian symbols, floated as though seated on an invisible cloud; he clasped a long rod in his hand, and on his breast the Eye of Horus and its golden chain glinted in the bright glow of the flames. Slowly, gracefully, he descended to the stage and stood beside his young apprentice to receive their public's excited acclaim.

Michael stepped away, abandoning the spotlight to the master, who leaned on his rod and glared appraisingly, mockingly, at the applauding audience. His usually pale face was flushed, and a look of terrible exaltation burned in his single eye. Different music began, primitive, sinuous, chthonic, like something played on instruments made of bone and hide before the dawn of what is referred to as civilization. He cast down his rod upon the stage, stooped, and picked it up; some people cried out, for he was holding an extremely long and madly wriggling snake. He flung this down in its turn, it clattered woodenly against the boards, and when he stooped and straightened, it was a rod again. He repeated these actions several times, moving closer and closer to the footlights as the barbarous music thundered louder, his grin growing more and more ghastly, the snake larger and more furiously wriggling with each successive transformation. He stopped at the edge of the stage, shook his rod, and waited.

He did not have long to wait, for screams began to erupt from the back of the auditorium, screams at first mingled with exclamations of disgust or disbelief, then turning into expressions of unadulterated primeval terror: a squadron of long, thick, garishly colored snakes, perhaps a dozen or more—though some who attended the show later claimed there were hundreds of them—was slithering along the floor of the theater toward the stage. Some were using the aisles, others making their way under the seats and between or over the feet of the audience. A few of them wrapped themselves briefly around ankles or ramped up the sides of the chairs, raising their wedgelike heads between the seat cushions and flicking out their forked tongues, but these quickly recovered from their confusion and returned to the pursuit of what appeared to be their single purpose: reaching the stage as soon as possible. The throbbing music was overlaid by piercing shrieks as people leaped to their feet, shoving, hopping from one leg to the other, climbing onto their seats, where they gaped and swayed; a few brave souls tried to kick or stamp on the serpents, but their feet rebounded as if from automobile tires.

In a short time, though it didn't seem short to the crowd in the Little Cairo, the lead snakes arrived at the front of the theater and began to wriggle and slither up the steps. When the swiftest of them reached the stage, the master, who had stood observing the scene with the rod clutched in one of his outstretched hands, dashed it down at his feet; whereupon it became a serpent of pythonlike proportions, charged its arriving fellow, and swallowed it in a series of horrible peristaltic gulps, repeating the process with each newcomer. All this ingestion required some ninety seconds, sufficient time for the audience to move from visceral fear to horrified fascination, and so no sound could be heard but the music—now a reedy, whining snake-charmer's air—when at last the master snatched up his bloated creature by the tip of its tail and snapped it like a whip against the boards. It became a rod, longer than before, and encircled by a leafy green vine. He held this innocent-looking pastoral instrument out to the cringing audience, while Michael, advancing to the footlights, announced with a theatrical sweep of his arm, "The Great Wurlitzer, ladies and gentlemen. Ladies and gentlemen: the Great Wurlitzer!" Then they waited for the applause that they knew would, eventually, come.

At length the master raised his hand for silence, and a drumroll rose in extended crescendo from the loudspeakers. Laying aside his rod—to everyone's relief, it remained a rod—he stepped to meet Michael at center stage and surveyed the house with a triumphant air, his single eye unblinking in the glare of the footlights. Flushed with excitement, standing next to the master, who was gathering himself to address a totally subjugated audience, Michael found that all his misgivings had vanished like smoke in the wind, and he told himself that this power, this incredible, transforming power, was the only thing worth striving for, the only thing worth having. "The only thing," the master whispered into his ear, echoing his thought and chilling his blood, and then the Great Wurlitzer began to speak aloud.

"Ladies and gentlemen," he said, "if I may interrupt the performance for a moment, I have a few things to say. First of all, I should like to thank you for your attendance here tonight at this, my farewell performance. I trust you are being entertained by our little spectacle. We have saved the best for last: the Tempest Illusion, the highlight of the evening, during which you will experience the four elements magically released in all their fury. I warn you: it may seem frightening, even pitiless, as storms are wont to be; you have come to this theater to see real magic, and real magic has no mercy. But before we bring the proceedings to a close, I wish to offer public thanks to my colleague and successor, Michael Hawke, alias Presto the Great, without whom it would not have been possible for me to make my exit in such a memorable fashion."

He paused, grinning abominably, while the audience cheered and Michael, standing off to one side, made a charming, deferential bow. Then, picking up the thread of his speech, the master went on. "I am convinced that Michael will be a worthy successor and will carry on the proud magic tradition of the Little Cairo Museum of Wonders. As a symbol of this transfer of power, and as a token of my final farewell, I hereby present Michael with my magic amulet." He removed the Eye of Horus, pressed it for a moment with both hands against his breast, and then, like a priest displaying the sacrament, he held it up for the audience to see before waving Michael to his side with a dramatic, summoning hand.

Michael approached and bowed his head, the drumroll sounded again, and the master, holding the golden chain with both hands over Michael's bent neck, said, "Michael, I give you the falcon-god's Eye. It is in some ways a heavy burden but also a source of great satisfaction. Wear it as a symbol of your power among men."

What a blowhard, Emily thought, watching with Lena from the wings. The drumming stopped; the master placed the chain around Michael's neck; and a blinding flash of light, followed immediately by a deafening roar, like an awful thunderclap, stunned the assembly. Emily reeled against Lena and clutched the curtain, watching Michael go chalk white, stagger, and sink to his knees on the stage.

The chain lay about his neck like a steel cable, and the weight of the pendant amulet dragged him down. He tried to rise, to go on with the part he had so carefully rehearsed, but his burden fettered his movements, confounded his memory, and spread open the boundaries of his consciousness. He saw the firmament, the fiery stars, the unspeakable void, and as he peered into those black depths he found himself staring up into the master's appalling eye, and through that eye he glimpsed a parade of hallucinatory images. He saw the inside of an ancient Egyptian funerary chamber, where a wizened figure bitterly embraced the mummified corpse of a dead prince; he saw the sleeping quarters of King Solomon, and laughed as he watched the great king, stupid with wine, heave himself upon the beautiful dark body of his desert queen; he saw a magus in a purple gown, a weary old man in druid's robes, a fetid dungeon, the gray fog settling like a shroud over the graceful arches of London Bridge. All these things he saw in succession, and all at once.

Meanwhile the audience perceived a sound as of rising wind, and the old man spoke again, in a penetrating, exultant voice. "Brace yourselves, ladies and gentlemen! A mighty storm is coming! I, for one, shall not survive it. Farewell!" He faced the wings where Lena and Emily stood. "Farewell," he said again, more softly. Then, turning once more to the audience, he shouted above the increasingly ominous sounds of the oncoming tempest, "Long live magic! Long live magic!" Spinning on his heel amid the sweep and flutter of his robes, he strode quickly upstage to where the Chinese cabinet stood.

With every step he took, the wailing of the wind grew in volume, turning into a drawn-out howl. Another lightning flash bathed the entire theater in a wash of lurid light, and, almost simultaneously, an earsplitting burst of thunder shook the building to its foundations. Suddenly it began to rain, big, pelting drops that the wind drove into the faces of the spectators, who sat as though chained to their seats, helplessly exposed to this elemental violence.

When the master reached the cabinet, he stopped and held up his outflung arms as though commanding the storm. Its fury redoubled; lightning struck one of the light fixtures, which exploded in a shower of electrical sparks; the footlights dimmed, flickered, grew very bright, went out; lightning lit up the house again, apparently striking the curtain, which began to burn brightly above the stage, despite the pouring rain and the howling, lashing wind; rolls of thunder swept through the hall like harbingers of utter destruction.

Michael knelt where he had dropped, nailed to the stage, his neck bent to the Eye's intolerable weight. Though it threatened to snap his spine, he accepted it, accepted the burden and the terror it brought, for he saw clearly the inevitable steps that had led him, compelled him, to attain his desire. He recalled his last glimpse of his parents, the hours of frightened waiting, the strangers who dragged him from the bus station; he experienced anew the horror of his frog-thralldom; he felt once more the same pitiless exaltation, the same monstrous panic he had felt at the sight of the desperate animals in Washington Square, he shivered at the memory of the naked corpse in the funeral parlor, in his mind's eye the statue in the garden once again nodded its cold stone head, and he gasped as the stone hand saluted him. Once he had fondly believed that knowledge would drive out fear, but now he saw that one of its functions was to incorporate fear. Fear was essential; if he strove against it, he could have no power. He sensed the audience's fear, sensed Emily's mounting terror, and the recognition of her suffering, and of himself as the cause of her suffering, made him bow his head still more profoundly.

"What's happening?" Emily shouted into Lena's ear. "What's he doing?" Her heart nearly stopped as she saw Michael, still on his knees, pitch forward as though yanked by the chain around his neck. "Did they rehearse this?" she yelled at Lena, but received in reply only a terrified stare. He's not acting, Emily thought; he's in trouble. She shook off Lena's restraining hand and hurried onto the stage, heading for the spot where Michael was lying, but a bolt of lightning that seemed to strike directly in front of her knocked her flat on her back. She rose at once, whipped to her feet by fear—for Michael, not for herself—but now she realized that the only way to help him was to make Wurlitzer stop whatever it was he was doing. Avoiding the charred, smoking hole in the stage, crouching against the wind and the rain, she ran toward the cabinet.

Wurlitzer was still standing before it with outstretched arms, his head thrown back ecstatically, savoring this final triumph. Emily's arrival interrupted his transports, and he opened his eye to see her standing between him and the cabinet doors. Around them the storm raged on unabated, but they were confronting one another at its center, where the air, though rank and sulphurous, was terribly still. His eye widened in disbelief as she grabbed the sleeves of his robe.

"Stop this!" Emily shouted at him with a fury so intense it made her temples ache. "Whatever you're doing, stop it!" She pulled at his robes with both hands, trying to turn him in Michael's direction. "Look at him!" she screamed. "Do you want to kill him too?"

With a furious jerk, he freed himself from her clutches. "Get out of my way, you little fool," he hissed, thrusting her aside. His face bore a look of consummate repulsion, as though physical contact with her filled him with loathing. "He's not dying," he snarled. "He has found his heart's desire."

The old man opened the cabinet doors and tried to step inside, but Emily flung herself past him into the dark space, braced her shoulders against the back of the cabinet, and held out both hands. "No!" she shouted, the blood pounding in her ears. "Help him! Don't let him die!"

A lightning flash lit up his face, black with scorn and rage. "He will live a long time!" he spat at her. "Save yourself! Get out of there!"

Emily lunged forward and blocked the entrance to the cabinet, shouting through the riot of the storm and her own thundering blood. "I'm not afraid of you! Make this stop!"

His contempt was absolute, his indifference to her fate like the indifference of the speeding vehicle to the little animal whose life it unmalevolently crushes out. "You are blind, you understand nothing," he said, beyond all patience. "For the last time: *out of my way!*"

"You're not going anywhere, you old fraud!" Emily yelled.

"So be it," Wurlitzer said fiercely. He sprang into the cabinet, sending her staggering into one of its murky corners, and pulled the doors shut behind him.

At that moment the tempest exploded in a paroxysm of violence, as though its manifestations heretofore, however tremendous, had but foreshadowed the ferocious apocalypse that now began. An eye-searing, hair-singeing lightning bolt, an electrical discharge of cosmic proportions, split the stage in front of the Chinese cabinet, and the white-hot flash was accompanied by a thunderclap whose gigantic pressure ripped gaping holes in the ceiling and the walls. Power cables, blasted from their moorings, fell to the floor, setting off shimmering blue-green bursts as they lashed the rising water. The burning curtain was rent in two and fell in twin fireballs to either side of the stage. The wind roared and raged, totally submerging the shouts of the audience.

From where he lay on his side, still pinned to the stage, Michael could see the two gleaming, lacquered doors of the cabinet slam closed. Ignoring the tempest—it was, after all, only an illusion—he fixed his mind on the Chinese cabinet, concentrating as he had been taught to do. He had the power to see into sealed boxes, locked rooms, enclosed spaces; it was only a question of finding the right formula and focusing intensely. He strained to penetrate that shiny exterior and enter that darkness. Thrusting aside his dread, the final obstacle, he passed inside the black cabinet, though he lay unmoving, and what he saw there blighted him forever. He saw Emily in mortal danger, fighting not for her life but for his, and he saw the master looming over her in the blackness, hardly bothering to fend her off, his single eye transfixed by his single purpose. Emily lashed and tore at her adversary, who seemed to grow larger, darker, amorphous, and Michael had a flashing vision of his own future, the new master, isolated by the power he had so tenaciously striven for, struggling in the loveless night, and Emily gone. He could feel her desperation, her mounting terror, all for his sake, all for him, and he cringed as he realized that his ambition had put her in that box with her worst enemy. Her eyes—he could see them, and the sight scarred his heart—shone like two points of heat, grew hotter and smaller, and then all at once the great darkness enveloped and extinguished them. Michael shrieked in agony, but the sound of his cry was swallowed by the howling wind.

And suddenly all was silent, the cataclysm was over. People looked at themselves and one another with incredulous eyes: they had been neither blinded nor deafened, neither scorched by fire nor struck by falling debris; they weren't even wet. The curtain hung suspended above the proscenium, unharmed, ready to fall at the end of the show; the boards of the stage itself, polished and shining, relected the bright footlights. An awed silence fell over the crowd as they watched Michael rise shakily to his feet. He looked about him as though dazed; then, with a lurch, he approached the front of the stage.

"The Tempest Illusion, ladies and gentlemen," he proclaimed by rote, his professional instincts almost completely masking the wobble in his voice. "Thank you for your attention, and we hope you'll come again. Good night to you all." Michael waved and bowed, then stood valiantly smiling until the first uncertain smattering of applause began, whereupon he bowed again and vanished into the wings.

There he found Lena, wild-eyed and speechless. Though he too was bewildered, he knew that the show must be closed and the house emptied before he could give his entire attention to the mounting dread he felt. He grabbed Lena's shoulders and shook her as gently as he could. "Bring down the curtain, Lena!" he commanded, staring into her stricken eyes. "Bring down the curtain." He walked back onstage to acknowledge the applause, which was growing steadily in volume, bowed once and then again, and finally the curtain began its slow descent behind him. There was a tumult of clapping now, and the houselights came on, and Michael could see Dazz standing in front of his first-row seat, shouting "Bravo! Bravo!" again and again and clapping as though he meant to cripple his hands forever. On either side of Dazz, Michael recognized the bulky figures of Samir and Beulah Wales, still in their seats, apparently being ministered to by a vaguely familiar figure, a tall man with thick blond hair who bent over each of them in turn. Michael bowed one last time and disappeared through the curtain.

Lena came up to him at once. "Where are they?" he asked urgently, ignoring the insistent clapping, shouting, and foot stamping on the other side of the curtain.

She seemed about to falter, but her voice was firm. "I don't know, Michael. I've looked everywhere backstage. Unless they're . . ." She hesitated, turned slightly, and simultaneously their eyes focused on the Chinese cabinet. Michael walked upstage toward it as Lena murmured, more to herself than to him, "But they couldn't possibly . . ."

When he grasped the handles of the double doors, his heart was already like a lump of lead in his chest, and the foreknowledge of what he would see flashed upon him the second before he saw it: Emily lay in an ungainly heap on the floor of the cabinet. "Emily," he gasped, and then the dread burst inside him, in his throat, and for several moments he couldn't speak. He reached inside the cabinet, shifted her carefully so he could get his hands under her arms, and drew her out onto the stage. A sob opened his throat, and without taking his eyes off Emily he said to Lena, "Get a doctor." She started offstage, but he was concentrating now, he knew how to concentrate under pressure, and he said to her in a tone of clearheaded command, "No. Not the telephone. Dazz was in the front row. He's with a doctor. Get him."

Obeying wordlessly, Lena passed through the curtain. Michael removed his coat, folded it into a pillow for Emily's head, shrinking from her blank, wide-open eyes. Both her hands were clenched into fists, one resting on each breast; Michael felt in vain for a pulse or a heartbeat. Her skin was cool. He wanted to go and find something to cover her with, to keep her warm, but he couldn't bring himself to leave her, so he knelt wretchedly beside her, uncertain of what to do. He passed his hand in front of her staring eyes; there was no response, and, pressing his fingertips on her eyelids, he drew them shut. She must be in shock; she couldn't be dead.

It seemed the applause had stopped a long time ago, he could hear the sounds of people leaving the theater. The curtain moved, and he looked downstage to see Lena enter, followed by the tall blond man Michael had seen with Dazz and Sami. Pale blue eyes, horsey face, not particularly friendly on the few occasions when they had met. What was his name? Mortimer, that was it, Mortimer.

With a curt nod, Dr. Mortimer knelt beside Emily, facing Michael across her body. He felt for her pulse, put his fingers on her throat, her temples, pulled back one of her eyelids, shone into the eye a small flashlight he had taken from an inside pocket, shut the eye again, moved her hands aside and laid his ear against her chest; then he looked at Michael with an expression of mingled rage and dismay. "I'm afraid she's dead," he said.

Lena cried out softly and knelt beside Michael, her hand on his shoulder. Michael shook his head, returning the doctor's stare. "She can't be," he said evenly. "It's not possible. How can you be sure?"

"In some cases it's hard to be sure, but I'm sorry to say this isn't one of those."

"But how? What could have killed her?"

"That I can't tell you. But we'll find out." He rose to his feet and loomed over them. "Meanwhile I must inform the proper authorities. Where was she when you found her?"

"In the cabinet."

"Ah. And where is the older gentleman, the one I take to be responsible for this"—he paused briefly, but seemed unable to restrain himself any longer—"this outrageous spectacle?"

"I don't know. I can't find him," Lena said in a voice broken by sobbing.

"I suggest you try again. The police will certainly want to talk to him. I'll come back shortly." He started to turn away, but stopped and looked sadly down at Emily's body. "What a terrible shame," he said, not attempting to disguise the anger in his voice. "Please cover her up." He gave the two of them a contemptuous look and left the stage.

As the doctor exited, Michael turned to Lena. "Have you looked upstairs?"

"No," she said weakly.

"I think you should take a look up there," Michael told her, patting her hand. "Maybe that's where he went."

"Maybe," Lena said, unconvinced and tearful. Bracing herself against Michael's shoulder, she rose heavily to her feet and padded toward the wings.

Alone with Emily, Michael knelt quietly beside her and stared at her body. A line he had read somewhere came to him: "No motion has she now, no force." How could she be dead? She looked beautiful, he realized, more beautiful than ever; her face was serious and serene, her lips tightly closed, her jaw set in that determined way she had, her hair startlingly black against the pallor of her skin. Overcome by sadness, Michael rocked back on his heels and moaned. He remembered what the master had taught him about the magic will, how the magician must perceive the will of others and attune his own will to theirs. He seemed to feel the strength of Emily's will to live, even as she lay there lifeless, and he closed his eyes and concentrated, focusing his entire consciousness, every ounce of his force, on the single object of his desire: that Emily might live. He could feel the power radiating from him, flowing out of him in a surge that burned his cheeks and blurred his eyes, and he leaned close to her ear and whispered her name, once, and waited, and then again.

He squeezed his eyelids together to clear his sight, and when he opened them again he saw that her lips were slightly parted, and when he moved his face close to hers he felt something warm, like a soft puff of breath, against his cheek. Straightening up a little, he saw that her eyes were still closed, but at the edge of his vision one of her arms twitched. He thought his brain would burst with the effort he was making, he clutched at his throat, at his clamped jaws, and raised his head, and then her eyes opened, not fluttering, not blinking, but all at once; he saw anger in them, and something like disappointment, but when they met his they filled with joy and a smile of ineffable sweetness spread over her face. "You're safe," she said. "I'm so glad. I thought you were hurt." Her voice was strong and natural, a hint of color tinged her cheeks.

"I'm safe," he said gently. "But what about you?"

"I'm all right. Just a little tired."

He put his hand over her breast and felt its soft curve, and underneath, her beating heart. "I was afraid you'd left me."

"I'll never leave you, Michael," she said. "But I think I have to rest a little."

"No!" he cried. "Don't! Stay here with me!"

She raised her left hand and stroked his cheek, then slowly drew her fingers across his lips. Her eyelids looked heavy. "Just for a little while," she said. "I'll be back soon."

She closed her eyes, and her body seemed to stiffen slightly under his hand. He tried to concentrate again, tried to will her back into consciousness, but he was exhausted, the power had drained from him. He snatched her up in his arms and knelt there swaying, rocking her gently, cradling her head against his chest as his tears fell onto her face.

There were sounds, footsteps, movement. Tenderly, he laid Emily's head back down on his folded coat. When he looked up, Dr. Mortimer was standing over him again. "The police will be here soon. Why haven't you covered her?"

"She was alive, Doctor," Michael said hotly. "I mean—she *is* alive. She opened her eyes and spoke to me."

"Please," Dr. Mortimer said. "This whole affair is absurd enough."

"But she spoke to me."

"She's been dead for at least half an hour," the doctor said, crouching down beside her. He touched her clenched right fist, paused, began to pry open her fingers. "What's this she's got in her hand?" Grimacing a little, he released the object she was clutching, but it eluded his grasp, fell to the stage, bounced, rolled a few feet, and stopped, shining dully in the lights. Mortimer, drawn by curiosity, stepped over to it, bending down to pick it up. While Michael watched him, the doctor extended his hand, then abruptly pulled it away, as if unwilling to touch the thing, whatever it was. From his place beside Emily's body, Michael scrutinized the object for several seconds before, with a shudder, he recognized what he was looking at: the master's glass eye.

There were plenty of offers, but after two frustrating though successful outings, Michael made up his mind; he wasn't doing television. It was like having a stone wall between himself and his audience, he told Lena. He needed to hear them breathing.

He did a few interviews for magazines, with the understanding that Emily's name was not to be mentioned. Sometimes these were gratifying. The interviewers were well informed about the history of magic and enthusiastic about Michael's place in it. "Your work is definitive," one wide eyed young woman told him as they sat over yet another cup of coffee in the little place across the street. "There hasn't been anything, I mean anyone, like you in a hundred years."

He toured for a while, greeted at each stop by two or three of the best magicians in the area, and these were often charming, competent performers, typically much older than Michael, but deferential, even respectful. His reputation preceded him, and there were times when he tired of the role assigned him, the wunderkind, the young master. After such excursions he was eager to get back home to his quiet, simple room at Lena's, to her heavy meals, endless cups of coffee, dull evenings in front of the television.

Magic absorbed and sustained him, as he had always known it would. He kept to a schedule of two shows a month at the theater. This seemed adequate to satisfy his faithful audience as well as the steady supply of newcomers, tourists, mostly, who had read about him, and students. He concentrated on refining his act, making it cleaner, using fewer props, less patter, but at the same time his love of theatricality kept him constantly on the alert for more dramatic effects. His audience was never bored, no matter how often they saw him. There was always something new, unexpected, and startling in his performance.

One evening, after a quiet dinner with Lena, he went to the theater downstairs, and then backstage, where he decided to go through his growing collection of music tapes in search of something delicate and suggestive for an illusion he had perfected, which used candles and mirrors. He never could, Lena said indulgently when he showed it to her, stop playing with fire. It was true, he thought, pulling out a rack of tapes he hadn't looked into for some time, he never tired of fire. Its paradoxical appeal was irresistible to him, as it was both a source of comfort and of danger, the perfect metaphor for magic.

The tapes were dusty from disuse, but he saw at once that they were unlikely to contain what he was looking for; they were all operatic overtures. He pushed the rack back into its space on the closely packed shelf, but it didn't go in all the way, something was blocking it. He pulled it out again, then reached into the space, fumbling at the back of it. As he suspected, there was a loose tape. He grasped it, pulled it out. It was dusty, like the others. As he turned it over to read the label he felt his heart sink, for in the moment before he saw the words *Grand Finale,* in Lena's fine, careful handwriting, he knew what it was.

Though he tried never to think of it, and refused ever to talk of it, Michael knew there was a way in which he never stopped thinking about that night. It had informed his life with two absences, a core of loss around which he fashioned a new life. He'd got through the inquest, the publicity surrounding the show, which, curiously enough, was largely positive, by saying as little as possible. Lena spoke for him when necessary. Max Wurlitzer was offically missing, though no one was really looking for him, and Emily's death was determined to be the result of natural causes. Though it was certainly unnatural for a strong, healthy young woman to suffer a massive cerebral hemorrhage, such things happened now and then, against the odds.

It was one of Michael's pleasures, one of the few, he thought, to sit at night on the stage of his empty theater and turn the music up so that it filled the place. He examined the tape in his hands, dusted it off against his pants leg, flipped open the plastic case. Why not, he thought, as he slipped the cassette into the player and adjusted the volume. Then he flicked the light switches so that the houselights were down and a single spot illuminated the center of the stage, like a disk of silver. A series of beeps issued from the powerful speakers as he dragged a wooden chair onto the stage and took his place, his familiar place, in the spotlight.

First came the stately, pompous *Music for the Royal Fireworks*, which the master had chosen himself as appropriate for their entrance. Michael could see him as he was that night, so confident, so pleased with himself, his hands flashing like precision instruments as he moved noiselessly across the stage to stand side by side with his protégé. His timing really was a miracle, or the opposite of a miracle, Michael thought, whatever that was. Then, as always when he thought of Wurlitzer, a sensation of bitterness mixed with awe made him clench his teeth. He battled down his anger and outrage at having been betrayed, because it was useless to be angry, as the master had taught him; anger diluted power, which was always focused and calm. Would he have gone through with it, the endless hours of preparation, the grueling practice, the concentration of will and energy that had resulted in the triumph of the Grand Finale, would he have done it if he'd known that on the other side of that triumph there was to be so much sadness, loss, and loneliness?

Probably not, Michael thought. But then there was the deeper question of whether he had really had any choice, ever, from that first moment when he had looked up into the wizened, comical face under the umbrella and pretended, for his own amusement, to be a frog. He still didn't know where the master's power had left off and his own begun. The music swelled around him, becoming more and more explosive, and Michael recalled the enormous satisfaction he had felt as he stood shoulder to shoulder with the Great Wurlitzer, the colored smoke billowing around them while the audience roared with pleasure.

There was a break in the music, then the cheerful fountain theme began, lighthearted and silly, as if to mock him.

"What a fool," Michael said. Emily had been right, the old man was using him all along. What Michael had perceived as affection, even admiration for his cleverness, his aptitude, was just relief at finding someone gullible enough to walk into his trap. As in some cosmic game of tag, Michael was now "it." The Great Wurlitzer had wanted to leave, and Michael was his avenue. How it must have amused him to see Michael's avidity, his greed, so undisguised and all-consuming, for power.

And he had given it to him, Michael admitted, that much couldn't be denied. It was the master, not Michael, who had made him what he was. He knew things ordinary people didn't, he saw things they would never see, could do things that astonished them, that challenged their disbelief. That had become vividly apparent to him from the first moment the Eye of Horus was placed around his neck, when its memory became his as well. When he walked into a room, he took the room, and when he left it, there was one subject on everyone's mind: Michael Hawke, who was he, what was he, where did such power come from? Was it natural or unnatural?

An interviewer had asked him that once. He smiled, feeling smug, as he recalled his answer: a little of both. It was ironic, also, that in another day and age, he might have been burned as a witch. Now, he was merely a celebrity.

Then the fountain music ended, there was a pause. The next sound drove the self-satisfied smile from Michael's lips. It was a high, almost shrill note, held, then dropped suddenly, entirely, to be replaced by another, a little lower, fuller, then a phrase of three notes, that declared to even the most unsophisticated listener its Oriental origin. It was the sound of Emily's flute, carried into the air by Emily's breath, as clear and direct as she had been. Michael groaned and covered his eyes with his hand, slouching in his chair as if recovering from a blow. Why hadn't he remembered that this was on the tape?

He listened quietly, helplessly, and the music was like a flood-gate that opened and poured in images of Emily. He could see the slight, ironic elevation of her eyebrows as she turned off the tape the first time she played this music for him, explaining that she had chosen it and arranged it in just this way because she thought it was "uplifting," didn't he agree? Then his memory wound backward, and he saw her as she was the night of Sami's party in her princely Tamino costume, her thick hair drawn up under the huntsman's cap, her flute carried jauntily in one hand; and as she appeared, breathless and indignant, that night she had tracked the master halfway across town only to lose him; and again as she leaned over him, her expression complicated by anxiety and love, as he struggled back to consciousness on the lawn in Central Park the day when she had stood by while he succumbed for the first time to the spell of the master. How brave she was, he thought, how strong and how honest. No one had ever loved him as she had, so sincerely, without question, though not without skepticism, for she knew him and she knew what he wanted and why, just as she knew, instinctively and surely, the difference between right and wrong.

And then the thought of that night, and of how she had looked, so peaceful and serene, when his will and hers had coalesced and she spoke to him for the last time. He didn't, wouldn't ever know how much of that strange, impossible event was attributable to his power, the power he had been given by the master, and how much of it was Emily's own fierce and determined spirit, her will, which was stronger than he had ever, until that moment, understood.

Useless tears filled his eyes, and he dashed them away with the back of his hand. How beautiful this music was. How he longed for her. Hardly conscious of what he was doing, he slipped one hand inside his jacket pocket and withdrew the pack of cards that was always there. There was a trick, a simple sleight, that she had always loved. His hands worked the cards without his really attending to them; it was so easy, and he could see her delighted expression. She never tired of this trick. The cards spread out, stood on edge, appeared to collapse one way, but then, when it seemed he'd lost control and they must cascade onto the floor, they leaped back into his palm as if on command. "Do it again, Michael," she said, as incredulous as a child. "How do you do it?"

"It's so easy," he said softly into the dark that hemmed in his spotlight, into the still theater, while the delicate, ethereal music continued, and the tears rolled down his face, and his hands worked the cards, back and forth, skillfully, magically, for the only audience he really wanted now.